knit one pearl one

WITHDRAWN

knit one

pearl one

Gil McNeil

voice

HYPERION / NEW YORK

Library of Congress Cataloging-in-Publication Data

McNeil, Gil
Knit one pearl one / Gil McNeil. — 1st ed.
p.   cm.
ISBN 978-1-4013-4167-1
1. Knitting—Fiction.   2. Single mothers—Fiction.   3. England—Fiction.
I. Title.
PR6113.C58K65 2012
823'.92—dc22
2011018110

Hyperion books are available for special promotions and premiums. For details
contact the HarperCollins Special Markets Department in the New York office at
212-207-7528, fax 212-207-7222, or email spsales@harpercollins.com.

Book Design by Jennifer Daddio / Bookmark Design & Media Inc.

FIRST EDITION

1   3   5   7   9   10   8   6   4   2

SUSTAINABLE FORESTRY INITIATIVE   Certified Fiber Sourcing   www.sfiprogram.org

THIS LABEL APPLIES TO TEXT STOCK

For Joe

··· Contents ···

knit one pearl one

I'm a Little Teapot

January

t's 6:30 on Wednesday morning, and I'm putting the finishing touches to a tea cozy in duck egg blue while Pearl is busy emptying all the saucepans out of the kitchen cupboard and carefully stacking them in the washing machine. She thinks I don't know what she's up to, and is happily humming her favorite nursery rhymes and snippets of hymns and show tunes, which she's picked up from Gran. She might only be fifteen months old, but it's amazing how much noise she can make.

"Would you like some breakfast, sweetheart? Juice?"

She ignores me and carries on clattering, moving forward slightly, so her head is hidden inside the cupboard. In Pearl world this renders her invisible; if she can't see you then you definitely can't see her. I think she's hoping I might forget about breakfast; surreptitiously putting things in the washing machine is one of her favorite ways to spend a happy half hour, which means I've washed the bloody car keys twice this week. If we were richer, no doubt we'd have one of those enormous black Jeeps which are always clogging up the High Street, and washing the electronic keys to one of those on fast spin would probably get you into the kind of trouble that no amount of four-wheel drive with heated seats could sort out. And at least the hunt for the car keys in the morning is a little bit more interesting, as long as I remember not to put the washing machine on just before we need to leave the house.

I usually spot the bigger stuff, I'm not completely hopeless, even at 6:30 in the sodding morning, but I'm still in trouble for washing one of Archie's Lego soldiers last week, complete with horse and shield. I've also got pretty expert at untangling the coils of pipes when the drain gets blocked, even though I haven't quite worked out how to undo the nozzle without gallons of water gushing all over the floor before I've got the sodding washing-up bowl in the right position. But at least the kitchen floor's a great deal cleaner than it used to be before Pearl arrived.

Actually, come to think of it that might be why she's so keen on kitchen appliances, since she was born in a blur of panic and swearing, right here in the kitchen, by the fridge, despite my plans for a nice calm cesarean in the local hospital and a few days' rest with no small boys jumping on my bed. I remember thinking how shaming it was the floor was so filthy. Not that Bob and Dave seemed to notice when they turned up in their ambulance; they were far too busy trying to unpack their bags and behave like they weren't desperately hoping the midwife would turn up before we got to what Dave likes to call the tricky bit. He came to her birthday party last October, with his wife, Sandra, and apparently he didn't stop talking about it for weeks, and to hear him tell it you'd think he was the one who'd given birth clinging to a fridge. Bob popped along too, with a pink rabbit wrapped in Happy Birthday paper, so it was like a little reunion, although without quite as much bad language as the last time we met.

But it all seems so much longer than a year ago; I felt the same way about Jack and Archie, once you've got them you can't imagine a world where they weren't around. They occupy such a huge space, it's like you were somehow living a different life. A less crowded and quieter life. Much quieter.

"Mum, I don't want Shreddies, and Pearly's putting stuff in the washer again."

"I know, love, just ignore her, and you don't have to have Shreddies. There's Weetabix too."

He tuts. Archie's been going in for much more tutting recently. He also appears to have decided to only wear one sock to school today.

"Where's your other sock?"

He looks at me like I've just asked him for a quick summary of quantum physics.

"I hate Weetabix. Why can't we have proper cereal in the little boxes? Gran always has the little boxes, they're much better."

Jack nods. "He's right, they are."

Great, so now I've got Jack lobbying for Variety Pack enhanced mornings. But at least he's got both socks on. Although no school sweatshirt.

"Jack, find your sweatshirt, and Archie, you need both socks on for breakfast."

"Nelly has Variety Packs, she told me."

"She does not, Archie, she has porridge, Connie told me. They all do."

Actually Connie said Mark made porridge one morning

last week and both Nelly and Marco nearly fainted with shock at being asked to eat something so revolting-looking, even with golden syrup on top. But there's no way on earth I'm falling for a Variety Packed school run every morning, and I'm not certain honesty is always the best policy with under-tens. I'm sure Connie would agree. Both Nelly and Marco give her what Gran likes to call a run for her money, particularly Nelly, or Antonella, which is what Connie calls her when she's being annoying. Which is pretty often; just one of the reasons why Connie quickly became my best friend when we moved down here. I've noticed before how mums with Lively children tend to gravitate toward each other.

"Why can't we have Frosties, or Coco Pops?"

I think I'll ignore this; if I want to see how many ways a seven-year-old and a nine-year-old can leap about with massive sugar highs while I try to get their coats on, I can just give them cans of Coke for breakfast and win the Top Mum award for the entire week.

"Go and find your other sock, Archie, and Jack, find your book bag too please; you took it upstairs last night to do your reading."

Everyone is glaring at me now. Even Pearl. Time for a spot of positive behavior reinforcement as the experts like to call it; bribery, basically.

"While you're both finishing getting ready I might have time to grill some bacon, but only if you get a move on."

They both cheer, which prompts Pearl to pause from stuffing the washing machine with unsuitable objects and clap her hands.

Jack smiles. "Thanks, Mum, and can we have egg too, like Gran makes?"

Perhaps a few grilled mushrooms and possibly a side order

of kedgeree? Am I running some kind of bed-and-breakfast operation and nobody has told me? Anyone for kippers?

"No. Just toast, and bacon, if you hurry up. Or Weetabix, if you don't."

They sprint for the stairs, followed by Pearl, who will start screaming in about five seconds, when she finds they've climbed over the stair gate and she is therefore trapped in the hallway while her brothers are free to roam. Time for me to nip in with a diversionary tactic or we'll have another school run where she's red-faced and furious and won't sit in her buggy without five minutes' wrestling.

"Can we take the saucepans out of the washer now, love?"

She charges back into the kitchen ready to defend all her painstaking efforts.

As soon as the bacon's done and I've got her into her high chair, she starts singing along to the radio, with her fingers in her ears so she can achieve maximum volume to annoy Jack and Archie but not have to enjoy the full volume herself. She pretty much has two volume settings does my gorgeous girl: Loud and Very Loud. And while her blond curls and dazzling blue eyes make her look like a poster baby for our new life by the seaside, her temper and steely stubborn streak are less enchanting. Especially at 5 a.m.

The phone rings just as I'm pouring juice, and trying to persuade Pearl to keep her bib on.

"I've been up since dawn. This motherhood thing's a total bloody nightmare, isn't it?"

"Morning, Ellen."

"The little swine was up three times last night. At least Harry says he was, I went back to sleep."

Alfred Arthur Williams-Malone arrived seven months ago and has shown no signs of letting up on the nocturnal activity front yet. Ellen wanted to call him Merlin, mainly to annoy her mother, but Harry used his paternal veto, so they settled on Alfred instead, in honor of Harry's favorite granddad, who used to collect lawn mowers, but endearingly also bought glass jars full of toffees whenever a grandchild was due to visit. They call him Eddie most of the time, or Fast Eddie, since he was born in just over an hour from Ellen reaching hospital and getting into the birthing pool. She didn't even have time to unpack her bags. And knowing Ellen like I do, I can safely say she'd have had quite a few bags. She's my best friend, and has been there for me for all my best and worst times, but she definitely doesn't travel light.

"Poor Harry."

"Oh yes, my heart bleeds. He's having a lovely time, moaning on about the night shift like he's the only man in the Western world who gets up at nights to feed his baby."

"He probably is, Ellen."

She laughs. "True. But filling the fridge with bottles was a masterstroke, if I say so myself, and I'm so glad we've got him on the stuff that comes in tins now. That bloody milking machine made me feel like a prize heifer, way too bovine for me, although it did freak out all the boys at work; there's something about a breast-feeding woman they just can't cope with. And the mummy mafia couldn't guilt-trip me about being back at work because he was still getting the good stuff, I just didn't have to actually be there. Perfect win-win."

"Less winning for poor old Harry though?"

"Oh please. One of you has to end up looking like the living dead with a new baby in the house, that's the rule. And it sure as hell wasn't going to be me, darling. Besides, so what if he's a bit tired; nothing most women haven't been doing for centuries. He says this house-husband thing is against the Geneva convention and we're breaching his right to sleep or something. He's thinking of hiring a lawyer."

"Who's he going to sue, you or Eddie?"

"Both of us, probably. Like being a freelance cameraman could keep us in wine and roses; he wouldn't even be able to cover the mortgage. He's got a job on next week, and by the time I've sorted out the child care, and rejigged my studio slots, it's costing me a bloody fortune. Christ, the things we do to keep our boys happy. Anyway, enough about Planet Boy, how's my Pearly Princess? Thinking of taking any legal action?"

"Probably. She's got a major issue with the stair gate at the moment, and I've told you, please stop calling her that, it makes me feel like I'm living in my very own remake of *Cinderella*."

"I loved that film."

"Yes, but it's not so great when you're the one doing all the sweeping up and cooking, but with no friendly squirrels sewing sequins on your frock."

"Or birds flying backward and forward twirling ribbons. Don't forget the birds. I loved that dress, I wanted it so much I was nearly sick."

"Me too, but less of the Princess please, or God knows what she's going to insist we call her by the time she's bigger."

"Madam?"

"Hang on a minute, Ellen. Jack, drink your milk, sweetheart. And Archie, stop doing that, please. Come on, it's nearly time to go to school."

"What's he doing?"

"Giving Pearl the crusts from his toast. They're always

foisting things on her. They treat her like a mini–vacuum cleaner, she's always trotting round with fists full of mashed-up toast."

"Handy though, a mini Hoover. I hope Eddie goes in for that when he's a bit bigger. So what are you up to today then?"

"Creating a fabulous new window display of tea cozies and knitted cakes. I hope. The patterns for the tea cozies are selling really well."

"Knitted cakes?"

"They look a lot better than they sound."

"They'd have to."

"They make great pincushions."

"And there are people out there who need special cushions for their pins? It's a whole new world, isn't it, darling?"

"You can mock, but they sell really well. Anyway, what's Britain's Favorite Broadcaster up to then? Annoying celebrities, having on-air fights with her coanchor?"

"He started it."

"Yes, but you didn't have to push him right off his chair."

"Bastard. He lodged an official complaint you know. I had to go to another meeting with Human bloody Resources. Idiot woman told me that it didn't set a good example to the younger staff."

"It *is* the second time you've done it, Ellen."

"Yes, and it won't be the last. I told her, if she's really concerned about good role models for younger staff, she'd better crack on with stopping the boys in senior management shagging young hopefuls and hiring them as their new protégées. Because sooner or later we're going to get hit with the mother of all sexual harassment suits, and I for one am perfectly prepared to be a witness for the prosecution. She went quite pale, and then I said I needed to go and lactate, and that really finished her off."

"I bet."

"So have you decided? Weekend away, health spa, but with booze, and proper food, none of that low-carb bollocks? What do you think?"

"I can't decide."

"About what?"

"Anything really. It took me nearly half an hour yesterday to decide whether to take my cardigan off."

"That doesn't sound good, darling."

"I know. Something's happened to my brain in the last few months. When I had Jack and Archie, it was my memory, so I had to write lists for everything."

"So that's where you got your addiction to lists from. But I know what you mean, I'm loving those sticky Post-it notes now. I'm on a couple of packs a week, and I'm sticking them everywhere. And you can get them in such fashion-forward colors. It's brilliant. I stuck one on Harry last night, to remind him to take the rubbish out. So useful. Anyway, what sort of decisions are you wrestling with, anything juicy?"

"Whether to take my cardigan off."

She laughs. "It can't be that bad, darling."

"It bloody is. My head's so full of the shop and the kids and what we can have for tea the bit where I can make decisions has fallen off, so now I just dither."

"Postpartum Dithering. I like it."

"Well I'm glad someone does, because it's driving me round the bend."

"A weekend away sounds like just what the doctor ordered."

"Yes, but it'll take so long to arrange everything, for the

kids and the shop. Why don't you just come down here for the weekend? I can have Pearl in my room and you can have her room, like last time."

"Ooh, that's a good idea. I love my weekends by the seaside, and so does Fast Eddie. He sleeps better, it must be all the sea air. And then we can do the spa thing another time. Perfect. How's Dovetail?"

"Martin's fine, thanks, and stop calling him Dovetail, he only told you about dovetail joints that one time, and that was ages ago."

"When was the last time he told you another fascinating fact about wood?"

"Yesterday, but—"

"I rest my case."

"Look, I've got to go or we'll be late for school."

"Okay, but I'll call you later, and I want a full report on the state of play with old Dovetail, I'm writing a Post-it note now, to remind myself. I'll stick it on Eddie; he's asleep at the moment. So sweet when they're asleep, aren't they? I can do the yummy-mummy thing when he's asleep, it's just when he's awake it gets a bit more tricky."

"Tell me about it."

Pearl is now throwing small pieces of toast, aided and abetted by her brothers.

I fob her off with a piece of peeled apple while simultaneously overseeing final school uniform checks and grabbing a last cup of tea. She adores pieces of fruit, and she'll pretty much eat anything as long as you put it in her current favorite plastic bowl. This week it's the *Toy Story* one. Last week it was the blue one, with the green stripes. She'll even eat mango and kiwi along with the usual toddler favorites of strawberries and grapes, whereas I had to practically force fruit into the boys when they were asleep. Although now they're being outclassed by toddler sister, they're considering apples and mandarins as possibilities.

I'm drinking tea as we have one of those golden five minutes that make it all worthwhile. Pearl is singing to her piece of apple, doing a little celebratory dance now she's been released from her high chair, and the boys are joining in, slowly and carefully so they don't knock her over. It's moments like this when it all makes sense. Until I realize we're going to be late and there's a mad rush to get out of the door.

"Come on, Archie, walk a bit quicker, love."

"I'm going as quick as I can. Honestly, Mum, it's boss boss boss with you. All the time."

It's only a ten-minute walk across the park to school, or forty-five minutes if Archie is allowed to dawdle.

"I bet I'll be the first to get to the gates." I speed up, walking as fast as I can toward the park gates.

Jack and Archie race past me.

Pearl temporarily abandons her battle with her hat in order to bounce in the buggy as an encouragement for me to walk faster. She hates wearing hats, so I've knitted her a balaclava for cold January mornings. She tries to get it off but only ends up turning it round, so we often arrive at school with a woolen-faced child. But at least I know she's warm.

Jack beats Archie to the gates, but only by centimeters, so they're both calling for a steward's inquiry as we cross the road, holding the handles of the buggy and walking properly, despite protestations.

"Horrible big liar. Tell him, Mum, lying is terrible, isn't it?"

"Yes, it is, Archie, and so is shoving your brother, and Jack, stop it now. It doesn't matter who won."

They both look at me like they've had yet another glimpse of Planet Mother and found it totally nonsensical.

"Of course it does, Mum. He's always saying he's faster than me, and he's not."

Pearl is shouting now too, random shouting, just so she doesn't feel left out. If I'm not careful we're all going to arrive at school mid-bicker.

"What do you want for tea tonight, Archie?"

"Not sausages."

"Okay."

"I'd love sausages, Mum, they're my favorite."

Time for a little bit of brother bonding I think.

"Okay, well, since you two can't agree, I'll choose. I know, macaroni cheese."

They both start to make being sick noises, which Pearl thinks is marvelous.

"Well choose something, together. Or it's macaroni."

They walk slightly ahead, whispering, all disputes temporarily put to one side while they rack their brains to try to come up with a mutually acceptable supper which will also annoy me.

"Can we have roast chicken with crispy potatoes and gravy?"

"Not on a school night, no."

They both tut, and Pearl relaunches Battle Balaclava.

Excellent.

Connie's already in the playground, and Jack and Archie run off for a last two minutes' playtime before the bell goes. She's looking tired, and I don't think being four months pregnant is helping; she says this is my fault, because seeing me with Pearl made her go all broody. Although unlike her and Mark, I appear to be missing the husband and father of course. Which was pretty tricky when the news first got round that I was pregnant; half the town seemed to think Martin was the dad, even though we weren't actually together then. At one point I thought I'd have to put a notice up in the bloody shop window: Martin Is Not the Father, something like that. And Elsie was driving me mad in the shop; not only has she worked with Gran for years before I took over but she's also Martin's mum, so it all got pretty fraught. But once I fed the gossip grapevine with a few snippets about an old friend who wasn't going to be part of our lives, things calmed down, thank God. Not that Daniel is an old friend, but I could hardly say it was a one-off magic moment in Venice with a handsome stranger. People round here don't really go in for that kind of thing. Especially not if they're recently widowed. Actually neither do I, widowed or not; it was my first experience of being the kind of woman who has affairs in foreign cities with glamorous photographers. It's just typical of my luck I ended up pregnant. Although of course now Pearl is here, I realize just how lucky it was. I wouldn't have missed being her mum for all the world. Even if she won't wear hats.

"Porca miseria."

"Good morning to you too, Constanza."

"Sorry, no, it is Annabel Morgan, she is giving us the evil eyes, again."

"What have we done now?"

"Just being here is enough, I think. Nelly, come, your coat is not done again."

Nelly races past, ignoring her mother.

"Antonella."

Connie's right, Annabel Morgan is definitely giving us one of her Looks. As president of the PTA and all-round snooter, she's an enemy you don't want to make, but that ship sailed quite a while ago for Connie and me. She's standing with her son, Horrible Harry, who is poking his tongue out at passing children whenever her back is turned. How charming.

I'm still not entirely clear why she dislikes me so intensely but I don't think my appearing with the occasional VIP has endeared her to my cause. Being Britain's Favorite Broadcaster does mean people tend to recognize Ellen when she turns up to meet her godsons from school, and my knowing our local film star Diva Grace Harrison is even more annoying, even if I am only her official knitting coach. It's all put me firmly on Annabel's do not resuscitate list. And Connie is far too Italian to put up with any nonsense, so she's definitely on the list too.

The nasty looks have definitely got worse since Pearl arrived; I think I'm meant to be embarrassed about appearing with what she'd definitely call an illegitimate child in my buggy. In fact, as far as she's concerned all my children are annoying. Archie is in the same class as Horrible Harry, and since Archie's not one to sidestep anything remotely resembling conflict, they clash pretty frequently, and Archie's a lot less sophisticated than Harry, so he tends to shove people over rather than going in for a bit of sly nipping when nobody is watching. If Annabel could work out how to get away with it, we'd definitely be subject to a lifetime ban from the PTA.

The kids are lining up now as Mrs. King rings the bell, with help from a rather enthusiastic small boy from the reception class who is trying to lift the bell above his head for maximum ringing. Jack runs over to grab his PE kit, while Pearl tries to undo the straps on her buggy and follow him into school.

"I just hope she's this keen when she's actually old enough to go."

Connie smiles. "Nelly was the same, always trying to be with Marco."

"You look tired you know, Con. Are you sure you're not doing too much?"

I think running the pub, and trying to keep up with Nelly and Marco, combined with keeping the new café stocked, might count as too much in anybody's book.

"I am fine, little rests, all the time, it is driving me crazy. Everyone keeps saying, sit with the feet up, but how can I, if I don't know everything is being done properly?"

"I know, but—"

"And Mark is telling me yesterday, when this baby comes we will have a little holiday. But he is mad; all I will want is to stay at home, not doing the holiday."

"Your mum will come over though, won't she?"

"Yes, but after the baby, and just her, not the whole family. I have told her, there are too many Italians in our house already."

"How's it going, with Susanna and Cinzia?"

"Cinzia, okay, she is a good girl; Susanna, not so much."

"We all love Cinzia, she's a total treasure."

Connie's mum and dad have decided that since they can't persuade her to come home to Italy, they'll send the younger members of the family over to her to lend a hand, and since none of them ever travel alone, they're sending them in pairs. They're meant to learn English, like a sort of family gap year, and now baby number three is on its way, Connie's mother is even more delighted with her plan. Both Cinzia and Susanna have been instructed to keep a close eye on Connie and report back in to La Mamma. They're both really sweet, although I think Connie does get a bit fed up with them following her around trying to Help. But it's been particularly fabulous for me, since Cinzia has become our semi–au pair: she wanted to earn a bit of money, and Connie practically insisted I take her on. It's been a total lifesaver; I get some cover for the days I'm in the shop, without having a homesick Italian in my house laughing at my attempts to make pasta, and Connie gets a break from Operation Mother. It's brilliant.

"Good morning, ladies."

Bugger. Annabel Morgan has executed a sneaky rear-guard action and circled the playground so she can pounce on us. I thought we might be able to make a swift exit.

"Morning, Annabel."

"Just to let you know, the committee meeting is next week, so if you do have any suggestions, feel free to jot down some notes. I know how busy you both are."

She trills out a little laugh.

"What time is it?"

Annabel gives Connie a very dismissive look. "Sorry?"

"The meeting. When is it?"

"Eight o'clock, on Monday, but I really don't—"

"So, we will come, and we can tell everybody about the walking buses."

"There's really no need to take time away from your restaurant, Mrs. Maxwell, I know you're always so busy, no need at all; and our committee meetings are not really open to the public. But as your president, I shall be more than happy to represent your views."

Damn. I really wish we hadn't started this now. I only mentioned to Jack's teacher, Mrs. Chambers, that I'd read an article about a new scheme to get kids walking to school, and before I knew it, Connie and I had been persuaded to raise it at the annual PTA meeting, and now we've been Volunteered.

"Thanks, Annabel, but Mr. O'Brien did ask us to make sure we went to the meeting. He seemed quite keen on the idea."

Let's see if she tries to outrank the Head.

She hesitates, and various parents who are lurking nearby lean forward slightly so they can hear her response. Oh dear.

"Yes, well, that would be super, of course, so important for everyone to play their part, if you're sure you can spare the time. Now you must excuse me, but I do have to get on, so many things to do, sometimes I don't know how I manage to keep up with all my PTA business, I really don't. But we all have to do our bit, don't we? Good morning."

She nods at us, like we're dismissed, as she marches across the playground in her twinset and smart skirt, stamping her medium-heeled court shoes with annoyance. Crikey. She's channeling a minor member of the Royal Family even more than usual; she'll be knotting a silk head scarf under her chin next. Or arriving at school on a bloody horse. If she gets her hands on one of those polo sticks, we'll all be in trouble.

"Bloody hell."

Connie laughs. "I know."

"I don't even want to do this stupid walking bus thing, and you'll be too pregnant."

"To walk?"

"Well no, but walking up and down the High Street collecting small people whilst wearing a fluorescent tabard isn't my idea of the perfect way to spend my morning if I'm completely honest, Con."

"A what?"

"It's a sort of vest. But longer, like an apron."

She mutters something in Italian.

"Exactly."

"Mark says we are mad."

"Well he might have a point there, Con. Come on, let's start walking to the shop or I'll be in trouble with Elsie for being late."

"She works for you, yes, so you can arrive when you want."

"Technically yes, or I can be on time and have a peaceful morning."

"I am with the car. I have to take Susanna to her language classes; she is not going, and my aunt Silvia, she is furious."

"Oh, dear. What's she been doing then, when she gets the bus into Canterbury?"

"Flirting."

"Fair enough."

"I know. But it is not teaching her the English vocabulary."

"Maybe not the kind of vocabulary your aunt had in her mind, but I bet it comes in a lot handier than 'What time is the next train to Cardiff?'" I was helping Cinzia with her homework last week.

Connie smiles and bends down to kiss Pearl as we reach the car. Poor Susanna is sitting in the passenger seat, looking pretty miserable.

"See you later, bella. She's turning the hat again."

"I know, leave her. It annoys her if I try to turn it back the right way, and she'll be asleep in a minute."

Connie kisses her again and puts her hand on her tummy.

"I hope this one, he is happy with hats. Or she. But Mark thinks it will be a boy."

"How does he work that one out then?"

"He says already there are too many Italian women in our house."

"I don't think you can ever have enough Italian women, Con, not if they're all like you."

She blows me a kiss and gets into the car.

'm trying to work out how we can rope in enough parents to make the bloody bus thing work as I push the buggy down the High Street, with Pearl having a nap, her hat half covering her face. I got details from the local council, and you can start off with a Walking Wednesday, which I quite like the sound of, and see how it goes just one day a week before you launch a whole scheme and find yourself pretty much permanently in your tabard marshaling small people around at the crack of bloody dawn. You need a minimum of two adults for each journey: a driver and a conductor, one to lead the kids, and one at the end to make sure no stragglers get left behind. Dear God. You have to set up a route, so parents bring their kids along rather than having to stop at each house, which would take all day. But even so. Jane Johnson says she'll help, and she works in the school office, so that will be an advantage when it comes to setting up rotas and getting notes out to all the parents. But Annabel is bound to meddle if we ever

manage to get the idea approved. So that'll be me stuck in a
bright orange outfit on a ten-mile walk that finishes at the
end of our rickety old pier if she has anything to do with it.
Christ. Me and my big mouth. Next time I read something
interesting, I'm going to write myself a note. And hide it.

It's still freezing cold, but at least the sun is shining. I love
Broadgate on mornings like this, with the sea sparkling at
the end of the High Street, even if it is a rather chilly kind of
sparkle. Mr. Parsons is hanging up metal buckets on the
hooks outside his ironmongers and arranging mops, and Mrs.
Baintree in the bakery gives me a cheery wave, which is good
because when we first opened the new café things got rather
strained. I think she was worried we'd be taking all their customers, but since we don't sell loaves of bread, or giant baps,
or multicolored biscuits with smiley faces on them, cordial
relations have been restored. She even came in for a coffee
last week.

Elsie's behind the counter as I wheel Pearl through to the
back of the shop.

"Morning, Jo, is she asleep?"

"Yes, but not for long. Unless you fancy a little walk?"

She smiles. "You're all right, dear. That girl will be along
soon, won't she?"

"Yes, she's due any minute."

Hurrah. The cavalry are coming.

Elsie doesn't entirely approve of Cinzia. There's something too flamboyant about her for Elsie's taste. But even she
has to admit the children adore her.

"It looks like you sold lots of that new cotton on Saturday."

"Yes, Mrs. Collins was in, she's making another blanket. I asked her if she'd like to knit orders for us, and she was really pleased. She said she'd think about it and let us know."

"Well, she's a lovely knitter, I'll say that for her, and we can always do with more things to sell in the shop."

"Morning, Jo." Laura walks through the new archway into the café, carrying a cup and saucer. "Thought you'd like a cup of tea, Jo."

"Bless your heart. That's just what I need."

Elsie stiffens. She and Laura have a running battle over who is in overall charge. And the truth is, nobody is. Or I am. But definitely not Elsie. Laura worked for Connie at the pub as a waitress before we spotted her as perfect for the café. She's studying textile design at college part-time and lives just off the High Street with her little girl, Rosie, and her mum lives a couple of streets away from Elsie. So she's perfect for popping in when we're particularly busy in the summer, and she sorts out all the orders with Connie, and arranges the rota for her college days. Her friend Tom does the days she can't do, which is working really well, even if he does play in a band in the evenings so he sometimes looks slightly frayed around the edges in the mornings.

Connie and Mark have been really clever about the menu too, keeping it simple so we don't need too much equipment or people wearing special hairnets; we do juice and smoothies, teas and coffees, and a selection of Mark's cakes and biscuits, and paninis. Nothing hot, so no grills or ovens, just simple, fresh food and great coffee, thanks to the huge machine Connie's uncle Luca brought over for us, which was half the price of anything we could find from the local suppliers. It was a bit terrifying at first, all that steam and wiping nozzles, but he was very patient, and now we all know how to use it, although Elsie isn't convinced it's not going to blow up and tends to steer clear of it.

"Would you like a tea, Elsie?"

"Well I don't mind if you're making one."

Laura winks at me as she goes back through into the café. I'm glad now we didn't spend a fortune and turn it into one huge space. It works well having the two shops connected, and if things ever get really tough, I can always sell the café and go back to just having the wool shop. But the café is definitely attracting new customers; people don't tend to go into wool shops unless they already know how to knit, but once they're sitting in the café, they see the notices we've put up about our knitting groups, or the tea cozies, and the blankets and shawls for sale, and it encourages them. And Laura often sits knitting at the counter, working on the designs for her course, like the bag knitted on huge needles with lots of bobbles, or the cape with the lovely cable pattern.

"Hello, poppet."

Pearl is waking up.

"Shall I give her a biscuit?"

"She's just had breakfast, Elsie, thanks."

In other words No, please don't be passing her chocolate digestives every time we're in the shop, particularly when she's wearing a balaclava, or I'll have to wash it again.

Laura brings Elsie her tea and shows us both a magazine she's got from college, with pictures of a knitwear show in Milan full of extraordinary sweaters with extra sleeves, or huge cowl necks, and wonderful soft wraps draped over tiny vests.

"Do you think that's cashmere?"

Elsie and I are both peering at the pictures.

"It looks a bit thinner than that, doesn't it? Maybe silk?"

Laura nods. "That's what I thought, but then I thought maybe four-ply?"

Elsie's finding her glasses while I pick Pearl up. She's not very good at waiting patiently in her buggy while people chat.

"Come on, darling, let's see the lovely pictures."

"More."

No and *more* are the top words at the moment. And it's surprising how far you can get with just two such useful words.

"Do you want a drink, sweetheart?"

Please let me have remembered to put her juice cup in my bag.

"No."

Excellent.

"Nice apple juice?"

She starts to wriggle.

"More."

She wants to be down, running about, but I'm not that keen; I'd prefer to avoid the bit where she pulls balls of wool off the shelves and I try to stop her if I can possibly avoid it.

"Let's have some juice first, love."

She gives me one of her why-is-my-mother-such-an-idiot looks, which she's learned from Archie, and is about to start yelling when Cinzia arrives, just in the nick of time. She's looking even more like Sophia Loren than usual, a young Sophia, like she was in *Houseboat*, although I suppose that would make me Cary Grant, so possibly not. But she has that gorgeous sway about her, and wears the kinds of clothes that regularly make most of the male residents of Broadgate stand with their mouths slightly open.

She's busy kissing Pearl, which Pearl is tolerating although she's not usually that keen on too much fussing.

"So today we go to baby gymnastica, yes?"

"Thanks, Cinzia, she'll love that."

"See, I am wearing the trousers."

It's amazing how many more dads have suddenly found time to take their toddlers along to the baby gym sessions in the Village Hall since Cinzia arrived. She wore a tiny denim skirt and black footless tights a couple of weeks ago, and Lucy Meadows says Mr. Dawes was so busy watching her he tripped over a mat and banged his knee so badly he had to go home. Mrs. Dawes is still giving me rather pointed looks in the playground, particularly if Cinzia is with us.

"Brava." I'm picking up a few more Italian words to add to the ones Connie's taught me.

"Rock Around the Clock" comes on the radio, and Pearl and Cinzia start to dance, with Pearl bobbing up and down and Cinzia shaking her enviable hips. Christ. I think the baby gymnasticals might be in for another tricky session. She's wearing skinny jeans, with a glimpse of a very flat brown tummy, and a minuscule pale blue T-shirt with a cashmere cardigan. It's always cashmere with Cinzia.

"Are you still okay for tomorrow night, Cinzia?"

"Sure, and we will make pizzas I think, with 'am?"

Ham on pizzas is Archie's favorite. And Cinzia's learned not to call it prosciutto, which Archie refuses to eat.

"Great."

"Say good-bye to Mamma, Principessa."

Okay, so the Principessa thing isn't ideal, but I put up with it because Pearl likes it, and she sometimes gives me a dismissive wave, like I have her permission to leave, which is so much nicer than the routine where they burst into tears at the slightest hint that you might be about to part.

I used to hate that with Jack; he went through a very

clingy phase, which basically meant I didn't go anywhere without him for ages. He even came to the dentist with me, which was particularly hideous, him sitting in his buggy looking at his baby books while I tried to avoid flinching when the dentist did that jabbing thing they do with the little prodder. Nick used to get really annoyed about it, and told me I was making Jack anxious. With hindsight I wish I'd told him to shut up, and if he spent a bit more time working on his relationship with his son, and less time on having an affair with bloody Mimi the French UN worker, he'd be in a better position to give me top parenting tips. Although I didn't know about that at the time, of course, I just thought he was busy being an up-and-coming television news presenter, and I was the stay-at-home mum who wasn't keeping up my end of the deal. Most of the time I remember feeling like I was somehow failing, not quite exciting or smart enough, not able to keep up with the pace. God, if only I'd known.

"Thanks Cinzia, and call me, if anything—"

"Yes, I will call, like every day; I will call if anything 'appens, but it will not. We will have a lovely day, and do our gymnastica, won't we, Principessa?"

Pearl waves. I'm sure she's going to have an Italian accent; she sounds very Italian when she's babbling, and she goes in for a fair bit of Italian-style tutting, often accompanied by a slight shrug of the shoulders. And she calls me Mamma, but then so did the boys and we didn't have an Italian au pair then. Or even the remotest hint of an au pair. Nick didn't like the idea of anyone else in the house; he liked to come home and completely switch off. Sometimes he just slept, and hardly spoke to us at all. Which I also used to think was somehow my fault.

"See you later. Have a lovely day, sweetheart."

G reat. Finally, I can start work. It's ten past ten and I've been up for hours. This working-mother lark is such a treat.

"I'm going up to the office, Elsie, and I'll check the website orders."

"Right you are, dear."

I think I'll make a list. That's always calming. I'll drink my tea and make a list. And then I need to sort out the window displays. I took out most of the Christmas things last week, but I still want to add in a few more hot-water-bottle covers, and the new tea cozies. And I should probably start thinking about a new display for February, with a Valentine's Day theme again; it worked really well last year, and I've still got the strings of pink heart-shaped fairy lights in the stockroom. The café window display is fairly simple, with knitted tea cozies and teapots, and knitted cakes on the antique glass cake stands I found in Venice, and the blue willow pattern one I found in a junk shop; with fairy lights and frosted glass sundae dishes, it all looks very pretty. Gran and Betty loved knitting the scoops of ice cream for the dishes, in dark chocolate and raspberry, with a few pale pom-poms in vanilla and caramel, and mint. So all I need to do is update it, adding in knitted mince pies and holly leaves at Christmastime, or more knitted cakes. Gran found a pretty cup and saucer in the jumble sale at the Lifeboats last week, so I want to put that in too.

Which reminds me, I must ask Gran if she can babysit on Monday, so I can go to the bloody PTA meeting with Connie. I'll ask her if she's decided about her cruise as well; she's been looking at brochures again with Reg, and there are some lovely looking ones that go round the Caribbean, but she says she doesn't want to be that far away, in case I need her. So I need to persuade her it'll be fine.

Right. List. Ring Gran. Get more details on the bloody bus thing. We'll need to set up one of those telephone charts for the mornings when the light sea mist is more of a torrential downpour and walking to school would involve lots of soaked children arriving sopping wet and chilled to the bone. I should ring Mr. Prewitt too, and make sure he's got everything he needs for the shop accounts; he's been impressed with the impact of the café; our profits were up nearly 500 percent for the last quarter, even after I gave Connie and Mark their share, which sounds great until you know how low it was to start with.

I want to check with him about the insurance too; ever since the fire I've been fairly obsessive about it. Thank God our policy was up-to-date, or I would never have been able to afford to buy Mrs. Davis out. Even though her florist business wasn't earning much, and the prices round here are still pretty low, it was a fair chunk of money, and being right next door might have made some people double the price. But she was so nice about it, and kept trying to lower it because her electrics started the fire in the first place. I sorted it out with Graham and Tina in the end, and he talked to his brothers. We saved a bit by not using an agent. But I thought I'd still need to take out a business loan, and I don't think the bloody banks are that keen on wool shops run by single parents with three kids. Although they seem perfectly fine with multimillion-pound gambles run by the kind of men who you'd pay serious money not to sit next to at dinner parties. Not that I go to dinner parties, but if I did I bet I'd end up sitting next to a banker boasting about his bonus. Despite taking us to the brink of financial meltdown, they all still seem to be awarding themselves massive bonuses. Bastards. But with the insurance money and a bit of help from Gran and Reg, and dipping into my rainy day money, I managed to buy the café without having to go the bank. Not that things aren't a bit tight, and I still can't work out how I managed to paint most of the upstairs while Pearl was newborn. I went into a sort of magnolia daze I was so tired. But things have always been tight financially, so I'm used to it. Nick and I never reached the bit where things got a little easier; he was gone long before that. Not that I realized it at the time. I thought he was just working, not off having an affair and taking out a bloody second mortgage behind my back. It's almost embarrassing how stupid I was back then. Still, you live and learn, as Gran would say. Although in Nick's case of course, not so much.

Damn, that's something else to add to my list. I need to call Elizabeth and arrange a time for us to visit the grave. Another opportunity for her to tell us all how marvelous her Nicholas was, and treat me like his driving his car into a tree was somehow my fault. It's been three years next weekend, but it feels so much longer than that. We've come a long way since those early days, when the police came round and everything fell apart. If Ellen hadn't been there for me I don't know how I'd have managed. The shock, the grief, the anger, all of it. Now it all feels much more distant. Maybe I've done that thing all the books say you're meant to do, and I'm into the acceptance phase. Maybe forgiveness is on the horizon, although on second thought, maybe not. I don't think I'll ever really forgive him. Not for crashing the car, he couldn't help that; although if he'd ever listened to me when I told him not to drive like a total nutter, well, who knows. But for planning to leave the boys, who idolized him. It was all so predictable, and unfair, and cheap, and he's already missed so much. And

I can't help wishing he'd met Pearl, although if he was still around I probably wouldn't have had her. I would never have gone to Venice for that first Christmas after he died, when I couldn't face our first family Christmas without Nick. I'd never have sat drinking whiskey with Daniel in his hotel room, talking about lost loves. Still, I wish Nick could have seen my gorgeous girl, I know he'd have got a kick out of seeing how like Jack she was when she was born. He'd have recognized her in a heartbeat. She's much more like Archie now, in temper and steeliness, which is probably a good thing. I think girls need a bit of steel, just in case.

Oh God, I'm feeling tearful now, and I really don't have the time for this. Not now. I'll check the order book, and if that doesn't work I'll do a mini–stock take. That always helps.

"Hello, pet."

"Gran, I was just going to call you."

"Reg has just dropped me off, he's on his way to the Bowls Club, there's a row on about who put the scoreboard away last time; silly fuss about nothing if you ask me. Did you want me for anything special?"

"No, just wanted to know if you've decided about your cruise."

"Not yet, pet, I like to take my time, and Reg is getting some new brochures. There's a lovely one goes round the fjords, and Russia."

"Why would you go there when you could be in the Caribbean?"

"I don't like it too hot, you know that, pet."

"Well, that definitely won't be a problem if you're cruising round Siberia."

She smiles.

"Gran, you're not fooling me you know. Go on a proper cruise. We can manage for a few weeks. I really want you to have a proper break."

"I know, pet, but I'm not even sure I want to go gallivant- ing off, spending all that money. I get lots of breaks now, and what I really like is being with you and the boys, and our Pearl. I never thought it would be so lovely you know, stuck in this shop for all those years with old Mrs. Butterworth mak- ing my life a misery, I never dreamed it would all turn out like this. I'm so glad I stuck it now. Reg was saying the same thing only the other day. And when you get to my age, if you haven't worked out what makes you happy, then it's too late. And for me, it's stopping right here."

"I know Gran, but—"

"I'll think about it, pet, that's all I'm saying. Anyway, it's not like I haven't been before, we had our lovely honeymoon cruise, which I still think is silly at our age, calling it a honey- moon. It was different with your grandad Tom, but we were so young we couldn't afford a proper honeymoon, just a night in a hotel in Margate. Terrible place, got bombed flat later in the war, and a good thing too. No, my holiday with Reg was lux- ury compared to that. And he does look nice in his blazer; I'll say that for him. So I'll think about it, I promise. Now then, when do you need me this week? I'm happy to come in, you know, or sit with the children, whatever you need, just say. Shall we have a cup of tea, love? I'm parched."

"Lovely."

"And then we can run through the next few days. I've brought my diary, Reg got me one, did I show you? Lovely leather one."

"Yes, you did, Gran." About ten times actually.

"I'll just put the kettle on then."

It's like a military exercise, keeping track of our week. Cinzia has her English classes in Canterbury, so Gran has Pearl on Monday mornings, and they go to baby music, which Pearl enjoys, particularly the drums apparently. Reg sits cross-legged on the floor with her because his knees are better than Gran's, while she catches up on the gossip with Mrs. Nesbit, who makes the tea. But all in all, despite the tricky timetabling, we seem to manage, unless anyone is ill, or the kids are on holiday, when it all goes pear-shaped and I have to make it up day by day. But Elsie is always happy to do extra shifts in the shop, and Gran's friend Betty helps out too, so we usually get there. And it's not quite as overwhelming as I thought it would be in those first few weeks after Pearl was born. Although there was one morning when I'd finally got her off to sleep, and I was sitting by the till, with her Moses basket by my feet, looking at the order book, and then I woke up nearly an hour later to find Elsie had draped a blanket over my shoulders and was making the customers tiptoe past while I was facedown on the counter, still holding the order book. Which wasn't a perfect example of entrepreneurship, but people seemed to like it.

"Right then, pet, you've got me for half an hour or so, what needs doing?"

"You could help me with the windows."

Gran loves doing the window displays with me. "Lovely."

We rearrange the hot-water-bottle covers, and adjust the
little wooden figures that are meant to look like they are
skiing down the cotton wool slopes, while I drape hats and
scarves over the partition along with a couple of mohair
shawls in dark forest green and apple green, with white fairy
lights in the cotton wool snow. I'm knitting another shawl in
soft cotton, in a dark orange marmalade color, but I haven't
quite finished it yet.

By the time Reg has collected Gran, and we've talked
about cruises again, and whether they do or do not want a
balcony, and I've talked to Mr. Prewitt and put in orders for
more cotton and the chunky tweed, it's nearly half past one
and I'm knackered. The café's busy, so I sit upstairs in the
workroom and light the fire. People often bring a drink and
a slice of cake up with them from the café while they look
through the pattern books; Elsie's convinced we'll end up
with sticky balls of wool from people browsing while they're
eating; she keeps a packet of wipes behind the till specially,
but so far she hasn't had to swoop in and demand anyone
wipe their hands.

It's so lovely watching the flames on the kindling wood,
with no customers, and no small people needing any attention. It's hard to believe you could see the sky through the
holes in the roof after the fire, when everything was black
and soaking wet. But with the new plaster and paint, you'd
never know it happened. Downstairs is still pretty much how
it was, only brighter and warmer, but upstairs is where there's
been the biggest transformation. The whole of the space
above the shop is now the workroom, with the fireplace and
the big table, and lots more shelves, and a new sofa and armchairs by the window where the old kitchen used to be. Above
the café we've made a small office in the front and a large

kitchen with the café dishwasher and huge fridge. We've managed to fit in a storeroom too, with floor-to-ceiling shelves for extra stock, which means we can order larger quantities and get better discounts. But almost best of all, we've actually got a parking space now, in the lane behind the café; the wool shop never had a back door because we're right on the corner, but the café does, so now there's somewhere for delivery vans, and I can leave the door open and nip into the shop for five minutes if Pearl is asleep in her car seat. Elsie keeps an eye on her, or Laura, so it's not as dodgy as it sounds, and it made a real difference when she was tiny and waking her up led to so much squawking.

I'm in serious danger of falling asleep when Mrs. Bullen comes up wanting to look at patterns for Fair Isle cardigans for her granddaughter. We're back downstairs choosing colors when Mark arrives.

"Afternoon, Jo. Connie said you were getting low on chocolate, and the pistachio, so I thought I'd bring some more stock over."

"Thanks, Mark."

He unloads the tubs of ice cream and puts them into the big glass-fronted display fridge in the café while Mrs. Bullen finally decides on purples and pinks to contrast with the grays and whites. The pattern has a lovely pale blue which we haven't actually got in stock, but apparently it doesn't matter, because her granddaughter is now insisting on pink and more pink since her new baby brother arrived. I find a pretty rose pink as a substitute, and a ball of pale lilac, which I let her have at half price since it's the last one on the shelf.

"I can't wait to get home and get started."

"Well don't forget, come back in if you need a hand with anything."

"I will, thank you, dear."

Mrs. Bullen often gets confused with patterns, and the last time she made a cardigan she ended up with two left fronts and no right, so now she tends to pop in and check she's on the right track. We're always happy to help, and Elsie loves it; she can give top tips and catch up on all the latest gossip at the same time.

"Here, Jo, try this, would you?" Mark hands me a glass dish and a spoon, and Laura's already started on hers. Great; I love it when we do tastings. The ice cream is still our best seller. I thought it might slow down in the winter, and it has a bit, but since Mark keeps to his mantra of seasonal food, and introduces new flavors every couple of weeks, demand has stayed fairly steady.

"Not too sweet?"

We both shake our heads; too busy enjoying it to waste time speaking.

He smiles. "Good. The first batch I made was too sweet. Clementines can be tricky like that. I'm glad it's okay."

"It's so much more than okay, Mark."

Each time he brings in a new flavor I end up revising my Top Ten List. Damson, blackberry, salt caramel, the peach one he made in the summer, lemon meringue, hazelnut, and the chestnut one he made at Christmas. The raspberry ripple with old-fashioned vanilla. And the gooseberry fool was pretty epic too. Actually, maybe I'll just have a Top Twenty, because the honeycomb is lovely too, and the black currant. I think I might need another mini-scoop.

"Looks like the sorbet is getting low too. I'll do some more tonight, I've still got stacks of frozen berries in the freezer."

"Lovely."

"I'll do some more sherbet too, shall I?"

"Perfect."

"Right, well I better be off, we've got a big group in for dinner later, and Con's on at me to pull out all the stops. Some family birthday, so they've ordered a cake."

"Lucky them."

Laura looks longingly at him as he goes out and sighs. "I wish I could meet someone like him. Maybe a bit younger. But basically just like him. The ice cream alone would make it worth it."

"Maybe you should check out the local catering college?"

She smiles. "Have you seen them? Either they're seventeen and nervous or they think they're God's gift. No thanks. Mark's so clever with the new flavors, you know; some of our regulars come in just for that."

"Actually, I think that was Connie's idea. They serve the ice cream at the pub too, and they like the menu to change so they can keep things seasonal. They've taken on a new apprentice now, just for the pastries and ice cream."

"I know, he was telling me. Actually, that's the only thing I don't like about him really."

"What?"

"That he's got such a lovely wife." She grins.

"Yes, that is a drawback, I can see that."

"It's bloody typical. All the good ones are married, or gay."

"Tell me about it."

She laughs, and then we realize Elsie has come into the café and has heard me. She's not pleased. Damn. Not only have I inadvertently cast aspersions on Martin, which is something only she's allowed to do, but we forgot to call her in for the Tasting. Bugger.

"You've got to try this, Elsie."

"I've just had my lunch, thank you." She sniffs, clearly annoyed. Great.

Laura winks at me as I follow Elsie back into the shop.

Things are still pretty frosty when Martin arrives.

"Hi, Jo. Hello, Mum. I'd love a coffee."

"I'm not using that silly machine; you can have tea and like it. Better for you."

"Okay."

She goes into the café, and Martin looks puzzled.

"What's up with her now?"

"Mark brought some new ice cream in, and I forgot to ask her to help us taste it."

"Oh dear, I'm sure she'll get over it."

"Yes, but how long will I be getting the sniffing routine?"

"Well, she's still not speaking to my aunty Doris over that shortbread."

"And when did that happen?"

"Three years ago."

"Thanks, Martin, that's very encouraging."

He grins. "Sorry. Look, have you got a minute? I've got something to show you."

Oh God, I hope it's not another bit of floorboard. Or a kitchen brochure.

Buying the wreck of a barn to renovate was definitely one of his better ideas. It combines his passions for carpentry and all things wooden with bargain hunting and reclaiming old materials, so it's eco-friendly too. I'm sure it will be stunning if he ever finishes it. But it does seem to involve me in more conversations about oak versus walnut than I ever imagined possible.

"I've got about fifteen minutes before I need to leave to get the boys. Can it wait?"

"I've found a new book—well, an old one really—with patterns, for cabinets and cupboards, for the kitchen. I got it at the library."

"Great."

"Do you think I need a plate rack?"

"Sorry?"

"There's one with a sort of rack, for plates, built into the cupboard. Would that be good?"

"Depends on how many plates you're going to have. You've only got three so far."

"Two actually, Trevor got a bit excited when the lorry turned up yesterday with the bricks, and he knocked the table over."

Trevor the bloody Wonder Dog is now fully grown, and even more enormous than when we first met him pulling our new neighbor Mr. Pallfrey up our garden path on the night we moved in.

"How's Mr. Pallfrey doing?"

"Fine, I think. He rang me last week from Spain. Well, I say me, but he likes to speak to Trevor too."

"Martin, you're completely mad, you know that, don't you?"

"Trevor recognizes his voice."

"Well he bloody should do, he's his dog. Which brings me to the question how come you're stuck with him, with us as backup? It was only meant to be temporary, you know."

Mr. Pallfrey is visiting his daughter Christine, in Spain, ostensibly recuperating from his second hip operation, but I think he likes it so much he's going to stay over there.

"I still can't work out how you've ended up adopting Trevor.

A few weeks were fine, but it's been ages now. And yes, I know you like dogs, and the boys adore him, and so does Pearl, although he does keep knocking her flat and sooner or later she's going to get fed up with that. Even bloody Cinzia loves him. I know you wanted a dog, but do you really want such a huge mad one?"

"I can't get rid of him now, it wouldn't be fair. I'm too nice, that's my trouble."

"And an idiot."

I lean across the counter and kiss him, which is risky, because if Elsie comes back in with the tea there'll be even more sniffing.

He's grinning now. "Anyway, enough of all that, I need to ask you something."

"No."

"You don't know what it is yet."

"Can we have Trevor for the night next week while you go to London for a freelance job that'll pay double your usual rate because their computers have all gone on the blink and you're the only person who can unravel them?"

"Crikey, that's almost spooky, how did you— Oh, right. Mum."

Elsie puts the tray on the counter and sniffs again. "There's only digestives."

"I thought you liked digestives, Elsie."

I've learnt from bitter experience that it's pretty vital to keep Elsie supplied with the right kinds of biscuits, particularly if she's already in a sulk.

"I do, but I like those jam ones you got last week, I was hoping for one of those. Still, never mind. Now what were you saying, Martin?"

"Nothing, Mum, just talking about Trevor."

She sniffs again.

"Martin can go and get some Jammie Dodgers, Elsie. Can't you, Martin?"

"What? Well I—"

"Yes. And I'll think about that stupid dog."

"Right. Jammie Dodgers coming up. Is that right, Mum? Or are these some new biscuits with jam that I don't know about?"

"Don't be cheeky, Martin, it doesn't suit you."

It does actually.

He kisses me on the cheek and then winks. Bugger. Elsie is definitely going to need those extra biscuits now.

By the time I've got the boys home, and we've had baked potatoes and tuna with grated cheese for Jack, and sweet corn for Archie, and a bit of both for Pearl, although most of the sweet corn ended up on the kitchen floor as usual, because she insists on waving her spoon about, I'm exhausted. I've managed to get through bath time without shouting at anyone, but I'm beyond tired. Pearl conks out in her cot nice and early, but Jack and Archie are still keen for another half hour of cartoons.

"It's a school night, come on, up we go, and there might be time for a story."

"Mum, that's just not fair. I'm the oldest; I'm nearly ten, so I should be allowed to stay up longer."

Archie is horrified. "You are not nearly ten, not for ages. You're nine, and I'm nearly eight, and that's only one littler than nine, so you're not that bigger. Stupid."

"Tell him, Mum."

"You can keep your light on and read for a bit, Jack, you know that. But it's bedtime now."

There is no way on this earth I'm falling for an extra half hour of someone sitting downstairs watching child-friendly telly every evening, thank you very much.

"Yes, but I'm not tired, Mum, I'm really not."

Archie's getting agitated now. "I'm not tired too, stupid."

"Well I am, so stop it, both of you. Or there won't be time for any stories. At all."

They both hesitate but recognize the signs of a mother close to the edge.

"You can choose one book each, and no, Jack, not a long book, one of your bedtime picture books. Or not. And I'll just have a nice rest and you two can sulk."

"Honestly Mum, there's no need to be so grumpy. Great big grumpypotamus."

"Thanks, Archie, I love you too."

Archie falls asleep while I'm reading to him, but Jack's sitting up looking anxious by the time I'm trying to tuck him in.

"Lie down, love."

"Mum, you know Dad is in heaven."

Oh God, not again.

"Yes love."

"If there is a heaven. That's what we say, isn't it?"

"Yes love."

"Well, is there?"

"What sweetheart?"

"A heaven."

"I don't know, Jack, nobody does. Not really. Some people think there is, but if you love somebody, like you love Dad, well, that never ends. They live in your heart forever."

"And that's a kind of heaven, isn't it, Mum?"

"Yes love."

And a kind of hell too, if you happen to have been on the point of leaving them and sodding off to live with a bloody French nymphet called Mimi. And now you're stuck floating about somewhere and watching your little boys trying to make sense of it all.

"Yes, but he can't see us, can he? Not all the time?"

"No love."

Please don't let him ask me any more tricky questions tonight, I'm too tired and I never feel I'm getting this right. I don't want to trot out the lines about heaven and angels, because I'm really not sure what I think about all of that, and it seems important to be honest about something so important. But I want them to have the comfort of it, like fairies and Father Christmas; that sense that magic things can happen and there will always be a happy ending. Even if it doesn't feel like it. Something that makes the darker moments a bit more bearable.

He's still thinking.

"Snuggle down, love."

"I can't see him now, Mum, when I close my eyes. Sometimes I can't remember what he looked like."

He's on the brink of tears now, silent crying in the dark while he tries to make sense of it all.

Bloody hell, I hate this. It's so incredibly unfair.

"I know love, neither can I, sometimes. But we've got lots of photographs, and our holiday films."

"It's not the same."

"I know, but when you look at the photographs, you'll see, you'll feel it straightaway, love."

"Feel what?"

"How much he loved you, more than anything in the whole world."

"Yes. More than anything in the whole wide world to infinity and back again."

There's a small smile now.

"Yes."

"Even more than Archie, because I was first, wasn't I, Mum?"

"He loved you both more than anything in the entire world; there just isn't anything bigger than that. Now, what story do you want, love?"

"*Owl Babies*. Just because it's one of our favorites. I'm too big for it really."

"Okay."

"And Mum."

"Yes, Jack."

"If I have one of my dreams, can I come into your bed?"

"Yes love. But very quietly. If you bring Archie or wake up Pearl, then the deal's off."

He nods and snuggles down.

So that'll be him in my bed by the time I come back upstairs. Great.

"Oh darling, poor Jack, he's always been such a trooper about it all, and they've coped so well, you know, you've done an amazing job."

"No I haven't, Ellen, I've done what any mum would do, muddled through the best you can and tried to keep the kids safe."

"Well, I think you're amazing."

"I should bloody hope so. You'd be in real trouble if your best friend thought you were crap."

"True."

"He hasn't had his bad dreams so much lately; I was hoping he might be getting over it. Well, not over it, obviously, but past worrying it was somehow his fault."

"Archie's never really gone in for that, has he?"

"No, nothing is ever Archie's fault. He gets that from Nick. But he minds. He told me the other day, how much he misses him."

"Did he?"

"Yes, but he wanted to play football in his pajamas, so I'm not sure he wasn't just guilt-tripping me, to see if I might cave and let him out into the garden."

"Why should you feel guilty? You didn't do anything. Christ."

"It's never just one person though, is it? And anyway, haven't you realized yet, the wonderful world of motherhood is one long guilt trip; it goes with the territory."

"True. I was looking at Eddie the other day, and he's definitely got Harry's nose, you know. You'd think I could have chosen someone with more aquiline features. Anyway, enough of all this guilt-tripping bollocks, tell me about you and Dovetail. What's up? I thought it was working out really well."

"It was, I mean it is. It's just. Oh, I don't know, but sometimes it feels like we've been catapulted forward ten years."

"You mean you're totally bored and you hate him?"

"No, but I think maybe we're in a bit of a rut, and it's quite early for that, isn't it? I mean, we haven't actually been seeing each other that long, not really."

"By seeing you mean shagging, right?"

"Ellen."

"Well, you do."

"I mean just the two of us, as opposed to with the kids, or in the shop, or with his mother."

"Kinky."

"Ellen, this is so not helping."

"Sorry darling. But seriously, maybe he's not the one for you."

"I don't want anyone who's the one for me, I haven't got the energy. The last thing I need is Mr. Right."

"Just Mr. Friday Night?"

"Something like that. I just want everyone to be happy, and go to sleep on time. That's about all I can cope with at the minute. And I do like him, you know, he's really—"

"Don't say nice, darling. It's the kiss of death."

"I know, but he is. A really decent, nice, kind man. He'll never cheat or lie, and he gets how important the children are, they're not just background noise for him."

"Stop it, I'm getting so jealous. The passion. I can't bear it."

"Yes, but maybe that's just the way it is, when it's more than a brief affair, for most people anyway, and I can barely make it through the day as it is; the last thing I need is too much passion."

"You can't have too much passion my darling, trust me. But I do know what you mean. Sometimes I look at Harry and I think, Really? This is it, forever? How's that going to work?"

"But it does."

"Not all the time."

"You say that, Ellen, but it does, with you and Harry."

"He's all right, I suppose. Moans a lot, but when I watch him with our beautiful boy, well, it makes up for a great deal."

"Exactly. But that's another thing. Martin's great with the kids, better than Nick ever was, but they're not his. He just doesn't have that extra bit of connection, and I'm not sure about that, longer term."

"Well, you could soon fix that."

"How?"

"Have another one, with him."

"Are you mad? I'm in enough trouble with the three I've got. Christ, four would finish me off completely. I don't think Martin wants kids actually; he's never said anything. And anyway, I'm too old."

"Forty isn't old, darling, haven't you heard?"

"It bloody is if you've got three kids under ten, and no visible means of support that doesn't involve you getting out there and working for it. And before you say it, yes, there's still a bit of my rainy day money left, and the money for the boys from Nick's work policy, and Daniel said he'd put some money aside for Pearl, when she's bigger. But that's up to him. I've told you, I don't want to be beholden. Not to anyone. I never want to do that again. That way the world can't come crashing down again. See, I've got it all worked out."

"Marvelous, darling. Talking of Daniel."

"We're not talking about Daniel, we're talking about Martin."

"Yes, but when Daniel rang you on her birthday, and then turned up bearing half of Toys 'R' Us in the car, are you really sure you're okay with that? Because I think you're mad. You should sue him for every penny."

"For what? It was my choice, Ellen, and anyway, the presents weren't useless. Well, not all of them."

"Nothing for you though?"

"Ellen, it was one night. A nice moment. Why would he be bringing me presents? He hardly knows me. I like it that he comes to see her. He's not going to be a major part of her life, and that's fine, Nick wasn't much different for the boys, not when it counted."

"I know darling, but wouldn't it be good not to have to work quite so hard?"

"Says the woman who went back to work six weeks after having Eddie."

"Yes, but that's different. The bastards are all after my job, you know that. If I'd left it any longer, I'd have been moved back to weekend slots. Anyway, don't change the subject. All I'm saying is keep your options open, with everything, including Martin."

"Well, that should be easy; he's not pushing me to do anything else."

"Do you want him to then? Ask if he can move in or something?"

"God, no."

"Well then."

"I know, ignore me. I don't know what I mean."

"It's not enough, that's what you mean, and I think you're right, I've told you before. He's sweet, but he's not enough for you. You need someone who can give you a run for your money."

"What money?"

"You know what I mean, someone more like Nick."

"Ellen, please. When I think how long I spent trying to work out what to do for Valentine's Day that year, and if he'd get the new foreign correspondent job and whether we'd get posted to somewhere with good schools for the boys. It would be ironic if it wasn't so tragic."

"I know, darling, but you were happy, at first."

"Until."

"Yes I know, until he came home and announced he was

having an affair and then stormed out and crashed the bloody car. Bastard. But look how far you've come since then."

"I didn't have much choice."

"Yes you did, darling, you could have gone under, especially with him taking out that second mortgage on the house and leaving you with no money and everything. You could have been in real trouble. But you didn't. You picked yourself up and carried on."

"Yes, straight into the next disaster."

"Daniel wasn't a disaster, darling, your first Christmas on your own was bound to be rocky, going to Venice to your mum and dad was a top plan. And having a magic moment with Daniel was just what you needed."

"Oh yes, perfect. Being wanton in a glamorous hotel. Very clever. Until I got back home and realized I was pregnant."

We're both giggling now.

"Yes, but I've told you that was just incredibly bad luck, that would never happen twice; condoms are usually completely reliable; trust me, I should know. God, if I'd gotten pregnant every time I had a magic moment I'd be like Old Mother Hubbard. But you don't regret having Pearl, do you?"

"Of course not, you know I wanted another one but Nick refused to even talk about it."

"Well then, and now Daniel's calmed down and stopped sending those daft letters from his lawyer demanding tests, it's all worked out fine."

"Yes, but it's not exactly an endorsement for boys who can give you a run for your money, is it?"

"I know, but Daniel was a proper match for you; he was an alpha male, that's all I'm saying, and you're an alpha female."

"Yes, but in case you'd forgotten, Daniel's got a Diva of his

own now, and I don't think Liv will take kindly to his attention straying too far."

"She sounds like a total cow to me, and she's definitely had
work done, you can see it on her face. Quite recently, if you
ask me."

"I think they all do, Ellen."

"Your Amazing Grace hasn't."

"She's not my Grace, she's our local Diva and I'm her
knitting coach, that's all. But she is amazing."

"I was looking at some paparazzi shots of her skiing, and
even in one of those hideous ski suits she looks amazing. And
they got her on the slopes; you could see she wasn't in full
makeup or anything. And she still looked bloody gorgeous."

"Are you still trying to persuade Harry to go on that skiing trip?"

"No, I've gone off the idea now. Tom Partridge came back
with his leg broken in three places; they had to air-ambulance
him home. His wife wheeled him into the studio yesterday
and he looked well pissed off. She was pretty chirpy though;
it's the first time she's been able to keep track of him for years,
he's such a shagger. And anyway the outfits are hideous, unless you look like your Diva; she had a great fur hat on actually, beautiful, but she'll have to watch it, I bet those animal
rights nutters can ski."

"I'll tell Maxine the next time she calls."

"When are they back from the States?"

"A few more weeks, I think. She's doing loads of publicity
for the new film."

"And you're the transatlantic knitting coach; see, you can
do stuff like that. Not many people could pull something like
that off. You just need a bit more après-ski, that's all. I can see

you might not want to tackle another black run like Daniel just yet, but you could still go off piste a bit more."

"Yes, and end up facedown in a snowdrift, being rescued by a Saint Bernard who's even more stupid than Trevor. No thanks."

"Yes, but keep your eyes open for new boys, that's all I'm saying. You never know, you still might get swept off your feet by a tall, dark, handsome fisherman or something."

"I'd need more than my eyes open round here, I'd need a bloody huge telescope. Anyway, you know we don't have fishermen down here, apart from a few old codgers on the pier, and getting swept off our pier isn't my idea of a good night out."

"Oh, I don't know. He could rescue you, mouth-to-mouth and off you go. I'm feeling it, darling. Just don't wear that tragic old sweater. Make sure you've got a cotton shift on or something."

"Good night, Ellen."

"Night darling."

Great. So now I've got to fall off the pier and hope I get rescued by a handsome stranger, rather than a pensioner with a folding stool and a thermos flask. I better get the timing right, because I could have quite a wait. A cotton shift would be hopeless; at this time of year you'd only last about thirty seconds in the sea, it's bloody freezing. Maybe a flannelette one would give you a few more minutes. I saw a pretty one in one of my catalogs, I think, with roses on. Excellent. I'll add it to my list. Or possibly not.

··· 2 ···

Toddlers, Tiaras, and Tantrums

February

'm kneeling in the window of the shop on Thursday morning, trying to hang little pink hearts on pink gingham ribbon. I've got cramp in my arm and I've just knelt on one of the pink fairy lights, so now I'm stuck dithering, leaning over the partition tweaking and trying to avoid kneeling on anything else. There's always a point when I'm doing the windows that I want to chuck everything out in the street and go and get a doughnut. I lit the fire in the workroom earlier, and the lure of one of Mark's chocolate croissants is growing: exactly what you need on a freezing February morning when you've just crushed a fairy light.

I'm worried I may have overdone it on the pink: I've knitted small hearts in pale pink and a crisp white cotton, and some cashmere and silk ones in tea rose pink, and filled them with dried lavender, and Gran's made some pom-poms, which I've hung from the partition, although they're a bit more shades of

Pepto-Bismol than I intended. Mrs. Marwell has just popped in to tell me she thinks it looks lovely, but I'm still not sure. Maybe when I drape the mohair shawls over the partition that will sharpen it up. Elsie's knitted one in bright candy pink with small silver beads knitted in along the edges, and I've made one in garnet, and one of the cotton ones in amethyst, so I hope that will make it all look a bit less My Little Pony.

"Have we got any headache tablets, Jo?"

Christ, all the pink must be getting to Tom as well. I thought he looked a bit under the weather when I arrived this morning; he was making himself a triple espresso and told me he'd been out with the band until 4:00 a.m., before retreating behind the counter to serve Maggie with her early morning coffee on her way in to the library. Mind you, I'd be needing way more than a couple of headache tablets if I'd been out until 4:00 a.m. I'd probably need those things people use to jump-start their cars—one more bit of proof, if proof were needed, that he's nineteen and taking his gap year while he works out what he wants to do with his life, and I'm forty, with three kids, and no gap year anywhere in sight.

"I think there's some aspirin upstairs in the kitchen cupboard."

"Great. That window looks brilliant by the way. Are those heart things hard to make?"

"Not really."

"Could I do one then? Only this Valentine's Day thing's a really big deal for girls, isn't it?"

"I think it depends on the girl, Tom."

He nods, and then winces. "Yes, but it's one of those things where they say they don't care and then they really mind if you don't make a big fuss, isn't it? My mum goes nuts if my dad forgets. She locked him in the garage one year."

"I bet he didn't forget after that."

"No, but then he forgot her birthday, and she locked herself in the garage, and that was much worse."

"Why?"

"We hadn't had supper."

He grins. "Anyway, I haven't got much cash at the minute, so I thought, Well, if I made something, a token gesture kind of thing?"

"That's a good idea."

"So would you help me then?"

"Sure."

Elsie's been hovering and can't resist joining in.

"Well I think that's lovely, making something for your mum. My Martin used to make me things like that, and I've still got them all. There's some of your lavender left Jo, you could put some of that in. And it's nice to know where it came from, so you be sure to tell her; Jo dries it herself and everything. And the price they charge for those little sachets, and most of them are dust, no real smell at all."

"Can we wait for the aspirin to kick in first, Jo?"

"Of course. I'm here until three today, or I've got my Stitch and Bitch group tonight if you want to come along to that."

"That's all women, isn't it?" He looks rather panicky.

"We might make an exception, just this once."

"No, you're all right; I think I'd rather have a go on my own if that's okay, without a load of women watching me make a total idiot of myself. Oh, sorry, Elsie. But maybe after lunch, when we're a bit quieter? Do you want a cappuccino, Jo, decaf, extra foam?"

"Perfect."

"Coming right up. Tea, Elsie?"

"Yes please, dear."

"There's still a couple of croissants left if either of you fancy one?"

"I'll just have one of my biscuits, thanks." Elsie doesn't hold with croissants, she thinks they make too much mess. Flaky pastry isn't something she encourages.

"Sounds like another good idea, Tom, I'll just finish off here, and I'll be right with you."

Excellent. This café lark is definitely working out way better than I'd hoped.

'm changing the roll of paper in the credit card machine when I see Martin and Trevor the bloody Wonder Dog are outside. Martin's trying to persuade him to sit while he ties him to the railings, but Trevor's having none of it, and by the time he's got him safely tethered, Elsie and I are both standing behind the counter, watching him.

"There's no need to stand there looking like that. He's still learning how to Sit, but he's getting better at it."

"Just not outside shops?"

"Yes, well, I wouldn't be quite so superior about it or I'll give him back."

"Well give him back then; send him to Spain to live with Mr. Pallfrey. I never agreed to adopt the silly thing."

"He just doesn't know his own strength, that's all. But he's getting much better; you've got to admit that."

Elsie sniffs. "Not by the state of your jeans he's not, he's always pulling you over. Anyway, some of us have got better things to do than talk about silly dogs. I'll go and sort that new stock out, shall I, Jo? Shall I put it on the shelves in the workroom?"

"Please, Elsie, next to the Scottish tweed."

"Right you are. And Martin, I've done those shirts, if you want to pick them up."

"Thanks, Mum."

He shakes his head as she goes upstairs. "I keep telling her, she doesn't need to iron them. I've got an iron."

"But no ironing board?"

"I did have one, it's just . . . Well, never mind."

"Trevor killed it."

"It was very old; Mum had been keeping it in the shed, for spare."

"A spare ironing board?"

"Don't ask."

"Well at least I know where you get it from."

"What?"

"Being bonkers."

"Thanks, I only came in to ask you out to dinner, and now I'm being told I'm bonkers."

"Sorry."

He's smiling. "I thought maybe on Saturday? Only I should probably book somewhere what with it being Valentine's Day. Do you think Connie might have a table?"

"I doubt it. They've been booked solid for weeks now, and this Saturday's not ideal, we've got Fiona on Sunday."

"Fiona?"

"My ex-sister-in-law. Married to James, Nick's brother. That Fiona."

"Oh, right. That's this weekend, is it?"

"Yes. I told you."

"Of course, well, if you've got other plans."

"Don't make it sound like we're off on a jaunt, we're having lunch with Nick's family and then visiting his grave. It's not my ideal weekend."

"No, of course not, I didn't mean—"

"I know you didn't, sorry. I'm just a bit nervous about it, that's all."

"Nervous? What have you got to be nervous about?"

Sometimes I wish he wasn't quite so literal.

"Just silly stuff like Fiona giving me her special recipe for lemon curd and showing me her cleaning rota again. She makes sure every bloody inch of her house gets polished at least once a week you know, and she hoovers twice a day. It's almost scary how perfect everything is; I feel like I'm up for a slattern of the year award every time I see her. And Nick's mother is still sulking about me having Pearl. It doesn't fit her image of the grieving widow. I think I'm meant to spend the rest of my life in black, sobbing."

"Doesn't she know, I mean, well, you know . . ."

"About her favorite son having an affair and wanting a divorce? No, she bloody doesn't. It didn't seem like the ideal time to tell her, what with it being his funeral. And then after that, well, it just seemed too cruel. So I'm the brazen hussy who isn't honoring her son's memory, and Pearl is, well, not a member of her family, put it like that. It's going to be a total bloody nightmare. But the boys want to go."

"Of course. God, sorry, I didn't mean to."

He leans over the counter and pats my arm, which is somehow mildly annoying and yet rather sweet at the same time.

"Does she really have a rota for cleaning?"

"Yes, she bloody does. It's up on the notice board in her kitchen, all color-coded and cross-referenced with her diary for the girls' school and that stupid Golf Club she belongs to with Elizabeth. She could handle logistics for a small country it's so complicated, but there's no way she's going to let a

Ladies' Match get in the way of her keeping her bathroom tiles sparkling. She shows it to me every time we're there; she even printed out a copy for me once, when Nick and I first got married. I think she was hoping I might finally see the light. Discover the joys of polishing things."

He laughs. "I could do with someone like that at the barn."

"You so couldn't, Martin, not unless you got a major supply of Valium. Either that or you'd find her collapsed in a heap, hyperventilating clutching her mop."

"It's not that bad."

"Is there still a big hole in the middle of the kitchen floor?"

"Yes, but I've told you, I haven't decided where to put the pipes yet, not until I decide about the new cesspit. There are some really good compost loos now, you know, with sawdust, and that way I wouldn't have to buy a tank."

"No, because nobody would ever come round, and you and Trevor could just make do with a bucket."

He smiles. "So you think I should hook up to mains drainage then, or replace the old cesspit?"

Since when did the merits of mains drainage become one of my specialist subjects?

"I'd rather not think about it at all, if I'm honest. But yes, since you're asking, I think you need a proper loo, not something that includes sawdust."

"Fair enough. I got those brochures, by the way."

Oh, good, more brochures. He must have practically every brochure in existence now.

"For what?"

"The bath. There's a great one, with jets and everything."

As well as being a budding eco-warrior, Martin loves gadgets. He's a sucker for anything electronic, especially with flashing lights and complicated programs. He'll spend days carving the perfect banister, even though the barn doesn't actually have any stairs yet, but he'll also spend an entire weekend installing what seemed like miles of cable, just so he can turn off all the lights with one click of a button on the remote-control unit. Unfortunately, Trevor then buried the remote control in the garden, so he's got to buy a new one, but in theory it'll be great.

"I'm off to the auction now, to get those panels. Well, I hope so anyway. Solid oak."

"Are you taking Trevor?"

"Yes."

"Watch out he doesn't bid for anything."

"I'll leave him in the car."

"Good luck."

"He's much better now I've got the dog mesh up in the back. He lies down and goes to sleep. Well, sometimes."

"Yes, and the rest of the time he rocks the car backward and forward and eats the backseat."

"He does not, well not lately. I'll ring you later, shall I, let you know how I got on at the auction?"

"Sure. I've got my Stitch and Bitch group later on though."

I'm not sure I can really face another conversation about Oak.

There's a sound of barking and aristocratic canine commands as Lady Denby arrives, with Algie and Clarkson in her wake. Dear God. Today must be Take Your Dog to Your Local Wool Shop Day and nobody's bloody told me.

"Is that your dog outside?"

Martin takes a step backward. "Yes, he's—"

"Get him trained then. Can't have dogs leaping up like that, spreads like wildfire, bad behavior with dogs. People too, come to think of it. Morning, my dear, know you don't like me

bringing mine in, but I can't leave them outside next to that
idiotic wolfhound."

"Morning, Lady Denby. I'm afraid we really can't have
them in here, not with the café. Martin was just leaving,
weren't you, Martin? So Trevor will be going too."

"Trevor? Extraordinary name for a dog. Always call mine
after staff, so much easier to remember. Excellent butler,
Clarkson, worked for my father for years. Can't remember
who Algie was—oh yes, the gardener's boy. Marvelous with
soft fruit. Not the boy, the father. The boy was hopeless. Had
a motorbike, used to make a terrible racket. Fell off it eventually,
much quieter after that. Now, where was I?"

"Good morning, Lady Denby."

Elsie's shot back downstairs and is now trying to keep a
safe distance from Clarkson, who likes licking people's feet,
while simultaneously attempting the half bob/half curtsy she
reserves for Lady Denby's appearances in the shop.

"Morning, Enid."

Martin smiles. If anyone else attempted to call his mother
Enid, there'd be ructions, but Elsie seems to have decided that
discretion is the better part of valor where our local aristocrats are involved.

"I'll ring you after the auction, Jo. Good morning, ladies."
Martin's whistling as he goes out of the shop, and he winks
at me, which Lady Denby spots. Trevor goes into a frenzy of
barking and tail wagging, leaping up and putting his paws on
Martin's chest so they end up doing a sort of dance until Martin finally gets the lead untangled.

"Did he say auction? Hope he's selling that ridiculous dog,
though I can't imagine who would buy it."

"He's restoring a barn, Lady Denby, so he's off to buy
wood. Shall I take the dogs outside for you?"

"Please, my dear. Restoring a barn? Excellent, got to keep our old buildings alive. So important. Now, what was it I wanted? Oh yes, told George I'd meet him here. Cup of tea, keeps him going, the promise of a cup of tea. Has he tipped up yet?"

"Not yet, but do go through, Tom will find you a table."

'm outside untangling dog leads and getting my hands and feet licked when Lord Denby wanders along, looking as vague as ever, and carrying a large metal bucket.

"Those dogs look familiar, got two just like that at home. Oh, right, Pru inside, is she? Meant to be meeting her, only I'm damned if I can remember when. Excellent. Got it right for once. Might treat myself to a bun."

Not if Lady Denby has anything to say about it, he won't. She tends to stick to cups of tea unless it's a special occasion.

I follow him into the café so I can wash my hands in the sink behind the counter. Bloody dogs. I can tell Tom is trying not to laugh.

"You can stop that right now or I'll make you do it next time."

"I'm allergic to dogs."

"Really?"

"Well no, but they seem to like you."

"Yes, and they'll like you too, once they've licked your feet a few times."

lsie is still lurking, ostensibly checking the stock of pattern books and knitting magazines on the shelf unit by the window.

"Good morning, Moira."

Lord Denby calls everyone Moira. He says it saves time.

"Cup of tea and a bun please, when you have a minute."

Lady Denby sighs. "There you are, George. Do sit down, I've already ordered. What on earth is that?"

He glances down and looks momentarily confused. "A bucket?"

"Yes, thank you, I can see that, but why have you got it?"

"No idea. Hang on; it's coming back to me. Need it for the drawing room fire. Other one's got a ruddy great hole in it. Nothing like wood ash for mulching round clematis. Hydrangeas love it too. Marvelous stuff."

She doesn't look convinced, but they're sitting sipping tea and enjoying a tussle over whether Lord Denby will or will not have cake while I add a few knitted jam tarts to the café window. Gran's knitted some slices of Battenberg too, just to keep the pink theme going.

"Excellent, that's the ticket, got to keep up your standards, key part of our plan, can't be doing with Silver again."

Lady Denby is determined to win the Gold Medal in the Best Seaside Town (Small) competition this year.

"Meant to ask, could you provide tea and cakes for the judges? They've changed the rules this year, coming down unannounced, sneaky trick, and then they return for the formal visit. But we'll have our scouts out, so we're bound to spot them. Just need to make sure everything is looking tip-top from early summer onward, and your windows always do us proud."

"Of course, we'd be happy to help."

Elsie's thrilled. "Fancy, the judges in our café. Won't that be lovely."

Lady Denby gives her the kind of look you'd give a parlormaid who was lingering too long over the dusting. I wish I could do it, because I'm sure it would come in very handy.

"I'll give you the dates, my dear, as soon as we get the official letter."

She pours the tea, and tops up their teapot with hot water from the jug. Connie and I were determined to have proper tea sets, there's something so cozy about the clink of china teapots and cups, even if it does mean the café dishwasher is on all the time when we're busy. We've got a few little glass teapots too, for herbal teas, not that there's much call for them. But if we ever get a rush of people needing peppermint tea, we'll be ready.

"Excellent pot of tea as usual. Do you know I ordered a cup on the train and they gave me a plastic beaker, with a tea bag floating about, and a plastic pot of milk that it was impossible to open. Absolutely revolting."

Lord Denby leans forward to pour milk into his tea and clangs the bucket against the table leg.

"Better watch out, Pru, nearly kicked the bucket."

He's so pleased with himself for making such an excellent joke he manages to order a slice of chocolate cake from Tom while Lady Denby is mid-chortle.

"Kick the bucket. Don't want any of that, do we, Pru, not yet anyway. Want to see us win the Gold first."

She gives him a fond look as he picks up his cake fork in readiness.

"Always been a devil for cake. Worse than the dogs. Goes back to tuck boxes at school, I shouldn't wonder."

"Only way we survived. Food at my prep school was absolutely filthy; used to have to bribe the porters to bring us in bars of chocolate, or we'd have wasted away."

They're enjoying a light bicker about whose school had

the most revolting food as I go upstairs to check on the website orders. Elsie is helping Mrs. Frencham choose a pattern for a sweater in the chunky tweed, and I want to look at the new shade cards for the summer cottons and try to work out why we seem to have ordered three packs of ten balls of the forest green and none in pebble, which is one of the most popular colors. I bet Elsie ticked the wrong box on the online order form again; she refuses to wear her glasses if she thinks anyone can see her, which plays havoc with her orders. But if I mention it, she'll sulk for days, so I think I'd better just return them and put in a new order. Either that or hope we get a sudden rush of people wanting to knit sweaters that make them look like Robin Hood.

By the time I've collected Jack and Archie from school and walked home, I'm in the mood for a nice little lie-down. But I've still got to feed everyone, and then get back to the shop for the Stitch and Bitch group. Connie's walked back with us, so the kids are watching cartoons while we have a peaceful half hour sitting at my kitchen table and trying to persuade Pearl not to keep bringing us saucepans. She's wearing the pink plastic tiara I bought at the supermarket on Saturday—it was either that or the full fairy dressing-up outfit—it's her new favorite thing. She even wears it on top of her balaclava, given half a chance. Diamanté, pink shiny stones, and pink plastic; it's completely perfect as far as she's concerned.

"Mum, tell him, he keeps singing." Jack's giving me a beseeching look.

"Just ignore him, love."

"He's doing it really loud."

Archie appears in the doorway. "I am not, and anyway, Mrs. Berry says I've got a lovely singing voice."

Jack shakes his head and puts his hands over his ears, which makes Cinzia laugh.

"You sing to us here, Archie, yes?"

"No. I want to watch cartoons with everybody else, and just do singing if I want to."

"Mum, tell him."

"Okay Jack, don't make such a fuss, and Archie, you can't sing while people are watching telly. Either sing somewhere else or sit with the others. But not both."

Please God, let him choose the telly.

He tuts as they both go back into the living room.

Sometimes I think I should get myself a special umpire's armband. Or a blue helmet, like the UN use for conflict zones. I wonder if bloody Mimi had one. Probably not. Too busy sleeping with my husband. But I blame him for that; she probably didn't even know he was married, not at first; he never wore a wedding ring, he thought they looked silly on men. But once she knew, she should have put her blue helmet on and posted herself somewhere else. Actually, I've never liked the French; they're far too snooty about food, and they don't seem terribly good at laughing at themselves, which is a pretty vital life skill as far as I'm concerned. Although that might be just my life.

Connie yawns. "I am so tired; this baby never sleeps, not at night."

"I'll give you a lift home if you like; it's a long walk up that hill."

"No, Mark is coming, with the biscuits for tonight. Lemon shortbread, I think."

"Lovely. But make sure you don't overdo it tonight okay?"

They've got a group booking in the restaurant, a design firm from Whitstable who've just completed a big job, so Connie can't make our Stitch and Bitch group tonight.

"I will be fine. Don't be fussing."

Cinzia says something in Italian, and Connie mutters something under her breath which makes Cinzia laugh.

"What?"

"She is reminding me, she was talking to my mother last night, and she made her promise. If I am tired, she must ring her, and she will come and make me stay in bed all day."

"Sounds good to me."

Cinzia nods. "Yes, and I will do it."

"You will not."

"Yes, I will. And you cannot stop it, because La Mamma, she always wins."

"Not round here they don't, Cinzia, I don't know if you've noticed. Pearl, please don't do that."

She's bored with saucepans now and is trying to open the cupboard under the sink, where I keep all the cleaning stuff. Reg has put a child lock on the door, so it only opens a few centimeters. It's a bugger to open at all actually, but at least it means I don't have to race across the kitchen every time she toddles toward the sink.

"More."

"No, love, we can't open it now. It's nearly suppertime."

She stamps her foot. "More."

"No, Pearl, we can't open it now."

She hurls herself on the floor and starts shrieking. Great. Time to launch Operation Tantrum, again. Fortunately, Cinzia knows the drill and goes into the living room to watch telly with the kids while Connie and I sit ignoring Pearl, pretending not to hear the earsplitting shrieking. Only another mum can really pull this off; with child-free people there's always that slight tension, where you know they think you should have some magic trick to stop the yelling, and if you don't you're clearly a crap mother. I'm giving Pearl the occasional arms-folded, have-you-finished-being-silly-yet look, which she's ignoring. It's quite hard not to laugh at my little princess with her tiara askew, throwing such a major stop, although I'm sure it's a scene repeated in palaces around the world. But at least in my kitchen I get to be the Queen.

She's running out of energy now, but still furious. This is the crucial bit. If I get the timing wrong, as I often do, she'll launch herself straight into round two.

"Have you finished, sweetheart? You can carry on being silly if you like, but the door has to stay shut. But when you've finished, I'd really like a cuddle."

She hesitates, and looks at me as I cross my arms again and try to look Determined. She gets up and readjusts her tiara. Trying to pretend nothing has happened, she saunters over for a cuddle, but she's still doing that hiccuping breathing they do when they've gone straight past being cross and right into hysterics.

I pick her up, and she snuggles into my shoulder, and her breathing starts to calm down as I pat her back.

"Brava." Connie winks at me.

I'm just about to make a start on supper when the unmistakable sounds of barking and scrabbling at the back door announce the arrival of Trevor.

Excellent. Another sodding canine moment, like I haven't had enough today.

"Porca miseria."

"Precisely."

Connie laughs, but Cinzia picks up Pearl and waves at an

increasingly hysterical Trevor, who is now leaping up at the kitchen window.

"No, it is good, we will play football, in the garden, and I will be putting on the coats."

"Thanks, Cinzia, but isn't it a bit cold?"

"No, it will be fine. And then the Principessa, she will not be screaming again, yes?"

"That's true. Well, okay then, but only for ten minutes?"

"Bambini, who wants to play football?"

There's a stampede from the living room, and before we know it we're all out in the back garden, and Trevor's in goal, as Mark arrives with the biscuits and joins in the fun. I'm trying to ignore how muddy everyone is getting. That'll be another load of washing to put on this evening, once I've checked to see what Pearl's posted in the bloody machine.

Martin misses a vital penalty and gets sent off by Nelly, who seems to have appointed herself as referee and player, which is proving to be a very useful role; it's a wonder some of the big professional teams don't go in for it.

"How did the auction go, Martin?"

"Yes, well, that's why I came round really. Only it was such a bargain, and I'd already started bidding when I realized, I thought it was the next lot, and then, well, anyway, I got it."

"Got what?"

"It needs work, but it'll be great when I've finished, and it's something I've always wanted, so."

"Martin, you don't have to explain it to me. It's your money, you can buy what you like."

"Yes, but it will take a fair bit of time, and—"

"What will?"

"The boat."

"You went to an auction to buy wood and ended up buying a boat?"

He grins. "What do you think?"

"What kind of boat?"

"A fishing boat, with an outboard engine and everything.
Well, I'm not sure that actually works, but I can replace it. And
the mast is okay, although I might need new sails. But it'll be
beautiful when I've restored it. Technically, it's called a smack."

"Which is exactly what your mum's going to give you when
she finds out, so that'll be handy."

He grins again. "I was hoping you might help me with
that."

He's looking so pleased with himself. Twit.

"Are you going to get a special hat?"

"Sorry?"

"One of those captain's hats?"

"I'm not going to be one of those wanky weekend sailors,
you know. I might even take up fishing."

"Right."

"I might."

"You don't actually like fish, though, do you, to eat I mean?"

"No, but I can sell it, and anyway I like grilled fish. It's just
all the sauces I'm not that keen on."

"Like your mother's parsley sauce? Honestly, I've never
seen a grown man make so much fuss about a bit of parsley."

Connie is laughing now, and then Mark gets sent off, for
arguing with the referee, and agrees that parsley sauce can be
a total travesty, but there's a great recipe for a sauce involving
capers and boiled egg, and would Martin like it, and what
kind of boat is it, and before I know it they're deep in conversation about what kinds of fish he might be catching in

between kicking the ball occasionally and trying to stop Nelly sending anyone else off.

As far as I know, Martin has never sailed a dinghy round the harbor, let alone a whole fishing boat out at sea. Dear God, I'm having visions of him in a South Coast version of *The Perfect Storm*. Which Elsie is bound to blame on me somehow.

"When are you going to tell your mother?"

"Sorry?"

"You heard me. When are you breaking the good news to Elsie? I need to know. So I can make myself scarce in the shop. And also, and this is really important, I want you to stress that this has got nothing to do with me, okay?"

He grins, and Mark nods. "Might be a good idea, mate; get her onboard, so to speak."

And they're off, using as much nautical phraseology as they can think of while Connie and I shake our heads and wander back into the house.

"I didn't know Mark was so keen on sailing."

"He's not, but he loves cooking fish, and the price is so high at the markets."

"Well I hope he's not planning on changing the menu anytime soon, because it's taken Martin two years just to get a roof on the barn. And even that's not finished. So I wouldn't be putting in orders for fresh fish just yet."

"Elsie will like it so much, I think."

"Oh yes, Con, she's going to be completely thrilled. Just what I need, her in a mega-sulk."

Mark finally rounds up everyone who speaks Italian and takes them home, and Martin manages to grab Trevor and drag him back down our front path. He goes off whistling, and promises to let me know when he's breaking the news to Elsie. Christ, I bet she goes nuts.

Jack and Archie are still in the back garden getting more mud over their coats, with Pearl in goal in her plastic trousers and anorak, which she loves because it's got a ladybird on the back. There's one on the hat too actually, but the hat has been inevitably jettisoned in favor of the tiara, which is sparkling in the dusk. It's really freezing now.

"It's time to go in now. Come on, it's getting really cold."

"It's not too cold for us, Mum; it's just too cold for girls. Take Pearl in, she keeps letting in goals."

"Pearl, don't do that, it'll hurt the plant." She's bashing one of the lavender bushes with a stick. And ignoring me.

I walk over and pick her up, amid rising levels of squawking.

"No."

Precisely.

She tries a bit more wriggling. "More."

"We can't do more playing if you're going to hit things."

She drops the stick.

"Five more minutes, and then we're going in, okay?"

She nods, and the boys pretend they haven't heard me. And since Pearl's concept of five minutes, or five hours, is still pretty shaky, I'm not sure anyone has really signed up to my five-minute warning.

Great. I've still got to give them supper, and get them into the bath before Gran arrives. Bloody hell. Perhaps a spot of bribery might be in order.

"There's shepherd's pie for tea, and if we go in now there might be time for jelly for pudding. But if you stay out here, there won't be."

Everyone races for the door.

Excellent. 1–0 to Mums United, and nobody sent off with a red card.

After a bath time blur of trying to stop Archie putting in so many bubbles they actually reach the ceiling while simultaneously trying to change Pearl's nappy and detach the sodding tiara, and then get the jelly out of everyone's hair after a rather lively supper, I finally get the boys downstairs and watching telly while I give Pearl her bedtime bottle and have a quiet cuddle. She's half asleep, and her hair is still damp from the bath. I can't resist nuzzling in and smelling the back of her neck, a combination of bath lotion and that indescribable smell of a newly washed baby. I've got no idea why this is so compelling, but it is. It's my favorite smell in the world. She's smiling now, a dreamy half-asleep smile as she snuggles in, back to her baby shape, with no angles, no elbows or knees digging in, all soft and round with little chubby wrists, and her fingers wrapped around her favorite blanket. I lay her in her cot and tuck her blankets in as she mutters her bedtime mantra.

"More."

"Night night, sweetheart."

"Mamma."

"I'm here, sweetheart. It's sleepy time now, time to go to sleep."

"More." But it's fainter now, softer as she slips away.

"Time to sleep now, sweetheart."

"No."

And she's off, fast asleep.

Hurrah. I love the way she falls asleep, fighting it until the very last second. I stand and watch her. My beautiful girl, my bonus baby, the one I thought I'd never have. But even so, like mums the world over, I can't help loving her just that tiny bit more when she's actually asleep. So far so good. Now for the boys. Although if I manage to get them into bed and fast asleep before Gran arrives, it'll be a bloody miracle.

By the time I'm back in the shop, arranging the lemon shortbread on a plate on the workroom table, I'm way past knackered and entering the twilight zone. But I know as soon as everyone arrives it'll be fine; it always is. I left Gran reading stories to the boys, and she promised she'd take them straight up to bed when she'd finished, so she can watch a bit of telly; the little swine have a habit of coming back downstairs when they know she's there, Archie in particular. He had her making him a tuna sandwich a few weeks ago.

I'm bringing in the glasses and a jug of water from the kitchen when Tina and Linda arrive with a bottle of wine. We take it in turns to bring the booze now, and Angela even brought a bottle of gin a few weeks ago; she says she's getting a taste for a gin and tonic in the evening, which is a pretty major transformation from when she first came along to the group and was so timid she hardly spoke, let alone had a drink.

Linda's opening the wine. "No Connie tonight, Jo?"

"No, they've got a big booking at the pub."

"She wants to start taking it easy, you know. Mind you, I saw her in the Post Office yesterday, and she looked lovely. She was wearing that new scarf she knitted, and her cream coat, and it really suits her. She always looks great though."

"It's a knack. Cinzia's got it too."

"Yes, well, tell her to keep it to herself a bit more, that's my advice. Mrs. Dawes was in the salon last week, and she got very huffy when Tina asked her how Mr. Dawes was getting on with his knee."

Tina smiles. "I was only trying to be friendly, mind you. If my Graham did something like that, I'd kill him."

Linda smiles. "No harm in looking."

"Yes, but they don't stop at looking, do they, Lind? Not that Cinzia would waste her time with someone like my Graham. Sometimes I wonder why I do."

"What's he done now?"

"Nothing. Which is typical. The light outside our garage isn't working, and it's handy when I put the bin out, so I asked him if he could have a look at it, and he went into a right strop. Moaning on about how he spends all day up a ladder and he didn't want to come home to be sent straight up another one. Silly sod. They spend most of their time sitting round the kitchen at that station anyway. Or driving too fast in that silly fire engine, when there's no need. He shot past me the other day, blue lights, sirens on, everything, and when I asked him, do you know where they were going?"

"To a fire?"

Cath is trying to be kind, but she's smiling as she takes off her coat and sits down next to Angela.

"Tesco's, because they'd run out of milk."

Linda laughs. "Yes, but they do put fires out, if there are any, Tina. Be fair."

"I suppose, and he did say they'd just finished a nasty job on the motorway, but still. He's so annoying sometimes."

Angela nods. "Sometimes Peter is so infuriating, with all his committees and that silly Golf Club, I just want to poke him with one of his golf clubs. I think his sand wedge would be best; it has such a nice pointed end."

She looks at Linda, and they both start to laugh.

Angela's husband, Peter, is very straitlaced, and takes his role as our local estate agent and Parish Councillor terribly seriously. If they had uniforms on the Parish Council, he'd definitely wear his every day. Maybe they should have special armbands or something, he'd love that. Mind you, if they did, he'd probably have us all saluting him every morning.

"I've got the photographs from Penny's wedding if you'd like to see them?"

Angela passes the photographs round, looking every inch the proud mother of the bride. I'm helping Cath with the cable pattern for the sweater she's making for her husband for a surprise birthday present, but we both pause to look at the photos.

"Doesn't Stanley look lovely at the wedding in his little suit, Ange? When's the baby due?"

Linda passes a picture of Angela's grandson, Stanley, looking adorable, standing holding his mothers' hands. Penny looks beautiful, and very happy, as does Sally, who also looks very pregnant. Angela's been knitting for the baby for a while now, a beautiful shawl and delicate tiny baby cardigans and hats, just like the things she made for Stanley when she first start coming along to the group.

"Next month. I'm so excited about it, and the wedding was such a lovely day. I was so proud of Penny."

Linda hands her back the photographs.

"Let's drink a toast to the happy couple. To Penny and Sally, and the new baby."

Angela goes pink as we all raise our glasses—in my case an empty glass, which I quickly fill with water from the jug.

"Don't you want some more wine, Jo?"

"I'd love some, but I'm driving Linda, so I better not."

The last thing I need is to be banned for drunk driving;

Annabel Morgan would probably get me thrown off the new bus even though we're bloody walking.

"Talking of new babies, when is Connie due, Jo? I thought we could have another baby shower. I don't know if they have them in Italy; actually, I don't think they're that traditional here either, but we can start a new Broadgate tradition."

Maggie's getting into local history in a big way since she started running the new archive section in the library. She gives talks with slides and notes full of tips on tracing your family tree, and she's really enjoying it.

"June, I think."

"Could we make something from all of us? A blanket maybe, where we all knit a square each? That was a local custom with patchwork quilts, for weddings or births; we could adapt that and do a knitted one, start a new tradition."

"That's a great idea, Maggie. I'll sort out some patterns."

Tina helps herself to another piece of the shortbread. "It'll be handy her having the baby just before the school holidays, give her a chance to get back on her feet before she's got the kids at home. Mind you, it won't be great for your bus thing, will it?"

"Thanks, Tina, I'd almost forgotten about that."

"What bus?"

"I told you, Linda. Jo and Connie are organizing a thing where they all walk to school, saves on pollution."

"Was that the meeting where Mrs. Peterson stood up?"

"Yes."

We all go quiet for a minute, and Tina puts her knitting down. "I'll never forget her face, you know. People do tell you stuff in the salon; me and Linda are always saying it's like they go into a trance when they're in front of the mirrors. Some of the stuff they come out with, well, it's hard to keep a straight face. But by the time she finished, I just wanted to run round to the school and give my Travis a great big cuddle."

"Connie said the same thing at the meeting; she said it makes you want to hold your children in one big cuddling and never let go."

Linda smiles. "I quite like the sound of one big cuddling. Poor woman, it just doesn't bear thinking about it, does it? It makes me go all shivery."

Mrs. Peterson, whose daughter Amy is in Jack and Marco's class, sent a letter to Mr. O'Brien which she asked him to read out at our PTA meeting, where she said that anything that kept cars away from the school gates was a good thing, and the reason they moved down here was to get away from the school in London where her eldest daughter, Alice, was run over, and killed. Everyone at the meeting went silent, even Annabel.

Tina takes a sip of her water. "She said it was right in front of the school, and all the parents and children just stood there. It was raining, and she was kneeling down in the middle of the road, holding Alice. But she knew there was no hope. Even though the ambulance was there and they were putting drips in her arm and everything. She said she knew. I can't imagine how you'd ever get over something like that, and please God none of us ever have to find out. Do you think it helps? Her knowing that we all know. What do you think, Cath? I'd hate it if it made it worse."

Cath puts her knitting down and gives Tina a reassuring smile; she's been a volunteer at the Citizen's Advice center in Margate for nearly a year now, and she's just started training to be a counselor.

"I think it's important, for something so terrible, for it not to be a secret. She was obviously ready to tell people or she wouldn't have said anything to you, Tina. And then writing to the PTA, well, that's another step in her processing. I don't think you ever get past something so terrible, but maybe, with time, she'll be able to accept it. Don't you think, Jo?"

Everyone's looking at me now, like I'm some expert on tragedy. I think they're worried I might find this upsetting because of Nick and the car crash, but it's completely different. Completely.

"I'm not sure. I think the best you could hope for was to be able to carry on. Somehow. Not that you'd have a choice, if you had other kids, you'd just have to, wouldn't you?"

Tina looks close to tears, and I'm not feeling that great myself.

Angela coughs. "I'm sure that's right, Jo, but let's not think about it anymore; it's far too upsetting and there's quite enough sadness around as it is. Let's count our blessings instead, that's what I try to do, there are so many. Tell us more about the walking bus, Jo. There was an article in the Sunday paper a few weeks ago, lots of councils have got schemes now, I cut it out for Peter to read. He's in a terrible sulk now you're doing it; he says he was going to propose something similar. Which is completely untrue, it's just sour grapes. When will you start it?"

"Next month. Although March wasn't my idea, it'll still be cold. But once we got Annabel outflanked, we thought we'd better get on with it. So if you see me trudging up the High Street looking half frozen, give us a wave, would you?"

Angela smiles. "Well, I'll be happy to help. Peter can get his own breakfast for once. It's such a good idea, and we should all do our bit. If it helps cut down pollution, it safeguards the future of all our children and grandchildren."

Linda nods. "Yes, Ange, but you can count me out; my

mornings are bad enough trying to get my Lauren out of bed and into college, thanks. It's a good idea though, be lovely seeing you all marching up the High Street. I'll look forward to it."

I poke my tongue out at her, and she laughs. "Is that a heart you're making, Jo? Feeling in need of a bit of romance, are you?"

"Yes, and before you ask, it's not mine, it's Tom's, from the café; he's making it for Valentine's Day and I said I'd sew the backing on for him. He made it earlier, and honestly, I've never seen anyone so hopeless in all my life, knit one, drop one, drop the needles, get the wool in a knot. The wool rolled under the ice cream fridge at one point, and he had to lie on the floor and poke it out with the pole we use to put the awnings up."

There's a chorus of "Bless his heart," and Tina says she'd love it if Graham made one for her, although the idea of him trying to knit makes her laugh so much she nearly chokes and Linda has to bang her on the back.

"Elsie thinks he's making it for his mum, but it's for some girl he's got his eye on, only he wouldn't say who."

We spend a happy ten minutes trying to work out who she might be. Linda's determined to keep a lookout, and then we move on to discussing the bed-and-breakfast on the seafront which has been bought by two men from London. Apparently they've nearly finished the renovations, and it's all stripped floorboards and rolltop baths in the middle of the bedrooms.

"Although why anyone would want a bath in the middle of their bedroom is beyond me, just think of the mess. And where would you put all the towels, that's what I'd like to know. Be very nice sleeping next to a load of wet towels, won't it?"

Linda picks up a piece of shortbread. "It's all the rage you know, Tina; meant to be romantic, wandering about stark naked, although they better watch out in those rooms facing the sea. I was on the bus the other day and you can see right in from the top deck. So that'll be something to look forward to."

"Trust you to spot that. And I'm not sure if I want to get an eyeful of people wandering about starkers when I'm off out shopping, thanks all the same. Not anyone from round here anyway. I see quite enough of most of them in the salon."

"Yes, but that's the point. It's for weekend breaks, isn't it, so they'll all be down from London, new, fit people who go to the gym and everything. Could be a real eye-opener. I wonder if it'll just be gay couples."

Everyone looks at Linda. "Mrs. Parsons saw them having a smooch, the two blokes that own it, down by the bandstand, and I think it's lovely, just what we need round here. Make a change from Mrs. Salter and her B and B, all rubber eggs and out by ten-thirty in the morning even if it's chucking it down with rain. I can't see any of the London types putting up with that."

Maggie nods. "It'll be a bit more expensive, though, won't it?"

"Yes, but it'll be worth it if you get to put on a show for all the people on the bus. Spread a little happiness, that's my motto. And anyway, it means we're going up in the world, doesn't it, what with Jo's shop and the new café, and Connie and the pub, and the new art gallery in the High Street. We're getting more like Whitstable every day. Property prices will go up, you mark my words, and we'll all be able to retire. Stands to reason. And we've got Grace Harrison, she's a local too, and Whitstable haven't got any big film stars like her, have they? So we're one up on them on that front. When is she back, Jo? They had that new film of hers in the papers again; it looks great, full of special effects and car chases."

"It's a thriller I think, an international diamond robbery and a huge budget and a cast packed full of A-listers. I can't wait to see it. I'm not sure when they're back, soon I think, I had an e-mail from Maxine the other day. I must call her and find out."

"I bet you've missed her."

"I have, Linda, but we've spoken on the phone a few times."

Being knitting coach to our local Diva has been one of the nicest things that have happened since we moved down here. And I have missed my regular tastes of glamour when I nip over to Graceland with the latest patterns and new yarns.

"Be a bit quiet for her round here after all that excitement, won't it, Jo?"

"Oh I don't know, Tina. Mrs. Palmer at the Post Office says someone has nicked her parcel tape off the counter again. She was keeping a very close eye on me when I was in yesterday sending off an order, I can tell you."

Cath smiles. "I wonder if *Crime Watch* will come down and do a program."

"I wouldn't hold your breath, Cath, but you never know."

By the time I've sorted out a pattern for Tina for a new sweater for Travis, and helped Cath work out where she's gone wrong on the increasing for the sleeve of hers, it's time to go home. I hope Gran's had a nice peaceful evening and everyone's fast asleep. Either that or I'm sleeping on the sofa downstairs, because I'm really not in the mood for a repeat of last night, when I ended up with all three of them in my bed, and about two inches of mattress and no bloody duvet. I seriously need to buy a bigger bed. Something else to add to my list. I'll have to save up. Mind you, by the time I've saved up, they'll probably all be teenagers, and wanting new double beds of their own. Actually, I'm not going to think about that.

t's Sunday morning, and we're finally heading to the churchyard. I'm feeling pretty close to slapping someone, possibly Fiona. I did manage to persuade her we didn't want to take a forty-five-minute detour to see Beth's pony, but her light buffet lunch was a bit of a trial, what with the boys avoiding the anchovy and olive salad like it was radioactive and Pearl throwing an epic tantrum when I couldn't find her pink juice cup. Fiona's in full Stepford Wife mode, and James has been even more annoying than usual, and given me a lecture about pensions and how to be clever about tax, even though he knows I haven't got the kind of money where worrying about tax is really an issue. We've had countless dramatic interludes from Elizabeth, the artist formerly known as my Mother-in-Law, including two tearful moments where she told us all that Nicholas was the perfect son, which James particularly enjoyed, since he was always pretty competitive with Nick. We've also had a major sulk when Archie announced he didn't like her special spinach quiche even if it was his daddy's favorite. Which it bloody wasn't, but never mind. Nick hated spinach, and his dad, Gerald, is semi-plastered as usual, after helping himself to an extra glass of wine while everyone was fussing over Elizabeth.

Christ. This is going to be a long afternoon.

Lottie and Beth are walking ahead across the field toward

the church with Jack and Archie. Pearl's insisting on walking too, so I'm holding her hand and trying to encourage her not to pick up sticks while dragging the buggy along with my other hand. It would be nice if someone offered to help, instead of just giving me top housekeeping tips or lectures about tax evasion.

"Jack, don't go so fast, love; you too Archie, wait for us."

I really don't want them to get to the grave without me. Jack will need a cuddle. Actually, I think we all will.

They wait for us to catch up, and Lottie, who is rather mesmerized by Pearl, particularly the fact that she's wearing a tiara, holds her hand and walks very slowly, while Jack tells us all how important it is to be a good big brother.

Archie nods. "Yes, and I'm her big brother as well, so she's got two."

He's hopping now, showing off another brotherly skill.

Pearl's impressed and has a go, but it's quite tricky in wellies, and thankfully a rather marvelous leaf catches her eye, and she picks it up and solemnly hands to me, like she's giving me a tremendous treat.

"Thank you, sweetheart."

She smiles, and I put it with the others on the hood of the buggy. I draw the line at muddy sticks, but collections of leaves seem pretty harmless to me, despite the worried looks from Fiona; I know she's desperate to whip out a tissue and clean Pearl's hands, but she's just going to have to get over it. Leaf collecting is one of Pearl's new passions.

We're at the gate now, and Jack's looking anxious.

"Which one is it, Mum? I've forgotten."

"Just over there, love, by the big tree."

"Oh. Yes. I think our pictures are silly, you know, Mum, because he can't see them, can he? So what's the point?"

He's getting tearful now, and Archie's very quiet.

"You don't have to leave them, if you don't want to, but I think they're lovely, sweetheart."

Archie nods. "Yes, and it shows you remember. We did it at school."

I don't think how to behave at family graves is now part of the National Curriculum, and Jack's looking a bit confused too. "With the soldiers, and the war, and we have to remember so they don't go down with the sun. That's right, isn't it, Mum?"

"Yes love."

That special Remembrance Day assembly last year must have really struck a chord.

We walk forward, more slowly now, and I kneel down to arrange our flowers. Elizabeth has already put hers in the marble vase, so we're relegated to the plastic one, but at least it's not raining, so I won't end up with muddy knees like I usually do. I'm wearing jeans today, in contravention of Elizabeth's preferred dress code, but I'm fed up with wearing black skirts and dark tights every time we visit. It makes the whole thing too formal. And muddy knees in tights feel so horrible.

"I make sure there are fresh flowers, every week."

"Thanks, Elizabeth, they're lovely."

She sniffs, a rather tragic sort of sniff.

I think I'm meant to feel guilty that we don't come every Sunday, but tough. We come as often as the boys need to.

"He always loved daffodils. They were his favorite."

I'm just going to ignore her. I can't remember Nick ever expressing a preference on flowers, except for not liking carnations. And buying me a huge bunch of tulips, actually about ten bunches; there were tulips all over the house when Archie was born, because Nick said they were so beautiful he just couldn't resist.

We've brought tulips today actually, and a little pot of hyacinths and drawings, in envelopes, so Jack doesn't fret if it starts to rain. They've both written "Dad" on the front of their envelopes, and Jack's drawn a heart.

Okay, I've got to stop this now. Take a deep breath. This is about the boys. This is about what they need, not for me to indulge myself and get upset, they need me to be calm.

"I'm not sure she should be doing that."

I don't think I've ever heard Elizabeth use Pearl's name. She's either the Baby or She.

"Perhaps she should go for a walk."

"We're fine, Elizabeth."

Pearl's picking up leaves in between the graves. Not exactly forbidden behavior in a country churchyard.

"Yes, but people might not like it."

I'm definitely going to ignore her. Silly old bat.

Jack puts his envelope down by the hyacinths and then stands holding Archie's hand, both of them silent.

Oh God.

"I just feel—"

"Elizabeth, can we have a minute, please."

"Of course, but I do think—"

"Elizabeth. We'd like a moment. On our own."

Actually, that came out a bit louder than I meant it to.

Fiona steps forward. "Perhaps we could go and say a prayer?"

"I don't see why I can't say something, I was only pointing out; he was my son, after all."

She's doing the Tragic Sniff again, and Fiona looks rather panicky; Elizabeth is definitely gathering momentum for

one of her little Speeches, which will end in tears and us
all making a fuss of her. Again. Or possibly not. Not today
anyway.

I turn to face her, trying to channel Lady Denby. "Thank
you, Elizabeth, the flowers are lovely. We'll come and find you
when we're ready. We just need a moment on our own."

Pearl hands her a leaf, which she pretends not to notice.

I pick up my gorgeous girl and kiss her cheeks.

"Thank you darling, another lovely leaf."

Elizabeth falters, but she's not done yet. "Perhaps you'd
like to come into the church and we can all say a prayer."

Bloody hell, what is it with her and trying to get us into
the church? We've been a few times, and she just starts crying
and making a huge fuss about lighting candles and showing
off the flowers, and the boys get totally left out. She's on the
flower rota, and we have to examine every display and make
suitable comments. It doesn't leave any space for them at all.
They just have to stand there and let her take center stage
like he wasn't their dad and this isn't hard for them.

"No thank you. You go in, and we'll see you later."

"More." Pearl wants to be down.

I turn back to the boys. Time for a strategic retreat, I
think, before I really lose it.

"Shall we go and sit on the bench for a minute, let Gran
have some peace, and then we'll come back, when she's gone
into the church. I need a cuddle. I don't know if anyone else
does."

Archie smiles, a small, pale smile, but it's a start.

"Come on, the last one to sit down is a squashed tomato."

They both start to run.

———

"She did not."

"She did, Gran. And then she sent the bloody vicar out, poor man, although that backfired a bit; I think she'd ordered him to tell us off for not going in to pray, but he was lovely. He said he was pleased to meet us, and Archie shook his hand, and then he said people had different ways of remembering their loved ones, and it was what was in people's hearts that mattered. And then he winked at the boys."

"He sounds lovely, pet."

"I know. It almost made me wish we'd gone in."

"Not with her carrying on like she does, terrible woman."

"It was good though. When she finally came out with Fiona and the girls, the vicar said good-bye, and then he turned to Pearl and said thank you so much for my leaf, I will treasure it. It made Archie giggle. Elizabeth was seriously miffed."

"Nasty woman. I've got a good mind to ring her and tell her just how lovely her son was, leaving you in a right old mess with two boys to bring up and a second mortgage he hadn't bothered to tell anybody about. You were lucky you had a penny left after selling that house you know."

"I know, Gran, but don't, please?"

"I know you're right, pet. Losing your son is a terrible thing, even if you aren't as nice a person as you should be. But that's no excuse to go trampling over other people's feelings."

"Yes, but whatever gets you through the night?"

"I suppose so. Only next time I'm coming with you, and that's final. I told Reg, I knew I should have come today. She spends so long in that church you'd think she'd have learnt a bit about Christian charity by now, but they're often the worst ones. I've noticed that before, too busy being holier-than-thou to bother with being decent or kind."

"Okay."

"I thought you'd say no."

"I think you might be right. Having you as backup would make it so much easier."

"Yes, well, grandmother to grandmother, if she starts kicking off, she'll get a piece of my mind and make no mistake about it."

"I know, Gran. And thanks."

"Good, well, that's decided then. I might get to meet your lovely vicar."

"If Elizabeth hasn't worked out a way to get him defrocked or whatever they do to naughty vicars now. If fraternizing with unmarried mothers and their illegitimate babies is still a hanging offense, that is."

"No, pet, they got past all that nonsense a while back, thank goodness. It used to be terrible. But that's all changed. Just look at that Robin Williams."

I think she might mean Rowan Williams, the Archbishop of Canterbury, although I'm sure Robin Williams takes a pretty tolerant line on unwed mothers too.

"He's a lovely man, you can tell just by looking at him. If they were all like him, I'd go every Sunday. Far more important things to worry about than who is married or isn't, or who is gay and who is, what's that other thing they say?"

"Straight."

"Yes, straight, silly word if you ask me, but still, thank heavens times have changed. People can choose now, and as long as they're not hurting anybody, it's nobody's business but their own, is it, pet?"

"No, Gran."

"Night, pet."

"Night, Gran."

I always feel better when I talk to Gran. Not that she

won't tell you if she thinks you're wrong about something. But deep down I know she loves us all, pretty much unconditionally. There's something terribly reassuring about knowing you have someone like her in your corner, come what may. I really want that for the kids, that certainty that I'm there for them, come what may. Only preferably not at 3:00 a.m.

'm in the kitchen on Friday morning at the crack of bloody dawn, and Pearl is on saucepan patrol again when the phone rings.

"Morning, Jo."

"Maxine, are you back yet? I was going to call you."

"Yes, we got back last night, and she wants to see you. Yes, Grace, I'm just on the line to her now, yes."

"Hello Jo. It seems ages since we've seen you. Come round, and bring the kids; Lily's really getting into playing with other children."

"I still can't believe she's two now."

"I know, and she's much taller than when you last saw her. She must get that from Jimmy. Let's hope that's all she gets."

There hasn't been much activity on the Jimmy Madden front for a while: he's busy on a World Tour, with a series of the kinds of young women who usually hang around rock stars. So hopefully there won't be any repeats of him turning up and wanting a paternal moment with Lily. I'm sure Grace is right and that was more to do with the launch of his new album. She handled it really well, but I could see she was upset. Thank God Bruno was there to escort him off the premises.

"Fix a time with Maxine. Oh, and bring some of the new colors, would you? I want to be inspired."

"Sure."

The line goes dead, and then there's a click and Maxine comes back on. "Sorry about that. I think she's missed you."

We both laugh, but it's an affectionate sort of laugh. That's one of the things I like most about Maxine, she's so loyal. However demanding Grace is being, Maxine always behaves as if she's being completely reasonable, with only a faintly raised eyebrow or the occasional mild aside to me when she's sure Grace can't hear. It makes me feel like I'm part of the team and I really like that.

"What time works for you today?"

"Well, it'll have to be after school if you're sure you want me to bring the boys."

"Great, I'll get Sam to make snacks, and they can have a swim if that works for you?"

"That would be lovely."

Sam's food is always fabulous; being personal chef to Ms. Harrison means his version of snacks is everyone else's version of a four-course meal.

"See you around four then."

"Perfect."

Bugger. So that'll be me in my tragic swimsuit making sure nobody drowns their brother while Grace will be looking divine. And Martin's coming round for supper later on, and I'd hoped I'd be looking halfway decent, rather than with my hair all tufty like it goes after swimming. Brilliant.

By the time I'm driving to Graceland after school, I'm seriously thinking of canceling. We were unusually busy in the shop with a group of women from Maidstone who'd come over specially to stock up, and then the till in the café jammed, and one of the reps came in to show me their new catalog and

I had to spend ages haggling to get anywhere near a decent price. Jack's got a special sticker for Good Helping, and Archie always hates it when Jack gets stickers.

"Mum, can we have ice cream, on the way home?"

"No, love, it'll be too late."

"Yes, but you said when we had an ice cream shop we could have ice cream every day and we don't and that's a lie. It's not fair."

"I did not, Archie, and stop whining. You're very lucky to be going swimming after school."

"I hate stupid swimming."

Excellent.

There are a couple of cars parked on the shoulder of the road as we get close to the gates for the house, and some bored-looking snappers who don't even bother to lift their cameras; they probably reckon exciting people don't drive such tragic old cars. Bruno is waiting by the gates to buzz us in, with Tom and Jerry standing by his side, looking every inch the perfectly trained guard dogs. I must get him to have a word with Martin. He waves at us as we drive in, suddenly transformed from the scary security person keeping a beady eye on the photographers. The gardens are even more manicured than usual, presumably in honor of Grace's return, as I park at the side next to a huge dark green Jeep and a silver Mercedes with tinted windows. They both look brand-new, sparkling in the last of the afternoon sunshine, and making ours look even worse than usual.

"Now remember, be polite, and no running, or shouting. Or singing, Archie. Let's just have a lovely swim."

He tuts.

———

Maxine opens the side door.

"Hi, Jo, Grace is on the phone, but Lily's in the pool with Meg, so go straight through. Gosh, hasn't she grown?"

I hand Pearl to Maxine, who looks pleased. She's got a soft spot for small people, even though she pretends she hasn't.

"Hello, Pearl, how are you?"

"More."

By the time we've changed into our swimsuits and I've persuaded Pearl that she really does have to wear her swim nappy, and Archie that he doesn't need his snorkel, I'm really going off the idea of a swim. But the water is lovely, and it feels very glamorous, swimming in an indoor pool surrounded by such opulence with views of the woods, and perfect lawns. Even the towels are superior.

"Hi, darling, how are you?"

Grace looks stunning, as usual, in a white swimsuit. I can't imagine ever choosing white, black provides so much more in the way of camouflage, but she looks lovely. Lightly tanned, and not a millimeter of anything remotely wobbly. Ellen's right, it's like she's from another species.

Lily takes a shine to Archie and paddles around the pool after him, much to Jack's amusement. Pearl is bobbing around in the inflatable baby seat Lily used when she was little, having a brilliant time. I managed to jettison the tiara during a nifty bit of footwork involving slices of apple or she'd definitely be wearing it.

"Ten more minutes, Meg. I think Sam has made some food, Jo, if that's okay with you. Chicken I think."

"That sounds lovely, Grace, thank you."

I enjoy a mini-daydream where I no longer have to cook suppers because my chef has them ready and waiting when I emerge from my pool. I can't really see it somehow, but it must be wonderful. Actually, I'd settle for someone to cook the occasional supper and do without the pool. No more pondering what to do with a packet of mince or how I can persuade Archie to eat omelets.

"I'll just do a few more laps, Jo. Take the kids out with Meg and I'll see you in the kitchen."

"Great."

"More."

I'm not sure Pearl is quite ready for her supper yet.

Maxine's sitting at the huge refectory table in the kitchen drinking tea by the time we're all changed. The kids are starving, but Sam has everything ready, so instead of the usual wait while I race to get a meal on the table and they get increasingly crabby, the food appears the minute we sit down. Roast chicken and mashed potatoes and green beans, and a toddler-friendly fruit salad with yogurt, with cartoons on in the background on the giant TV screen. Everyone is blissed out, and I half wish I wasn't eating later with Martin because the chicken looks so lovely.

Grace reappears in jeans and a pretty cotton shirt, with bare feet. Even her feet are beautiful, with perfect red nail varnish that she definitely didn't do herself.

"Let's go and sit by the fire. Meg will watch them for a minute."

"We'll need to leave as soon as they've finished eating or Pearl will start kicking off. She's tired and that's always tricky."

Meg smiles and nods at Lily. "Same here. But they'll be fine for a bit, Jo."

"Max, bring us in some more tea, would you. I want my herbal stuff, and did you bring the wool, Jo? I want to see the new colors."

I lift the basket I made up in the shop earlier, with a selection of the cashmere and silk mixes she likes, and the soft baby cotton.

"There are some lovely new Italian ones, really fabulous colors, and they knit up beautifully. Connie helped me with the order, so the price isn't that bad either."

I follow her across the hall and into the small living room, which has new sofas and armchairs, in a lovely mix of blue florals and pale greens.

"She's the one who's pregnant, right?"

"Yes."

Grace sits down in an armchair by the fire. "Show me. Oh, I love the pale lilac, pretty. Get me some of that, I want to make her another ballet wrap; she looks so sweet in them, and they're so easy."

"Okeydoke. So how was the trip?"

"The usual madness, hard work, but pretty good overall. We saw Daniel Fitzgerald in L.A., did Maxine say?"

"No, how was he?"

"Fine, busy being the jet-set photographer, surrounded by models as usual, but he showed me a picture of Pearl, the one you sent him from her birthday. He was very discreet about it, but he seemed very proud of it, it was sweet. So you've sorted it with him?"

"I wouldn't go that far, and I'm sure it will get more complicated when she's bigger, but so far so good. He calls, to check in how she's doing, that kind of thing. It's fine."

"What about money?"

Grace is very up-front on stuff like this, just like Ellen. I'm not sure what I've done to deserve both of them on my case though.

"I really don't want his money, Grace. It feels important that I'm taking care of us, all of us. It would be different if I couldn't manage, but I can, and he did offer. I've told him to start a savings account for her, if he wants to, for when she's bigger. I've still got some of Nick's money for the boys, so that'll give them all the same."

"Good for you, darling. Sisters are doing it for themselves, yes?"

"Yes. Or doing it for their kids. And that reminds me, I keep meaning to say, you really don't need to keep paying me, for the knitting coach thing, not when you're so busy. I've hardly done anything lately, and that doesn't feel right."

"Yes, well, get over it. You're my supplier, and I need my fix now, and anyway, us single parents have got to stick together." She smiles.

"Thanks, Grace, that's really kind, but seriously, I'd hate you to think you had to—"

"Darling, I don't have to do anything, I know that. But I like having you on call, and that's final. I'm surrounded by people taking a cut of my money, I know the type, and it's just not you. Anyway, this new film I've just signed up for involves knitting, so you'll be back in action before you know it."

"Well, if you're sure. What new film?"

"It's not public yet."

She gives me one of her Megastar looks. She moves backward and forward between being an ordinary person and suddenly going all VIP, and you have to be careful to mind the gap.

"Of course."

"*Brideshead* meets *Upstairs Downstairs*. I'm the servant who becomes the Lady of the house, like that ever happened. They used to pack him off to the colonies, and she got the sack. But this is set around the First World War, so they're running out of heirs. The scripts are written by two women, rather than one of those middle-aged men who all secretly yearn for the good old days when you could buy a scullery maid and still have change from sixpence. I can't be bothered with that lot, they're such snobs. We've spent ages getting the script right; I'm Exec-Producing this one too."

"It sounds brilliant."

She smiles, one of her megawatt smiles.

"I am pretty excited about it. She's the gardener's daughter, but she ends up the Toast of Society, instead of just Toast, which is what the dowager countess wants. So there's comedy too, and I get to knit, in the gardener's cottage, to show I'm a proper working-class girl. We're shooting in the U.K., thank God, I'm so over living in fucking hotels. You can never get what you want, however much you pay. I'm so pleased to be home. Oh, great, tea. Thanks, Max."

"Sorry I took so long. Ed rang, and he'd like to speak to you."

"I don't want to know. He's my agent; he should be fixing things, not ringing me up with questions all the fucking time. Ring him back and say I'll talk to him tomorrow."

"Okay. Have you asked her?"

"Sorry?"

"About the party."

Grace smiles. "I was just coming to that. I want to have a tea party for Lily. We had her birthday party in L.A."

"I know, I saw it in the papers."

"Yes, well, that wasn't my idea, some fucker tipped them off. Probably Ed."

"There weren't any pictures of Lily, just people arriving, stuff like that. It looked very glamorous."

"It was ridiculous. Some idiot from the studio actually bought her a diamond tiara, can you believe it, and she got a diamond tennis bracelet, although why anyone wears diamonds to play tennis is beyond me."

"To show off?"

She smiles.

I'm so glad I left Pearl's tiara at home.

"I thought an old-fashioned English tea party would be nice. This is her home, after all."

Maxine looks nervous. "Ed wants to invite lots of VIPs from London too, Grace. Have you decided about that?"

"Fine. A few. But I want locals too, people with kids, if you can help us with that, Jo. I want it to feel like a family event. Next month sometime."

"I'd love to. Why don't you do it on a Sunday? Actually, Mother's Day's coming up, isn't it? Would that work?"

"Brilliant. Max, check the dates, would you?"

Maxine is already tapping away on her BlackBerry.

"Mother's Day is April the third this year, and then Easter is toward the end of April. We're in Milan on the second, but we could do the weekend before that?"

"Perfect. An early Mother's Day tea party. I like it. Sort it with Jo, would you, Max?"

"Of course."

"And Jo, get me some of that lilac, and the peppermint, and the raspberry, and bring those patterns for blankets over again, I want to make something for her new bed. Evenings by the fire knitting, that's exactly what I need right now. Fuck, who's that?"

The phone on the table by her chair is beeping.

"It's Ed. He really wants to run through the interview bids with you, Grace."

"Christ, why can I never get any peace? Okay, I'll take it. Thanks, Jo. Hi, Ed, don't hello-darling me, I'm not in the bloody mood."

Maxine nods toward the door, and we tiptoe out. Blimey. It sounds like Ed might be in for a bumpy half hour.

"Oh, before I forget, I've got a couple of bags for you, just a few things Lily's too big for now."

"Thanks, Max."

Cinzia will be thrilled. She loves dressing Pearl in clothes which Lily has grown too big for, little designer T-shirts and denim skirts, with soft cotton tights that cost a fortune, and gorgeous old-fashioned flannel nightgowns with embroidered yokes.

"It's our pleasure. It's lovely knowing someone else will get the benefit. And Meg says we've got stacks of cot-size sheets and blankets if you can use them, now she's in her new bed."

"I'm fine, I think, but thank her for me, would you? Oh dear, I think that might be Archie."

There's the unmistakable sound of "If you're happy and you know it clap your hands" being sung very loudly as we head back toward the kitchen. Lily and Pearl are clapping and having a lovely time, despite being covered in yogurt.

Jack gives me a desperate look. "Is it home time now, Mum?"

"Yes, love."

"Good."

———

t's nearly half past eight by the time I've finished the baths and bedtime routine. Thank God I took the lasagne out of the freezer this morning, so I only need to make a salad and supper is ready. I've brought some of the clementine ice cream home for pudding—Martin's not that keen on puddings, but he makes an exception for Mark's ice cream.

I'm lighting the fire in the living room when he arrives, with a bottle of red wine and a bunch of red roses. He's still wearing the bobble hat Elsie knitted him as we go into the kitchen.

"I know they're soppy, but I thought you might like them."

"Thank you, they're lovely."

He leans forward for a kiss, but I move sideways.

"There's something I need you to do first."

He looks slightly worried.

"Take your hat off."

He takes it off and throws it on the floor. "Better?"

"Much. Now we've both got tufty hair."

"Tufty? This is tousled, proper men have tousled hair. Nothing tufty."

"If you say so. Supper's nearly ready."

"Great. I'm starving. It smells great, what is it?"

"Cod in parsley sauce."

I open the oven door and carry the lasagne to the table.

"Great. You had me going there for a minute."

"Good. Because I need to know when you're going to tell her. You can't keep a great big boat a secret for much longer, you know, and if she finds out, well, it'll be much worse, that's all I'm saying."

"I know."

We talk about his plans for the boat, in slightly more detail than I intended, and the sailing course he's going to book, where you learn how to read charts and not sail into things, and use the radio, and then he gives me another lecture about how we can improve the website for the shop and I need to take far more pictures, and upload stuff. Or possibly download.

"This lasagne's great. I'll need to get some flares too."

"I'm assuming you're talking distress signals now, rather than special sailing trousers."

"Yes, thank you. You won't be so superior when we're onboard in some little deserted bay catching our own supper and watching the stars."

"I might be. It depends on the weather."

"Well yes, not this time of year obviously. But in the summer. I can't wait. I bet the kids will love it."

"I'm sure they will. Once we've got them into their life jackets, just in case. Actually, do they do life jackets for girls in tiaras? Otherwise Pearl won't be coming."

He smiles. "I'm sure they do. Safety is paramount, even for princesses, every good skipper knows that."

"Skipper?"

"Shut up."

He's helping me put the plates in the sink. "That was lovely."

"The fire's on in the living room. Why don't you go through and I'll make the coffee."

"No, you go and sit down, you made the meal, I'll make the coffee."

"Ahoy, Captain."

O h, God. How mortifying. I've just woken up, and it's half past twelve and I'm on the sofa. The fire's gone out, and Martin's left a note.

Tried to wake you, but you were out for the count. Let's do this again, only next time where we're both awake.

Martin x

P.S. You looked very lovely fast asleep.

I text him, just in case he's still awake.

SORRY. BEEN A LONG WEEK. PROMISE TO STAY AWAKE
NEXT TIME. JO X

My phone beeps while I'm putting the washing machine on.

HAVEN'T ACTUALLY SENT A GIRL TO SLEEP BEFORE. AT
LEAST I KNOW YOU DON'T SNORE. :) M.

I text him back.

I DO. PS—YOU LEFT YOUR HAT. TWIT. X

· · · 3 · · ·

Let It Snow

March

It's a quarter to nine on Monday morning, and we're about to start the inaugural journey of the walking bus at the bottom of the High Street. We've already got fifteen kids, and Pearl's singing and trying to get her balaclava off, thrilled to find herself with such a large audience. Bloody hell; it's so cold the kids are all wrapped up in wooly hats and scarves, which they're trying take off when their mums aren't looking. Connie's holding the we're-walking-to-school lollipop which Mark made for her, and Jane Johnson is already festooned with PE kit and book bags. We've got a stop set up at the Post Office on the seafront, then one at Mr. Parsons's shop, where he's hung a special sign in among his buckets and mops, and then one just past our shop on the corner. The last collection point is by the bandstand in the park, which is only a few minutes from school, but we didn't want anyone to feel left out. It's cloudy, and it looks like it'll rain any minute. Bugger.

Jane counts the kids and lifts her green flag; her husband, Bob, collects model trains, and he's got a bit carried away with all the planning. He's lent us his whistle too.

"Fifteen."

Connie and I nod, and we're off.

Parents stand clapping as we straggle up the High Street, and I spot Lady Denby standing waving a Union Jack, for some reason best known to herself, with Algie and Clarkson wagging their tails. By the time we reach our shop, we've got thirty-one kids, and there are more children and parents waiting, alongside Gran, with Elsie and Laura.

"Here you go, Jo. I can't wait till my Rosie can do this, it's brilliant, isn't it?"

"You can take my place on the rota anytime you like, Laura."

She smiles. "No, you're all right."

"You look very smart in your jacket, pet."

"Thanks, Gran."

Jane is raising her flag again.

"Forty-two."

I start counting, which is harder than you'd think when everyone keeps moving.

Connie blows her whistle, and the kids all stand still; all that PE training at school is definitely paying off.

"We need to count."

Everyone stops talking, including Gran and Elsie.

"Forty-two."

Jane raises her flag and we're off again, to a little chorus of clapping.

I'd be touched if it wasn't so bloody cold and I wasn't wearing a scratchy fluorescent tabard with I'M WALKING TO SCHOOL stenciled on the back.

The tricky bit, where we have to cross the road at the top of the hill, goes without a hitch; partly because we got so anxious about it last week we came and practiced with Jane after school. We wait for the lights to go red, and then Connie leads the kids across, while Jane plants herself in the middle of the road and holds her green flag firmly down by her side in case some idiot mistakes it for a signal to drive forward. I follow slowly to make sure nobody gets marooned on the wrong side of the traffic, and a man in a Range Rover toots and looks annoyed. Luckily, Trent Carter's dad is behind him and leans out of his window and gives him a hand signal which I don't remember from the Highway Code.

"The kids are crossing the road. What's your problem? Wanker."

The driver in the Range Rover tries to ignore this, but it's quite hard when you've got three women, forty-two mixed infants, and various onlookers laughing at you. The kids are all thrilled, particularly Trent.

"That's my dad, and that bloke is a wanker, isn't he, miss?"

I'm not sure what our policy is on swearing on the bus, I'm guessing we're not keen, but I think I'll just ignore it. And anyway, I quite like being called miss.

"That's a lovely scarf you're wearing, Trent."

"It's crap, but my mum said I've got to wear it or I'll get one of my chests. Is the baby's face meant to be like that?"

Pearl is woolen-faced again. Fortunately without her tiara this morning. Although the balaclava-with-tiara look is one she's definitely working on.

"No, not really."

I lean forward and adjust her balaclava, amid shrieks which make Trent laugh. "She don't like that."

He wraps his scarf over his face, and then drops it, which Pearl thinks is hilarious.

Archie is watching Trent, who's one of the tougher boys, and someone he'd usually steer clear of.

"She does that with her hat all the time, and she takes her socks off and throws them away when she hasn't got her wellies on."

Trent's obviously rather impressed by Archie's fraternal boasting. "She can throw my scarf away if she likes. I don't think boys wear scarfs, they're more for girls, but my mum makes me wear it."

Archie tuts and Trent grins at him, and whispers something which makes them both giggle.

Jane's looking anxious. "We're going to run out of armbands if we get many more."

She's got a stash of fluorescent armbands in her bag for every child who joins the bus, so we can spot the ones we're meant to be shepherding.

"I never thought we'd get this many."

"I know. It's great, though, isn't it?"

She nods and starts counting her armbands again.

There's another group of parents waiting by the bandstand, including Mrs. Peterson and Amy. I stand up straighter, trying to look like the kind of überefficient person you'd trust to walk your child to school, and there's a round of applause as we stop and Connie and Jane start counting again. Angela is waiting with Peter, who's looking very pleased with himself, like this is all down to him and the Parish Council; he's got his suit on and looks like he'd make a Speech given half a chance. Bob's taking photographs with his digital camera for the school newsletter, and Peter's making sure he gets into every shot, much to Angela's obvious annoyance.

"It all looks marvelous, Jo, I'm quite looking forward to Wednesday."

Angela's volunteered to be on the rota for Wednesdays, with Tina and Sophie Lewis's mum.

"Thanks, Angela, and it's very kind of you to help out."

"Not a bit of it, it's helping me really. I always mean to go out walking, but somehow I never do, so this will be the ideal opportunity."

Connie blows the whistle again, and we start counting; it's vital we don't linger here, as there's a slide and swings beckoning in the playground by the fountain, and if we let them start wandering off, we stand no chance.

Jane lifts her flag. "Fifty-six."

Crikey. That's nearly a third of the whole school.

Connie shouts "Fifty-six," and we start moving and Mrs. Peterson suddenly looks very anxious, like she's changed her mind and wants to walk with us. I think this is an important moment for her, letting Amy go. Oh, God.

"Would you like to help me push the baby, Amy?"

She nods and puts her hand on the buggy handle as we start to walk, while her mum stands still, clearly willing herself not to race after us and retrieve her child. Jane's noticed too, and we both smile at her encouragingly, and she tries to smile back. Just when I think she's not going to be able to bear it, Angela steps forward and puts her hand on her arm, and she turns, with one last look at Amy, and starts talking. Good for Angela. Amy seems oblivious, but I put my hand on her shoulder, just in case her mum's having one last look.

Jane starts singing "The Wheels on the Bus" as we walk

through the gates and down the road to the school. We're
not going to sing every morning—we don't want to annoy
the entire town—but we thought on the first day we'd indulge
ourselves. The playground is lined with parents and teachers,
and Mr. O'Brien rings the bell and says how pleased he is to
see the bus arriving right on time, and how every car journey
we avoid will help save our planet, and while there won't be a
walking home bus after school just yet, he hopes parents will
get into the habit of walking. He asks the kids to give themselves a round of applause, which they do, so enthusiastically
he has to ring the bell again to get them to stop.

"And now everyone is warmed up and ready to learn, let's
all line up, quietly please."

There's a bit less enthusiasm for this, but it's starting to
drizzle, so we divest ourselves of book bags and PE kits and
packed lunch bags as quickly as we can. I'll have to get some
of those plastic clips you put on the handles of buggies or I'm
going to look like a luggage porter. We're not really meant to
carry things according to the guidelines we got from the local
Education Department, but some of them are so little it seemed
mean not to. Maybe we should get a trolley. Or a donkey.
The kids would love that, or we could train Trevor, he'd be
perfect for a couple of panniers full of kit. I might mention it
to Martin.

Annabel Morgan is standing by the main doors, looking
Annoyed. She's talking to her usual coterie of Gina Pres-
ton and Mrs. Nelson; I think we were supposed to crawl in
with a dozen kids, preferably having lost one of them in the
sea. Not fifty-six with nobody gone AWOL.

Jane's very pleased. "That was brilliant."

"Yes, largely thanks to your organizing it all, and thank Bob too, for the flag and the whistle."

"I'll have to get him new ones, I'm keeping these. I draw the line at the hat though; he was still trying to get me to wear it this morning."

Connie smiles. "A hat, it might be good, for the rain?"

"Yes, but not one with STATIONMASTER on it. Oh, and I meant to say, Mr. O'Brien's found a bit of money in the budget and he's giving me a promotion. It's not much, but still, I'm really pleased. It'll be after Easter, and I'll be office manager and school secretary, isn't that great? And I know doing the bus helped, so thanks, Jo, it was such a good idea."

"Don't thank me, I just mentioned it at the meeting. I didn't think we'd end up doing it."

"Be careful what you wish for?"

"You're telling me. Trust me; being fluorescent in the mornings was never top of my list. Do you want the tabards, for tomorrow?"

"Please, and can we have your sign, Connie, it was really handy. We could have hit that idiot in his Range Rover with it if we'd needed to."

"Sure, but it is, how do you say, it is not straight, in the wind. It bends."

"No problem, Bob will soon sort that. I better get in, no rest for the wicked. See you later. I'm going to order some more armbands just in case."

Annabel gives her a very haughty look as she walks past holding the lollipop and the tabards, but Jane is fearless.

"Morning, Annabel. Isn't it marvelous? Such a huge success, Mr. O'Brien says the governors are really pleased."

Jane shakes the lollipop and smiles at Annabel, which completely infuriates her. Just like she knew it would.

"She's a brave woman, that Jane, I've always liked her. Come on, Con, I'll race you to the café. There's one of your lovely husband's croissants waiting for me. I can hear it calling. Here, give me your bag and I'll put it in the buggy."

The atmosphere in the shop is rather fraught: Elsie's furious about Martin getting a boat; he told her at the weekend, and she's still not speaking to him, or her husband, Jeffrey, who made the mistake of saying he thought it wasn't such a terrible idea and he'd help with some of the carpentry. Big mistake. She's barely speaking to me either, since she thinks I should have stopped him.

"I think I'll change the window, Elsie. I thought we could do something for Mother's Day."

As soon as I've said it, I realize this is a pretty stupid thing to say with her in tragic mother mode.

She sniffs. "Nice Mother's Day I'm going to have, worrying myself sick about him on that silly boat. He was sick on the ferry that time we went to the Isle of Wight, he never liked boats. I don't know what's got into him, I really don't."

"Well, it's got nothing to do with me, Elsie, but he can spend his money on what he likes, don't you think?"

"Yes, but how would you feel if your Archie bought himself a great big boat?"

"Not that thrilled, but he is only seven, Elsie. Martin's thirty-eight."

"Yes, so it's about time he grew up and got that barn finished; there's still a hole in the middle of that kitchen floor."

"I know, but he's still working out the plumbing, it's not going to stay like that."

"He's always been the same, starts things and never finishes. Just like his father. I don't know how I've put up with it
for all these years, I really don't."

"Because you love them?"

She sniffs again, but she doesn't look quite so cross.

"It could be worse, you know, Elsie."

"How?"

"They could be into morris dancing or something."

There's a trace of a smile.

"Well, I will say they've never been drinkers, and they can
make your life a misery. I was talking to Mrs. Marwell the
other day, and she said she saw that Mr. Nelson coming out of
the Star and Garter along by the pier, and he could hardly
walk straight he was that far gone."

"Oh dear."

Actually, if I was married to Mrs. Nelson, I might have the
occasional tipple.

"Yes, they'd had one of their silly meetings, that Navy
thing they all belong to, and they always come out three
sheets to the wind after one of those."

"Oh dear."

"Mind you, for all I know my Martin will join them now
he's got a boat. And his father will go along too. Hasn't got
the sense he was born with."

"I can't see them sitting around with a load of old codgers
getting legless."

"Well, maybe not. I'm just saying I wouldn't put it past
him, that's all. Do you want a hand with the window? We've
got those baby cardigans we hung up last year on that little
washing line upstairs in one of the boxes in the stockroom,
shall I bring them down?"

"Thanks Elsie. And if you see the flags, bring them down as well, would you?"

We knitted a set of little flags last year, in pretty colors with initials on, to spell out MCKNITS, so I'll hang them up too. The flag kits are selling quite well now, with the gingham ribbon and the pattern for each initial, so you can knit the name of your child. Short names are easiest, of course. Christopher takes quite a few flags; Mrs. Hirst said she wished she'd gone for James, her other top name, by the time she'd finished knitting all the flags for him. But it did look lovely. The kits are popular on the website too, so people obviously like them. They're one of the things I'm most pleased with, the beach bag kits in summer and the shawl kits, in the mohair made famous by Grace, and the easier crepe one, which is lovely and warm. We do a cotton one too, and a simple baby cardigan, all knitted in one so you only have to sew up the sides, with no tricky shoulder seams or neckbands. But the best sellers so far are our blanket kits; we do a cot-size one, and smaller ones for the buggy or car seat. We sell quite a few ready-made too, and Mrs. Collins is knitting for us now, as well as Elsie and Laura, and Gran and Betty if we get busy, so we're just about keeping up.

I'm ready to start on the window when Maggie comes in to collect the wool for Connie's blanket.

"I'll take Tina and Linda theirs, and Angela's coming into the library later on. They're such lovely colors, Jo. Butterscotch and vanilla, it sounds delicious. How may squares do we need?"

"I thought twenty, with hearts and stars knitted into each square; it's all in one color, so it's pretty easy. I'll sew them together and do the border once everyone's finished."

"I'll copy the pattern at lunchtime. I can't wait to see her face. I hope she likes it."

"All her friends knitting a blanket for her baby? She'll love it, Maggie."

Elsie's nipped out to get some shopping for supper while I'm behind the counter untangling flags when Maxine calls.

"Hi Jo. Have you got your final invite list?"

"Sure, I'll e-mail it over. I thought Connie and Mark with Nelly and Marco. Tina and Graham Davis, he's the local fireman I told you about, and their son, Travis; and Jane and Bob Johnson and Seth; and Laura from the shop and her little girl, Rosie."

"Perfect."

"I can think of more if you want me to?"

"No, that sounds about right. What about your friend Ellen?"

"I was going to ask you about that. She'll kill me if I don't get her an invite, but you know she works in telly?"

"That's fine, as long as she knows it's a private event. Although it'll be full of people from London and they all gossip like mad, so we'll be on our best behavior. Anyone else you'd like to add?"

"Gran and Reg obviously, if you're still sure that's okay, and Cinzia, and Martin, and I was going to ask you, could we invite his mother, Elsie, from the shop? Only it would save me no end of bother if she can come."

"Sure."

"She's quite annoying."

"So are most of the other guests, don't worry about it."

"Thanks, Max."

xcellent. I think I might have a way to get Elsie out of her
Sulk.

I think I'll text Martin first, just to gloat.

HAVE JUST WANGLED INVITE FOR YOU AND YOUR MUM
TO GRACELAND MOTHER'S DAY PARTY. YOU NOW OWE
ME BIG-TIME.

My mobile rings.

"I always knew you were brilliant, although Dad and
I are getting the hang of the silent thing and we quite
like it."

"How ungrateful. Well, I'll just leave it then, shall I?"

He laughs. "No, sorry, it's great. I wish I could see her face
when you tell her. Say I asked you to fix it, would you? I seriously
need to get back in her good books."

"Sure, and by the way, it's fancy dress."

"Bloody hell. Do I really need to go? I'm hopeless at parties, and if it's fancy dress it'll be even worse."

"It's fine. Just rent a sailor suit."

"Are you serious?"

"No, you twit."

"So it's not fancy dress then?"

"No, well, apart from you. Look, I'll call you later, I can't
talk now, we're just about to sort the window display."

"Is that Mum?"

"Yes."

"Don't forget, tell her I asked you specially, whatever it takes."

"I think I've got it covered, speak later."

Elsie's thrilled.

"Isn't that nice of her, asking local people. Fancy. And just a few of us; put some noses out of joint, that will. I'll get Martin's suit to the dry cleaners."

"It's just people with children really, Elsie, and a few friends."

She nods. "I know, dear, but just think, that Mrs. Morgan's going to be so annoyed."

We both smile.

"Either she invited hundreds or it had to be just a select few."

She mutters "select few" to herself as she hands me the box for the window.

"I'll go and make us some tea, shall I, dear? I'll just put these chops in the fridge; my Martin loves chops for his tea."

"Great."

Mission accomplished.

Half an hour later I'm still balanced in the window pegging cardigans on the washing line with the little wooden pegs, and hanging the flags across the partition. Gran and Betty have arrived and are sitting in the café talking about what Gran will wear to Graceland, with Elsie joining in and then nipping back into the shop whenever anyone comes in. Tom's looking lovesick, mainly because he hopes Cinzia might be coming in; it turned out his knitted heart was for her, so that's something else for me to worry about. She seemed delighted, but I've got visions of half of Connie's family descending on me to complain that I've encouraged a dalliance with a would-be musician-waiter, and they've probably got enough of those at home. Connie's pretty relaxed about it, and so far they've only been for a walk, with Nelly and Marco as chaperones. But you never know. He's doing a fair bit of lovesick lolling about, so I'm predicting Trouble.

"It all looks lovely, pet." Gran's peering over the partition.

"It's getting there."

"The colors are so pretty."

I've chosen some of the nicest pastels, buttermilk and caramel and blush pink and powder blue, with peppermint and primrose, and none of the nasty sickly green that Elsie's always trying to order, or the acrylic peach four-ply. And there's an old-fashioned layette, with a fancy shawl, and a tiny sleepsuit with mittens and bootees. I've swathed white and cream muslin over the partition so everything looks fresh, but it's still a bit sparse. I've got a few cardigans in brighter colors to fold on the shelf at the side, in the baby cotton, a lovely bright pink, and one with navy and white stripes, and one in damson, so that'll help. And then the blankets, in creams and pale coffee colors, with borders of nutmeg, and a pretty oatmeal one with a catkin border.

"I'll put the knitted animals in too, Gran, and can you and Betty make a few more, they sell really well. I'll save the ducks and rabbits for Easter, but a few more of the little teddies and the elephants would be great. Oh, and the penguins, with proper beaks this time."

She smiles. I knitted one of the penguins a few months ago, but I managed to get the decreasing for the beak wrong, so it ended up a bit more like a puffin than a penguin.

"Of course we will. I like to have a bit of knitting on the go in the evenings, you know that, pet."

"I'm going to play around with some new blanket designs for Grace; she wants something a bit bigger, so I might need your help with that."

"Right you are."

For larger blankets I prefer knitting squares; it's so much less daunting than casting on vast numbers of stitches on a circular needle. I usually sew a flannel sheet to the back to help keep the shape, or thinner cotton or muslin for a new-born blanket. I've already got one to sew onto Connie's blanket when it's ready, in pale yellow brushed cotton with little ducklings on it.

"I thought we could do some new motif patterns for the squares too, like the seaside blanket I knitted for Jack when we first moved down here. Ice cream cones and lollipops, flowers, boats, the letters of the alphabet, that kind of thing."

"Well, let me know if you need a hand."

"Thanks Gran."

Gran and Elsie often help me write the patterns, and then we make up the kits in our posh new McKnits boxes, with bright pink tissue paper. And unlike the bigger companies, who make you buy a ball of every different color you need, we divide up balls into smaller skeins: Elsie loves winding them onto our new little McKnits contrast cards. So we can keep the prices reasonable and still make a decent profit.

I'm just about finished when Mrs. Peterson comes in. She smiles at me over the partition as Gran comes through from the café. "Do you need any help, dear?"

"I was just, I'm not sure, I used to knit, I made things for both the girls and they loved them."

She hesitates.

"Did you? And now you're thinking of starting up again, are you? I think that's a lovely idea."

"I see the colors, in the window. I often stop to look when I walk by, and they're so pretty. And Amy's friend Nelly, at school, she's got a lovely cardigan her mum made for her, so I thought I'd try to knit one for Amy, if it's not too difficult?"

"It's the pattern with the flowers on the pockets, Gran, the one Connie made, in the cashmerino; we've got most of the colors on the shelves, just over there. Hang on a minute and I'll show you."

I show her the pattern, and the wool, and help her choose the colors and make sure they're from the same dye lots.

I'm putting the wool and needles into one of our shopping bags while she looks at the pattern book.

"I can't wait to get started. I just hope I can manage it, I'd hate to disappoint her. She's been so good, and, well. It's been difficult."

"I'm sure you'll be fine, but why don't you sit in the café and I'll help you make a start. Have a coffee, and we can read through the pattern together?"

"Oh, would you? That would be so kind."

"Of course, no problem, that's what we're here for."

"It's hard, when children are so young, and they have to cope with such terrible things, isn't it?"

She looks at me, and I know she's trying to say something, about Nick; Tina will have told her, and she's trying to let me know that she knows, about Jack and Archie, losing Nick, as well as her Amy, losing her sister. So much loss, for such little people.

"Yes. But they cope, somehow. It doesn't stop you minding, though, does it?"

"No."

She puts the pattern book into the shopping bag.

"Shall I sit anywhere, in the café?"

"Yes, I'll be through in a minute, I just need to take these boxes back up to the storeroom. And I can highly recommend the cake, if you're in the mood for a treat."

Gran and Betty have got her sitting with them when I get back downstairs, and Betty's reading the pattern, and explaining how healthy our smoothlies are.

It doesn't matter how many times I say smoothies, they just nod and then carry on calling them smoothlies. Even I've started doing it now.

"They're very good in the mornings, if you don't eat much breakfast. I often pop in for one, you should give them a try, dear. Shouldn't she, Mary?"

Gran nods and pours me a cup of tea and tops up Mrs. Peterson's cup.

"Tell Jo about your Valentine's card, Betty. She got ever such a lovely one, with a big red satin heart on it."

"Yes, only I haven't worked out who it's from yet, and it's driving me demented, I can tell you. I think it's that Ted Mallow from the Lifeboats, but I'm not sure. Silly to send one and then not make yourself known if you ask me, just making a nuisance of himself, but then he's always been like that."

Mrs. Peterson is smiling at Gran.

"Did you get one this year, dear?"

She looks surprised. "Er, yes, from my husband."

"Isn't that lovely? Nice when they still bother. Mind you, lovely-looking girl like you, you can't blame him, dear."

Gran winks at me. "Has Her Majesty calmed down about the boat yet? She seems a bit happier."

"Sort of, but don't mention it."

"It'll cost him a fair bit, I shouldn't wonder, and he's got that barn to do as well. He'll have to be careful."

"He's taking on extra consultancy work, in London."

"Is he? Well, that won't go down well. She was just saying she's going to ask him to drive her into Canterbury for late closing on Thursday, see if she can find a new frock."

"Right."

"What will you be wearing, pet?" Gran turns to Mrs. Peterson. "We're off to a special tea party at the weekend, only I've got no idea what to wear."

"I don't know, Gran. Something that won't show stains? It's a tea party with children. There's not a lot of point in wearing anything too special."

"Yes, but that's half the fun, isn't it, getting a new outfit. Have you been into Debenhams? They've got some lovely things. Have you been in lately, dear?"

I hope Mrs. Peterson's not going to regret coming in today. But once Gran and Betty have got you in their sights, there's little chance of escape.

"No, not lately."

Betty puts her cup down. "You should do, love. You've got such a lovely figure, and they've got some pretty spring colors in now. We saw a nice blue blouse that would suit you. What would you call that color, Mary?"

"What color?"

"That blouse we saw in Debenhams."

"Petrol blue?"

"Yes, although why do they call it petrol? Petrol isn't a color."

"I think there's a bird with that color plumage, a seabird I think."

Betty gives Mrs. Peterson a very approving look. "Is there,

dear? Fancy that. Did you hear that, Mary? It's a bird. Well, I bet it looks very smart when it's flapping about, it's a smart color. They had it in pink too. But it wasn't a very nice pink. More salmon than you'd want in a blouse."

Mrs. Peterson appears to be trying not to laugh now.

Oh God. I think I might go back in the window.

Ellen and Harry arrive at lunchtime on Saturday with Eddie asleep in his car seat.

"He's so much bigger, Ellen, I can't believe how much he's grown."

"Never stops eating, that's why. Total little porker."

"He's gorgeous."

Harry grins.

"Can I park him upstairs? He usually has a couple of hours around now, and if he wakes up he'll be hell on wheels."

"Sure, you're in the same room as last time. I've moved Pearl's cot into my room and put the travel cot up, I've put a sheet in and a couple of blankets. There are more on top of the chest of drawers if you need them."

"Thanks, Jo."

So what's the plan for today, darling?"

"Lunch, and then I need to go into the shop. So I thought we could all go, and then maybe a walk on the beach?"

"In this weather, are you joking?"

"It's warmer than it's been all week, Ellen, and it's not pouring. That's top weather round here. And anyway, I've got to take the kids out for a run; it's a bit like having dogs; lots of fresh air and exercise or they break the furniture."

"Okay, a bit of fresh air, dump the kids and go out club-bing later, yes?"

"Or come home, make supper, do bath time, and then collapse in a heap by the fire?"

"And then we go out clubbing?"

"Sure."

She grins. "This motherhood thing is rubbish, isn't it?"

"Totally."

We're enjoying a cold but sunny walk along the beach, and I've even remembered to bring a carton of milk and the keys to the beach hut, so we can have a cup of tea while the kids race about and Eddie gets to look at the sea, which he seems to find completely mesmerizing. Pearl has let Ellen wear her tiara, for about thirty seconds. All in all, it's going very well indeed, until Trevor bounds toward us. Great.

"Hi Jo. Mum said you were down here. Look, I've brought a new ball, to replace the one we broke."

Ellen smiles. "Hi Martin, or should I say Morning, Cap-tain? How did you manage to break a beach ball?"

"Trevor bit it, by mistake."

"Naturally."

I think I'll make the tea now. We may be here for quite a while.

Harry's carrying Eddie in what looks like a baby rucksack and playing football with the kids; Eddie seems delighted to be part of the action, though less convinced about Trevor. Martin's in goal, and Pearl is digging a small tunnel. I don't really blame her.

Ellen and I are sitting in the loungers, covered with bright orange parrot fabric, with jaunty flip-top sunshades with orange fringing.

"I hope to God nobody sees me."

"I'll have you know Gran's very proud of these loungers, and you've got to admit they're comfy."

"They'd have to be, darling."

"Tea?"

"Sure, unless you've got something stronger?"

"Black currant?"

call halftime in the football match and make everyone have a hot drink.

"Thanks Jo, and I'm really sorry, but I can't make it tomorrow, to the tea thing. That insurance client wants me in all day tomorrow, the whole system has crashed."

"On a Sunday?"

"I know, but they're paying double time, and I really need the money. Dad's going to go in and feed Trevor, and I should be back by late Monday, but if you could pick Mum up, on the way to the party?"

"My car will be full, but I'll ask Reg, or I'll see if Max can add your dad to the guest list, would that be better?"

"That would be great."

"Such a shame, when you rented your fancy dress outfit."

He smiles. "I know."

"Fancy dress? Christ darling, you didn't tell me it was fancy dress."

"It's not, that was just for Martin."

"It's a shame, I was looking forward to it."

Harry laughs. "You don't need a hand, do you, mate? Not

that I know anything about computers, but it's got to be better than a tea party with the Diva and a load of media types. I get enough of that in town."

"Harry. I've told you, you're coming. Someone's got to hold our beautiful boy while I network. Get over it."

He pokes his tongue out at her, then asks Martin about the boat, and before we know it they're talking about rope and special kinds of varnish, and Eddie starts getting fed up, so Ellen takes him down to watch the waves before coming back quite quickly and handing him back to Harry.

"It's even colder down there. Why don't you finish your game? He loved it when you were running around."

Harry sighs. "Girls can play football now, you know, darling, if you fancy a game."

"In these shoes? Go on, before he starts yelling."

I've made a fish pie for supper, which is Ellen's favorite, and after a fairly lively bath time, where I de-sand Pearl, she conks out with her bottle really early, and the boys do too, after so much running around on the beach. Archie's battling to stay awake, but he's in bed, with only his night-light on, so he won't last five minutes. Ellen's giving Eddie a bath and brings him downstairs wrapped in a baby towel with a hood, looking angelic.

"Here you are, one gorgeous boy. Ready for his good night kisses."

I kiss him as she hands him to Harry.

"I don't know if he'll settle, he had quite a long sleep today. I'll give it a go though. Come on, my boy; let's see if your old dad can work his magic once again. Good night, ladies. I may be some time."

"God, I need a drink. I love giving him his bath, he's so adorable, but it's knackering, isn't it?"

"Yes, especially if you made the supper and are now doing the washing up."

I hand her a tea towel.

"Are you serious, darling? What am I meant to do with this?"

"Dry the dishes?"

"And you haven't got a dishwasher because?"

"There isn't room, without moving all the cupboards around, and I haven't got the money for that, or the time. I needed to get the shop and the café sorted first."

"Fabulous ice cream today, darling; that blackberry sorbet was seriously good. That Connie's a very lucky woman. I wish Harry could cook like that; maybe I can send him on a course or something. He is good with our boy though."

"He's great."

"He wants us to get some backup child care sorted. He keeps on about how his life's not his own anymore, and he needs to do the occasional freelance cameraman gig just to keep his eye in. Any views on au pairs versus nannies?"

"Au pairs are much cheaper, but they usually live in, and I don't think you'd like that, would you?"

"If we had a bigger house maybe, and yes, before you say it, I know the new house has five bedrooms, but I think you need a special servant's wing to really pull off having staff living in."

"You'd only want someone part-time, wouldn't you?"

"Yes, but still. I might delegate it to Harry. If he wants a nanny, he can call the agencies and come up with a short list, and I can just meet the ones he likes."

Sometimes I'm amazed at how different Ellen is to me; I'd never have let Nick choose a nanny, if we'd ever had one. But then Nick would have just picked the most attractive one, whereas Harry is much more in tune with his boy. And actually, I don't think there's a law that says mums are responsible for sorting out the child care.

"Then if we have another one, we'll be all set."

"Two nannies?"

"No, you twit, another baby. Harry thinks we should; he thinks they work best in matching sets."

"Do you want another one?"

"To be perfectly honest, no, not really. I adore him, obviously, more than life itself and all that, but I feel like I've done it now. I've got my motherhood badge. I'd quite like to be working on something new."

"It's not like the Girl Guides, Ellen."

"It bloody is. There's the Have a Proper Career badge, tick, Live Somewhere Smart, tick, Partner You Can Take to Dinner Parties, Not the Size of a House, Produce an Infant, tick tick tick. Now I want something new."

"What about a Learn to Dry Up with a Tea Towel badge?" She laughs. "Not really what I had in mind, darling."

"If you go by those rules, I've hardly got any badges at all."

"I know, darling, but you don't care."

"True."

"It's very annoying, actually."

"What is?"

"How you always make the best of things, like a maternal version of fucking Pollyanna."

"Well, there's not much point in making the worst of things."

"There you go again. When life gives you lemons, some of

us hit the gin and tonic and use the lemons as a garnish, but not you, you're off making bloody lemonade every time, aren't you, darling?"

"I don't like lemonade."

"Do try to keep up. I mean you're genuinely happy, aren't you, and the kids are central to that."

"Yes, I suppose I am. I love living here, being part of things and close to Gran. I felt so invisible when we lived in London, and I definitely didn't have all my badges. Well, apart from a husband you could take to dinner parties, but we didn't go to any."

"Bastard."

"Yes, but it takes two."

"Oh not that again, it does not take two. It takes one to be doing the right thing, and one to be a bastard."

"Maybe, but I did get stuck in a comfy little rut, and I really don't want to do that again. I hardly thought about whether I was happy, let alone Nick. You're much happier too now though, aren't you?"

"Yes. I'm not sure I'd spend the rest of my life with Harry if we didn't have Eddie, but we do. And it's great, brilliant actually, but it is strange, you know, how we've all gone right back to staying together for the children."

"Not all of us. Nick and I would have been divorced by now, for sure."

"I know, darling, he was such an idiot. But what I meant was when did we miss out the bit where we got to choose? It was meant to be so liberating, but most of us just have to do three jobs now, the day job, and the wife and perfect bloody networker and hostess, and then we get to do the mother-hood thing on top of all that. Most women I know are either stuck with some master of the universe, terrified he's going to leave them, or they're earning more than the boys, faintly bored but putting up with it because he does all the child care. My friend Liz, you remember the one who had that fling with that actor, she's got two kids now, and her husband is such a prat. She's not allowed to put anything in their dishwasher, he's totally OCD about domestic stuff, practically washes your glass before you've taken your first sip."

"But Harry's not like that."

"No, of course not, I'm not completely hopeless. The day I shack up with Domestic Demigod, who makes his own bread and won't let you open the fridge in case you put the milk back on the wrong shelf, well, just shoot me. But I sometimes hanker, that's all."

"For?"

"I don't know, that's the point, something new. Don't look at me like that. I work bloody hard, and sometimes I think, Is this it? Don't you?"

"Of course."

"Thank God for that. Even Pollyanna has her moments. And what do you decide?"

"Yes. This is it."

"Great, that's totally bloody inspirational."

"What do you want me to say? It's okay to go off and have a fling? I don't think it is."

"No, and neither do I, that's the problem. If Harry ever did that to me, I'd kill him."

We're both laughing now.

"Every silver lining has its cloud, Ellen."

"Yes, and I've got my new series to obsess about anyway; that'll keep me out of trouble."

"Is that definite now?"

"Yes. Signed off and everything, contracts done, half an

hour weekday mornings, starting next month. Just me and no bloody has-been male anchors cluttering up my set."

"That's fantastic, Ellen, well done."

She sits down at the kitchen table, still holding the tea towel. I've nearly finished the drying, but I hand her a glass. "Dry it, and we can have a drink to celebrate."

"You're on. Just what I need, nice large vodka and tonic. And I think your Diva would be an ideal first guest you know, darling."

"Ellen, you promised."

"I know, but she'll be doing PR for her new film. Have a word, would you?"

"What, ask her to agree to go on your new program and spill the beans on her personal life like she's never done before, that kind of thing?"

"Ideally, yes."

"No."

"I am your best girlfriend, darling, there must be some perks."

"I'll knit you something."

"Actually, that might work."

"Sorry?"

"She can come on and knit, and you can be on too, as her official knitting coach. It would be fabulous for business, darling, and it would give it a hook, add to her general profile stuff, they'll like that. Is her agent going to be there tomorrow?"

"Ed, yes, I think so."

"Fine, I'll have a quiet word."

"You will not. You promised. Bruno will throw you out."

"Okay, okay. God, you're bossy. When did you get so bossy?"

"When I woke up one morning and found I'd got three kids and a shop to run?"

"I know, it's a complete choker, isn't it? The other day I woke up and I was still half asleep and there was this terrible noise. Harry was having a bath with Eddie and singing to him, and I thought, Christ, how did that happen? It was a bit scary, like I was in a parallel universe, and I'd been having this great dream about Brad Pitt."

"And you were?"

"Angelina, obviously."

She hands me a vodka, with very little tonic.

"God, that's strong."

"It's meant to be, darling, otherwise it doesn't work. So how are you and Dovetail then?"

"Fine."

"I think we need a bit better than fine, don't we?"

"It's good. It's just, well, the last time he came round, I fell asleep."

"Fell asleep in the middle of—"

"Yes, thank you. I really don't want to go into details."

She's trying not to laugh. Which is annoying.

"Well, that happens sometimes, darling."

"He was making the coffee, and I fell asleep, that's all. Look, let's talk about something else."

"What, like how lovely our babies are? Boring. How crap work is? Boring. Sex and drugs and rock and roll are my specialist subjects, darling."

"What drugs?"

"Well okay, mostly vodka, but come on, Share. I'm not going to let this one go."

"There's nothing to share. He was really sweet about it, left me a note and everything. It was just, well, it can't be a good sign, can it?"

"But you do have passionate moments?"

"Yes, sort of. It's not really Martin's style, or mine, but we have our moments."

"Maybe you need to dress up as a tree or something, since he's so into Wood. Makes a change from those bloody nurse uniforms."

"Ellen, shut up."

"Sorry darling. But honestly, you have to make a bit of an effort, you know. Role play, surprise him, that kind of thing. Dress up as a French maid in the middle of the afternoon, although why they have to be bloody French escapes me, the only French women I know would give you very short shrift if you tried to get them into a black nylon miniskirt."

"And what do I do with the children then, when I'm surprising people in fancy dress at teatime, tell them to put their hands over their eyes and count to one hundred?"

"What about the shop? You could come up and have a great time there, dress up as a nurse and show him all about proper First Aid in the Workplace."

"That's a brilliant idea, and then when his mother wanders in and has a heart attack, it'll be handy to be in the right kind of uniform, for when the ambulance turns up."

We're both nearly hysterical with laughing now.

"It's tricky, Ellen. I can't leave the kids, and he can't be away all night or Trevor will eat the barn. So we end up having supper at home, and then we sit in front of the fire—"

"And shag like rabbits."

"Ellen, please."

"Just spice it up a bit."

"Spicy things make my mouth go numb, and then I'm sick."

"Well don't put anything in your mouth, darling."

Oh God, we're both cackling again.

"And that's another thing; there's usually someone small in my bed. It's just too complicated, until the kids are older. Let's talk about something else now. This is so not helping."

"Well it's helping me, darling. I thought I had problems with Harry. But at least he's never actually made me fall asleep."

"He didn't make me fall asleep, Ellen, I was just really tired. We have been talking about booking a couple of nights away somewhere though."

"Well get him to bloody book it then. When was the last time you had a break away from the kids?"

"Pass."

"Seriously?"

"Not since Jack was born."

"Christ, I didn't realize. Well no wonder you fell asleep, darling. Seriously, didn't you and Nick go off to that festival thing one year, in Italy?"

"Yes. And we took Jack, and I spent most of the time in the hotel room trying to get him to sleep in the world's most useless travel cot."

"Okay, well there's your problem then, darling. You need a mini-break more than any woman I know. Nice spa, buy the kind of lingerie you don't want anyone to see hanging on your washing line, and away you go."

"No thanks. I like the idea of a passionate interlude now and again, but I'm not dressing up, I'd feel like a total fool, and Martin wouldn't like it, I know he wouldn't. It would probably make him laugh."

"If you found the right outfit he wouldn't be laughing, trust me, darling. But whatever floats your boat. He does though, doesn't he? Float your boat, at least for the occasional day trip?"

"Yes, and can we please not talk about bloody boats."

"Okay, so keep him for Mr. Friday Night for now, and see how it goes. Just try to stay awake, darling. Now enough about you, let's talk about special me. Because I need a top motherhood tip, I really do. He threw porridge at me this morning."

"I'm sure he didn't, Ellen."

"He bloody did. I'd just finished getting dressed, and I wanted a little kiss, he looks so sweet sitting in his high chair, and the next thing I knew the little sod had dolloped porridge all over my new tweed skirt. I had to get changed."

"Oh dear."

"He thought it was fabulous, he was chucking stuff everywhere. I think we're going to have to rethink giving him a spoon. He can fling stuff right across the bloody kitchen now."

"You wait until he works out he can chuck the whole dish. I've had to get those bowls with suction cups on the bottom so I can stick them to the high chair, which is all Archie's fault for trying to teach her how to throw a bloody Frisbee."

"I'll watch out for that one then. Maybe I could avoid mealtimes altogether."

"Coward."

"Too right. I don't have the kind of wardrobe for spillages."

"Well get one then, that's my top tip."

"Charming. Maybe I can get some of those trousers with elasticated waists and give up altogether."

"They're very comfy."

"They'd bloody need to be. Talking of which, what are you wearing tomorrow? Not those jeans?"

"What's the matter with them?"

"They're completely the wrong shape."

"They're the same shape I am."

"You know what I mean. You're not wearing them. What else have you got?"

"A Vivienne Westwood gown, with six-inch heels."

"Perfect. Out-Diva the Diva, that's the spirit."

Great. So now all I've got to do is stop Maxine throwing Ellen out of the party for pitching interview bids in the middle of the tea and cakes, and work out what to wear that will be up to Ellen's exacting standards. I might as well stay in bed.

Christ. It's snowing. It's the tea party this afternoon, and it's definitely starting to bloody snow.

The kids are hysterical, and charge around outside collecting snowflakes in outstretched fingers. Pearl's transfixed, and Eddie seems to be enjoying it too. Thankfully it's not really settling, so they soon get bored and come back in for cartoons. But still. Bloody hell. Poor Maxine.

She calls, sounding panicky. "Grace is thrilled, but what will we do if it really snows and everyone gets marooned? Where on earth will we put them all?"

"Don't worry, it never gets that bad round here, and the forecast only says light flurries."

"Well I hope they're right, because the caterers are already driving Sam nuts, and Mr. Magic has called me twice already this morning."

"The children's entertainer?"

"Yes, although what would make him really magical is if he could just get on with it and stop calling me. Oh, and Grace says she wants you to get here early. Come around two, that'll give us an hour before anyone else arrives."

"Can I bring Cinzia and Gran and Reg? Only that way they can watch the kids if Grace wants, well, anything."

"Wants you all to herself you mean, which she will. So yes, bring them. Just not anyone else, not until we're parade ready."

"Sure."

"I better go. Bruno seems have sacked two of the event security team."

"Event security?"

"Just extra muscle to stop the snappers climbing over the walls."

"Why did he sack them?"

"They made fun of Tom and Jerry I think. Who knows? But I better sort it out."

"See you later."

"If I haven't run away."

"Max, it'll be fine."

"It better be. She's in a funny mood. She usually obsesses about the tiniest detail, but today, well, she's not. It's very disconcerting."

"That's because she knows you're doing it for her."

"Thanks Jo, see you later."

"On a sledge if necessary."

"Sledges, God, do you think I should have sledges on standby?"

"Max, it was a joke, and anyway, the place will be seething with Range Rovers and Jeeps. They're meant to be able driving through arctic forests; a light flurry isn't going to stop them. We can drive people out in shifts if we have to."

"That's true. Okay, I feel better now. See you later."

Poor thing. If I'd got a mixture of VIPs from London and locals descending on me for tea with a light dusting of snow for extra drama, I think I might be a little bit panicky too.

Gran is astonished at how grand it all looks as we drive into Graceland. She even waves at the photographers outside, and one waves back, which is a bit mortifying. Reg is following us with the boys in his car, which he's washed specially for the occasion.

"Isn't it lovely, it's like something out of a film, and the snow looks so pretty, it's almost settling."

"Yes, Gran."

Cinzia says something in Italian. "When I am the grown-up, this is the house I want."

"Good plan, Cinzia. Can we come and see you when you get it?"

"Yes, you and the Principessa. The boys, maybe not so much. Archie, he tell me today I am stupid horrible. Because I cannot find the flipper."

"They're too small, I've told him. He doesn't need his snorkel either really, but he definitely doesn't need his flippers. I hope you told him he's not allowed to be rude to you like that."

"No, I was laughing."

"That works too."

"I hope I look smart enough."

"You look lovely, Gran."

She's wearing the suit she bought for her wedding. She said she'd been saving it for a special occasion, and now she's got one. When I spoke to Elsie earlier, she was still deciding between her new blue dress and her old wool crepe, which she says makes her neck go red. Jeffrey's bringing her along later, poor man; she made him race out and buy a new suit yesterday after I got him added to the guest list.

Maxine's waiting by the side door as we park. Bruno is standing next to her with Tom and Jerry looking spotless. Bugger. The boys will want to say hello, and I was hoping not

to arrive at the poshest event we've ever attended covered in
dog dribble.

"Hello, Bruno."

"Hi, Jo. You got your lads with you? Brought the dogs round
specially."

"Lovely."

"Come on, Grandad, come and see Tom and Jerry."

Reg doesn't look that convinced that two enormous Rottweilers really are the ideal dogs for Jack and Archie to be racing toward at full pelt, but Bruno shouts "Lie Down!" and both
dogs hurl themselves to the ground and start rolling around
for tickling, which is more than Trevor ever manages.

Maxine raises her eyebrows. "Will this take long, Bruno?
Only I'd quite like to get Jo inside. It's rather cold. You may
have noticed, what with the snow and everything."

"They're just saying hello."

A pair of security guards in smart blue uniforms walk past
and make a determined effort to look the other way.

Bruno stands up. "Update in ten minutes at the gate-
house, yes?"

"Yes, guv."

I'm sure I can see them exchanging a smile as they walk
away. I just hope Bruno didn't spot it.

"What on earth are you doing out here?"
Grace has got huge foam curlers in her hair and is
wearing a kimono, which while being very beautiful, clearly
signals she's not actually dressed yet. But I've noticed before
how she's very relaxed about wandering around half dressed,
looking gorgeous, even in curlers.

"Bruno, the boys can see the dogs later. Isn't there something more important you should be doing now?"

"Yes, of course, I was just—"

"We'll put that on your tombstone, you know, 'I was just.' Max, write that down. 'Here lies Bruno. He was just.' Anyway, hello everybody, lovely to see you, please excuse the chaos. Jo, I need a few minutes."

Maxine steps forward. "Would the boys like a swim? And Cinzia, isn't it?"

Cinzia smiles, one of her biggest, most stunning smiles, which even Grace notices.

Maxine gives her an admiring look. "Could you take them swimming, Cinzia?"

"Yes, of course."

"Actually Maxine, I'm not sure she can take all three of them. Maybe later, when I can go in too."

Or not, if I can think of a way to get out of it.

Maxine gives me a slightly anxious look. "Oh, right, it's just, well, Meg's taking Lily down, and she'd love it if the children joined her."

Gran puts her hand on Archie's shoulder. "You're all right, pet; me and Reg will go in too. Well, not in, but if there's a seat, we'll sit by the edge and watch, so Cinzia's not on her own."

"Thanks, Gran."

She's in for a nice surprise; there's a range of posh loungers, so they'll be able to watch in comfort.

Grace gives everyone another megawatt smile as we walk across the hall, and they head off toward the pool.

———

"Where did you get such a gorgeous nanny, darling?"
"She's more of an au pair really; she's over from Italy staying with Connie."

"Italian, that explains it, such gorgeous hair. Let's go and grab some tea before we go up. Sam is in meltdown, and that's always fun."

Maxine shakes her head as we walk toward the kitchen and points to the stairs. I think I'm meant to get Grace upstairs as soon as I can and away from poor Sam. Although how she thinks I'm going to manage that is anybody's guess.

Sam's looking Stressed. "I'll send someone up with the tea, is that okay? Do you need anything else?"

"Jo, would you like something to eat? I'm sure Sam can rustle you up something delicious."

Sam gives me a beseeching look over Grace's shoulder.

"No thanks, Grace, I'm fine. Just a cup of tea would be lovely."

I turn to walk toward the door, hoping Grace will follow me, and miraculously, she does.

Maxine's very impressed and gives me the thumbs-up sign as we walk back across the hall. At least I've done something to help, even if it's only keeping Grace occupied.

"Did you bring the wool?"
"Yes, it's in the car. I've found some lovely new organic angora mix from Wales, and some grays and slate blues from that Scottish mill, the one in that article I showed you. I've brought some more of the baby cashmere too. Shall I go and get it?"

"No, bring it in later. I need a favor first."

"Of course."

She smiles. "You don't know what it is yet."

"No, but I'll give it a go."

"It's rather personal."

Oh, God, I hope it's not anything to do with wax. Ellen asked me to help her do an emergency leg wax once, and it was a complete disaster.

"Okay."

"When you were having Pearl, when did you find out?"

"Sorry?"

"That you were pregnant."

"In the car park, at the supermarket. Well that's when it first dawned on me. I went in and got a test, and then had a mini-meltdown in the customer loos and rang Ellen."

"Can you buy some more?"

"Sorry? Oh. Right, well yes, of course."

"Just make sure nobody sees you. There's press everywhere, and I can't ask Max, I don't want her to know, not until I know, and there's nobody else I can ask."

"Of course."

"Can you go now? And bring the basket in with the wool when you get back. Yes?"

"Sure."

"And be as quick as you can."

Bloody hell, I'm not really cut out for clandestine missions, and I'm sure there's a car following me as I drive back into town, but then it turns left as I go right, and I start to relax. But still, bloody hell. Gran didn't seem at all bothered that I was nipping back to get some more wool for Grace, but even so. I really don't know what I'll do if I see someone I know while I'm tipping pregnancy testing kits into my trolley. I think I'll head to the retail park on the road to Fordingham; there's a big chemist's there, and less people go that way. Crikey, I wonder who the father is, if it's someone who'll be around or not. Maybe it's one of the actors from the last film. God, the press are going to go nuts; the whole town will be besieged by hacks wanting snippets. I must remember not to ask her, not even show a hint of curiosity about it. I really hated that when I was having Pearl. People are so rude, even the nice ones, asking questions about what's going on, when you're not even sure yourself. But still, I wonder who it is. Bloody hell.

pile a large bottle of shampoo, a couple of bottles of baby lotion, and a big pack of baby wipes on top of the tests and then stagger with my basket to the tills. I've got six tests, because I'm thinking Grace will be just like Ellen and one test will definitely not be enough. The woman gives me a strange look and smiles at me like I'm one of life's tragic people, which I can't quite understand until I suddenly realize she thinks I'm buying baby supplies before I've even done the tests. Bloody hell, it comes to £92.78; I'd forgotten how expensive they are. Great, this is all so mortifying, all I need is to bump into Annabel Morgan and it'll be perfect. Gran will be round knocking on my front door tomorrow morning and asking me if there's anything I want to tell her.

By the time I've driven back to Graceland, arranged the balls of wool over the top of the tests, and walked through the hall, I'm almost having a full-blown panic attack. I'll have to breathe into a paper bag if I carry on like this.

"I can't believe she sent you back for more wool. Honestly, sometimes I think she lives on an entirely different planet to the rest of us. Do you want a drink?"

"Please Max, that'd be great." Preferably a triple vodka.

"Go straight up, she's in the blue room. I'll send up some tea and tell her the first guests are arriving, so if she could get a move on we'd all be very grateful."

"Sure."

I half race up the stairs, so I'm out of breath by the time I'm walking down the corridor.

"I'm in here, Jo. Could you give me a minute, darling? Actually, make that ten. I just need a time-out with my knitting coach. Moment of calm, yes?"

The makeup woman nods and closes the door behind her.

"Maxine is sending up some tea, and she says the guests are starting to arrive."

Grace takes the bag from me, gives me a rather shaky smile, and goes into the bathroom.

Christ, I'm so nervous that when there's a knock on the door I nearly jump out of my seat.

"Tea?"

"Thank you."

I take the tray from a gorgeous-looking waiter. He must be part of the catering team. God, I wish she'd hurry up; I don't think I can take much more of this. Although I don't actually know what result she's hoping for, so that's going to be tricky, and I really don't want to get this wrong. Bloody hell, I'm definitely going to have to find a paper bag in a minute. Either that or pass out.

The door opens.

"Tea. Great."

She looks very calm.

"Everything okay?" Damn. I've crossed the invisible line again, where she can tell you things but you never ask. Too many people ask her things, all the time.

"Absolutely fine."

"Good. Shall I pour the tea?"

Right. Okay, she doesn't want to talk about this, and that's fine. Of course she bloody doesn't. My hands are shaking as I pour the tea, but I manage to avoid blurting out "Tell me, tell me" or anything mortifying like that. She needs peace and calm. I must get a grip and give her some space.

There's a silence, quite a long silence actually, and then she smiles. "Aren't you going to ask me then?"

"It's none of my business, Grace, as long as you're okay."

I'm quite pleased with this answer, but not as pleased as she is. She walks toward me and kisses me on my forehead, and then sits down.

"Absolutely fine. And absolutely positive."

"Oh Grace, how lovely. Sorry, I mean, is it? Because if it's not that's fine too, well, of course it is. Christ, sorry, just ignore me. I'll pull myself together in a minute."

I'm gripping the teapot so hard now in an effort to shut up I'm at serious risk of snapping the bloody handle off.

"It's perfect. Only I don't want anyone to know, anyone at all. It's very early."

"Of course."

"Promise? Nobody. Not Max, not yet, and definitely not your friend Ellen."

"Of course."

I hand her a cup of tea, and she smiles. "Thanks. It should probably be champagne, but here, let's raise a cup to new beginnings. And snow. It always brings me luck when it snows."

"Does it? Well, I'll definitely drink to that."

We clink our cups, and she does one of her Diva smiles that seem to light up the whole room, and I realize she's completely delighted, so deep down happy she doesn't really know what to do with herself. She puts her hand on her tummy, just for a second, when she thinks I'm not looking.

"Thanks Jo."

"My pleasure."

"And—"

"I promise. Relax Grace, I'm not a blurter. Well, with you I am, I do admit that, but sometimes I can't help it. But unless there's another major film star about to quiz me, I'll be fine. I can keep things secret squirrel when I need to, I promise I can."

She smiles. "What's a secret squirrel?"

"When I worked in news we had a whole list of secret stuff, it was part of the job, and Ellen and I used to call it our secret squirrel file. I didn't care about most of them of course, so it was different. But I can definitely keep things secret. And I know what it's like, people asking you questions when it's none of their business. I hated it. So subject closed. Now please, can you get ready? Because Maxine is going to kill me if I don't get you downstairs soon."

She's smiling again. "Sure, get the makeup girl back in, would you, and tell Max I'll be ten minutes. And we'll do the knitting thing later. I think I might be doing quite a bit of knitting in the next few months."

There are quite a few guests milling about as I go downstairs.

"Is she on her way?" Maxine is looking anxious.

"Ten minutes."

"Really?"

"Yes, she's almost ready."

"Good. Oh, and it's bloody snowing again. So we might need those sledges after all."

"It'll be fine, Max."

"She was banging on about snow being lucky this morning, although for who is beyond me."

"Was she? Well, it's lucky if you like snow, I suppose. Are the kids still in the pool? I'd better go and rescue Cinzia."

"Don't worry; she's got quite a few of the waiters trooping in and out checking if she needs anything."

"Has she? Sorry, that does tend to happen."

"I bet. No, she's fine, nice girl actually. She adores your kids, doesn't she? Really sweet."

"Yes, but they do tend to take advantage. Particularly Archie. I better go and get them out."

Good God, I'd be such a hopeless spy. I feel like blurting and nobody's even asked me a bloody question yet. Time to calm down. Get the kids and calm down. I know nothing. I'm going to wipe it from my mind. Keep calm and carry on.

Christ.

I'm having a quiet moment with a pistachio meringue when Ellen wanders over.

"Fabulous party, isn't it? The kids are having a lovely time with the magic show. Harry's just taken Eddie in; your gran's in there, with Elsie."

"I know, I just asked them to go in and help Cinzia. Not

that she needs any help, but they were starting to wear me out."

She laughs. "I don't blame them, darling. I've just been talking to Luke Baker, and I've always had a bit of a thing about him. I almost went a bit wobbly. Why is he here, do you know?"

"He was in the *Bedknobs and Broomsticks* film with Grace, wasn't he?"

"Oh yes, of course, she was great in that. Particularly the knitting scenes."

It was rather thrilling, sitting in the cinema and seeing her up on the big screen, knitting while the children are fishing; it was the scene they were filming when I visited, when I was pregnant. Except I'm trying to avoid thinking about anyone being pregnant.

"Yes, she looked great, didn't she? But then she always does."

"Hello ladies. Enjoying ourselves, are we? I gather this was your idea, Jo. Great theme, Mother's Day, right on target."

"Thanks Ed, but it was Grace's idea really."

"Well, she's loving it, so that's a relief. She can get a bit full-on when she's not happy. You may have noticed."

"Really?"

He grins and turns to Ellen. "I hear the new series has got the green light. When do you start?"

"In a couple of weeks, and I wanted to have a word with you on that, I was—"

"Ellen, you promised. No work today."

"Relax, darling, I promised not to badger your Diva, but I can have a little quiet word with her agent surely?"

Ed gives her a rather hard look. "Depends what the word is, darling."

"Just an idea for Grace. I thought she might like to join me, on the program. We could do it around the launch of the new film. We'll avoid the forbidden questions, all the usual. We could do Amazing Grace at home, or maybe in her local wool shop with her knitting coach, taking part in her local community, not too snooty to join in, something like that. We could do a prerecord, you can have approval, all the usual, or she can come in and join me on one of my new exquisite sofas, whichever you prefer."

"I'll add it to the list."

"Seriously?"

He grins. "Sure, I quite like it."

"Like what?"

Oh, God.

"Hi Grace, just pitching a little idea to your agent."

"So I heard, and the knitting angle is nice, Ed, let's look at it."

I'm giving Ellen a furious look, or my best attempt at one, which just makes Ellen laugh.

"I should probably say this wasn't Jo's idea, Grace, before she kicks me. You know what a shrinking violet she is. She made me promise not to ask, but if you would like to do it, I'd be thrilled, I—"

"I adore violets. Lovely to see you again, Ellen, so glad you could join us. Jo, walk with me for a minute, would you?"

Bugger. I really didn't want Ellen to ask her, and now I'm going to get Told Off.

"I'm really sorry about that, Grace. She promised me she wouldn't pitch anything, but she just can't help herself."

"It's fine, darling, I quite like the idea, but don't tell her that. But I'd put yourself on standby for a bit of filming in your shop. Be great for business, wouldn't it?"

"Yes, but only if you really want to."

"I never do anything I don't want to, darling. You should know that by now. Keep walking, and talk to me, like there's something urgent we have to sort out. Emma Fox is on her way over, and I can't stand her."

Naturally I can't think of a thing to say.

"Sorry, I can't think of anything, but the party is wonderful, everyone seems to be loving it, and I'm sorry about my gran, she's not usually like that."

Gran got so overawed introducing Reg earlier she held Grace's hand, and didn't let go, for what felt like hours. And Elsie did one of her special half curtsies, which she usually reserves for Lady Denby, who actually sold this house to Grace, so it was rather apt in a way, but she got so carried away she was practically on the floor, and Jeffrey had to help her back up.

Grace leans forward and nods as if there's just been a domestic calamity. "Don't be, I thought she was sweet. Let's go into the kitchen, we'll safe in there."

She blows a kiss to Emma, who very theatrically blows a kiss of her own, as we walk past her toward the kitchen.

Mark is inevitably deep in conversation with one of the caterers, talking about cakes. He promised Connie he'd be only five minutes, about half an hour ago.

Grace goes into full Diva mode.

"I just wanted to say thank you all, so much; everything is perfect. At least so I hear. I haven't actually tasted anything yet. So I'm taking a five-minute break. Sam, can you choose a few things for me, darling?"

How clever of her. She's given Sam the upgrade of being

her proper chef, and the two caterers and the waiters milling about are all looking thrilled with the compliments.

"Let's sit over here for a minute, Jo. Max will be here in about thirty seconds; once I've gone off radar, she usually tracks me down."

The view from the French windows is lovely, down toward the lake.

"Would you like a drink, some water perhaps?"

"Lovely, thanks darling."

Maxine appears, as if by magic. "Do you need anything, Grace?"

"No thanks, Sam is sorting me out a taster plate, and Jo's getting me some water. I think we've got it all under control. How's it going? They all seem to be enjoying themselves."

"Mr. Magic is about to start the children's disco."

"Oh God, I better get back in there, Archie can get a bit carried away when he's dancing."

Grace laughs. "Off you go then. Maxine will get me a glass of something cooling. Have we got any of that elder flower? I like that."

"Coming right up."

She's extraordinary. I've been watching her, for most of the afternoon, greeting her guests and being every inch the megastar, like she's got nothing on her mind except making sure everyone has a great time.

The disco is in full swing, with a bubble machine for extra excitement.

"Hasn't it been lovely, pet? Look at our Archie dancing with Pearl, aren't they a picture?"

"Yes Gran."

Cinzia's dancing with them, and attracting very longing looks from assorted dads and waiters. She seems oblivious to this and is trying to encourage Jack to join in. Which he won't, but that's not stopping her from trying.

"I've had such a nice afternoon, pet."

"Where's Elsie?"

"Over in the corner, with her Jeffrey, talking to your Ellen."

"Oh. Right."

Ellen is giving me one of her get-this-nutter-off-me looks, which I ignore. Serve her right.

Tina comes over. "We've had such a nice time, Jo. Thanks ever so much for getting us invited, Travis has loved it. Have you seen my Graham? Only he went off a while back with that security man."

"Bruno?"

"Yes, to look at the fire alarm. I told him, they don't need you poking about checking their circuits, but you know what he's like."

"I'm sure Bruno will bring him back soon."

Unless Graham is keen on dogs, in which case he could be ages.

"I better go and get Travis; he's trying to get the magician to tell him how he does his tricks."

Travis is very clever and likes to get answers to his questions, proper detailed answers, with diagrams if required. Sometimes I don't know how Tina copes.

"He's on at me to get him a rabbit now; he says it would be interesting."

We exchange slightly nervous looks.

"I'm sure he wouldn't hurt it."

"Of course he wouldn't, Tina. He's very gentle."

"I know, but he gets carried away, that's the problem. He wants a rat too, he says he can train it to do tricks. Can you imagine? My mum would faint dead away. Mind you, Graham thinks that might be handy; they don't really get on."

One of the media types from London, in a smart black suit, is handing his card to Cinzia. I think it might be time for us to gather our things before she ends up with the promise of a screen test.

I walk over and pick up Pearl, who snuggles in for a cuddle. She's got cake in her hair, and seems blissed out but very tired. I know the feeling.

"I think we should probably get going, Cinzia."

"Yes, and did you see the Principessa dancing? She is so happy, all the kidlings are, with the swimming and the magic."

"Yes, I did, and thanks for taking them swimming."

"I love it, the pool, it was so beautiful."

"Can we go swimming again, Mum?"

"No, it's nearly home time now, love."

Jack sighs. "I've had a lovely party, Mum, really lovely."

"Have you, sweetheart? Well that's good."

Archie's eating more cake. "We should have a party like this. We could have it in the shop and everyone can have ice cream."

"Maybe, let's see."

Archie tuts. "No, let's not see, let's just do it."

Actually, I think a collection of parents and children having an ice cream party would seem like a walk in the park compared to an outside broadcast crew crawling all over the shop, trailing wires everywhere, with Britain's Favorite Broadcaster and the Diva. Christ. I'm half hoping it doesn't happen.

It would be great for the business, obviously, but still. Bloody hell. Gran will need to take one of her tablets, and Elsie will probably self-combust.

"Let's go home, and we can talk about it."

"Yes, and I want a rabbit too, Mum, for my birthday. I really really do."

· · · 4 · · ·

Now We Are Seven

April

"Morning, darling."

"Ellen, do you know what time it is?"

"It's seven, but I knew you'd be up. Guess what I was doing this time last year?"

"Giving birth?"

"You were meant to guess."

"Sorry."

"It was such a perfect day."

Actually, it was, apart from the racing up the motorway in the middle of the night having a panic attack. I remember standing holding Eddie, so tiny in his little hospital blanket. Harry was in tears, we all were, even the midwife, but that may have been because Ellen had promised to get her fired.

"I can't believe he's already a year old. Is he having a lovely birthday?"

"He's still asleep, so not so much with the Fast Eddie this

morning, although he's definitely getting the hang of the crawling, in typical speedy fashion. It's terrifying; one minute he's there and the next he's off. I'm going to have to get some stair gates, I always said I wouldn't, but I see the point of them now. I've got a huge pile of presents waiting for him. Honestly, I'll have to wake them up in a minute, I can't wait. Harry's got me something too, I know he has."

"Clever Harry."

"Well it stands to reason the mum should get something. Didn't Nick used to do that?"

"He barely got me anything on my actual birthday, let alone the boys' ones."

"Well I'll get you something, for Archie's birthday, and I've got that Lego set for him. What shall I bring for you?"

"Drugs? I've still got an ice cream party and magic show to get through before you descend on us with your bloody film crew."

"It'll be fine, darling, I've told you, just relax."

Relax. Is she mad? Ellen, Grace, Gran, Betty, and Elsie, and a film crew. What could possibly go wrong?

"What shall I get for Eddie? You still haven't told me."

"A nanny. Harry's making a complete mess of it, as if I haven't got enough on my plate with the program launch and half the boys in suits from the top floor trying to screw things up for me. Mind you, getting the exclusive with the Diva has shut a few of them up."

"Well if I can't track Mary Poppins down, shall I get some Duplo? The boys loved that when they were little."

"That's baby Lego, isn't it? That would be perfect. Give him something else to chuck at Harry."

"Pearl, don't do that, love, that doesn't go in there."

"What's she doing?"

"Trying to put my milk saucepan into the washing machine."

"Bless."

"Oh yes, it's delightful. I nearly put the lid from the casserole dish on fast spin yesterday, and God knows how much that would have cost to fix."

"You should get a new machine, one of those top-loading ones, and while you're at it, get a bloody dishwasher."

"It is possible to live without a dishwasher you know."

"Yes, if you want to be a kitchen maid. How's Archie coping with his birthday countdown? I used to hate all the waiting when I was little, I still do. Have you got the rabbit yet?"

"Gran and Reg have got him at their house, in a small hutch. Martin's making a grander version, only I hope he gets a move on, because the last I saw it, it was just a pile of wood."

I'm still not sure about the rabbit, but Archie was so struck by Mr. Magic at Grace's party he's been begging for weeks now.

"It's very sweet, black and white with lovely ears, only a baby, but I'm sure it won't stay tiny for long. And guess who'll be the idiot feeding it long after everyone else has got bored. We got him from one of Reg's friends at the Bowls Club; he breeds them and takes them to shows and everything. It's a whole new world."

"Rabbit world, who knew?"

"You wait until your boy wants a pet."

"He can want all he likes; I'm not having anything that needs feeding or walking. He can have a virtual pet."

"'Please, Mum, please, I'd be so happy; it's all I ever wanted. Please.' You stand no chance."

"Peas."

"Was that my gorgeous girl?"

"Yes, it's one of her new words. She's not really that keen on *thank you* yet, but I live in hope. Look, I better get her some breakfast, before she rearranges the whole kitchen."

"Bye, darling, speak later, and happy birth days to us, yes?"

"Definitely."

'm enjoying a cup of tea, and a quiet moment with Pearl and our slices of toast and honey, her breakfast of choice at the moment, when the phone rings again.

Bugger. It's Mum.

"I've just been talking to your brother, darling, he's back for a few days after Easter before he's off messing about on one of those silly boats again."

"Vin's a marine biologist, Mum, and so is Lulu; they're not messing about, it's their job."

"Yes, well, they're back, and please call him Vincent, darling; it's such a lovely name. Vin sounds like he drives a van. Anyway, your father and I need a break, or rather I do, your father's fine, wandering about as usual with not a care in the world; the time he takes to do a simple job, anything at all, is completely ridiculous. But I've got so much restoration work on I just can't cope. My herbalist man says he doesn't know how I manage so much pressure."

I'd still quite like to know how mixing up a few sage leaves means he can charge her such exorbitant prices, but I don't think this is quite the right time to mention it.

"Is Dad's back any better?"

"It's absolutely fine; he was just making a fuss. And my elbow is starting to improve, thank you for asking."

Mum always invents a mystery ailment when anyone in the family is ill. Dad's had a bad back for years, and spending hours up a stepladder doing repairs to that stupid palazzo hasn't helped. Why they can't find a normal apartment is beyond me. But Mum loves it because the rent is so low and the Milanese banker who owns it lets them use the whole place when he's not around, so she can show off to all her arty Venetian friends. Most of whom are British or American; the Italians are far less impressed by collapsing palazzos.

"Maybe you should look for somewhere else to live, Mum, where he doesn't have so much work to do?"

"You father's fine, and living in the right surroundings is important to me, you know that. I'm not like you, I can't just live anywhere. I must feel inspired. Still, a little holiday should help."

"I'm sure it will. Where are you going?"

"Honestly, Josephine, are you listening to me at all? I've just told you, Vincent will be back, so we'll come over for a few days, after Easter, the flights will be cheaper then. Your father and I can have your room, and Vincent and Lulu can use your spare room, and you can have the baby in with you and the boys, they'll love sharing. I've planned it all for you, so there's no need to make a fuss. Won't it be super? You and Vincent used to adore it when you were little, one at the top of the bed and one at the bottom, I think we've got a photograph somewhere. So sweet."

Actually we didn't, we hated it, and spent most of the night kicking each other. And why do I have to get turfed out of my bedroom just because she's decided to pay us a visit? Time for a bit of quick thinking on my part or I'll be stuck in a single bed for a week, trying to stop the boys bickering. It's also vital I don't tell her about the forthcoming television appearance or she'll be over like a shot, demanding a starring role.

"I'm not sure, Mum. I think you might be better off staying with Gran. She's got a lovely spare room, and Pearl's not
sleeping that well at nights. She'll wake you up. Or there's a
new bed-and-breakfast opening, on the seafront, it's very stylish, if you'd prefer that?"

"You make far too much fuss of those children. I never let
you or Vincent get up at nights. You can't let children rule
your life; just leave her to cry for a few nights, she'll soon
settle."

"They don't rule my life, Mum, but I don't believe in leaving babies to cry. She's just little, that's all. The boys sleep
really well, and she will too."

"Yes, but—"

"Anyway, you and Dad always used to get us drinks or
read us stories if we woke up, don't you remember?"

Actually, Dad did most of that, but never mind.

"Well, I need my sleep now. Perhaps you're right. Talk to
her, will you? And I don't want a fuss, just a nice relaxing few
days. There's no need for any big meals or anything, this isn't
a royal visit."

She trills out a laugh. In other words, there had better be
a three-course lunch every day, with Mum and Dad as guests
of honor, or she'll be kicking up a major fuss.

"That sounds great, Mum."

"I must go. Your father's making coffee and you know
what a mess he makes. Derek, please put that down, I've told
you before. Bye, darling. I'll call you later to confirm the
details."

Bloody hell. So now I've got Archie's party, an outside
broadcast going on in the shop, and then, just to top it all off,
Mum will be landing on us. I wonder if that herbalist has
got any little bottles to cope with that level of stress. You'd

probably have to be on some sort of herbal drip. Dear God, I better make a list.

"All gone."

Pearl has finished her toast.

"More."

"Okay, love."

She's added quite a few words to her vocabulary in the past few weeks, but *more* is still a favorite. She must be having a talking spurt, just like they have growing spurts. *Up, down, cup, mine,* and *all gone* are new additions, along with *bella,* which is definitely down to Cinzia, and *geddy,* for spaghetti. She also says *juice* and *bear,* and *shoes,* which is useful given her new passion for rearranging all the shoes in the hall cupboard. And she loves it when you get a word wrong, and she can correct you.

"Here you go, sweetheart. I'll put it on your plate, shall I? Lovely plate."

I hand her more triangles of toast and honey in her yellow dish.

She grins. "Dish."

"Oh yes, dish, sorry."

She claps her hands.

It must be very nice being able to correct your mother occasionally. If only I could manage it.

"Mum, tell him he can't come to my party unless I say he can."

"Of course he can come, Archie, he's your brother. Brothers and sisters always come to parties. If they don't, there's no party. And why have you got your sweatshirt on inside out? Come here, love, and let me fix it."

"It was like this on my chair."

"Yes, well, you're both meant to put your uniforms out properly on school nights, so they're ready for the morning. It's on your list."

We've got new sticker charts up on the kitchen notice board in an attempt to release me from running around like some demented lost property monitor, endlessly searching for socks. There are stickers for having all clothes ready, having your book bag by the front door, making your bed, or at least picking your duvet up off the floor, and for brushing your teeth before school without spitting on your brother's arm. So far Jack has twelve star stickers, and Archie has three. But we're working on it.

"Mine is the right way out, Mum." Jack's smirking now.

"Good. You've got the rest of your things right though, Archie, so here, let's put a sticker on your chart. And one for putting your book bag on the hall table as well. Well done, love, just let me fix your sweatshirt."

"And me, Mum, I get a sticker. I've got all my uniform on."

"Okay Jack."

"I've got the most stickers."

"Where's your book bag?"

He gives me a blank look.

"Go and find it, love. You can't have a sticker if it's not on the table. But there are lots more to get."

Archie's doing a celebratory dance around the kitchen. Two stickers, and only one for Jack. It's all too perfect.

"Mum, when I have my ice cream party in the café, when Mr. Magic does the tricks, I'll be the one that gets to hold the rabbit, won't I, because I'll be the birthday boy."

"Yes, but it's not Mr. Magic, remember; he's another magician."

"What's he called?"

"Alan."

"That's not a very good magic name, Mum."

"He's good at magic though, and he has indoor fireworks."

"Oh, yes, I'd forgotten about that. It's going to be great, isn't it?"

"Wonderful. Now sit down and have some breakfast. Shreddies or Weetabix?"

"Toast. Like Pearly, only I want jam, not honey."

"Please."

"Yes, and cut up, in triangles, like Pearly's got."

I give him what I hope is a Firm Look.

"Please."

must find out if the bloody magician has a stage name, because Alan does seem a tad low-key. Tina found him for me; apparently he's a friend of Graham's who works at the fire station in Margate, which will be handy if the indoor fireworks get a bit lively. Graham says he does children's parties all the time, and he's brilliant; my budget couldn't run to Mr. Magic, who's booked up months ahead anyway, so I'm really hoping Alan and his rabbit will be a hit. Mark is making us a special cake, in the shape of a top hat, with a rabbit, and sparklers. Actually, that's something else for my list, paper plates; I want to keep the clearing up to a minimum.

Jack wants toast with just butter, and I distract Pearl with slices of apple while the boys have a light bicker about whether Jack will or will not be allowed to touch Archie's birthday rabbit, if he gets one.

"Stop it, Archie, you're being horrible. And Jack, stop whining. Just ignore him and he'll get bored. We share things in this family, so everyone will be able to stroke the rabbit, if Archie gets one. Which if he carries on being nasty, he won't. Now come on, or we'll be late. Go and brush your teeth."

They both earn stickers for noncombatant teeth brushing, and peace is restored.

"Get your shoes on, Jack, or we'll miss the bus."

"Are you walking with us this morning, Mum?"

"No."

"Good, because I don't like it when you wear that jacket, it's embarrassing."

I think it's going to take Jack a while to get over Archie getting two stickers when he only got one.

"He's right, Mum, it is."

"Thanks, Archie. I could wear much more embarrassing things than that."

Like Mum used to, artistic caftans and clogs to parents' evenings at school, when the other mothers worse sensible skirts and blouses. I rather admire her for that now, although I could admire her so much more if she stayed in bloody Venice.

"Like what?"

"My swimsuit?"

They both look appalled.

"Mum, you can't wear that, people could see you."

"I know, Jack. But I might, if people don't hurry up and get their shoes on."

They put their school shoes on in almost record time, while Pearl lines the rest of our summer shoes in a neat row all the way down the hall.

Excellent.

———

'm in the shop by ten past nine; this walking bus lark is definitely saving me loads of time in the mornings when I'm not
actually on the stupid thing. Last week it rained so torren-
tially, just after we'd set off, we thought we might need to rope
ourselves together so nobody got washed down the hill.
Luckily lots of the kids have got plastic trousers to wear over
their uniforms, although Archie hates his, but even he had to
admit they were good when he saw how wet my jeans were.
Mrs. Lenning has taken over from Connie now; she's far too
pregnant to be schlepping up and down the High Street,
even though she thinks she's fine. But Mark and I insisted, so
Jason's mum is blowing the whistle, and loving it. Jason's in
the same class as Archie, so they're commiserating about their
mothers wearing fluorescent tabards in front of the whole
school.

"Do you want a drink, pet?"
    "Thanks, Gran."
Reg has taken Pearl to feed the ducks in the park, before
they go to their baby music group. I'm thinking this might be
a good moment to break the news about Mum to Gran; Elsie's
upstairs sorting out the orders.

"Hang on a minute, Gran, before you make the tea. I've got
some good news and some not so good. Which do you want
first?"

"The not so good, get it out of the way."

"Okay. Mum's coming over after Easter, and she's staying
with you."

"Is she? That'll be nice, if she manages to behave herself,
that is."

"I'm sure she will."

We both smile.

"We can ignore her, when she gets narky, and it'll be fine. Vin and Lulu will be around too, so that'll help, and she was okay at your wedding, wasn't she? We thought she'd be a nightmare at that."

"Yes, pet, she was. Well, apart from that horrible orange outfit she was wearing. All my photos are lovely, you know, everyone in nice outfits in pretty pastels or smart navy like Betty, except for her. And she made such a fuss about arranging the flowers I thought we'd never hear the end of it."

I tried to keep out of the flowers drama, but I know Gran got very close to throwing one of Mrs. Davis's buckets at her. Mum wanted modern arrangements, a couple of twigs and one giant flower. And Gran wanted freesias.

"I'm sure it'll be fine, Gran."

"Well, it'll be nice to see them both, although how your father has stuck with her all these years I'll never know. I shouldn't say it about my own daughter, but she's always been a right little madam. It'll be lovely to see our Vinnie though. Are you sure that's the bad news, pet?"

"Yes. I was joking, Gran."

She smiles.

"You weren't planning to go on your cruise around then, were you?"

"No, we're still looking. We're thinking about June, for our wedding anniversary. Do you think that's silly, at our age?"

"No, not at all."

Elsie's coming back downstairs; she's got a sixth sense for gathering interesting news. She puts the order book down on the counter.

"Another cruise, Mary? It's all right for some, isn't it?"

"Nothing's decided yet, we're just looking."

After years of battling with her in the shop, Gran's still reluctant to confide too much potential gossip to Elsie, not least because she likes to save her top nuggets for Betty.

"There is something else I wanted to tell you, both of you actually."

They look at me.

"Ellen's got a new television series, in the mornings. She's starting the week after next, on Monday."

"Isn't that lovely? Well tell her congratulations from me, pet. She works so hard, you'd think she'd slow down now she's got the baby. Tell her I'll make sure I watch it, or Reg can record it for us, can he? We've only done that with programs in the evening so far. Is it the same during the day?"

"Yes, Gran, he'll be able to record it. But that's not all of the news, because she's going to come down here to film, in the shop, next Wednesday. An interview, with Ellen and Grace, and me, hopefully only a bit of me. I don't really want to be in it at all, but Ellen's insisting, and you know how bossy she is."

"Oh my Lord."

"In our shop, Mary, did you ever?"

Gran seems stunned. "Our shop, on the television, I never dreamed in a million years. Well, I just hope old Mrs. Butterworth is watching; not watching the telly, of course, I mean looking down. Although if she's in heaven, then someone up there needs their head's examining, that's all I'm saying. She'll drop down stone dead all over again when she sees how well you've done. She always said I ruin everything, and now look."

Reg comes back from the ducks, fussing about them being late for music.

"Yes, but Reg, you'll never guess what our Jo's done now. Go on, guess. We're going to be on the television, that's all."

"Gran, calm down, it's days away yet."

"Yes, but I'll need to get my hair done, and I've got nothing to wear. I can't wear my wedding suit for something like that. Oh, Elsie, isn't it lovely?"

They hug, which I'm not sure they've ever actually done before. They both seem rather shocked, and pause, mid-hug, and then smile at each other, and Elsie pats Gran's hand.

Reg looks like he's trying quite hard not to laugh as Elsie beams at me.

"I always said your Jo would work miracles, Mary, and she has. I feel quite faint, you know. I think I better sit down."

By the time I've calmed everybody down and got Gran off to music, Elsie's eaten half a packet of chocolate digestives and is still sitting behind the counter in a daze. I've promised they can all be in the café, for background interest. I'm not sure they'll actually appear on telly, but I'll ask Ellen to make sure they film them for a minute or two, because it's the only way I can think of to keep them out of the way. I've sworn them all to secrecy: I've said if the news gets out, the filming will probably be canceled, so they've invented a code word, which was Reg's idea, Operation Double Knitting.

Christ, this is going to be a long day.

I'm adding the knitted egg cozies into the window, with some of the flower brooches Elsie's finished, bunches of primroses mostly, and a few of the mohair flowers in fresh spring colors, to move the Mother's Day theme on toward Easter. I'll put the rabbits and chicks in after the party; I don't want anyone small being tempted to help themselves to a knitted rabbit. Laura's knitting some more egg cozies; they sold well last year, so we need as many as we can get. I'll knit a few more flower brooches too, if I can find the time. Sitting knitting in the evenings, with the feel of the wool between my fingers and the regular rhythm of the stitches, is very calming, and I can use as much of that as I can get at the moment, even if I am only knitting a daffodil.

"It's Maxine on the phone for you."

Elsie's almost quivering with excitement as she hands the phone to me, and I can tell Maxine is smiling.

"Have you told them yet?"

"Yes, why?"

Oh, God, what has Elsie been saying?

"Nothing, she just said she expected she'd be seeing me soon, so I thought you'd probably told her. We're not going to announce it yet, but it's not a problem if it gets out. Just put any press calls through to me as usual, yes?"

"Of course, but I've told everyone that filming is likely to be pulled if it gets out. So I'm sure we can be discreet about it."

She laughs. "You're trying to keep the excitement levels down, is that the idea?"

"I think that ship may have already sailed, but we need to avoid half the town knowing, or they'll all be lining up desperate to get on the telly."

Elsie is listening and nodding, looking furtive, like she's on a secret mission in enemy territory and is keeping a lookout for snipers.

Maxine laughs. "Well, good luck with that one. In my experience, everyone likes to tell someone, and before you know it you've got snappers everywhere. The local paper is bound to get wind of it, but we're happy with nice local stuff."

Luckily, Mrs. Marwell tries to wheel her trolley in at this point, and Elsie has to go and help her, so she can't keep listening in. I'm not sure Mrs. Marwell has ever found herself helped into the shop quite so quickly though.

"So if that boy from the local paper who did the library knit-in turns up, I don't have to wrestle his camera off him?"

"No, you're fine. And anyway, we've got Bruno if we need any wrestling."

"When are you back? You're still in London, I take it?"

"Yes, but Grace wondered if you're around at the weekend. Actually, here she is now. Yes, I'm on the line to her now, I was just—"

"Sunday would be great, if you're around, darling?"

"Sorry Grace, it's Archie's party that day. You're welcome to join us, of course. I think Maxine already has it in the diary."

Please God, let her say they can't make it. We're already going to be packed in quite tightly, without adding Grace and Lily and Maxine and Bruno into the mix.

"Oh yes, of course. I don't think we can do that, I'm meeting the studio people, and Monday is out, we've got a lunch, so I guess I'll see you for the interview. Anything special you'd like me to say, apart from how much I love the shop, spend hours there, that kind of thing?"

"That would be lovely."

"Sort me out some knitting, would you, darling? I've just finished that cardigan for Lily, and I won't have a chance to start anything else; this premiere is getting ridiculous. One of your shawls would be perfect."

"The mohair ones are rather fiddly. Shall I go for the cashmere?"

"Perfect. Max, what am I wearing for this interview? No, I don't want that, that's totally wrong; honestly, you're hopeless. One of the new dresses, the green one. Okay, so that pale gray color you were showing me would work with that, Jo."

"The pebble or the slate?"

"Pebble. Thanks Jo. Ed's really pleased we're doing this; it fits in perfectly with the media strategy. We were going to have to do another bloody At Home piece, and now we don't. "

"And you're feeling okay? Sorry. I don't know why I said that, but are you? Oh God, sorry. Just ignore me."

Bugger. I've catapulted myself into babbling now, just like Gran and Elsie.

She laughs. "Wonderful, darling, thank you, see you next week."

Phew. I'm glad she didn't mind, you can never tell with Grace. Sometimes the shutters come down so quickly you practically have to watch out for your fingers. But I keep thinking about her and the baby, I can't help it. It will be so lovely for Lily; at least I hope it will, it can be a pretty major blow for the firstborn. I think Jack is still trying to get over the arrival of Archie. Actually, we all are, not that we don't adore him, of course. But I'm so pleased for her, even though I can't help wondering who the father is, which is awful because I hated that, all the gossip when I had Pearl, and it's got to be so much worse when all the national newspapers cover your every move.

Everyone seems to have a view on how other people live their lives, especially in a small seaside town where not much else is happening. But everywhere really, not just in Broadgate, people seem to love dissecting other people's lives. Like most of us aren't just doing the best we can. I didn't plan to have Pearl, but then I didn't particularly plan to have Jack either. Married, single, gay, straight, or haven't made your mind up yet. With a partner, solo, or going the turkey baster route, I can't see that it matters as long as you really want the baby and you do your very best for them when they arrive. When you see some of the terrible things that happen, you realize that's the only thing that matters. That you love them. And anyway, it's Grace's business, not mine, and I need to stop thinking about it, or I'll probably end up blurting at the worst possible moment, probably in the middle of filming, like those anxiety dreams where you're halfway round the supermarket when you realize you haven't got your trousers on.

Right. I need to put those orders in from Saturday, and have another look at the workroom; the light's much better upstairs, so I'm guessing they'll want to film up here. Elsie's already writing a list of jobs she thinks we need to do, under the heading of Operation Double Knitting on the top of her notepad.

"I'm just going to put little notes to myself, and that way if someone finds it, they won't know. Should I use code, do you think, like shorthand?"

"Do you know how to write in shorthand, Elsie?"

"No."

"Probably not then."

I'm not sure those biscuits were such a good idea now.

"Can I tell my Jeffrey, and Martin?"

"Sure."

"We'll need to clean those windows. I know they were only done a few weeks ago, but I've said it before and I'll say it

again, he doesn't do a proper job. Dirty old bucket of water
and that windscreen wiper thing; you need to do a proper
polish to get windows clean."

"They look fine to me, Elsie."

"I'll bring my cloths in from home and give them a good
going-over."

"Okay, if you want to. Crikey, look at the time. The mums
group will be here any minute."

'm hoping our new mums group will be a nice diversion
from Operation Double Knitting. I love the way we get different people using the café at different times; in the mornings, people on their way to work, like Maggie, or pensioners,
out getting their shopping early. At lunchtimes there's a nice
mixture of mums meeting up for a coffee or people on their
lunch breaks, and later in the afternoons we get the teenagers,
on their way home from school, who come in to deconstruct
their day; Betty says it reminds her of when Gran and her were
young and they used to spend hours in the old coffee bar on
the pier. But Mondays are my favorites, with all the new mums
who met at childbirth classes. They come here once a week
now, and sit in the workroom upstairs; there's more space for
the buggies and baby kit. It's a hassle helping them up the
stairs, but once they're settled it's fine, and quite a few of them
have started knitting, so Elsie and I help out with that. Since
I'm older than most of them, and have three kids, they seem
to have rather sweetly adopted me as their amateur baby
whisperer. Talk about the blind leading the blind.

Elsie's even got over her initial horror at the prospect of
them breast-feeding; they're all very discreet, but there's no
way I'm making anyone go and sit in the loos to feed their

babies, not in my shop. I've spent too long perched in cubicles myself to want to inflict that on anyone else.

"Hi Jo. Look, I finished it."

Clare holds up the blanket she's been making for Ava, who's fast asleep in her buggy, wearing a very fetching pink and purple hat Clare knitted for her a few weeks ago.

"That's great, Clare."

"She loves it, it's so soft, and it makes me feel like a proper mum, knitting things for her. What can I make next?"

I'm showing her some cardigan patterns while Helena gives everyone another one of her pep talks about the importance of reusable nappies.

"Dylan loves his nappies, and they're really not that much trouble to wash."

"They are if you've got mummy's little helper adding crockery to your washing machine."

Clare laughs. "Is she still doing that?"

"Yes, and I did try the reusable ones, Helena, but it was just one thing too many, having nappies soaking in a bucket. I know they're a good idea, and I do recycle, as much as I can."

Helena doesn't look that impressed and starts telling us all about landfill sites and the water table. God, she can be tedious sometimes. She's always banging on about something; last week it was the wonders of baby flash cards, to stimulate our budding Einsteins. She reminds me of all those mums in London, who used to make me feel like Jack was practically on the at-risk register because he wasn't learning Japanese or special baby boffin maths. No wonder Dylan always looks so tense, although his eczema can't help with that, poor little thing. I pass Clare the shade cards for the cardigan so she can choose the colors.

"I'm sure you're right, Helena, but to be honest, I think we should sort out the big oil companies, and air travel, things that make a huge difference, before we start guilt-tripping mothers about nappies. Although obviously it's much easier to guilt-trip mums. I know we should all be doing our bit, but until they stop making cars that go two hundred miles an hour when it's illegal to go over seventy anywhere in the whole country, I think it's okay for me to use disposable nappies."

Lucy laughs as her son, Oliver, starts yelling and she lifts him out of his buggy. "I still can't get him to go anywhere near four hours between feeds, you know. Three is my record so far. Do you think I'm missing something, Jo?"

"God, no. I don't think breast-fed babies go that long between feeds, unless mine were just greedy. I don't care what the books say, they don't. It might be nature's perfect design, but it was designed for mums who never put their babies down in case a woolly mammoth trod on them. Feeding them all the time wasn't really a problem for them; you could still do the hunter-gatherer thing, and just shift the sling round."

She smiles. "Oliver hates his sling. I got the one with the sheepskin and everything, but he hates it."

"So did Archie, and Pearl. In fact, Pearl squawked so loudly, Jack made me promise I'd never try to put her in it again."

"I can't imagine how you cope with three."

"I don't. I just hang on in there and hope that one day soon they'll all be big enough to make me breakfast in bed."

They all smile, even Helena.

I think it's important to try to be reassuring; I used to look at women with older babies when I had Jack, and wonder how they did it. They all seemed so capable, so much better at it than me. But actually there is something quite liberating about third babies; you still have the usual fog of exhaustion, and bliss, but at least you're more prepared for it. I didn't read any of the books with Pearl, I just didn't have the time, so I went with the flow, literally, since she fed pretty much non-stop for the first few weeks. And it did feel a lot less terrifying, less like you've wandered into completely new territory and nobody's given you a map.

"Oh, look, they're playing."

We all watch Ruby and Oliver, who are sitting on their mums' laps, smiling at each other. Ruby's always been a smiley girl. It's been lovely seeing them develop from tiny newborns, with unfathomable stares, to little smiling people starting to sit up. You're so up close and personal with your own you don't see it. Lucy kisses Oliver on the top of his head.

"How's she doing at nights now, Nicky?"

Clare is still feeding Ava, who seems to have fallen asleep, but every time she tries to put her down she fusses.

"Better, well, a bit better. But as soon as I finish cooking our supper and sit down, she kicks off. I think it might be the cooking smells. We had salad the other night, just to see, and she was a bit better. We'll have to barbecue all our stuff in the back garden if she carries on like this."

We all smile.

"Try giving her one of those baby rusks, that should keep her quiet while you eat."

"I might try that, Jo, because it's really getting on my wick."

There's been a lot of talk about when to start on the baby rice. None of them are quite six months old yet, and the new rules say you have to wait six months before you start introducing solid food.

"When did you start Pearl on solids again, Jo?"

"Around four months, like I did with Jack and Archie. Mind you, that was Pearl's idea really; she was helping herself to Jack's mashed potato, so I missed out the tiny spoonfuls of baby rice thing. I don't know what I'd have done if I'd had to wait for six months. I think it depends on the baby. I mean obviously you have to be careful, but I reckon a bit of baby rice works wonders. It was the first time Archie ever slept for more than two hours."

We're all watching Ruby as she twists round and tries to grab a piece of a cake. Nicky kisses her on the cheek. "You might be right. She watches you sometimes like she's starving. Phil won't eat in front of her now; he says it puts him off."

"There you go then. Give her a plastic spoon and she'll be away, eating your supper before you know it."

She laughs.

"I'm going downstairs for another coffee, anyone want anything?"

"Do you have any peppermint tea, Jo?"

"I think so, Helena. I'll come down with you, Nicky. I know we've got lemon, or green tea, or rose hip if you prefer?"

"Lemon would be lovely."

I knew those glass teapots would come in handy.

We're halfway home after school when I realize Archie is walking rather oddly, and on closer inspection, it turns out he's wearing two left shoes, and someone else has gone home in two right ones.

Jack is delighted. "He doesn't get a sticker for that, does he, Mum?"

"Be quiet, Jack. Archie, you must know who you were sitting next to after PE."

"Well I don't."

I still can't work out how he managed to put on someone else's shoe; it's the same color, but it's entirely different. Archie's got two Velcro straps on his, and this one only has one.

Bugger. I'll have to ring round; I wonder if Jane has everyone's phone numbers at home. I've only got some of them.

"Honestly, Archie, you need to be more careful. Come on, let's get home and I'll try to find out who's got your other shoe."

He's walking like a duck. Things must be so simple on Planet Boy. Two left shoes, just waddle home and your mum will sort it.

Jack's walking like a duck now too.

"Stop it, Jack."

"No, he likes it, don't you, Arch? Don't be so grumpy, Mum, he didn't do it on purpose. Grump, grump, grump."

"Gump."

Great, another new word for Pearl.

Jake Palmer's mum rings as soon as we get in, and luckily Jake isn't quite as dopey as Archie and remembered who he sat next to while they were getting dressed. Still dopey enough to go home in the wrong shoes though.

"Shall we do a swap tomorrow morning then, Jo?"

"Good idea."

"You wouldn't credit it though, would you? How could they not have noticed? I wouldn't mind but Jake's are a size smaller than your Archie's. Boys are hopeless, aren't they?"

"Tell me about it. I've got two of them."

"I'm not sure I could do that. At least with my Charlotte she always comes home with the right shoes on, although the fuss she makes about her clothes drives me mad. I suppose it's all swings and roundabouts being a mum, isn't it?"

"Yes, where you end up dizzy and all the money falls out of your pockets."

She laughs. "That sounds about right."

"What's for tea, Mum?"

"Omelets and salad?"

"Yuck." Archie's making being sick noises.

"Or scrambled eggs on toast, if people eat a small bowl of salad first."

"Scrambled eggs with cheese?"

"Yes, or not for people who don't like cheese."

"Jack, she says we don't have to have omelets."

There's a cheer from the living room, and Pearl claps her hands, and then trots off down the hall, only to return with one of my flip-flops, which she puts into the washing machine. How helpful.

It's half past nine on the night before Archie's party, and I'm trying to finish the party bags. There's no need to spend a fortune like the mums did in London; we keep things fairly simply round here, thank God. So I've got some little packets of sweets and a magic wand each, and a magic writing pen with invisible ink, along with a bath bomb, which fizzes in the water, and a tiny flannel, which unfurls into a normal-size one. I'm hoping these will be popular with the parents. Perhaps I should write a little note and pop it in each bag: "I'm sorry your child is covered in ice cream, but there's a flannel in the party bag." Martin should be here any minute, he's putting the finishing touches to the hutch, and then Gran and Reg will be round at the crack of dawn in the morning with the rabbit. Martin's bringing fish and chips, and I'm starving. I should have eaten with the kids, but I'm trying to avoid having two suppers, however tempting, or I'll have to buy new jeans again.

The phone rings just as I'm thinking about making an emergency sandwich.

"Hi Jo. Look, I'm sorry about this, but I think I'm going to have to bring the hutch round first thing in the morning. I'm not quite finished. Is that okay?"

"Of course. Are you on your way now?"

"Well, no, there's a bit of a problem with that. I've got a bit behind with the laundry, so I've got nothing to wear."

"Sorry?"

"I was round at the boatyard, and well, to cut a long story short, I fell in, and before you ask, Trevor was at home. I just tripped, that's all."

"You tripped?"

"Yes. And stop laughing."

"I'm trying not to, I really am. Shame you weren't wearing your new anorak."

"Shut up."

Elsie's bought him an oceangoing anorak; it's bright orange and looks like it would turn into a life raft given half a chance.

"I'm just saying, you could have tried it out, seen if it really was waterproof."

"Yes, thank you. Don't tell her, will you; I'll never hear the end of it."

"Okay, I promise. What are you wearing now then?"

"Is this going to be one of those rude phone calls? I've never done one of those."

"Neither have I."

"Shall we give it a go?"

We both laugh.

"Seriously, what are you wearing?"

"Shorts, it's the only thing I could find, and that sweater Mum knitted me."

"The one with the stripes in all those different colors?"

"Yes. I bet you're glad I didn't turn up now. The problem was there was so much mud, my jeans were covered in it, and by the time I'd sorted them out I'd soaked my spare pair too. I must get a dryer."

"Martin, you haven't even got the washing machine plumbed in yet."

"I've got a sink though. And stuff dries pretty quickly in front of the fire."

"I'll get you a mangle and then you can do the whole Victorian laundry maid thing. I'll get you some carbolic soap too if you like."

"Thanks, I knew I could count on you to make me feel better."

"You can always bring your washing round here, if you don't mind the occasional item of crockery in with your delicates. Although she seems to be moving on to shoes now."

"I don't have delicates, at least not the way I do the washing, and anyway, I'm not entirely useless, you know. I've got a system, it's just I got a bit behind this week."

"You mean Elsie didn't pick up your dirty washing and return it neatly folded."

"Basically, yes. I'm sorry about supper though, I was looking forward to it."

Not as much as I was.

"Never mind, we'll see you tomorrow."

"Yes."

"And, Martin . . ."

"Yes?"

"Get your washing tub ready. It's a kids' party, with ice cream, so whatever you wear will probably need a rinse when you get home."

"You can get enough of sarcastic women, you know."

"Can you?"

"Not tonight apparently. But I'll let you know."

"Night, Martin."

t's half past four on Sunday afternoon, and the party's in full swing. Archie insisted on only inviting boys, apart from Nelly and Pearl, and they're all having a marvelous time constructing ice cream sundaes, with Tom and Cinzia handing out the chocolate flakes, mini-sprinkles, and assorted sweets, including jelly babies and chocolate buttons. I've avoided nuts, not that any of them are allergic, as far as I know, but this would be the perfect moment to find out. We've got chocolate sauce, and strawberry and toffee, and I've also bought a couple of cans of that horrible squirty aerosol cream, which the boys love. Tom is giving Cinzia very longing looks in between passing out the flakes, and trying to grab the cream back off Archie. He's been on two proper dates with her now, according to Connie, so I'm still expecting a visit from a large group of irate Italians.

Gran's made mini-sandwiches, and I've done sausages on sticks, so we've made a token effort to balance out all the sugar, and we've had two rounds of pass the parcel and a rather brutal session of musical chairs, just to get everyone in the party mood. Alan the magician is sorting out his equipment upstairs in the workroom; he understandably chose to avoid performing his magic show in full view of the High Street through the café windows, so Reg is upstairs lighting the fire. Apparently Alan's got a special powder to throw on it at a crucial moment, which makes a loud bang and produces lots of green smoke, so I'm hoping Elsie isn't upstairs for that bit, or Gran either, come to think of it.

"Shall we do the cake now?"

"Yes, Con, that would be great."

"He will love it, I think. It has the rabbit, in icing. Wait until you see."

"Thank Mark again, will you? It's such a shame he couldn't get away."

"Yes, but this evening we are closed, in the restaurant, so he will be fine. I want to talk to him about the room for the baby, but he doesn't know yet. If he did, I think he would be going out."

"I'll help if you like. I'm quite good at wallpapering now after I did our hall. Well, if you don't look too closely."

'm trying to wipe ice cream off Pearl's face, ready for Reg to take the photos, when Gran dims the lights and Cinzia carries in the cake, with the eight candles. Archie's thrilled, and sits looking very pleased as we sing "Happy Birthday" and he blows the candles out.

"I get the first bit, Mum, and then Jack, because he's my brother."

"Okay love."

"And then Pearly, and then you."

"Bless him; he says the nicest things sometimes, doesn't he?"

"Yes, Gran."

"And, Mum."

"Yes Archie."

"Only give Jason Lenning a small bit, because he shoved me right off that chair, and I was nearly winning. And can we take some home for my new rabbit?"

"I'm not sure rabbits like cake, love."

"I bet he does. He's going to be a magic rabbit, I've told you, Mum, and I bet they like cake."

"I still think they prefer carrots, however magic they are."

The magic show is a huge success, and despite his lack of a catchy stage name, Alan does us proud. Long silk scarves appear and disappear, and giant chocolate coins pop out from behind the birthday boy's ear before the card tricks receive a rapturous reception. The indoor fireworks produce a thrilling series of bangs and showers of colored sparks, and the special powder in the fire makes such a huge bang that Archie jumps about three foot off the floor, as does Elsie. She's been hovering with a damp flannel in case anyone with sticky fingers touched any of the stock, but even she's been pretty transfixed.

Cinzia is kissing Pearl, with Tom watching her devotedly.

Connie mutters something in Italian.

"What?"

"He needs not to be so, how do you say?"

"Lovesick?"

"Yes, exactly."

"Poor boy."

"Yes, and poor Aunt Lucia when she finds out her daughter only wants the older men. She was telling me, she thinks they are better."

"It doesn't bear thinking about it, does it, when Nelly and Pearl are that age?"

"No, I hope this one will be a boy. One daughter will be enough, I think, for my nerves." She pats her tummy.

"But as long as everything is okay, I don't mind. But I wish it was tomorrow. It is so much longer this time."

"It better not be tomorrow, we haven't done the wall-papering yet."

"Great party, Jo."

"Thanks, Tom."

He sighs. "I think I might need to shake things up a bit with Cinzia. I might have overplayed my hand a bit."

"Oh, right."

"Time for Plan B."

"Which is?"

"Go cool. Don't return her texts, drives them mad."

I think Cinzia might give him a run for his money on that one, but let's see. I'm not going to tell him she's already announced she only likes older men.

She's putting Pearl down now, and walking over to us.

"Right, I'm off then. Start as I mean to go on sort of thing."

"Thanks Tom. Beyond the call of duty to come and help, but I'm really glad you did."

"No, I enjoyed it. Bye, Cinzia. I'm a bit busy next week, but I'll call you, okay?"

He winks at me and Connie as he leaves. Cinzia looks puzzled. Maybe he's not quite as daft as I thought.

"Thank you too, Cinzia, for helping with the party."

"I have loved it. An English birthday party."

"We don't always have quite so much ice cream."

"Look at the Principessa, she is dancing."

Pearl is bobbing round in a circle, wearing her tiara.

"She looks like Philippe, he is terrible at dancing. But he has the eyes. So the dancing is not so much."

"Who's Philippe?"

"He is French, at my course."

Connie smiles. "But Tom, he is nicest, yes?"

Cinzia shrugs. "He is okay, but now he is too young. Philippe is older, and French."

Poor Tom.

"Thanks Mum, it was my best party ever. And I think I've decided on my name for my rabbit. I want to call him Peter. The magic man said you don't want anything fancy for rabbits, you have to keep it simple."

"Did he?"

"Yes. And his rabbit is called Peter, and he can do magic, with the hat and stuff."

Thank God we haven't got a top hat, or the poor thing would probably find itself spending quite a bit of time stuck inside it.

"All right."

Peter Rabbit it is then. I'm going to feel like I'm channeling Beatrix Potter every time I feed it. Knowing my luck,

Jack will start lobbying for a hedgehog, and we'll be Mrs. Tiggy-Winkling before we know it. And I'll be the horrible Mr. McGregor chasing everyone round the garden. I'll probably end up with busloads of Japanese tourists coming round to photograph our pets.

"I'm going to be a magic man when I grow up, Mum."

"Are you, Archie, that's nice."

It'll probably come in handy if he knows a few diverting tricks when Jack tells people he called his rabbit Peter.

"Come on then, let's get home and you can open the rest of your presents."

"Yes, and Mum, I need a top hat, to practice my tricks."

"I think you have to start with simpler tricks than that, Archie."

He tuts.

By the time it's finally Wednesday morning, I've gone off the whole idea of the television thing, and I'm seriously thinking about going home and hiding. Gran and Reg and Elsie have been in the shop since dawn cleaning and fussing, and Cinzia's raced back from the school run and is lurking before she takes Pearl to baby gym, hoping for her three minutes of fame. It's only a quarter to ten and I'm already exhausted. Even Pearl has picked up on the tension and is throwing a mini-strop because she wants to go upstairs. But Elsie's just finished hoovering up there, so I don't want Pearl rearranging things.

"Cinzia, maybe you should take her to her class now?"

She pretends she hasn't heard me.

Actually, I've just had a brilliant idea. I'll go to baby gym with Pearl and leave them all to it.

"They'll still be here later, Cinzia, I promise."

Just when I think things can't get any tenser, a huge white outside broadcast van pulls up outside, blocking the High Street, even though they're meant to be parking in the lane behind the shop. I'm giving them directions when Ellen arrives in a swish silver car with a driver, and her producer, Scott, who is looking as nervous as I feel.

"Hello darling. Why is the truck here, Scott?"

"I'm not sure, I'll just—"

"It's fine, Ellen, they're just about to move."

"Well make sure they don't park in the wrong fucking street, would you, Scott? I'll be with Jo. I need a coffee. Come on, darling, let's get inside."

"Gran and Reg are here, and Elsie, and they're a bit excited. Just so you know."

"They'll be fine. We'll film them for background shots and then they can relax. Sweet windows, I love the little flowers."

"They're primroses, Elsie made them."

"So they are. You look brilliant, by the way; the skirt suits you. Are those the boots we bought last year?"

"Yes."

"Well, they look great. Once we get some makeup on you, you'll look fabulous."

"I'm wearing makeup."

"Yes, for normal life, darling. Not a six-foot HD telly."

"Thanks a lot, that really helps."

"Don't worry, I've brought Elaine, she'll sort you out. She does all my makeup, and she's a genius."

"She's going to have to be."

"Your hair looks nice. Top marks, darling."

Tina did it for me yesterday, so it's a bit sleeker than usual, and I hope my dark green velvet skirt and the cardigan I knitted in the pretty catkin color look okay with my best cream silk shirt. I looked all right at seven o'clock this morning, but I still feel wildly underdressed compared to Ellen. And Grace hasn't arrived yet, which will ramp up the fashion gorgeousness to a whole new level.

"Morning, my dear. Left the dogs at home, thought they might get in the way, shall I go through? Sit at any table, is that the drill?"

Great. Lady Denby has arrived. Just what we need. She must have a network of spies; she always seems to know about anything remotely exciting happening in the town.

Ellen gives her one of her Britain's Favorite Broadcaster smiles. "Good morning, I'm Ellen Malone."

"Are you? Marvelous. So exciting, putting Broadgate on the map, do carry on." She gives Ellen a dismissive wave and goes inside.

"Is she the mad old bat who showed up at the knit-in when they were threatening to close the library?"

"Yes."

"Great. Well, if your Diva doesn't turn up I can always interview her. I bet she's got a few stories to tell. Barking old aristocrats always do."

"True, but it would probably be something about the Prince of Wales in 1913. Or a special moment during the Blitz."

"We'll meet again? I love all that. Great, that's my backup story sorted."

"Maybe I should ask her to bring the dogs along after all, and Lord Denby. He calls everyone Moira, and the dogs like licking people's shoes. That way you can get the full experience. "

"Well, they better not bloody try it with these. They're Stella McCartneys."

"Well give them back to her and you can borrow a pair of mine."

"Highly amusing. Will you be cracking duff jokes on air, darling, only I'm not sure—"

"Stop it. I'm nervous enough already."

"I know you are, but I'm here now, it'll be fine and anyway, get a grip, darling, you worked in news, you know how to handle yourself on camera. We did all those bloody training sessions, it'll all come flooding back."

"The ones where you and Nick were brilliant and I fell right off that swivel chair?"

She kisses my cheek. "You only did that once, and you did it very beautifully. Come on, get me a coffee. We need caffeine."

I think I might be needing more than caffeine, but I'll give it a go.

Scott is busy setting up in the workroom upstairs, rearranging the furniture and moving the wicker baskets, which I've filled with a selection of wool in the nicest colors. Elsie's standing by with her duster in case anything needs another polish, and Al, the cameraman, has filmed Cinzia until Scott made him stop, so now he's wandering around outside taking shots through the café windows, with everyone looking very bright-eyed over their teas and coffees. Lady Denby has even put on extra lipstick. Gran and Betty are having a lovely time with Reg, who's wearing his best suit, giving me the occasional wink. And Tom's behind the counter, with his white apron wrapped tightly round what look like new jeans, and a clean gray T-shirt, which also looks a bit tighter than the ones he usually wears. He's making coffees like his life depended on it. Laura is sitting at one of the tables with Tina, knitting and chatting like they've got all the time in the world. I just hope to God they use a second or two of the footage of Elsie behind the counter, or I'll never hear the end of it.

"You didn't tell me he was so gorgeous, darling."

"Who?"

"Your Tom, very nice."

"He's not my Tom. And anyway, he's pining; he's got a crush on Cinzia."

"Bless. Well, you could soon take his mind off that. They say every man needs an older woman in his life at that age, show them the ropes, that kind of thing."

"Only if someone shows me first."

"I can get you a book, darling."

"Do shut up, Ellen."

"Suit yourself, but I'm just saying, gorgeous, right under your nose, can make a decent cup of coffee. The words *gift horse* and *mouth* come to mind."

"Only to your mind. He's just a few years older than Jack."

"Oh stop it, he's got to be twenty if he's a day."

"He's nineteen. Jack is ten this year. See what I mean?"

"Haven't you heard of MILF, darling? Very popular amongst teenage boys."

"No, and I don't want to know what it stands for. They don't go in for things like that round here."

"I bet they bloody do. Mothers I Would Like to—"

"Go Fishing with?"

"I give up."

"Good."

Oh, God, I'm never going to pull this off. Ellen can snap into broadcast mode effortlessly, but I haven't been near a studio in years. I'll sit there dumbstruck, and look like a nutter. Oh God.

We're sitting upstairs now, and I've practically inhaled two chocolate croissants, which strangely seems to have helped. Grace has arrived, and looks breathtakingly beautiful, in full Screen mode, although Maxine is a very calming presence. She's been very fierce about reminding Ellen what the agreed parameters are: knitting, the new film, no personal life questions, nothing about Lily, no follow-up questions to anything Grace might say. But just seeing her standing there is strangely comforting. Ellen's looking at her notes, and then suddenly we're sitting down, with Ellen and Grace on the old leather sofa I found in a junk shop in Margate, and I'm sitting in the armchair. The sun is in my eyes, but I daren't move after Scott spent so long setting everything up. The chair is quite slippy actually, so I'm sliding forward while Ellen and Grace seem to manage to stay beautifully upright. I'll probably slide onto the floor at some point. Bloody hell.

"Remember to breathe, darling. Okay, here we go."

Ellen winks at me, and Grace gives me one of her Diva smiles. Oh God.

"So here we are in beautiful Broadgate, with Grace Harrison. You live nearby, don't you, Grace?"

"Yes, Ellen, we love it here. The light is so beautiful."

And they're off, chatting away like old friends, with Grace saying that the British coastline is such a treasure she feels very lucky to be so near to it.

"We used to get the bus and go for days at the seaside, me and my mum, so it brings back lots of happy memories. She used to knit, and sew, she made most of my clothes, so when I saw this fabulous shop, I just couldn't resist. It makes me feel closer to her somehow, making things for Lily. Mum did try to teach me, but I didn't have the patience back then. But now I'm a mum myself I love it, and Jo is such a great teacher; it makes all the difference having someone to call on when you get in a muddle, although that happens less now. But knowing she's nearby means I can tackle more complicated patterns. I love sitting by the fire in the evenings with my knitting. I know it's not very Hollywood, but then I'm not really a Hollywood kind of girl. And there's something so timeless about it. It puts things into perspective. There's a danger when you work in the film business that you can start to take yourself a little bit too seriously. Connecting to something so elemental is very important to me."

Bloody hell she's good. It's like she's got a script in her head, which Maxine and Ed have worked on for her, so it covers all the messages she wants to get across, and she just delivers it, perfectly. Actually, that's exactly what she's got, but, God, she's good.

They move on to talking about the film, with amusing snippets about costars and filming car chases and what it was like being suspended by wires to film the diamond robbery scene. I'm meant to be sitting knitting, presumably with a relaxed smile on my face, but I seem to have forgotten how to knit. I manage a series of random stitches, on the cotton square for Connie's blanket, before I drop a stitch entirely and have to try to surreptitiously pick it up. So that's obviously terribly impressive for someone who's meant to be a knitting guru. God, I hope nobody writes in to complain.

"So, Jo, how does it feel to have such a famous customer? Actually darling, why are you slumped like that? Sit up, can't

you? Cut. Scott, sort her out with a cushion. For God's sake
don't just stand there. Help her out. She's my best friend, I've
told you, I want her to look fabulous, not like she's deformed,
for fuck's sake."

Grace looks like she might be about to laugh.

"Jo."

"Yes, Grace."

"Talk to me. Just forget everybody else and talk to me and
Ellen. Actually, do you all need to be here? It is rather oppres-
sive. Bruno, go downstairs, you're putting Jo off."

Actually it's the camera and the soundman and the sight
of Scott looking anxious which is putting me off, not poor
Bruno, but never mind.

"Jo."

"Yes Grace."

"What am I meant to be doing now with this, casting on
or casting off?"

"Just increase a stitch at each end of each row."

"In the knit stitch, in the border, yes?"

"Yes."

"That's a shame. I've been doing it on the purl stitch."

"It's fine, it won't matter, as long as you do it in the same
place, so it forms a pattern. It's quite loose, that's why the needles are so big."

"Are you sure? I love this color, I want to get it right."

"I'm sure."

Grace gives me one of her biggest smiles and then looks
down at her knitting as Ellen leans forward slightly.

"So, Jo, how does it feel to have such a famous customer?"

"It's lovely."

"And why do you think knitting is making such a come-
back?"

"Well, once you've got the hang of the basics, it can be very relaxing."

"And you sell kits, with everything you need to make a simple project, is that right? So if people don't live nearby, they can still have a go? Blankets for babies, and your lovely shawls. Like the one Grace is knitting?"

"Yes. We write our own patterns, and try to keep them as simple as we can. And people can phone us, if they get stuck."

Grace smiles, a major Diva smile that makes everyone look at her.

"Jo is absolutely right, it is relaxing, and you're also reconnecting to a traditional craft which women have perfected over the centuries. So you feel part of a long line of women, knitting to keep their families warm, and that's very special."

Bloody hell, that's a good answer. Even Ellen looks impressed.

"There's something so special about making things for the people you love. Jo has helped me make so many things for Lily. I knitted blankets for her when she was tiny, and toys. The little duck I knitted for her is one of her favorites, and I'm terribly proud of that. And when I'm working, well, as you know, Ellen, there's a fair amount of hanging around when you're filming, so it's great to have something productive to do."

"And is being part of the local community important to you, Grace?"

"Very. There's such a wonderful atmosphere, I love living somewhere so normal."

"So no plans to move to Hollywood just yet?"

"Never. I'm a Kentish girl and proud of it."

"So what's next, Grace?"

"Well, Jo and I are looking at some beautiful new yarns, from British producers, I'm keen to support that, it's so important that we keep our rare breeds, and they produce beautiful tweeds and organic wools in natural colors. Great for when it's chilly."

Ellen smiles. She meant what's the next film project, and Grace knows it.

"And I'm working on a new film I'm very excited about, I'll be producing this one too, we're working on the script now. I can't say too much, but I get to knit. So that's a good start."

"Can you give us a hint?"

"*Upstairs Downstairs,* with a twist. I think it's going to be fabulous, at least I hope it is. People are always so lovely about my work, so I really hope they're going to like it."

I can see Maxine is moving forward now. I think she'll probably stand in front of the camera if Ellen doesn't finish soon.

"Well thank you, Grace, and Jo, this has been lovely. Who knows, maybe I'll get my knitting needles out again."

"Not at all, and thank you, Ellen, this has been such a treat. I'm sure Jo can find you the perfect project, you've got a little boy, haven't you? Why don't you make him something in this blue? It's such a beautiful color, just like a pale seaside sky."

She picks up a ball of wool from the basket on the table and hands it to Ellen. "It would make a beautiful blanket."

"I might just do that. Thank you, Grace."

She smiles.

There's a silence.

"Thanks, Grace, that was great."

Maxine steps forward. "Can you turn the camera off, please?"

Al tuts but puts the camera down. Clever Maxine.

"There's a photographer downstairs, from the local paper. I said we'd do some shots of you leaving."

"Thanks, Max, was that okay?"

"Perfect."

"Jo?"

"Amazing. I don't know how you do it."

She smiles and turns to Ellen. "It's all part of the job. Thanks, Ellen, that was nice, lovely to see you again. And Jo, I'll see you later in the week."

A few of the photographers who lurk outside Graceland have turned up, and there's a flurry of cameras flashing as she leaves, and then she stops by the car so the local reporter, who looks about twelve and doesn't seem that confident with his camera, can get a decent picture. Gran and Elsie are waving through the café window, and he takes their photo too.

"Can I have a quote, from Grace Harrison? What did she say?"

Ellen fixes him with a very beady look.

"If you're asking me did she say anything during my exclusive interview with her, well, funnily enough, yes, she did. Am I going to give it to you? No, I'm bloody not."

He's looking rather terrified now.

"I tell you what, though. *I'll* give you a quote, will that do?"

"Oh, would you? That would be great."

"Sure. Ellen Malone said she was thrilled to have such a major guest for the launch of her new series next week, and she was very impressed that, what's the paper called?"

"The Whitstable and Broadgate Gazette."

"Very impressed that the *Gazette* were waiting outside the shop. It just shows that local journalism is alive and kicking."

"Oh, thanks, that's great."

"My pleasure. Now bugger off."

"Right you are. And thank you, Miss Malone. I really appreciate it. People are so rude sometimes."

"Are they, darling? What a shocker."

We're still giggling when Tom brings us a coffee.

"That was great, Jo. She's a total star, isn't she? Thanks, Tom. If you ever want a job in town, let me know, great coffee. We could use you at the studio."

Tom looks pleased. And rather interestingly, Cinzia does not. Which is probably a good sign for Tom.

"No, you're all right, but thanks, I've got my band, you see, we're starting to get a few bookings, so this is just to tide me over. Oh, sorry Jo."

"It's fine, Tom. I didn't think this was the height of your ambitions."

"Did it go all right then?"

"Well, apart from me nearly sliding off my chair, and getting completely tongue-tied, yes, it was great."

Ellen laughs. "You weren't that bad, darling. Trust me, I've had worse. At least you didn't say *fuck*. Or throw up. Or both."

"It was a close-run thing, that's all I'm saying."

"I might knit one of those blankets, you know. She's right, that was a great color. Can you sort me out with all the stuff?"

"Sure. Don't you fancy knitting a duck then?"

"No, sounds too tricky. Did she really knit one for Lily?"

"No comment."

"Oh stop it."

"I signed a confidentiality clause. Of course she did. It was lovely."

"And if she hadn't?"

"Of course she did. It was lovely."

"Great. You're meant to be my best friend you know, darling. Don't let the Diva dazzle you."

"I'm not. But I do like her."

"I do too. She's pretty normal, for a megastar. And her skin, Christ, not a trace of anything toxic. It must be natural, lucky cow. Beautiful eyes too."

"I know. It's amazing she's not in films really."

$\cdots$ 5 $\cdots$

From Here to Maternity

May and June

t's ten past two on Monday afternoon, and I'm wedged in the window with cramp in one arm and sand up both my sleeves. I'm finally changing the Easter display to our summertime seaside one, after the chaos of the last couple of weeks. Ellen's interview caused a sensation locally, and we've had loads of new customers coming in. The website's gone mad, and we've had so many orders for knitting kits we've had to set up a mini-assembly line in the workroom. I've put in an order for more of our McKnits boxes, and I've even been able to push the suppliers for a much higher discount. It's all been completely brilliant.

"That looks lovely, pet."

"Thanks Gran."

"You should ring the paper and tell them about the new window, now the shop is so famous. I bet that they'd come back."

"I think we've had enough excitement for a while, don't you, Gran?"

The local paper sent another would-be reporter round last week, a young woman this time, and Elsie wore her multicolored cardigan for the photographs, which was a shame as I wasn't really aiming for Nutter as our design motif. But Gran and Laura looked lovely, sitting knitting in the café with Tom in the background, and the reporter bought some wool before she left, so that was encouraging. "You're probably right, pet. If she tells me one more time what she said to the reporter, I don't know what I'll do."

Elsie's been in seventh heaven, giving media snippets to anyone who shows the slightest interest. She's even got a scrapbook of cuttings, which she keeps under the counter. It's her afternoon off today, but I'm guessing she's probably out getting more prints made for her album.

"To hear her talk, you'd think none of us were there; she's always been the same, taking center stage when there's no call for it, she's always been a—"

"Bugger."

Gran giggles. "She means well, pet."

"No, it's just I've just stapled the cuff of my shirt to the bloody partition again."

"Shall I put the kettle on? Let's see if Madam has left us any biscuits, shall we? But I wouldn't hold your breath if I were you."

I'm trying to fix swathes of dark blue net into artistic waves. I've already got the silver net up, and the fronds of seaweed Laura knitted, in different shades of green, which are rather beautiful, so I'm trying to make sure they aren't completely covered with the bloody net. But every time I get it into the right position, someone taps on the glass to say hello, and I have to start all over again. Clare has just held baby Ava up to do smiling and waving, which was sweet, but you do have to wave back unless you want to look like a total snooter. I need one of those curtains like the ones the big shops in London have when they're doing their windows. Although round here, people would probably just come in and open them, so they could see what you were doing.

All the knitted fish are bobbing around on their nylon thread, looking very nautical, and I've knitted a couple of starfish to dot in among the pebbles and sand. The papier-mâché ones the boys made when we first moved down here are in the box ready to put out, along with the lobster and little crabs I knitted last year, although admittedly some are more crablike than others. Laura's knitted some coral too, and a giant shell, in lovely shades of cream and gray, with a pale pink lining: she's really getting into knitting things for the windows, and we're taking pictures so she can put them in her Project folder for college. I'll hang up the string of flags I knitted last year, in bright, jaunty colors, although Martin says he's going to look them up in his new boat-owner semaphore book in case they're signaling something rude. I'm not sure people actually do semaphore anymore, but if they do, at least he's got the book. He better not let Elsie see it though, or she'll be hoisting signals up for the entire town to see. Come home and get your washing. Have you got your coat on? That kind of thing.

"It looks great, Jo. I love those fish; they must have taken you ages."

"Thanks, Laura, but the first year was the hardest; now I only have to add in a few new pieces, like your lovely coral."

"My tutor said she might come in and have a look. Can I take some photos of the café window too?"

"Of course."

I've already put the old cream jugs and the knitted roses in, and I'll add in a few more woolen cakes and the bowl of knitted strawberries as the summer season really kicks off. Gran's knitting some more sandwiches and some little fairy cakes, to go in the old wicker picnic hamper, and that got a lot of nice comments last year, particularly the woolly ham-and-egg pie, which took me bloody ages.

"I meant to say, Jo, I've had a think about it, and I'd love to, do the group I mean, if you're still sure."

I've asked Laura if she'll run a beginners' class on Saturdays for me. She's got a real eye for color, but she's also very gentle and patient, just the kind of person you want to start you off knitting. I need to get more classes going which don't involve me having to be there every minute, especially at the weekends.

"You'll be great, Laura, I know you will, and Elsie will be around, and Olivia too, she's in on Saturdays, don't forget. I usually nip in as well, if I can park the kids with Gran or Cinzia, and Tom's happy to do the café as long as you're around for the lunchtime rush. Let's try Saturday afternoon, shall we, and see how many people sign up."

"I'm really looking forward to it, and I can write it up for my course work, so that'll be a real help. I'm a bit behind. I never get time in the evenings what with Rosie and everything, and my tutor says I need a lot more written stuff."

"I've got some notes I did for the school knitting project, I'll bring them in. There's lots on the history of the Guilds, and all the different traditions of knitting socks and lace, and some great photographs."

"That would be brilliant, thanks."

W e're standing drinking tea with Gran and writing a notice for the board about the new class when Mrs. Marwell comes in.

"Hello Mary. We don't see you behind the counter so much
now. Hasn't your Jo done well, I bet you're pleased as punch.
I've been meaning to ask you, Jo, can I have your autograph, for
my book?"

Oh God, this is getting ridiculous.

"I like to get one from all the famous people in Broadgate.
My book will be worth a few bob one day I shouldn't wonder.
Look, I've got Mr. Parsons from the ironmongers, and he stood
next to Angela Rippon in a queue at Waterloo Station once.
She always had such lovely outfits on when she read the news,
and she was a lovely dancer, you know."

"Right, well, that's very kind, but—"

"When I was younger I used to go up to London, to the
Palladium. There were proper stars in those days, and if you
waited at the stage door they'd always take the trouble to sign
your book for you. Give you a kiss too, if you were lucky. Not
that I went in for that sort of thing, well, not much anyway,
but I did have my moments."

Gran smiles. "I bet you did, Florrie."

Bless. Now we'll have to look at the pages in her book with
signatures from a load of people we've never heard of, although
Gran might recognize a few.

"Let's see, oh yes, he was one of my favorites."

"Who's that, Mrs. Marwell?"

"Frank Sinatra. And there's Dean Martin. Such nice
boys. Have you got a pen, dear? I've got one in here somewhere."

Bloody hell. She starts unpacking her basket onto the
counter, which I know from previous experience can take a

while. Gran is looking at her feet, trying not to smile as a tin opener and a glove join the growing pile.

"I've got a pen, thanks, Mrs. Marwell, if you're sure."

"Oh right you are then. What's that, on top of that box?"

"A starfish, for the window, the boys made it."

"Did they? Well, isn't that lovely. I didn't know they were that purple color. Are you still doing your charity basket, dear?"

"Yes, we've moved it upstairs though, and it's a bit of a mess up there."

"Bit of a muddle never hurt anyone. I've got all sorts in my front room at home, but I like to have a few bits and pieces around me. Now, where did I put that? Here it is, I want to put this in, I never really liked the color, but it does knit up nicely. I just need a bit of green, to finish off the neckband of one of my sweaters for the orphans, poor little things. The church is sending off another parcel soon and I don't like to let them down."

"I'll come up with you, Florrie, see what we can find."

"Thanks Mary."

Gran winks at me as they go upstairs. The charity basket was definitely one of my better ideas. People are pretty good about putting something in if they take anything out, odd-ments of wool left over, sometimes nearly a whole ball. I've put little plastic bags in too so things don't get in a tangle, and we put old stock in, especially when we're not reordering. Elsie likes having shelves full of bargain wool, but I think it looks tatty, so the charity option is much better. Mrs. Mar-well buys a few new balls of wool for her sweater, and uses the basket for the contrast colors. She's only got a small pension, and she's knitting for charity, so it doesn't seem right to make her pay more than she needs to. So everyone is happy; well, apart from Elsie.

B loody hell, it's five past three.

"I better go and get the boys, Laura, can you tell Gran?"

"Sure. She'll probably be up there ages. I'll keep an eye out for customers; the café's pretty quiet. Who knew, though, Mrs. Marwell and Frank Sinatra?"

"I know. Still, it goes to show, you never can tell. Just because she gets her wheelie trolley stuck in the door doesn't mean she didn't go in for a fair bit of razzle-dazzle when she was younger."

"Razzle-dazzle? I like the sound of that."

"Me too."

T he sun is shining as I walk to school: Easter was freezing, and wet, but today it feels like summer might finally be on the way. We might be able to have a picnic at the weekend, after Mum arrives, and I can lock her in the beach hut if she gets too annoying.

Connie's in the playground, sitting on the bench under the chestnut tree. She looks tired; the combination of heartburn and the baby kicking is stopping her from getting much sleep. I'm so glad I'm not pregnant; one look at her and I remember just how knackering it was.

"How was last night?"

"Three weeks, with no sleeping. It is not possible."

I think once the baby arrives she might find it is, but I want to be encouraging.

"Did you try the milk of magnesia?"

"Yes, and it helps. But then I lie down, and it does not."

"Have you tried sleeping sitting up, sweetheart? It was the

only way I got any proper sleep at all with Archie, and Pearl too come to think of it, in that old pink armchair I've got in the living room, the one with the roses. Nick hated it, he said they should call it bourgeois floral instead of Peony Parade, or whatever they called it in the shop, but it was worth every bloody penny. You're welcome to try it if you like."

She smiles. "If I don't sleep tonight, then yes, I will."

"Good."

"Porca Madonna."

Annabel is barreling across the playground toward us, with Mrs. Nelson in her wake.

"Christ, it must be serious if she needs backup."

She's clutching her clipboard and her fountain pen, which isn't a good sign. She hasn't actually spoken to me since the television thing, but she's been giving me particularly furious looks for the last few days, so I'm pretty sure she saw it.

"Afternoon, ladies. I just wanted a little word about the Summer Fayre, although I do realize Mrs. Maxwell is likely to be otherwise engaged with her happy event."

She pauses and glances at Connie's tummy, and then looks away, as if she's just seen something unpleasant.

"But if you did a knitting stall, Mrs. Mackenzie, I'm sure that would be popular."

A knitting stall: is she mad?

"I'm so busy at the moment, Annabel. I really don't think I could manage a whole stall. Are any of the other local shops doing stalls this year?"

She looks at me like I'm a complete idiot. Which I would be if I agreed to run a stall at her bloody fayre. Connie and I already got stuck doing the White Elephant a couple of years back, standing in the boiling heat trying to flog a load of old tat. Never again.

"People are always so generous. I'm sure you want to do everything you can to support our school."

Connie stands up. "Yes, we do, with the walking bus, and with all the other things, but so. Enough. We will come to the fayre, and we will buy things, like the other people do."

Mrs. Nelson looks rather pale now, but Annabel isn't going to be diverted so easily.

"Of course I quite understand how busy you are, running your little businesses. Sometimes I don't know how I fit everything in, being President of the PTA does take an awful lot of my time, but of course I am lucky enough not to have to work."

She pauses, and Mrs. Nelson gives her a simpering smile.

"If you can't do a stall, then I'm sure you'll both want to join our Auction of Promises? It's such a super idea; we'll be sending round a leaflet. I've already arranged for my tennis coach to offer an hour's tuition, and he does get terribly booked up. Perhaps you can offer a meal in your restaurant, Mrs. Maxwell."

"I will talk to Mark, and we will see."

Lucky enough not to have to work? God, she's annoying.

"And I did want to mention"—she's looking rather pointedly at me now—"if our local celebrity wanted to join in our little auction, that would add a great deal of excitement. Perhaps a lunch, or dinner of course. And may I just say, strictly entre nous, I can guarantee that there would be a very respectable bid. I've already spoken to my husband, and we'd be very happy to contribute most generously."

Mrs. Nelson nods encouragingly.

I think the plan is for me to persuade Grace to be auctioned, like that's ever going to happen in a million years, and then Annabel will make her husband put in a hefty bid, and bingo, Annabel gets to have lunch with Grace, and can boast about it to all of her friends at the bloody Tennis Club. Oh dear. I may have just found yet another way to annoy her. Still, in for a penny, in for a pound as Gran would say. I might as well enjoy it.

"That's so sweet of you, Annabel, really, I'm very touched, but I don't think I could do anything like that. People would think I was getting above myself. It was only one little television interview after all, I'm sure nobody would want to have lunch with me."

"I didn't mean, well, I was rather hoping . . ."

She glares at Connie, who is trying not to laugh, and Mrs. Nelson coughs nervously before she rallies.

"I think Mrs. Morgan was thinking of Grace Harrison, although of course I'm sure people would, it's just, or perhaps Ellen Malone, she's a friend of yours, isn't she?"

"Yes, she's Archie's godmother."

Annabel stiffens. She's not keen on any of my children, but if she had to pick the most annoying one, she'd definitely choose Archie. To be fair, I think we all would.

"I could ask her, I suppose."

Mrs. Nelson nods encouragingly.

"But I have to say I think it's a nonstarter. Definitely for Grace. I happen to know her diary is completely full. And as for Ellen, well, I know she doesn't do things like that, she gets so many requests, I'm sure you understand. No, I think I should probably say no, there's no point in wasting everybody's time, is there? Look, Connie, the kids are coming out, and Nelly's got a Gold Sticker, she must have done one of her lovely paintings, they had art this afternoon, didn't they? Unless Archie has just painted his face green for fun."

Archie is swinging his lunch box around above his head, with a large splodge of green paint on his chin.

"Hello darling, did you have a lovely day?"

"Yes, we had a spelling test and I came top. Of the whole class. It was great."

He glances at Annabel and gives her one of his Best Smiles. Oh dear.

"Harry did good too, just not as good as me or Nelly. But we're in the top group, on the acorn table. Harry's only a walnut. Acorn is top for spelling. What's for tea, Mum? I'm starving."

I think we better beat a hasty retreat, before she demands a recount on the spelling test. Or implodes, and we all get to learn some new words.

Connie and I are laughing so much on the walk home she has to sit down in the park so she can get her breath back.

"Her face, it was so. So."

"Gobsmacked."

"Yes. And it is serving her right, horrible woman."

"Who's horrible, Mum?"

"Nobody, love, and Archie, did you really come top in spelling?"

"Yes."

"That's very good, love."

"Well, I did have the spellings in my book; I just forgot to turn the page over."

"Archie, that's terrible. That's cheating."

"No it's not, I know them. Go on, test me, I bet I know them."

"I will, later, and you better know them, Archie, or we'll have to talk to Mrs. Berry."

"I already told her, and she said I was very good for being truthful, and because I'm so good at spelling, this time she'll make a reception."

"Exception."

"Yes, so it's fine."

"It is not fine. And you must never do it again, Archie."

"All right, keep your hair on."

"And don't say that either."

"Why not? It's not swearing, it's not like saying—"

"Archie, that's enough, thank you. Pick your bag up, it can't stay there. We need to get home, Cinzia and Pearl will be waiting. Come back with us for a cup of tea, Con. You can try out that chair, give it a test run."

Archie ignores his bag and runs off to join the others on the swings.

I pick the bag up, and Connie smiles. "He is so, your Archie. So."

"I know, Con, thanks. Trust me. I know."

"He will go far."

"I'm sure he will, but I pity the person who has to run along behind him picking all his things up."

Cinzia is nattering away in Italian to Connie while I make the tea. Tom's Plan B seems to be slowly having an effect. Connie says she went out with the new French boy, but only for a coffee, and apparently he was too French, so now she's keen on a German student called Sebastian. It's like she's doing her very own version of the Grand Tour, only instead of crates full of paintings and marble statues, she's collecting admirers. But I think Tom is still the favorite, so maybe he's on the right track after all. Although she's due to go home at the end of the year, so it's not going to be a very long track.

She's looking particularly gorgeous today, in a short summer frock over pale pink leggings, which on anyone else would make their legs look like uncooked sausages, but on her look rather fetching. And if there's a chance Tom will be around, her outfits definitely get tighter and skimpier. She caused another stir at baby gymnastics last week, according to Tina. And Mr. Dawes has only just stopped limping.

"Cinzia, do you want tea or juice, love?"

"Juice please, I'll get some for the kidlings too."

"Great."

"Cup."

Pearl's joining in with the Italian, waving her hands and having a lovely time, while she plays with the plastic tea set I bought at the weekend at the Brownies' jumble sale. I can't wait for her to be a Brownie; Mum wouldn't let me join. She said the uniform was too depressing.

O nce everyone has had a drink, Cinzia takes them outside to stroke Peter Rabbit, while Connie tries out the famous armchair, and promptly falls asleep. She looks so peaceful I close the curtains and the door to the kitchen. I'm trying to get everyone to keep quiet, which is a Mission Completely Bloody Impossible, and then Martin arrives with Trevor the Wonder Dog, and the inevitable football game is launched. Peter's safely back in his hutch, and miraculously Connie's still asleep when I check on her, which just goes to show how utterly exhausted she is; nobody but a heavily pregnant, sleep-deprived woman could sleep through the kind of racket the kids and Trevor are making.

"Who wants a picnic for tea?"

Everyone puts their hands up, even Martin.

"Toasted cheese sandwiches?"

I might sneak in some tuna, and a few slices of tomato, just so there's something vaguely nutritious going on in among all the melted cheese.

"I love picnickers, Mum, they're my favorite."

"I know, Archie."

"Can we have one every day after school?"

"No, we can't. But today we can, okay?"

"Have we got crisps?"

"I think so."

"Peter likes crisps."

"No he doesn't, and you mustn't feed him stuff like that. Remember what the vet said when you went with Grandad Reg. He's a very healthy rabbit, and we want to keep him that way."

"Yes, but salad is boring and he's a magic rabbit, so you don't know what he likes."

"He likes salad, however magic he is. And don't be rude, Archie. Being rude isn't magical at all. But it might make the crisps disappear."

He tuts.

"I beg your pardon?"

"Sorry."

He tuts again, when he thinks I can't hear him.

We're sitting on the terrace at our rickety old wooden table when Mark arrives. The kids are finishing their yogurts.

"Thanks for giving them their tea, Jo. I've brought you the bread, whole meal and some white rolls, is that okay?"

"Perfect. I suddenly realized I've got nothing for their packed lunches tomorrow. Thanks, Mark. I'll drive Con back when she wakes up. Or Martin will."

"Great, and the baby shower, that's this Thursday, right?"

"Yes, are you still bringing cake? I think she needs all the treats she can get now, poor thing, this last bit feels like forever."

"Tell me about it. She went tonto at me last night, just because I said I'd give her a hand to get out of the bath, if she got stuck."

"That was subtle."

He laughs. "I know, I thought that, as I was saying it, I thought, You total idiot, shut up, now, but it was too late. She hit me, with one of my big wooden spoons. Quite hard actually."

"Oh dear."

"I'm not getting much sympathy here, am I? Is this one of those sisterhood things?"

"Definitely, so you better take the kids home quick, before she wakes up and we both hit you with our wooden spoons."

Jack wants to play more football, but it's starting to get chilly.

"Five more minutes and then it's bath time. And we've got to be very quiet, because Aunty Connie is still asleep. Quiet like mice. There'll be a prize for the quietest person."

"Because she's having a baby?"

"Yes, Archie."

"Is she going to the hospital to get it out, or will she do it in the kitchen, like you did with Pearly?"

"I think the plan is to go to hospital to have the baby, Archie, but you never know. Babies sometimes arrive at home."

Martin grins and puts his cup down. "Remind me not to go to the pub for the next few weeks; I don't think I could cope with another home delivery. Not that I coped all that well last time."

"You called the ambulance."

"Yes, and gibbered down the phone like a madman."

Actually, he was great when Pearl was born, pacing up and down the garden in a terrible panic, looking like he'd gone into some sort of proxy shock. It was sort of nice seeing someone else almost as freaked out as I was.

"You were fine. Do you want more tea?"

"Please. I'd forgotten how much I love picnics, well, the way you do them. Mum always used to make such a fuss, with Tupperware boxes for everything; I'm surprised she didn't have some sort of box to pop me into for a quick wash before she got the sandwiches out. We never went anywhere without a damp flannel in her bag. But you don't fuss about stuff like that, do you? They can get as grubby as they like."

"Thanks, Martin, that makes me sound like a very strong contender for Hopeless Mother of the Year."

"I like it, it's relaxing. I put those new photographs up by the way, on the website. Are the new windows finished?"

"Nearly. I've got some pictures on the camera, only Laura's got it at the moment, for her college work. I'll e-mail them to you, shall I?"

"Sure. See, once you get into the habit, it's easy to keep updating the site."

"Yes, as long as someone else does it for you. I did try, you know, but it went into a weird shape."

"I'll fix that, it's just the format. To be honest, you could do with a total redesign."

"Tell me about it."

"I didn't mean it like that."

Trevor bounds over and licks Martin's hands.

"That's not very hygienic, you know, talk about people getting grubby. Just think what your mother would say."

Jack giggles, and Martin winks at him.

"Well, we better not tell her how he wakes me up in the mornings then, jumping on the bed. Better than any alarm clock."

"You shouldn't let him do that. It might give someone a nasty surprise."

"Someone? I can't think who."

"Yes, thank you, not in front of Mummy's little helpers, if you don't mind. Dogs jumping on beds is not a good thing, okay? Or rabbits. Who like living outside."

"Fair enough. But everyone loves Trevor, don't they, boys?"

"Yes. But I love Peter most, because he's my magic rabbit, all of my very own. And he *is* magic; he can push his bowl right out the door now. And I'm going to teach him how to jump through hoops. And then I can set fire to them."

Oh God. Poor Peter. Just when you think you've got one thing sorted in the wonderful world of Pets, something else comes along.

"Mum, can I wake Uncle Vin up yet?"

"No Archie, they didn't get here until really late last night. He'll be awake when you get home from school though, love."

"It's not fair."

"Today's Thursday, Mum, isn't it? We've got our special assembly."

"Yes Jack."

Archie's not impressed. "I hate stupid assemblies."

"Well, I don't, I'm reading a poem."

"Are you, Jack? You never said."

"Well, I am, my whole group are doing it. I say 'And hand in hand, on the edge of the sand, they danced by the light of the moon.' And then we all say 'the moon,' twice. And then the whole class says 'They danced by the light of the moon.' We've done pictures too. I did a moon, and a green boat. I didn't do the cat or the owl, because I don't like drawing animals."

"Well, it sounds lovely, Jack, and you said it very well. We've got 'The Owl and the Pussycat' in one of your books I think."

He gives me a rather pitying look. "I know, Mum, it's a very famous poem."

"Well, it's very nice."

"What's nice?"

Both Archie and Jack launch themselves at Vin.

"Steady on, chaps, give me a chance. Any coffee going spare, Jo?"

"Sure. Does Lulu want one?"

"No, she's still in the Land of Nod. That girl can sleep through anything."

"Uncle Vin, I've got a rabbit, come and see, he's called Peter."

Vin gives me a look.

"Yes. Peter Rabbit. We like it. We're getting a Mrs. Tiggy-Winkle next, okay?"

"All right, calm down. Who rattled your cage?"

The boys giggle. You can always count on their uncle Vin

to say unsuitable things to their mother; it's one of his many attractions.

"Up. Up."

Pearl has decided she wants to join in the action, now she's taken a long, hard look at Vin, who she's only actually seen once when she was tiny.

"All right love, come and say hello."

"Shoes."

"I know, he hasn't got his shoes on, has he. Naughty Uncle Vin. We'll have to get him some slippers."

"You will not."

"We might. Like the ones you had when you were little. What were they, Batman or Superman?"

"Shut up."

"Up."

"Don't encourage her, Vin. Do you want toast?"

"Please. So does Mum know you were on the telly yet?"

"No. I thought if I said anything, she'd come over and insist on a starring role."

"Well Gran will soon take care of that. Honestly, we could hardly get a word in last night."

"I bet. Look, are you sure you're okay to collect Mum and Dad from Gatwick? Gran and Reg will do it, you know. They quite liked coming to pick you up, they got really excited about it. It'll just take a couple of hours longer."

"A couple of hours? Even the caravans were overtaking us. No, as long as I can drive your car, I'd rather do it myself; that car Reg drives would probably blow up if you tried to get it over fifty. We'll never hear the end of it from Mum if she has a slow journey in from the airport; you know what she's like. Gran was very chirpy though; she was telling us they're off on another cruise?"

"Yes, next month, for a late wedding anniversary."

"Well, we might as well alert the traffic police now, so they know when he'll be back on the M25 causing havoc."

"He's not that bad, Vin."

"He is, and I want butter on my toast, nothing else thanks."

Great, it looks like I've got one more guest for my bed-and-breakfast operation. How marvelous.

"You can have what you like. The butter dish is on the table, and the knives are in the drawer."

"You won't get a tip."

"No, but you will. Don't mess with a woman trying to make breakfast for three kids on a school morning."

"I'll give you a Chinese burn in a minute."

"You will not."

"What's a Chinese burn?"

"Vin, don't you dare, or you'll be sleeping in the garden. He's joking, Archie. Go and find your shoes, love."

He tuts; in fact they all do, even Pearl.

Excellent.

'm tidying up the workroom for our Stitch and Bitch baby shower for Connie when Cath arrives with a beautiful parcel wrapped in silver tissue paper, followed by Maggie, who's carrying a Tupperware box.

"I've made some sausage rolls, nothing like Mark's standard, but it's the thought that counts, isn't it?"

"Thanks, Maggie, I'm sure they'll be lovely."

"Oh look, doesn't the Moses basket look beautiful. Is that the one you had for Pearl?"

"Yes, the one you gave me at my baby shower, so I thought

I'd return the favor. I bought a new mattress, and Gran bought the sheets, and look, I've sewn up our blanket. It looks great, doesn't it? She's going to love it."

I hold up the blanket, with the pale cream brushed cotton sheet with little ducks on, and everyone strokes it, including Tina and Linda, who put their presents on the growing pile on the table.

"Makes you want to have another one, doesn't it?"

"Not really, no."

Tina laughs. "What's she done now?"

"Who? My Lauren? Nothing, apart from driving me demented; if she tells me one more time to get a life, I think I'll clock her one. I wouldn't mind, but if she'd settle down I could get a bloody life instead of worrying myself sick about what she's up to, out there with her skirts so short she might as well not bother wearing them."

"She does look nice though, Lind."

"I know, Tina, that's what I'm worrying about. You've got all that to come with Pearl, you know, Jo."

"She already has views on what she'll wear. If I try to dress her in the mornings in anything she doesn't fancy, she just goes all stiff so I can't move her arms. She's so stubborn. That doesn't bode well, does it?"

Cath smiles. "Well at least she won't be a doormat, Jo, and that's got to be good. The only problem is the first person she'll stand up to is you. Olivia is just the same. I know you think she's lovely, and butter wouldn't melt when she's in the shop with you, but honestly, she says the most crushing things sometimes. She told me I had to walk behind her when we went to the supermarket last week, because my coat was too embarrassing."

"Archie and Jack already do that, all the time. They're

trying to get me banned from the walking bus because they think my tabard is too tragic. Mind you, I agree with them on that one."

"Girls are much better at it, trust me. My Lauren's an expert. Last night she said if she thought she'd end up looking like me, she'd throw herself off a cliff. Just because I asked her to take her bag upstairs."

"Christ. There's so much to look forward to in the wonderful world of mothers and daughters, isn't there?"

We're arranging the presents on the table when Angela arrives. Mark's bringing Connie in about ten minutes, and so far I don't think she's guessed. I can't wait to see her face.

"Is Mark doing one of his cakes?"

"Yes, her favorite, chestnut meringue, with caramel and cream in layers, I've been thinking about it all day. Did you finish your shawl, Angela?"

"Yes, it's the same one I knitted for Stanley, and for Iris, so I've got a sense of the pattern now. I find them quite relaxing to knit."

We all admire the intricate pattern, and Angela goes pink. She's been spending a fair bit of time with Penny and Sally and her new granddaughter, and Stanley's apparently delighted with his new sister.

"He's so gentle with her; it's lovely to watch him. He supports her head so carefully. He's such a sweet boy."

I can't help smiling. "Just wait until she touches his Lego, that's all I'm saying."

Cath laughs, and tells us Olivia and Toby once fought so bitterly over a Monopoly game that she threw the board up in the air, and all the cards and the money went everywhere, and neither of them spoke to her for nearly a whole day. She said it was great. I must try it.

"Didn't you have to pick all the bits up though?"

"Yes, Tina, I did, but it was worth it, just to see the looks on their faces."

A ngela's showing us her latest photographs when Connie arrives, takes one look at the pile of presents, and bursts into tears.

"Oh, God, Con, it was meant to make you happy."

"I am. Happy. It is so kind. To have friends."

I give her a hug, and she calms down and starts opening her presents, and holding tiny cardigans and sleepsuits over her tummy. She's completely delighted. Mark has stayed too, and gets quite emotional when she hands him the Moses basket to put in the car.

"I'll be back in an hour, love."

"Yes."

He kisses her, and Linda and Tina exchange glances as Linda raises her glass.

"Look at them, picture of love's young dream. Makes you sick, doesn't it?"

Mark laughs. "I think that's my cue to leave, but I hope you like the cake."

"You know we will. God Connie, you've got a good one there, you know, looks half decent and he can cook too. You haven't got a brother, have you, Mark?"

"Sorry, and I'm definitely leaving now. But thanks, Linda, always nice to be appreciated."

'm collecting up wrapping paper.

"Everything is so lovely."

"Do you want more tea, Connie? Tina?"

Tina's on a new diet. Not that it's stopping her having cake.

"Yes please, and I've got top gossip. You know that Mrs. Churchill, the one whose husband ran off with the milkman—I'm not kidding, he did, they've got a bungalow now, outside Brighton—anyway, she was saying there were rows the other day, in the car park at Waitrose. Annabel Morgan and some woman in one of those great big cars were arguing about a parking space and neither of them would reverse. They had to call the manager in the end. I wish I'd been there, I could have taken a photo on my phone and we could have put it in the next PTA newsletter. Be better than those stupid puzzles she does, which her Harry always seems to win. Mind you, people do get agitated in car parks, don't they, Lind?"

"I just told her what I thought."

"I know you did. We all heard you telling her."

"She was parked in a disabled parking space, and there was nothing the matter with her."

Angela puts her glass down. "Oh, good for you, Linda. It really annoys me when people do that. What did you say?"

"I just said, I hope you can sleep at night, being so selfish, and if someone in a wheelchair needs that space, what are they meant to do, wait till you've done your shopping or what?"

"She did. It was great, actually; the woman went bright red and everything."

"Well good for you, Linda."

"I know, I was quite pleased with myself, Ange. Normally you only think of it when you get home, don't you?"

We all nod, and Maggie puts her knitting down. "We should have badges. Like the white feathers they gave out in the war, although that was horrible, I don't approve of that at all. But badges we could give to people being selfish would be useful. I could use stacks of them in the library."

"What, like a badge saying 'Put That Book Back'?"

She laughs. "No, Cath, more like 'Stop Being So Rude.' So when you saw someone behaving badly, you could just go up and give them a badge and walk away."

"Brilliant idea, Maggie. We could use them in the salon, couldn't we, Tina?"

"Yes, we bloody could. Especially with that Mrs. Collins. She comes in with pictures cut out of magazines and says, 'Do it like this,' but she's sixty if she's a day, with a face like a wet weekend, and then she gets all huffy and says I haven't done it right when she doesn't end up looking like Jennifer bloody Aniston."

Linda tuts. "You should tell her, Tina. You're a hairdresser not a bloody magician."

Connie laughs so much we have to bang her on the back, but rather carefully because she's so pregnant now none of us are keen to start anything off.

"More cake, anybody?"

Tina winks at me, and we go into the kitchen

"Smile and the Whole World Smiles with You."

"Sorry Ange?"

"That would make a useful badge. People look so miserable sometimes. 'Politeness Costs Nothing,' that would be a good one."

Maggie nods.

"'A Stitch in Time Saves Nine.' Actually, I've never understood that one."

Linda cuts herself another sliver of cake. There's not much left now, so we're all having tiny slices, to make it last.

"I think it's when you notice the button on your new coat is a bit loose, and you're meant to sew it back on tight right away. So it can't come off when it's pouring with bloody rain. I looked like I'd been swimming by the time I got in last week."

Maggie looks sympathetic. "'What Goes Around Comes Around,' that's a good one."

"I could give that one to my Lauren. God, I'm really looking forward to that, when she has kids and they start giving her hell. It's the best bit of being a gran as far as I can see."

Cath nods. "I'm looking forward to that too. Not yet, though. We could knit some 'Get a Life' badges too, you know. I'm sure Livvy would like one of those."

"My Lauren could use a whole bag full; mind you, I'd end up wearing most of them, so maybe not."

Cath laughs. "I think we all would, Linda."

I love our Thursday group, and it's great to know we might be doing badges. Maybe I should knit some and see if they sell. "Keep Calm and Carry On," or "Things Are Getting Worse, Send Cake" might be good. Or "Make Mine a Large One." I think Ellen bought one of those, we saw it in a shop in London. You could knit them in pretty pastels. I'll add it to my list.

Mum has arrived, and we're all trying to be Nice, especially Gran, but it's been fairly hard going.

"Honestly, I've never heard a grown woman make such a

fuss about a couple of tea bags. Why didn't she bring more with her, if they're that important?"

"I know, Gran, but they're her special herbal ones, from that man she sees in Venice."

"Well, he definitely saw her coming, the prices he charges, and they do all sorts in the supermarkets now, you know, me and Reg were looking at them. Tea to make you sleep, tea to perk you up."

"Tea to shut you up?"

"No pet, we didn't see any of that."

"Oh well, she'll just have to make do with chamomile then."

She's been here for a week now, and so far she's told Elsie that blue isn't a good color for older women, asked Lulu when she and Vin are going to stop faffing around with boats and get proper jobs, and told Gran and Reg that their bungalow is suburban and has the most uncomfortable bed she's ever slept on, and the living room carpet brings on her migraines. Gran's particularly hurt about the bed because they bought a new mattress specially, and I've tried it and it's lovely. I'm half hoping I can work out a way to "borrow" it once Mum and Dad have gone home; mine's got a great big dip in the middle, and some mornings when all the kids are in, I can hardly move.

Fortunately, the end of the visit is in sight, so I'm making Sunday lunch and they go back to Venice early on Tuesday morning. Hurrah. Vin and Lulu have been great, even if Vin does keep disappearing to go and see Martin and the stupid boat. Lulu's been keeping out of Mum's way by spending time with me in the shop. I didn't know she was such a computer genius, but she's moved all the photographs around, and changed the colors and the fonts on the website, and it looks much better. She's knitting Vin a sweater too, because he loved the last one she made for him, and wore it nearly every day until he got paint stripper on it, helping his friend who's into old cars. So one way or another we've all managed to survive Mum wanting to be the center of attention, although we're definitely feeling the strain.

"I don't know how your father puts up with her. Reg says he must have the patience of a saint. Still, at least our Pearl seems to like her."

We both smile.

For some reason best known to herself, Pearl has decided Mum is hilarious. It might be her fondness for Bright Colors, or her insistence on being called Mariella. Mary is far too boring apparently, and calling her Gran is completely out of the question. The boys call her Mariella automatically now, but since Pearl can't quite manage this, she's shortened it to Ella, which by happy coincidence is also the name of one of her favorite bedtime books, about a naughty elephant. So that's been an unexpected treat.

"Josephine, is that tea ready?"

"Nearly, Mum, sorry."

"If you leave it too long to infuse, it's undrinkable."

"Okay Mum."

"And call Vincent on his mobile and tell him to hurry up, would you? I've hardly seen him."

"The signal isn't that great at the harbor, Mum, but I'll try."

"Why on earth did you paint the kitchen this horrible yellow color?"

"It's primrose, Mum, and I like it."

"Did you make those curtains?"

"Yes. On Gran's sewing machine."

"You should have gone for blinds, darling, gingham is so old-fashioned. Blinds are so much more stylish."

"And expensive."

"Yes, but surely you must be earning money now from that silly shop, with your television appearance and everything. I still don't know why you wore that skirt, such a flat color, but then I am very sensitive to that kind of thing. I suppose most people wouldn't have noticed."

"Nobody else has mentioned it, no. Here's your tea, Mum. Lunch will be a couple of hours. Why don't you go and read the papers?"

"Don't make too much, I may not be able to eat anything, darling, I can feel one of my heads starting. And could you keep the baby out of the living room, please, she keeps interrupting me and I've no idea what she wants."

Gran puts her potato peeler down. "For heaven's sake, she just wants to play."

"Yes, but I'm not feeling well."

"Well, go and sit down then. Can't be doing your headache any good standing here moaning, can it? Unless you'd like to do the carrots, take your mind off it?"

V in makes it back for lunch with about fifteen minutes to spare.

"Thanks, Vin, I don't know how we'd have managed without all your help."

He kisses me on the cheek. "Sorry, we got a bit carried away. That boat's going to be beautiful, you know; that stupid dog is a bloody liability, though, in and out of the water all the time, getting everything soaking. Oh, and I got some champagne, for a treat. I'll put it in the fridge; we can have it with Gran's trifle."

Vin's been lobbying for Gran to make one of her sherry trifles ever since he got here; it's his top pudding, and she's made a nonsherry one too, for the kids.

"Is there anything needs doing?"

"No Gran, I think we're fine. Lulu's set the table and Vin's going to help me dish up. Just go and sit down, thanks; not you, Vin, I meant Gran. Here, take the lamb through while I do the gravy."

"Are there Yorkshires?"

"Yes."

He kisses me again.

"Mum, do I have to eat all my carrots?"

"Yes Jack, you've only got three little pieces, and anyway you like carrots."

"Not today I don't."

"Well maybe you won't like trifle today either."

He picks up his fork.

"I do."

"I know, Archie."

"I like trifle, and I like lamb, and the minty sauce, but I don't like the green stuff, so I'm not eating it. And you can't make me, because you're not in charge of the trifle, Gran made it, and she won't make me eat horrible green stuff."

Jack puts his fork back down.

"It's cabbage, Archie, and you haven't got very much. You like cabbage, and Jack likes carrots, so let's not have any more fussing."

Gran smiles at him. "You better do what your mum says, Archie. It doesn't matter who made what, your mum is still the boss."

He tuts, and Jack picks up his fork again.

Excellent.

"That was lovely, pet, that's one of the things I'm looking forward to on our cruise, all the lovely food. Betty's excited about it too. Makes a change from cooking every day."

The chance to be on holiday would be a fine thing.

"How come it's just the three of you going, Gran? I keep meaning to ask you, weren't you going to ask that man from the Lifeboats, the one who sent her that Valentine?"

"Ted Mallow? Yes, we were, but she says she'd rather wait and see who turns up on the boat. She says she can see him any time, and she quite fancies the idea of a nice young sailor. She's terrible, she really is. But to be fair, we're not sure if the card was from Ted, that's the thing. And Reg won't ask him."

"I can't, Mary; it's just not the sort of thing men talk about."

Vin nods. "That's true, Gran. Be handy, though, having someone familiar with lifeboats."

Lulu hits him on the arm.

"Sorry, I didn't mean it like that, you'll be fine, they're great big huge things, there's no way you can get into trouble on one of those in the Med. How long are you in Venice, Gran?"

"A day, and your father's going to take us to a fancy restaurant, so that'll be another treat."

Mum sighs. She'd been talking about taking them on a tour of all her favorite restoration projects, until Dad stepped in and said they wouldn't have time to be dragged all round Venice in and out of buildings covered in scaffolding, and he'd book lunch somewhere nice where they can all relax instead.

"Jack, help Uncle Vin with the plates, love, and you too, Archie. Take them into the kitchen one at a time."

Vin stands up, and so does Lulu. "Shall I bring the trifles in, Mary?"

Gran gives Lulu a very fond look, which seems to irritate Mum.

"Yes please, pet, the bowls are all ready, on the side."

Mum takes another sip of her wine. She made a fuss about it being too rough for her palate, but she seems to be drinking it quite happily now.

"I'm not sure I can manage dessert, your trifle is far too rich for me."

"Well, sit there quietly and don't spoil it for the rest of us then."

Gran's definitely getting to the end of her tether.

I think it might be time to give Mum an opening into her favorite subject.

"I know you said you've got lots of work on at the minute, Mum, what will you be working on when you get back?"

She starts telling us all about some plaster panels in a church, and how hard it is to mix the perfect colors, and we all listen politely; we've had quite a few History of Art lectures over the past few days, so none of us are paying terribly close attention apart from Pearl, who's joining in, waving her arms and giving Mum adoring looks.

Dad winks at me. "I think she's going to miss your mother."

This is a bit risky, but luckily Mum just ignores him and tells Reg all about her special brushes.

"Ella. More."

Not for much longer, thank God.

Lulu brings in clean glasses and the bottle of champagne, and the boys do their best impression of a fanfare of trumpets as Vin carries the trifles in on a tray.

"Before we start— Be quiet for a minute, Mum, I want you to hear this. Before we start, I have an announcement. Have you got that open yet?"

Lulu nods and smiles.

"Well, pour it out, woman, chop chop."

She pokes her tongue out at him.

"Same to you. Now, where was I? Oh yes, well, apart from thanking my clever little sister, for such a great lunch, and for taking such good care of us this week, I just wanted to say that I've finally come to my senses, and she's taken pity on me and said yes. So here's to Lulu, poor girl, my future wife."

He's gone pink, and so has Lulu.

"Oh Vin, how lovely."

I'm hugging him, while Gran gives Lulu a kiss, and Reg pours the champagne. Dad kisses Lulu on her hand, which is sweet. Mum's smiling, even if it is a careful sort of smile.

"Can we have champagne too, Uncle Vin?"

"You haven't got a glass, Arch."

They both drain their juice glasses and hold them up.

"A tiny sip, Vin, okay?"

He pours them both a mouthful.

"Cheers."

They raise their glasses, and Pearl waves her beaker.

"Shoes."

———

Mum puts her glass down.

"I've just had a marvelous idea; you should get married in Venice. I know the perfect church, with the most beautiful ceiling, well, it is now, the priest was so overcome when I finished, so sweet, I'm sure he'd agree, as a favor to me, and—"

"No thanks, Mum."

"It would mean a great deal to your father and me. I don't think you should dismiss it quite so quickly, Vincent. And anyway, where else could you possibly want to get married if you have Venezia as an option?"

"Here. We love it here. Or on a beach somewhere, just the two of us, and no fuss, we haven't decided yet, Mum. But we'll let you know, as soon as we do. We might have the baby first anyway."

Baby? Bloody hell, I don't think I can stand much more excitement.

"What baby?"

Mum's looking less happy by the minute.

"We're thinking of going in for a sprog, and by the way, I blame you for that, Jo, seeing you and the boys and our gorgeous girl here, so I thought I should do the honorable with all my worldly goods routine. So it's all your fault actually."

Gran's laughing. "I think you're meant to do it the other way round, pet."

Mum nods. "Exactly, and a wedding in Venice would be so perfect."

"No, I meant I think it's lovely, that they're going to do it the way they want. Far too much fuss about weddings, if you ask me, it's only one day. It's the rest of their lives that matters."

"I know we're meant to do the ceremony first, Mum, and I have asked her, I want to make that clear, but she's cool about it, aren't you, light of my life?"

Lulu smiles at him, a very sweet, calm smile, like she knows she can trust him, totally, and nods. "I don't want to get all obsessed about weddings. I've seen some of my girlfriends do that. They're totally normal, and then they get engaged and go sort of insane. It's totally bizarre. We'll know when the time is right. There's no rush, it's just a piece of paper, but I think we're ready for a baby, whenever it happens, I really do."

Gran pats her arm.

"And Jo?"

"Yes Vin?"

"We're counting on you, okay? We thought we'd drop the sproglet off with you. Have a few weeks off. Will that work?"

"Sure, and then when you come back we can do a swap, it'll be like a three-for-one deal."

He raises his glass. "I'll drink to that. To the newest member of the clan. Four can't be that tricky, surely?"

Gran laughs. "Reg, take some pictures. We should have some for the album on an important day like this."

"Hang on, Reg; I'll get my camera too."

I used to take loads of photos when the boys were little. I've got hundreds of Jack, and quite a few of Archie, but I haven't taken nearly so many of Pearl, and she's growing up so fast.

"Dad, can you wipe Pearl's face for me?"

"Of course I can. She liked that trifle, didn't she? Reminds me of you when you were little, you could never get between you and a pudding."

The boys giggle.

"You still can't."

"Thanks, Vin."

'm in the kitchen making coffee when Jack comes in, carrying his bowl.

"Well done, love."

"Can we look at our photographs later, Mum?"

"I'll need to get them printed first."

"No, not the ones from today, our old ones, with Dad in."

Oh God. Here we go again. He looks worried.

"Of course we can, darling. We can watch the films too if you like, of you both in the sea, remember, when you were little and just learning to swim?"

I'm not in many of the photographs, or the films. I was always the one behind the camera, which feels right somehow. In lots of ways it feels like it was someone else's life, and I was just taking the pictures.

"And the Christmas ones, when Archie got in that big box and he wouldn't get out."

He smiles, and nods. "And the one with us in bed and Dad's reading us a story."

"Yes."

"When the little bear can't sleep and the big bear has to keep getting him lights and he's jumping on the bed."

"Yes love, we can watch them tonight if you like."

"He was the best dad in the whole wide world, wasn't he, Mum?"

"Yes love."

I give him a hug, and I can feel him relax.

"Can I do my Lego now, Mum?"

"In your room, but not downstairs or Pearl will get it, and you know how cross you get."

They're pretty good with Pearl crashing into their games, particularly Jack, but they both draw the line at her "helping" with their Lego models.

"And can I have a biscuit first?"

"No love, it'll be teatime soon. Nice try though."

He grins and wanders off upstairs.

I hate this; I don't want him having to worry that he can't remember what his dad looks like. It's still so shocking, the complete and total end of someone who's running out of the sea with a small blond boy on his shoulders; it can still make me feel dizzy, for a second or two, when I least expect it.

I'm standing at the sink when Gran comes in. "Are you all right, pet?"

"It's such a waste, Gran."

"I know. Life can be very cruel; we all learned that in the War. But you just have to look at your lovely boys to know it was worth it."

"True."

"Silly man."

"That's also true."

Jack and Archie are upstairs building Lego spaceships while Pearl is half asleep on Lulu's lap, watching *The Little Mermaid*. I'm half asleep myself. Actually, what I really want is some tea.

"Anyone fancy a cup of tea?"

"I'll do it, pet."

"No Gran, stay where you are, I'll do it."

"I'll help you, darling; I want a little word anyway."

Great. Vin winks at me as Mum follows me into the kitchen.

"I've been thinking about this wedding."

"Mum, you heard Vin, they haven't decided."

"I thought when your grandmother arrives on that ghastly

cruise, I could show them the chapel, and then she can tell Vincent."

"She won't, Mum, she doesn't like to interfere."

"Yes, well thank you, Josephine. I know you think I'm meddling, but I am his mother after all. I do have a right to take an interest in my own son's wedding."

"I know, Mum, but he knows what he wants, and so does Lulu."

"Which reminds me, I did want to have a little chat with you about Martin."

Fabulous. This is just getting better and better.

"Yes?"

"Are you completely sure about him, darling? Why would you want to get saddled with someone who has no real ambition? He's so like your father, it's almost uncanny, all that DIY, and carpentry. Your father can take a whole morning just to change a simple plug, you know, if I let him. And all the time life is passing them by."

"Mum, that's totally unfair. Dad's not like that, and neither is Martin."

"The times I've regretted, well, let's just say I could have had a very different life. At least Nick was ambitious."

"Yes, before he drove his car into a tree. Very ambitious."

"That was an accident. A tragic accident. But at least he had some goals in life."

"I know, Mum, it was just a bit of a shame they didn't include us, though, don't you think?"

"I do realize this has been hard for you, of course I do, dreadful, but for heaven's sake don't hide away down here in this backwater. You need a proper career; do something important with your life."

"I am, Mum. I love our life here, and so do the kids. And I like the shop, I really do."

"You should have told me you were friendly with Grace Harrison you know, that was very thoughtless. She came over for the film festival, and if I'd known she was a family friend, I could have invited her to one of my little drinks parties. But you've never been that good at networking, have you, darling?"

Oh sod this.

"Well, I seem to have networked my way into being on speaking terms with a major A-list star and Britain's Favorite bloody Broadcaster, haven't I? So I can't be that crap at it."

"There's no need to be rude. I'm just trying to say you could be doing so much more."

"No, I couldn't. Because I don't want to. I want to do this. This is huge. The kids are happy, I'm happy, Gran's happy, we're all bloody happy. So why can't you be happy too, Mum?"

"I do realize she's always walked on water as far as you're concerned. But she likes living here, she always has. It doesn't mean you have to."

"Just leave it, Mum."

"No, I won't. It's about time someone told you."

"Mum."

"When I think about the sacrifices I made, it's high time you stopped wasting your time."

"And it's high time you stopped telling people about your amazing creative life and how we all need to get proper careers so you can show off at your stupid parties. Because that's what it's about really, isn't it Mum? It's not about what we want, what makes us happy. It's about showing off to other people; my daughter works in television, my son is, actually, what is it you want Vin to do? Because I'd have thought being able to boast about having a marine biologist in the family would go down rather well in Venice. After all, someone's got to work out how to keep the bloody place from sinking into the sea."

"I'm sorry you've taken this so badly, I was only trying to help."

"Were you, Mum? Well that's funny, because it didn't sound like it. Anyway, let's leave it. We're all happy, doing what we want, and if that's not good enough for you, then I think that's your problem. So just give it a rest. Here, carry the tray in, and I'll bring the teapot."

Gran gives me an extra-long hug as Mum and Dad walk to the car with Vin.

"Well done, pet, you told her, and we all heard you, and it needed saying."

Reg smiles and pats me on the shoulder. "I knew you would. You're a strong woman just like your gran. You don't get to my age without learning a thing or two, and I can tell you this, I'd bet on a strong woman against pretty much anything if she sets her mind to it."

"Well that's good, Reg, because I think you're going to need all the help you can get when your cruise stops in Venice. She's determined to show you that bloody church, you know. You'll get dragged round to see every bit of work she's ever done."

He smiles. "Don't you worry about that. Mary's already arranged it all with your dad. We're there for two days, but we're telling her it's only one. That way we can see the sights, and do the things we want to do, and then we'll see her on the second day, and your dad's booking a restaurant. So she won't have long to take us to see all her triumphs."

Gran nods. "Sometimes it's easier to go round the other way as long as you get there in the end."

"That was clever, Gran."

She smiles.

I'm still betting they spend a fair amount of time inside that church though.

'm in the shop on Tuesday morning when Grace calls.

"Hi darling, just wanted to let you know we've closed the deal on the new film. So I've had a talk with Maxine, and Ed, and we'll be announcing soon."

"That's great. Is that the *Upstairs Downstairs* one?"

"No, I meant the other announcement."

"Oh, sorry. Well that's—"

"We're keeping it under wraps for now, but probably in the next week or two. So stand by."

"Right, and was Maxine okay about it, that you hadn't told her earlier?"

"No, she was furious. I may have to let her go."

"Oh no, that's such a shame. Shall I call her, and try to explain?"

"I'm joking. Christ, why does nobody ever think I'm joking? She completely understood, she said she'd probably do the same, talk to you first, which by the way is totally unacceptable, so if she ever calls you, I expect you to tell me, instantly. Anyway, thanks darling, for keeping it, what did you call it?"

"Secret squirrel?"

She laughs. "Yes. Secret squirrel, I love that. We're back in a few days. Come over, I'll get Max to fix a time."

Bloody hell. So that'll be hordes of snappers parked at the gates again, and journalists wandering around too probably, trying to see if they can pick up any clues as to who the dad-to-be is. I bet one or two will come in here, to see if we've got any snippets. Christ, I'll have to practically gag Elsie. Not that she knows anything, but that doesn't usually stop her talking. I'll have to have a quiet word, and explain that less is definitely more on the trusted confidante front. Grace will drop us like a ton of hot bricks if we turn into blabbers. That might work. She loves boasting about our VIP connections. Still, I think I better buy some more custard creams, soften the ground a bit first.

"Shall we take our Pearl back to ours for lunch then, pet? Connie looks like she could sleep for England at the minute. Be a shame to wake her."

"Thanks Gran. I'll collect her on my way to get the boys from school. And Cinzia's fine to have the kids tomorrow so we can go shopping. I'll pick you and Betty up and we can get the last few things you need."

"Lovely. I think I might get a new bag for the evenings; the dinners are quite posh, you know."

"Okeydoke."

Beam me up, somebody. The endless planning of what they're going to wear on their cruise, and whether Betty wants a pair of shorts, has been driving me round the twist.

Connie's taken to coming round midmorning for a nap in the armchair. I've given her a key so she can let herself in whenever she fancies. I think she finds the combination of the chair and the lack of a busy pub and Mark fussing very relaxing.

"Right you are. Come on, poppet, let's get you into your buggy, your gran's got some bread for the ducks."

"Ducks."

Great, a peaceful hour or two at home is just what I need. I'll get some ironing done, the basket is getting beyond a joke now; in fact it's two baskets, in a teetering pile. I might even clean the bathroom.

"Jo."

"Yes Con? I thought you were asleep."

"Not really."

"Are you okay?"

"Yes. But I wanted to wait until your gran has gone. I don't want any fussing."

She looks pale.

"I think maybe, but it will be hours. I want to be calm."

Bloody hell.

"Okay. Are you having contractions yet?"

"No, just the little things."

"Okay."

She's sitting in the chair, but she's got that look, a mixture of relief that it's finally happening and a touch of panic. And there's something else, a kind of focus, like she's not quite here in the moment. She's starting to zone out. Oh God.

"Shall I ring Mark?"

"No. He will fuss. Not yet. Is that okay? If I stay here, in peace?"

"Of course it is. Do you need anything?"

"A glass of water?"

"Sure. Anything to eat? A sandwich? I can do you some toasted cheese and tomato if you like."

"Perfect."

Bloody hell. If Martin were here, he'd probably faint. There must be something about this house that makes pregnant women go into labor. I'm going to keep a very close eye on her, and if things start to speed up I'm calling Mark and an ambulance, and not necessarily in that order. The house is in a complete state, and there's no way I want anyone else giving birth here. It was bad enough when it was me, and I had a much better excuse then for the place being such a tip.

She's dozing when I carry the tray in.

"Thanks Jo. It is so quiet here. Mark, he is driving me crazy."

"He's just trying to take care of you, Con."

"I know, but I need to breathe."

Actually, breathing sounds like quite a good idea. She's not looking like she's Breathing yet, but she keeps zoning out. Mind you, that might just be tiredness.

"Just pretend I'm not here."

"Like I'm going to be able to pull that one off."

She laughs, but I know it's going to stress her out if I sit looking at her.

"I think I'll do the ironing, if you're sure."

She smiles, and looks sleepy.

Right, ironing it is then.

Christ, I've been standing here for ages; I've nearly finished all the ironing. If I rang Guinness World Records I could probably get a certificate for ironing while monitoring the onset of early labor. She's dozing again, and occasionally getting up for a little wander.

"Would you like a cup of tea?"

"I will make it."

"Great."

Oh God, this is starting to really get to me now; she seems very calm, which is good, because I'm pretty near to hysterics myself.

I follow her into the kitchen. If she's leaning over the fridge like I did when I had Pearl, I'm going to completely lose it.

She's fine.

"Tea?"

"Please, Con."

She smiles. "But maybe you."

She pauses.

"You carry the tray."

Okay, I see what she's doing now. She's breathing through the first few contractions, the little ones, the little ripples before the big waves start, and she thinks I don't realize what she's up to.

I give her what I hope is an encouraging smile.

"I'm onto you, Constanza Maxwell, so just you bear that in mind. And I'm going along with it. For now. But I'm watching you, and the minute things speed up, I'm on that phone, do you hear me? Deal?"

She smiles. "Deal."

Weirdly, I keep thinking about Nick as I potter about putting the ironing away. I put the phone and my mobile next to her on the table, just in case she fancies a chat with anyone, like a midwife possibly. But she ignores them and carries on dozing. Nick was so great when I had Jack and Archie, even when I shouted at him; he just stood there, for hours, and made me laugh and held my hand. I've never really thought about it before, but it's quite a tricky role to get right. Being too jovial would be annoying, but too tense and terrified-looking isn't that encouraging either. It's a pretty long haul usually, so it's hard to remember that something extraordinary is going on in among all the hanging about with nothing happening and people getting tired and irritable, something huge is happening. Something potentially life-threatening, and you need to be on high alert. Just in case.

"Is your back sore, Con?"

She nods.

"Lean forward a bit and I'll rub it for you if you like."

"Please."

She's completely bloody zoning out now.

"I think it's time for me to make some calls, sweetheart."

"A few more minutes."

She's holding my hand now, and she's not letting go.

"Okay, a few more minutes."

I reach for my mobile, still holding her hand, and dial Mark's number. I try to pass the phone to her, but she shakes her head.

"Hi Mark."

"Is she still asleep? Honestly, it's like living with Rip van Winkle at the moment."

"Not exactly. Maybe you should come round."

"You mean— Bloody hell, right, I'm on my way, tell her I'm on my way, the bag's in the car, I'll just—"

"Mark, she's fine, calm down, everything's fine, I promise. She's being very chilled out."

"Yeah, she does that, right before the serious stuff starts to happen."

Christ, I wish he hadn't told me that.

"I'm on my way."

"Okay."

She still won't let go of my hand.

"He's on his way, Con. Do you need anything?"

"Maybe, in a minute."

Bloody hell.

Mark arrives looking nervous, as well he might.

"Where is she?"

"Upstairs, in the bathroom. Go up, but she's fine."

God, I hope she's fine.

She starts walking down the stairs toward us, very slowly, smiling.

Mark gives her a hug.

"Right, let's get you in the car."

She ignores him and wanders back to the armchair.

Mark gives me a puzzled look.

"She's zoning out, it's a game she's playing, she's fine, just call the hospital and say we're on our way. The contractions are about every five minutes."

"Okay."

She's sitting in the armchair, with her eyes closed. Christ, maybe the only way we're going to get her to the hospital is if we can work out how to take the bloody chair too.

She's breathing harder now.

"Con."

She ignores me.

"Constanza, either we go or I'm calling your mother."

She takes my hand again. "No."

"Con. It's time."

"No, I will stay here and maybe I will sleep."

"Sure, we could try that. I'll just call the ambulance, in case the sleeping thing doesn't work out, shall I?"

She smiles, and I squeeze her hand.

"You're ready, sweetheart, you know you are."

"Will you come with me?"

"Of course I will."

I've already called Gran. Cinzia and Susanna can pick Nelly and Marco up from school, and Gran will have my three. Right. Off we go.

Mark drives to the hospital so quickly I've hardly had time to work out how to get my seat belt done up before I've got to undo it.

She wants to go for a walk.

"Walking is good."

"Yes, but let's get in, Con, and let them have a look at you, and then we can go for a bloody walk, all right?"

She ignores me and takes my hand again. "Jo."

"Yes love."

"Walk with me."

At least we're near a hospital if anything involving the word *delivery* starts to happen. But I wish she'd just go inside.

We walk toward a patch of grass with a few rather straggly looking bushes.

"It doesn't feel. It's not like it was with Marco and An-tonella."

She looks frightened, for the first time.

"The midwife said everything was fine at your last appointment, didn't she? It'll be fine, Con."

"Yes. But if . . ."

"If?"

"You will stay, yes?"

"Of course."

"And you will help Mark if . . ."

"Stop it right now. There's no if."

"Yes, but."

"Of course I will. Now stop it, or we'll both be in tears. It's going to be fine. You finally get to meet the baby today, and it's all going to be wonderful, okay?"

We pause, so she can breathe. Her hand is definitely clenching mine now. Christ. It's crucial we get inside soon, so someone else can lose the use of their fingers. I wish she'd let her mum come over.

"I'm sorry I can't speak Italian, Con, I really am."

She smiles.

"But porca bloody Madonna, yes?"

She nods.

Once we're in a room and the midwife has had a look and said she's already at seven centimeters and doing brilliantly, things calm down for a bit. We all listen to the baby's heartbeat. It sounds fast, like they always do; there's something disconcerting about it, even when you know it's exactly how it's meant to sound. Christ, this is really getting to me. I think I'm better at being the one giving birth than the one standing by trying to be supportive. There's a large pale green rubber birthing ball, which Connie takes an instant dislike to, so Mark sits on it, holding her hand and chatting, while I go off in search of coffee. I want to give them some peace, so I sit in the canteen, staring into space.

An exhausted-looking woman walks toward my table. "Is it all right if I sit here?"

"Sure."

The canteen is pretty busy, but in a hushed hospital sort of way, with quite a few people sitting with just a hot drink, looking vacant.

"My daughter's just had a baby."

"Has she? How lovely."

She smiles, but looks terribly sad at the same time. Oh, God.

"My first grandchild. They said he's holding his own."

She looks at me, and I can see the worry, and the fear.

"He's so tiny."

Christ, I don't know what to say.

We sit in silence. And I can't think of a bloody thing to say. I'm close to tears now, and that's the last thing she needs.

She puts her cup down. "He's in the special care unit."

I put my hand on hers.

"They can do amazing things now."

She nods. "I know, love. But he's so tiny. He's a fighter though. One of the nurses said that. He's fighting."

Oh God. I wonder if they ever say anything else. I wonder if they start letting you down gently, preparing you. If they ever say he's fighting as hard as he can, but he can't win, the odds are just too high for him. I wonder if they ever know, or if it's always totally heartbreakingly random.

She looks at her bag.

"I got him a teddy, but it's too big. I can't give him a teddy

that's as big as he is, can I? One of the nurses said I can give it
to him later, when we get him home. Do you think?"

"That sounds like a lovely idea."

We sit in silence again.

"I better go. My friend's having a baby, I should get back
to her."

"Good luck, love."

"Thanks. And to you."

She nods. And looks worried again.

Fucking hell.

I find a loo, and sit in a cubicle, having a silent weep,
blowing my nose and trying to pull myself together. I'm
washing my hands when the tears start again, and I can't
seem to stop. This is ridiculous. But that poor woman, and
her daughter, somewhere, sitting by a plastic incubator.
Hoping.

Right. I've got to stop this; a nice, relaxed, smiling person is
what Connie needs, not some pink-eyed woman sniffing.
She'll think something is up, that they've told me something
about the baby. But still. What I really want to do is race home
and cuddle the kids, and thank my lucky stars.

Connie and Mark are still holding hands when I get back,
but something's changed. She wants to stand, leaning over
the bed. She's talking, and breathing, and seems fine, but I
know things have changed.

And then I realize she's standing in exactly the same position as I was when I had Pearl. Exactly. Christ.

"Mark."

"Yes?"

"I think it might be good to press that buzzer. I think we might need the midwife back."

Connie gives me a look, and smiles. "Yes."

She's using the gas and air nearly all the time now. Mark's rubbing her back, and tucking her hair behind her ears when it falls forward. Which I think is starting to annoy her.

I'm guessing we are now in what the books like to call transition. Where anyone within a five-mile radius is likely to get an earful.

"Stop. It."

The midwife comes in, and suddenly there's a flurry of staff in white plastic aprons, wheeling in a crib and opening packs of sterile sheets and spreading them on the bed.

The midwife is trying to get her onto the bed, and I can see she's annoying Connie. She ignores her, and shrugs her off when she tries to get her to lie down.

Mark's looking panicky. "Why don't you try it, love, just get on the bed and see if—"

She shoves him. Very hard. It's a miracle he stays upright really.

Oh dear.

She's shouting, in Italian now, and I'm guessing these are the kinds of phrases you don't find in the average phrase book.

"Stay where you are, Connie, if that's what feels best. I'm sure the midwife can cope, can't you?" I'm doing my best to look firm. The midwife has been pretty useless really, just appearing and disappearing and not really taking the time to talk to Connie at all. But if Bob and Dave could cope with me standing by my fridge with a grubby kitchen floor, then surely it can't be that difficult for her to help Connie give birth in whatever position feels right for her.

The midwife gives me a cross look but stops hassling Connie and kneels down.

"Keep going. Can you move your foot a bit please?"

Christ, it better not be much longer.

"You're doing so brilliantly, Connie; you're just amazing, well done, keep going, keep breathing. Nearly there, sweetheart."

The midwife gives me another frosty look, and I give her one back.

"Yes, you're doing very well. Keep going."

Connie's gripping my arm now. Bloody hell.

"I can't."

She stops as another contraction hits her.

"I can't."

"I know, Con, but you're doing so brilliantly, and you can, you're amazing, just hang on. And breathe."

Another midwife joins us, and this one's older, and much nicer.

"Look at you, you clever girl. Thought you'd just get on with it, did you, my lovely? That's it, now pant, can you pant for me? There you go, perfect, you're nearly there."

Pant? Oh, God, if we're doing panting, we really are nearly there. Please let everything be all right. Please.

She's making those elemental noises now, the ones you never hear in normal life. The kinds of noises you make when you're in the midst of something extraordinary, or something terrible. Or both.

———

And then suddenly, she's not. And there's a baby. We're all in tears, and the midwife passes the baby to her, wrapped up tight in a green sheet.

Connie's lying down now, finally, and she smiles at Mark, one of those deep-down everything-in-my-entire-world-is-perfect kinds of smiles, which you only do when it's all over.

"A boy."

"Yes, and he's so beautiful, my darling, so beautiful, just like you."

And he is. With lots of dark hair, and those deep navy blue newborn eyes that are locked on to his mother, like he's checking her out, seeing what he's won in the lottery of being born. He's been very lucky, not that he knows it yet.

"I want to talk to Marco, and Antonella, to tell them."

He smiles. "I'll get my phone, is that all right?"

The midwife nods. "Fine, my love, and then let's get this woman a cup of tea, shall we?"

"Gran."

"Yes pet, is she all right?"

"Yes, she's had a boy, and he's beautiful."

"Well thank heavens for that. I've been on tenterhooks all afternoon. And they're both okay, are they?"

"Yes, she's tired, but she did brilliantly, and he's gorgeous."

"I should think she is. I'll never forget how tired you looked after our Pearl, I've never seen anyone that pale. I'll send Reg to get you, pet, and tell her well done from me, and I can't wait to meet him."

"It was amazing, Gran."

"Was it? Well, come home and tell me all about it. I'll put some soup on, I bet you haven't eaten."

"Are the kids still up?"

"Yes, and they've been as good as gold. They're sitting watching a film, our Pearl's half asleep, but I tried taking her up earlier and she created merry hell, so I thought I'd leave her a bit longer."

"That's perfect, I want to see them. I'll do bedtime when I get home. I need a cuddle first."

Somehow I think we might all end up in my bed tonight. And then we'll go cruisewear shopping tomorrow, and normal life will carry on. But for tonight, I just want to be home, with all three of them within arm's reach.

· · · 6 · · ·

We Do Like to Be
Beside the Seaside

July and August

'm in the shop on Monday morning when Ellen calls.

"How's Connie? Has she decided on the name?"

"She's fine, and yes, definitely Maximo Luca. Maximo because he weighed nearly nine pounds, which is more than Marco or Nelly were, and then Luca after her favorite uncle, the one who brought our coffee machine over for the café. Her mum's making her have a sleep every afternoon, so she's not too tired; actually, she looks better than she's done for weeks."

"Christ, I wish someone would do that for me."

"Me too."

"Anything else happening on the baby front, apart from Vin and Lulu thinking about taking the plunge?"

"No, Connie will be at the Summer Fayre this weekend, so you'll get to see the baby then."

"Great. So no more locals going in for sprogs?"

"Not unless you mean Mrs. Chapman, but you haven't

met her, have you? And Tina thinks one of the women in the baker's—"

"No, you idiot. But I've met Grace bloody Harrison, haven't I?"

"Oh."

"Yes. Oh indeed. How long have you known?"

"Known what?"

She's laughing. "Don't play that game with me, darling. I know you're meant to be discreet, but that's not supposed to include me."

"I think Maxine might disagree with you on that one."

"Well, don't tell her then. Look, I need details, boy or girl, who's the daddy, that kind of thing."

"No idea."

"And if you did?"

"No idea."

"Well stand by for a bumpy day, darling. All the tabloids will be in to ask you for snippets; you're the closest anyone is going to get to Amazing Grace for the next few days. They'll want to see what they can get out of you."

"Christ."

"What?"

"I better launch Operation Custard Cream with Elsie."

She laughs. "You've got a couple of hours; the news has only just gone out. And good luck, because you're going to need it. Serves you right for not telling me. Now, on to my specialist subject, Me. Because I need to find a new producer on top of everything else."

"What happened to Scott?"

"I fired him. He was driving me crazy, always standing about looking terrified. I need a grown-up, who can stand up to me."

"Is Attila the Hun looking for work in telly then?"

"Piss off, I'm not that bad."

"Didn't that woman in Human Resources say they've got a special file for complaints about you?"

"Yes, but that was before I got my own series; they probably need a whole bloody filing cabinet now. I just have high standards, that's all. I don't fire people who fuck up, I fire people who fuck up and try to make it my fault. So do you fancy a new job?"

"Never in a million years."

"We'd have such fun, darling, and you were a brilliant producer."

"Several lifetimes ago, maybe, and why would I want to get fired by my best friend? What would I do with the kids, leave them down here and see them once a fortnight?"

"Works for the boys, darling. Tom Parker hasn't seen his toddler for months now. I saw him at a drinks thing last night, just back from another trip following up leads, and not all of them suitable for broadcast, I can tell you, and he said when he got home the kid went into hysterics, thought he was a burglar. His wife's going nuts."

"I don't blame her."

"No darling, she's going all Perfect Mother on him, making her own muesli, all that bollocks. And the kid's a total nightmare, allergic to everything under the sun, including the sun, and highly neurotic. He screams so much he nearly passes out apparently. Mind you, she was always a bit highly strung, and now she's convinced he's cheating on her."

"And is he?"

"Not yet, but he will be soon, if she doesn't pull herself together."

"Ellen, that's awful. Why is it always the woman who has to pull herself together?"

"Because if she doesn't, he will. Anyway, she's always been a total cow, that's why. Gorgeous Georgia, my arse."

"Is she the one?"

"Yes. So serves her right."

"Oh, well, that's different. Definitely serves her right."

We're both cackling now; Georgia once nicked a man from Ellen in a most unladylike fashion, at a party; lots of tequila and a very short dress were involved.

"So if you won't be my next producer, will you do some of these interviews with me? The Wonders of Knitting, Me and My Woolly Friends, we've had stacks of requests. And I need to do some more publicity for the series; the figures are dropping, like they always do after a launch, but it's making the boys upstairs nervous, wankers."

"I'm not sure, Ellen. It was bad enough last time, and that was you doing the interview. God knows what I'd be like with someone I don't know."

"Yes, but it'll just be print stuff, not telly; there'll be no danger of you sliding off your chair onto the floor. I do loads of the glam stuff all the bloody time, but this needs to be more me and my normal life, so my audience can bond with me. Knitting for my boy. It's perfect. Anyway, I've already said you'll do it, so you may as well get the benefit for the shop. It won't take long, and we can have the afternoon to ourselves, maybe fit in a nice shopping session."

"I hate shopping, Ellen."

"I know, darling, but you need some new clothes."

"You sound like my mother."

"No, I mean you need a treat, some new stuff you fancy,

and we can check out wool shops if you like, I know you love doing that."

"Actually, that might be good. There's a couple of new shops I'd like to see. If they've got anything good we can do our own version, but for half the price."

"Okay, a couple of wool shops, and then shoes, great. I'll tell Amy to organize it."

"Who's Amy?"

"My new producer. But I would have fired her if you were up for it."

"I believe you. Thousands wouldn't."

"Any more texts from your gran?"

"Yes, they're having a brilliant time; Betty's still flirting with all the crew, even though Gran says most of them are young enough to be her grandsons, and Gran's learning how to sculpt, while Reg learns Hawaiian dancing."

"Bless."

"I know, but they haven't got to Venice yet, so Mum will soon put a stop to all that. Look, I better go; I should probably be having a word with Elsie in case any press turn up. I'm still not sure they'll bother coming all the way down here, you know."

"Trust me, they will. Good luck with the custard creams, darling."

"Thanks."

Elsie's thrilled that we might be having another round of attention from the press. What with the television interview, and now the breaking news about Grace having a baby, she's clearly finding it all completely thrilling. Which is slightly worrying.

"Yes, but it's really important we don't say anything, Elsie, otherwise they can twist it; we just need to say we know nothing, and would they like to buy some wool? Otherwise we'll have to ask them to leave the shop, okay?"

"Of course dear. I know what they're like, those papers, terrible some of them."

She buys most of them on a regular basis, so she should know. But I'm still not sure she really gets it. She's tapping her foot and looking excited, and that's probably not a good sign on the calm, no-comment front.

"If we get this wrong, Grace will drop us, very quickly, and everyone will think we tried to trade on her name, which would be awful."

"She knows she can trust us. We've been to her house and everything."

"Yes, but we won't mention that, will we? Or they'll ask all sorts of questions, which we don't want to answer, unless we want to read them in quotes, with whatever rubbish they want to say sandwiched in between so it looks like we've given them an interview. Seriously, Elsie, we do need to get this right if anyone does turn up, which they may not. We'll have to wait and see."

A large van pulls up outside. Christ, surely they can't have got here already. A man staggers in carrying a large wooden crate, filled with pots of summer flowers: daisies, geraniums, marigolds, and tall ones with pretty bell-shaped flowers, like mini-delphiniums. There's also a small brown velvet squirrel, nestled in among the flowers. I sign the delivery note, and the man goes back to his van, whistling, while Elsie stands watching, agog with excitement.

"There's a card."

"So there is."

Thought you might like another squirrel to add to your secret collection. G.

"Is that from her? Isn't that lovely? Do you like squirrels then, dear? I didn't know that."

"No, it's just a little joke."

She looks at me, wanting details.

"Pearl saw the one that Lily's got, and she tried to take it home, that's all."

I'm very pleased with myself for this bit of quick thinking. Perhaps I'm not so completely out of practice at batting back questions as I thought. I used to have to do it all the time when I worked in news. I bloody hope so, because I think I'm going to need to be on top form in the next few hours if Ellen's predictions are right.

"Isn't that nice? Shall we have a tidy-up then? We should take this lovely box up to the office; don't want anyone seeing it and asking questions, do we? You can plant them all out in your garden, dear; they'll look lovely. I'll just give the counter a polish. If we've got the press in, we want it looking nice, don't we?"

"Thanks Elsie."

Bloody hell. Double bloody hell actually, we've just got rid of the woman from the local paper when another one arrives, from a Kent paper I've never heard of, and I'm on the phone to someone else asking for a quote. I'm giving him the lines Maxine told me to say when I rang her to thank her for the flowers. We're delighted at such happy news but have no further information. In other words, we have no snippets, now bugger off.

"So last time you saw her, how was she?"

"Thanks so much for calling."

"I could come down and do a piece on your shop; we'd pay you for your time, and put a link to your website in the paper, which would be great for your business."

"That's very kind, but no thanks."

"I might be able to get my editor to agree to—"

"Look, thanks for calling, but I really need to go now."

I press the call waiting button on the phone; it's so much easier to end a call by pressing a button rather than actually putting the phone down. You feel more like a busy person and less like someone just being rude.

Elsie's talking to a young man who has just come in.

"We never discuss our customers, confidentiality is very important to us."

"In a wool shop?"

"Yes, dear, this is a wool shop, I'm glad you noticed. So if you're not going to be buying anything, I shall have to ask you to leave. I can't have you annoying my regular customers."

Elsie escorts him to the door. He seems rather surprised to be ejected from a wool shop so firmly by a middle-aged woman wearing such a tragic cardigan.

"Well done, Elsie, that was great."

"I wish your gran was here, and Betty; they'd have loved all this, wouldn't they? We could text them, you know, on your phone. Jeffrey was showing me how to do it on his new one, after that stupid dog broke his old one. You can send all sorts, you know, pictures and everything, and Reg has got a proper mobile phone, hasn't he, I know your gran never got one."

"Yes, I think so. Maybe later, Elsie."

Poor Reg. I think he might be getting a fair few texts from Elsie over the next few days.

The mums are starting to arrive for their group, and Elsie helps Helena upstairs with Dylan's buggy. The phone rings again, and I repeat the same drill as a young woman I haven't seen before comes in. Elsie comes back down and keeps a close eye on her while I answer the phone again. God, this is getting annoying.

"Aren't they terrible? Why can't they just leave her alone? It's nobody's business but hers, is it?"

The young woman has come up to the counter with an armful of balls of wool and is smiling at Elsie. "It must be so awful, having them all descending on her like that. But it must help having people like you, people she can trust. How much is this, it's such a pretty color."

I can see Elsie is falling for this routine and is about five seconds away from getting her album out. I step forward, slightly blocking Elsie's way.

"Six pounds ninety-five, and it knits up beautifully."

"Does it? How many balls would I need to make this gorgeous shawl?"

"About ten."

Actually the pattern only takes six, but since I'm pretty sure this will be going on expenses and she's got no intention of casting on a single stitch, I don't really care.

"I love all the colors."

I smile at her, but I didn't work in television news for so long without being able to spot other journalists on a story; she must think I'm a total idiot. She's scruffy, but in an expensive way, and she's got the look, there's a steeliness to her eyes. I'm sure she thinks she's being very clever, dressing down and dealing with the locals, but she'd stitch you up like a kipper in ten seconds.

She smiles back at me. "You seem very familiar, have I seen you on the telly or something?"

Bingo. I knew it.

"I don't think so."

"Is this hard to make?"

"Not really."

The pattern is fairly tricky, but since she's not going to be knitting, it won't matter.

"You've got such a lovely café, I might treat myself."

She's doing lots of smiling, but the smiles don't reach her eyes.

"Will you want needles?"

"Sorry?"

"To knit with?"

"Oh yes, of course. Great."

I put the needles into the bag.

"That'll be seventy-eight forty-eight please."

She hands her card over and taps in her number.

"Thank you, here's your receipt, I hope you enjoy your knitting."

"Thank you, I'm sure I will. I don't suppose you see her very often, do you?"

"Sorry, who?"

She's getting annoyed now. "Grace Harrison."

"No, hardly ever."

"Her little girl looked lovely, in those pictures. What's her name again?"

Elsie stiffens; I think she's finally worked out what's going on.

"Thanks again for coming in, but we must get on."

"I think it was Lily. She looked so sweet, she had a little cardigan on, I remember thinking how gorgeous it was. I bet Grace made it for her. If you've got the pattern, I'd buy that too, and the wool, my niece would love it. I could buy loads of stuff, if you'd like to make some suggestions?"

Actually, sod this. I've had enough.

"Which paper do you work for?"

"What?"

"I just wondered."

She glares at me. It's quite scary actually.

"All that stuff on the telly, about you being friends, that was all fake, was it? I might write my piece on that, how you were lying and she doesn't know you, just another wannabe. Or you could tell me your side of the story."

"There's no story, no side. We're delighted with the happy news. But aren't you supposed to say your name and the name of the newspaper you work for, if you're asking for a quote?"

"Fuck off."

That'll definitely be one of the tabloids then.

"I don't think you know her at all, and that's what I'm going to write. You'll seriously wish you'd given me a quote. I'll make you a laughingstock."

"Good luck with that."

She hesitates. "Good luck with what?"

"Writing a libelous piece. I think Ms. Harrison's lawyers are pretty fierce, aren't they? And so are mine. My friend Ellen Malone has sorted me out with some firm in London. Always suing the papers for a fortune. So you go for it. Only do it from outside my shop, would you?"

She slams the door as hard as she can as she goes out, and one of the teddy bears falls off the shelf in the window.

Charming.

———

"$\bigcirc$ood heavens."

Elsie's very shocked. Actually, I'm a bit wobbly too. It's years since I've had to deal with people like her. I'd forgotten how stroppy they get when they don't find what they want; they seem to think the whole world is just waiting for them to write their grubby little pieces.

"How did you know, dear?"

"She was far too pleased with herself, that kind of journalist always is, they think they're superior to the rest of us. The good ones are much cleverer than that though, or busy writing real stories. This isn't that big a deal or they'd have sent someone senior. Not unless the dad turns out to be someone interesting."

"And *is* he someone interesting, dear? I mean, of course, don't say if you—"

"Elsie, if I knew, I wouldn't tell you, and I don't. Can't you see how it's better not to know? Even if you do."

"Yes, I suppose I can. Well, I call that shocking, coming in here and lying like that. She was like butter wouldn't melt, and all the time— Well, just think, if we'd said anything, Lord alone knows what she would have written. I'm so glad I didn't show her my album now."

So am I.

"I think I'll go upstairs now, if you're sure you can cope for a bit."

"Of course dear. They'll be back outside on the pavement very sharpish if any more of them come in."

I think she's got it now.

"Thanks Elsie."

Great. So far, so good on Operation Custard Cream. I'll

call Max and report in later, but I think we've handled it fairly well so far and nobody will be demanding their squirrel back. Christ.

C lare and Nicky are full of the news about Grace.

"I think it's lovely. Tell her, Jo, if she wants to join our group, we'd love to see her."

"Thanks Clare, I will."

She grins. "We can hold the baby for her, while she gets on with her knitting. Although she probably has staff for things like that, doesn't she?"

We all agree that having a full complement of domestic staff would make our lives a great deal better, and Nicky says her mum comes round once a week, at half past seven in the morning so she can have a lie-in, and we all decide she deserves a Top Mother of the Year award and if someone doesn't give her one we'll knit one for her. Be far more useful than a badge with "Get a Life" on it. Helena is slightly irritated by all the talk about Grace and tries to move on to a conversation about the wonders of having a compost heap, but then Dylan gets bored and starts yelling.

"I better go. He's finding group activities rather challenging at the moment."

Clare and Nicky exchange amused glances.

"I'll take the buggy down for you, Helena."

"Thanks Jo."

"Anyone want more cake while I'm downstairs?"

There's a chorus of "Yes please," including what sounds like a yes from baby Ava.

Clare smiles, looking very proud. "She loves cake."

Great. That's another new customer sorted then, and

hopefully with better language skills than the last one who I've just thrown out of the shop. You win some, you lose some, I suppose. And to be honest, Ava is much more my kind of girl.

t's Saturday morning, and we're officially launching Martin's boat.

"I name this boat the *Broadgate Belle*."

Everyone claps as Harry sprays Martin with fizzy apple juice. Elsie stands well back. She's worn her best navy suit, with a hat, and she's loved doing the Regal thing naming the boat; it's all we've heard about, for days.

We're standing on the dockside in the harbor, and Martin's strung bunting up and polished everything so the whole boat looks gleaming in the sunshine. Elsie's made new blue and white striped cushions for inside the little cabin, and new curtains in the same material, and Martin's looking very pleased with himself, wearing the new captain's hat I bought for him as a joke. Even Trevor's behaving himself, looking every inch the nautical dog, with a blue and white spotted scarf tied round his neck.

"Right, come on, Mum, let's get you onboard."

He holds out a hand, and Elsie steps across.

"Are you sure you'll be all right, Ellen?"

The thought of Pearl and Fast Eddie on the deck of a small boat is too much for all of us, so Ellen and Harry are taking them for a tour round the shops.

"Of course. Pearl, sweetheart, do you want to come with your aunty Ellen and see if we can find some ice cream?"

Pearl claps her hands. "More."

"Thanks Ellen, we'll see you later. Come on, boys, and hold Martin's hand."

"I've got the lifeboat on speed dial, darling."

"Very funny."

t's lovely chugging round the bay on a dead calm day. It's warm in the sunshine, and Martin's letting the boys have a go at steering, while Elsie and I sit watching.

"So what do you think, Mum?"

"It's very nice, Martin, and you've made a proper job of it, I'll say that for you. The boys look very smart in their life jackets. Sensible of you, to think of that."

Actually, that was me, but never mind. I'm putting more sunscreen on Archie while Martin tries to fend off a rather persistent wasp. In fact, there've been quite a few wasps buzzing round him since we left the dock.

"You don't normally get wasps at sea, do you, Martin?"

"No, not usually."

He's waving his arms about, which is making Trevor bark.

"Maybe it's all that apple juice you're wearing?"

"Well, I wish they'd bloody pack it in."

Archie's thrilled. "Martin said bloody."

"I know, Archie, he's very naughty. Let's have a mutiny and make him walk the plank."

Martin laughs, and even Elsie's smiling.

"There's no need for language, Martin. I've got some wipes in my bag; here, use one of these."

I wonder how old your son has to be before you can stop carrying wet wipes in your handbag; if Elsie's anything to go by, it looks like I've got a few years yet.

"Thanks Mum. And nobody is going to make me walk the plank on my boat, thanks very much."

"Don't you be so sure, my boy. If anyone can it's our Jo;

you should have seen her with that horrible woman from the papers."

Elsie's still telling everyone about the journalist in the shop, even if they've heard the story before, quite a few times. She didn't write anything in the end; none of them did really, apart from a few wool-shop-owner-delighted lines in the local paper. Maxine was very impressed.

Martin grins. "I know, Mum, she's a marvel. How was Grace when you saw her, Jo? There were still quite a few photographers parked outside when I drove past last night."

"Very happy, and they're doing something this weekend, I think, so they'll all get their pictures and then they'll leave her alone. Oh, and that reminds me, Elsie, we'll need to get a move on with that order, for the Italian silk and cashmere, because she's off soon, for a couple of weeks in France, I think, or maybe Italy, she hasn't decided yet. Anyway, she wants to take some knitting with her, she's really getting into it again. We'll have to call that company in Milan again."

"I'll call them first thing on Monday. Will your Cinzia be around, so she can do the talking?"

"Yes, she should be, good plan."

"Can't it go any faster, Martin?"

"No Arch, it's not a speedboat, it's a fishing boat."

"Can we come fishing with you, later?"

Martin is taking his dad and Harry fishing this evening, but I'd quite like to see how he manages the boat on longer trips before he takes the boys out. Heading out to sea in the dark is a bit different from a tour of Broadgate Bay when it's dead flat and sunny.

"No Archie, he can't. Not tonight, but soon, okay? Does anyone want a drink?"

Elsie stands up. "I'll make us a cup of tea. I've brought

fresh milk in my thermos, and there's water in the kitchen-ette, isn't there, Martin?"

"Yes Mum, and it's a galley."

"I won't be a minute." She goes into the cabin, humming.

"She's loving that galley, Martin."

"I know. She's even given me a special washing-up brush, and I haven't even got one of those at the barn."

"You haven't really got a sink yet though, have you?"

"True, but that old tin bath is brilliant; it's multipurpose. I even gave Trevor a bath in it last night. And I'll be starting on the kitchen soon, now the boat is sorted."

"Well, it is lovely, the boat, and she's right, you've done a great job. I'll knit you a proper fisherman's sweater if you like. I was looking in one of my books, and they used to make them with special family designs on, so they could recognize them if— Well, never mind. But they looked very nice."

He laughs. "Recognize the body if they got washed over-board. Lovely. For God's sake, don't tell Mum."

"I could knit you one with a message of my very own."

"Like?"

"I told him not to get a boat."

"Oh ye of little faith."

He leans forward and kisses me, and Archie makes pretending-to-be-sick noises. "Yuck."

"Sorry, Arch."

He grins. "It's okay; everyone has to do kissing sometimes."

Jack shakes his head. "No they don't. I'm never going to. And that's final."

They have a mini-duel with their fishing nets until I threaten to snap any bamboo poles that are wielded in anger.

"Would you like a biscuit?"

"Yes please, Elsie."

"I've got custard creams, and there's Ribena for the boys. I got those little cartons they like."

Perfect. And we've still got the Summer Fayre at school to look forward to; there might be a cake I can buy for tea, one of Mrs. Pickering's coffee cakes, if Jane Johnson has remembered to put one aside for me. Even more perfect.

The Summer Fayre is heaving by the time we arrive, and everyone's having a marvelous time, particularly Annabel Morgan, marching round with her clipboard, barking out orders, in a floral outfit with matching hat that makes her look like she's in the Royal Enclosure at Ascot rather than a school playground. Ellen wins a plastic duck in the tombola, which Eddie loves, particularly the squeak, and the Auction of Promises goes particularly well. Mrs. Peterson bids a hundred pounds for the flag knitting kit that I donated, and Cath bids seventy-five pounds for one of Mark's cakes.

"She was trying to get me to put you in the auction, so watch yourself."

Ellen laughs. "Bloody cheek. I'm not reduced to renting by the hour, not yet anyway."

Harry grins. "What was she meant to be doing, if you bid for her?"

"God knows."

"Well, I'd have put in a bid, my darling. Just to see the look on your face would have been worth a hundred quid of anyone's money."

She pushes him, and he laughs.

"I could have put in a bid to stop you doing that for a start."

"Hang on, look out, here she comes."

Ellen has been attracting the usual amount of sideways looks and nudging, and a few people have told her how much they love her new series. But Annabel hasn't formally greeted us yet, although I knew it was only a matter of time.

"Good afternoon, I'm Annabel Morgan, President of the PTA; I just wanted to welcome you to our little school. I do wish I'd known you were available this afternoon"—she pauses, to give me a furious look—"I would have asked you to perform our opening ceremony. We're all enjoying your new series, so super."

Ellen gives her one of her Britain's Favorite Broadcaster smiles.

"People do seem to like it. Nice to have met you, Mirabelle. Come on, Jo, you promised to show me that banner you knitted with the kids."

It's times like these when I remember why I love Ellen so much.

"So that'll be Mirabelle giving me the evil eye again on Monday."

Ellen laughs. "Just tell her to bugger off. Women like her are terrible bullies, but they always back right off if you stand up to them. It's the ones like Connie or Tina, or that other one?"

"Linda?"

"Yes, they're the ones you have to watch out for. They stand their ground, if it's something they believe in, and nothing gets past them if they've made their minds up."

"That's true."

"I know, darling, I'm a very clever woman."

Harry snorts, and she pushes him, again.

"Shame I didn't get that bid in while I had the chance."

———

W e find Connie, and Ellen cuddles Maximo, who's attracting a fair amount of attention too, so there's a slight lull
in the hubbub as people watch Ellen and the Baby. Someone
even takes a photo, which I think is a bit much until I realize
it's Tina.

"That's a lovely one. I'll get you a copy, Connie, and Jo.
Shall I do an extra one for you too, Ellen?"

"Please darling."

"I love your series by the way, I just wanted to say that. I
record it so I can watch it when I get in from the salon, and
your hair always looks so lovely. Can I ask you a question, do
you mind?"

"Sure."

"Is that Steve Sumner as gorgeous as he looks?"

"More."

Tina's thrilled. "I knew it, I've always liked him, ever since
I was a teenager. I've got all his records, but some of them go
all seedy, don't they? All leather trousers and girls half their
age, but he seems to get better and better."

Ellen smiles. "Definitely, darling, and he smells divine too,
sort of lemony and cedar, expensive but not over the top.
When he kisses you, it's very hard not to swoon."

Harry puts his arm around her. "Hello? When did he kiss
you then?"

Tina laughs. "Well, if you need a—what do they call
them?—a stunt double, for any of the kissing, make sure you
let me know. Isn't the baby getting big, Connie? He's grown
loads since you brought him into the salon, you must be feeding him nonstop. He's a happy little thing, isn't he? Look at
him smiling."

Connie nods and mutters something in Italian. "He is happy today, but the afternoons he is usually grumpy."

A seething throng of parents and mixed infants is clearly diverting his attention.

"Never mind, love, they don't stay tiny for long."

"No, and if we can do this every day please, my afternoons will be much better."

"What, two hundred people with music and balloons?"

She smiles. "Perfect."

'm sitting in the kitchen with Ellen, with all the kids finally asleep, even Eddie, who slept so much this afternoon he's been wide awake this evening. It's half past eleven, and we're opening our second bottle of wine.

"Shouldn't they be back by now? They went off bloody hours ago."

"I'm sure they're fine, Ellen."

"Maybe we should go down to the harbor, wear our shawls, do the whole fishwife thing?"

"They'll be back soon. And anyway, we can't leave the kids."

We've nearly finished the bottle when I hear the front gate open.

"Talk of the devil."

Harry comes into the kitchen and kisses Ellen. "Sorry we're late, the engine stalled."

Martin and Jeffrey are both looking rather sheepish.

"Who wants a drink? We've drunk most of the wine, but there's tea."

Martin grins. "Have you got any brandy?"

"No. There's vodka."

Jeffrey sits down. "Tea for me, please. Your mother's going to be bad enough as it is without me going home smelling of drink."

Martin nods as I put the kettle on.

"Sorry it took us so long, Jo, only the engine stalled, and I didn't want us to call the coast guard, so we used Harry's special intercontinental phone and got a tow back. I'll have to get one of those phones, Harry. Mine doesn't get a signal in the harbor, let alone out to sea."

"So who towed you back in then?"

"Ted Mallow, when we finally got hold of him. It took a while because he doesn't answer his phone; you have to leave a message and then he calls you back. I don't know why he screens all his calls."

Jeffrey smiles. "Sending a Valentine to Betty would be a good enough reason for me. He's probably regretting it and is trying to go into hiding."

Harry laughs. "We should have brought your dog, Martin; we could have chucked him in, got him to swim back to shore. How far out were we?"

"About four miles."

"Maybe not then."

"I think water got into the engine."

Ellen laughs. "Isn't that something they're meant to cope with then, engines on boats, a bit of water? Doesn't that sort of go with the territory?"

"Technically, yes. I'll need to strip it down again, see whether the casing has got cracked."

Harry nods. "Either that or train that dog up for endurance swimming."

———

B y the time Martin and Jeffrey leave, it's ten past one, and we've had to almost physically restrain Ellen from dealing out the cards for a round of strip poker. Jeffrey's still chuckling as he gets into Martin's car, although I think Elsie might take care of any vestiges of amusement as soon as he gets home.

I 'm lying in bed trying to get to sleep, and failing. It's all very well them coming home like it's been a great lark, but being adrift in the dark isn't ideal, especially not so close to bloody Dover and the busiest shipping lanes in Europe. I'm trying to make a list in my head of all the things I've got to do next week, which is my version of counting sheep, but it's not working, so I may as well go downstairs and make some tea and write a proper list. Then maybe I can get past my visions of having to identify Martin by his anorak and get some bloody sleep.

"Mum."

"Yes Jack?"

"I had my dream again, the one where I'm in a boat and it's sinking and I can't find you."

"All right, snuggle in, but be quiet. Pearl's in the travel cot, and if you wake her up you can go back to your bed and take her with you."

He giggles, quietly.

"Night Mum."

"Night love."

Great. Bang goes my cup of tea. Bloody boats.

———————

'm in the shop on Monday morning, and it's already hot; the
weather's definitely turned into proper summer now, all clear
blue skies and gentle sea breezes. I'm putting the knitted
Teddy Bears' Picnic on one of the shelves in the window,
complete with the little picnic hamper which Betty made for
me. She loves knitting miniature accoutrements for the windows; she's even knitted a tiny white tablecloth for the picnic.
I've put another cotton beach bag in pretty pastel stripes on
the shelf above, with one of our flag kits, and I've already arranged the rocks at the side of the window, and put in the
bathing scene with the jolly Beryl Cook ladies and the little
bathing huts. And I've knitted a small orange seahorse,
which I've attached to the blue net in the window. I've always
been rather fond of seahorses, they look so jolly, and they're
the only animals on earth where the males have the babies,
and that definitely deserves a place of honor in the window in
my opinion.

I want to freshen up the window before the official judging for the Best Seaside Town (Small) later on; the judges came
down for their unofficial tour a couple of weeks ago. Lady
Denby's got us all on full alert, and poor Mrs. Cox backed her
Volvo into Mr. Dawes's new van yesterday, trying to get two
tubs of emergency petunias down to the pier. So it's all been
rather fraught.

Cinzia's on the phone, haranguing the Italian silk supplier
again, while Pearl "helps" me before they go off for a walk.
Great. Now Lady Denby has turned up, with those daft dogs.
I think we better go outside, before she tries to bring them in
with her again.

Pearl toddles over and starts patting the dogs.

Lady Denby fixes her with a Look. "Is she one of yours?"

"Yes, Lady Denby."

I'm feeling like a scullery maid again. I'll be bobbing a quick curtsy if I'm not careful.

"Used to be the same at her age, spent half my life in the kennels. Nice-looking child."

I smile.

"Well, can't stop chatting. All ready for the off?"

"Yes, we've reserved the table in the window."

"Excellent. Give them some of your cakes, that should do the trick."

She gently disentangles Pearl from Clarkson, and they end up holding hands, whereupon Pearl launches into her new party piece, which is a little dance loosely based on the "Oh, We Do Like to Be Beside the Seaside" routine that she learnt at her music group. She particularly likes the bit where the brass bands play tiddly-oom-pom-pom.

Lady Denby is delighted. "Charming. You must come round to tea, my dear."

Pearl smiles, completely oblivious to the high honor of being invited to Lady Denby's house, and launches into "Beside the Seaside" one more time. Lady Denby looks like she's accidentally pressed Play on a tape recorder and can't work out how to switch it off.

"Just ignore her, Lady Denby. She loves dancing, she'll go on for ages."

She nods. "Right you are my dear. Charming, quite charming. I'll be back later with the judges. Best foot forward and all that. Excellent."

———

inzia takes Pearl off for a wander, still singing, and I'm trying to concentrate on the till receipts for Sunday when
Mrs. Peterson comes in.

"Hello, I've been meaning to thank you, after the school
fayre, for making such a generous bid for the flag kit. I'd have
been really embarrassed if nobody had wanted it."

"Not at all. I need more projects, for the evenings, I find it
really helps when Amy's asleep. Look, I finished the cardigan."

She holds it up to show me, looking very proud. As well
she might, she's done a great job on it.

"That's lovely. If you're looking for more projects, we can
always use extra knitters for the shop you know, if they can
knit as well as you can."

"Seriously? What a lovely thing to say, I'm very flattered. I
want to make some dolls' clothes for Amy. My mum used to
make them for me and I always loved them. I want to make a
bedspread for her too, like the ones you've got in the shop, but
I want to keep it a surprise, for her birthday."

"That's no problem; you can keep it here, in our stockroom, just work on a square at a time and bring them in here
if you like?"

"Really, that would be so helpful. It's been such a long
time since I've done anything creative. It's the colors, I think;
they make me feel, well, hopeful. I'm so glad I started again. I
didn't realize how much I missed it."

"It's relaxing, isn't it, once you get back into the habit?"

"Yes, I find it very calming."

So do I, or I would do if I could get more time to knit seahorses and less time looking at bloody till rolls.

"And have you got any of the chunky tweed? I've signed
up for a knitting magazine now, and there's a lovely pattern
for autumn, for a little jacket."

"Sure, it's upstairs. Elsie's up there, she'll show you."

She goes up, looking so much happier than when I first saw her. Not that anything's really changed, of course, but somehow she seems lighter, like it's not such a huge struggle to get through the day, which is great. I hope the knitting has helped, a bit. Sometimes I really love working here.

'm having a coffee break with Tom, who's filling me in on the latest with Cinzia.

"She's driving me crazy, to be honest. One minute she's up for it, the next she goes all distant."

"A bit like you did?"

"Well yes, sort of, but that was a plan to get her interested. With her it's real. And there's this other girl. She comes to our gigs, she's always giving me the eye, but I'm not sure I want to try and cope with two of them; it can get really complicated if you start all that."

"I'm sure."

He grins. "Does she ever say anything to you?"

"No, and I wouldn't tell you if she did, Tom."

"When she's in the right mood, she's adorable, you know."

"I know."

He's looking lovesick again.

"Still, no point fretting, that's what my mum says. If she can't make her mind up, then I don't have to either. Looks like you've got a couple of customers."

walk toward the counter as a man turns and smiles.

"We're from the Bay, the new bed-and-breakfast?"

"Oh, right. It looks so great every time I drive past, I keep meaning to come in and have a proper look. I love the color."

They've painted it a beautiful gray.

"Well aren't you nice? Come in any time. We love people who say nice things. So the thing is, we were wondering, one of our friends from London was asking, and we thought if we did a package, a knitting weekend, we could do group bookings? You could do a class for them, maybe one on Saturday afternoon, and one on Sunday. Would that work?"

"We're pretty busy at the minute, but yes, we could look at doing something like that, I'm sure we could. When were you thinking?"

"The autumn, when the summer season starts to die down a bit. We're fully booked for most weekends until then. But I should warn you, our friends are pretty high-maintenance types, but you're probably used to that, what with your famous clientele. We adore our Gracie, such marvelous skin. Gus, isn't that tea cozy perfect? We've got to have it, and the blue one, so on trend. And you do a Stitch and Bitch group, don't you? Our lovely Tina was telling me. I popped in for a quick trim the other day, what a nice woman. Stitch and Bitch, sounds perfect, bitching is one of my favorite things."

Gus shakes his head. "You'll have to excuse Duggie; he gets a bit carried away when he's had a new idea. But we do think autumn mini-breaks would be popular. I'll run through some figures with you if you like, make sure we all earn a few pennies. Are there things you can make in a weekend? Only I think they'd need a project they could finish, and all these lovely things look like they'd take weeks."

"I've been thinking about doing something similar actually, and there are quite a few things that you could knit—a tea cozy, or a pair of egg cozies, or a lavender bag—small things, so people have something to take home."

"I knew you'd get it. I can tell from your windows you're a girl after our own heart. Get the credit cards out, Gus, I need some of these gorgeous things. They'll look perfect on our breakfast trays."

"We can knit you some with 'The Bay' on if you like."

He shrieks, a proper squealy shriek, which makes us all laugh, and even Gus admits that this is a fabulous idea and they'll think about colors, but in the meantime they'll take one of the blankets in gray tweed, and a matching cushion, and a couple of the tea cozies, and six egg cozies. I give them a discount, which goes down very well with Gus.

How lovely. Elsie's going to be pleased, since she knitted the last batch of egg cozies. Actually, if I ask her to be in charge of one of the classes, she'll be even more pleased, and Laura can do the other one so I only need to be around for extra-high-maintenance helping. Perfect.

'm on the phone trying to explain to an annoying rep why I don't want to order vast amounts of their nasty nylon economy range, however tempting the price might be, when Lady Denby sweeps in, with two men and a grumpy-looking woman. Elsie is already lurking by the door and ushers them to their table by the window. We've put vases of summer roses on all the tables, and Tom's already got an arrangement of cakes ready on one of our china cake stands.

Lord Denby has clearly been fully briefed. He wanders in shortly after they arrive and sits down at their table.

"Chap makes all his own biscuits, you know, and cakes and things. Had a crack at custard creams a while back, made a jolly good job of it too. Can't beat a custard cream in my opinion. One of the worst things about the War if you ask me, couldn't get them for love or money. Well, money, sometimes, if you knew the right chap. And as for cake, have you ever tasted cake made with powdered egg and carrots? Absolutely ghastly."

He pauses to smile at the judges. "Come here quite often, decent cup of tea, not that easy to find nowadays you know, great boon. Excellent. Thank you, Moira."

The judges look confused, having just been introduced to Elsie.

Lord Denby looks over the top of his glasses. "I call all the girls Moira; find it saves a great deal of time. Apart from Pru of course. That wouldn't go down too well, would it, my dear?"

Lady Denby raises her eyebrows and sighs, which the judges seem to enjoy.

Tom brings the cakes to the table, and Lord Denby practically claps he's so pleased.

"How long have you lived here, Lord Denby?" The grumpy woman judge finally seems to be enjoying herself a bit more; she's had two slices of cake and is finishing off an almond macaroon.

"Nearly six hundred years, give or take, couple of duds along the way, one got into a spot of hot water with one of the Henrys, forget which one, not the Eighth, too busy with all those wives, think it was the Sixth, anyway, picked the wrong side, nearly finished us off, but we managed to hang on. Had to be careful back then, make sure you knew what was going on. Important not to lose your head."

He pauses, so everyone can appreciate his joke.

"Decent place to live though, wouldn't live anywhere else, and you can still get a decent cup of tea. Can't say that about some places I won't mention, strong drink, yes, all the food you could possibly want to eat in a paper bag wandering about the streets, yes, but nowhere to get a decent cup of tea. I'd avoid them like the plague in the evenings if I were you, all sorts wandering about completely pickled. No harm in enjoying yourself of course, had a few adventures myself, old Teddy Barchester nearly landed us all in the clink on more than one occasion, he had terrible taste in women, that was his trouble, and—"

Lady Denby puts her cup down. "Yes, thank you George, that's quite enough of that. Shall we continue with our tour, if everyone is ready?"

The judges look torn between staying here and seeing what other gems Lord Denby will impart and finishing their tour of the High Street.

Lady Denby stands up. "We're very proud of all our local shops; some of them have been in the same families for generations. This wool shop for example, three generations. Marvelous."

Lord Denby pipes up again. "Must go and see old Parsons. Ironmongers you know, family's been here for years, saw a bit of action in the War, until he got shot in France, nice chap. Good bowler, when he had full use of his legs, not so good after that, of course, stick slowed him down a fair bit. Although he does make a very useful umpire, quite happy, standing there for hours. Decent chap, old Parsons. Salt of the earth."

They wander off up the High Street, with Lord Denby telling the lady judge about his exploits with Teddy Barchester.

"The problem was his father; being an archbishop did rather complicate things."

I'm half tempted to follow them, and I can see Elsie is too.

"Well, I think that went well, don't you, dear?"

"Yes, Elsie, or should I say Moira?"

She smiles. "He's a card, isn't he?"

"He is, Elsie."

"He was a handful when he was younger by all accounts."

"I'm sure."

"I might just nip out to the baker's if that's all right, dear. I need a white loaf."

"Sure."

"I'll only be five minutes."

She's back half an hour later, without any bread. But apparently the judges are now heading toward the pier, and Lord Denby is telling everyone about the bombing during the War, and how much fun you could have in an air-raid shelter if you put your mind to it. Elsie says he'd got the lady judge in fits of giggles, so I hope that bodes well.

"I'm off now, Elsie."

"Right you are, dear."

"I think I'll plant out those flowers Grace sent. I keep meaning to do it, and they're starting to wilt in the heat. Cinzia's going out later on this afternoon, so I'll be at home if you need me."

"They need to be in the ground, dear, not just those little pots. Well enjoy yourself, but don't overdo it. You want to be sitting in the shade on a day like this; good day to dry your washing though."

"Yes, I put some out this morning."

"Gets your whites nice and bright does good strong sunshine."

"Yes."

Especially if you've washed them with a stray flip-flop.

'm kneeling in the back garden, covered in mud, digging holes in the bed by the terrace and trying to remove miles of bloody bindweed from the shrubs before I put the new plants in. I'm starting to wish I'd listened to Elsie and was sitting in the shade when the garden gate opens.

Bloody hell, it's Daniel. Dear God, he's the last person I expected to see.

"Hello angel. I've just been looking at locations near here, Tony's gone on to look at the next lot, so I thought I'd call in, on the off chance, kill two birds with one stone. Sorry, that doesn't sound right. I probably should have called first. That woman in the shop said you were at home. She's not very friendly, is she?"

"Elsie? She's all right, once you get to know her."

Actually, I wish he'd called. At least I wouldn't be wearing such tragic trousers. Not that it matters, but still. Bloody hell. We haven't seen him since Christmas, when he brought all the presents down for the kids. Christ knows why he can't pick up the phone like a normal person.

"How's my girl then, still bossing everybody around?"

"Pretty much. Cinzia will be bringing her back any minute; they're feeding the ducks."

"That's the Italian girl I met at Christmas, right? Great, well, I'll hang around then, if that's okay?"

"Sure. Do you want a drink? There's water in the fridge, or juice?"

"I'm fine. I didn't know you were such a keen gardener."

"I'm not really; it's just a few things to brighten up the terrace."

"Nice."

make tea, and we sit in the shade.

"Sorry I didn't call first. It was a spur-of-the-moment thing."

"It's fine, Daniel. So how are things? How's Liv?"

"No idea. Thank God."

"Oh, right."

"Yup, all over, so I left. Well, technically she dumped me. But I was about to leave."

"That's a shame. I'm sorry, Daniel."

"It's fine actually, she's well and truly out of my system now, thank God. I should have known better. Actresses are a total nightmare, egos like canyons. So I thought I'd come and see my gorgeous girl, do something real."

"More tea?"

He grins. "I'd forgotten about you and tea. Yes, please. What's that, in the basket?"

"Lavender, from the front garden. It's been so hot, and the front garden is in the sun all day, so it blooms early. I dry it, to make lavender bags for the shop."

"It's like something out of Jane Austen. Shouldn't you have a muslin frock on?"

"For digging the garden? Nice state that would be in after five minutes."

He grins. "I never thought of that. I wonder how they managed."

"Same way they did most things I guess; they took their

time, didn't do any heavy lifting, and employed hordes of servants."

"Sounds good to me."

Cinzia comes back with Pearl, asleep in her buggy, still wearing her tiara.

"Christ, she's grown."

Cinzia gives him a rather cool look. I'm not sure she entirely approves of Daniel. Which is fair enough, I suppose; she's so besotted with Pearl I don't think she approves of anyone taking such a hands-off approach to being her dad. Actually, I'm not sure I do either.

"Why has she got a tiara on?"

"She likes it."

"Fair enough."

"Thanks Cinzia, and have a lovely time. Where are you going?"

"Just Canterbury, with friends. There are boats, on the river, so we will see."

"Sounds lovely."

"Yes, so I'll see you tomorrow. The Principessa, she will be hungry when she wakes up. She drank the juice, but she has not eated."

"Great, thanks."

She nods at Daniel as she leaves.

We stay in the back garden, and I make sandwiches and crisps, which Pearl adores, and then I finish planting out the flowers while Daniel watches Pearl, trotting round with her plastic watering can and getting in my way. It's all rather peaceful until the stupid rabbit starts hopping round trying to eat all my new plants, so I have to put him back in his run, which involves a fair amount of diving about until I can catch the bloody thing using my soon-to-be-patented technique of chucking a tea towel over him. Daniel is finding this all very amusing and chats to Pearl as she retrieves her squirrel, one of her new favorite things, from the buggy.

"Is that a squirrel?"

"Yes. Mine." Pearl holds it a bit more tightly.

"And the rabbit is called Peter? Great name, angel."

"Yes, and it wasn't my idea. Thank God she doesn't call the squirrel Nutkin, or we'd have to start searching for a hedgehog, and look like a mad Beatrix Potter family."

"So you're not a Beatrix nutter then?"

"Nutter." Pearl kisses her squirrel.

"Great, now look what you've done, you've just taught her to say *nutter.*"

"Happy to help, angel."

"Well in that case start digging a few holes with this trowel, would you, so I can get the rest of these planted before the boys get back."

"I don't really do much digging."

"Well now is a good time to start."

"It looks great."

"It does, doesn't it? Thanks Daniel. I better go and get the boys from their football camp in a minute. They're loving it. Yesterday it was dribbling, and I think they're doing penalties today, which is great, except I'm not that into football if I'm honest, and I have to be in goal. Sure I can't persuade you to stay for tea?"

He smiles. "I'd love to, but I'd better head back to the seafront. Tony will be back, and he's hopeless with one-way systems, always going in the wrong direction and getting shouted at. Nearly got us shot in Rome. Idiot. Those cara- binieri can get very irate, you know. I'll see you on Sunday though."

"We'll be on the beach around four; you won't be able to miss us. It's the last beach hut, and Gran will probably have balloons up, but bring a hat, it gets hot on the beach. I can lend you one if you like, because we all wear our hats in the sun, don't we, Pearl?"

"Nutter."

"No, Pearl, hat. We all love our sun hats."

He's trying not to laugh now. "Sorry, angel. Hat. Defi- nitely. See you Sunday."

As soon as I get the boys back from football, I ring Ellen. "Christ, Daniel Fitzgerald? What did old Fitzcarraldo want then?"

"To see Pearl. He came to the house actually, and helped me plant out those flowers that Grace sent. It was nice, but, well, I don't know. He's split up with Liv."

"Has he? That's very interesting. So is he going to be around more then?"

"I don't know, maybe, to see Pearl, and that will be great, obviously, but I'm not sure I want everyone to know that he's her dad, not yet, not until we see how it's going to work, if he's around more. I mean Gran knows of course, and Vin, and Martin. Well, quite a few people, I suppose, but they're all people I trust. But I don't want everyone to know, especially not Mum; she thinks it was just a one-off with an old friend when I was still deeply grief-stricken and all that, which in a way it was. Nobody special."

"Oh yes, not special at all, apart from the international reputation, being surrounded by supermodels everywhere he goes, and him winning all the major awards, that kind of thing."

"I know, but that's my point. She'll drive me mad trying to get him to one of her bloody cocktail parties."

"True. But you can cope with that."

"Yes, but, oh, I don't know."

"What?"

"I'm worried about the kids."

"Surprise surprise."

"This might just be some kind of rebound thing, Ellen, to help him get over Liv, see if being a dad appeals, and announce to the world you have a daughter, and see how that goes. I want him to be just Daniel. I don't want us using the dad word, not yet. The boys will find it hard, after Nick and everything, it's a tricky word for them, and Pearl won't care, not yet, she's too little."

"Tell him that then, he'll get it."

"I know, I sort of did, and he did get it."

"So what's your problem then? Are you worried about how Dovetail's going to react?"

"No, he understands it's important for Pearl to see him. We talked about it at Christmas, and he was fine about it. No, it's not that. I just don't want things getting complicated."

"Complicated is where all the fun is, darling."

"Not in my world. Anyway, he's coming on Sunday, to my birthday thing."

"Bugger, I wish we were coming now."

"You'll be in Italy, Ellen, at your luxury villa. I'll swap, if you like."

She laughs. "No thanks darling, and I'm sure it'll be fine. Just relax."

"I suppose."

I'm sure she's right, but still. Bloody hell.

We're at the beach hut by half past three on Sunday afternoon, and Gran's put up bunting and balloons, and a rather mortifying Happy Birthday banner. My birthday barbecue has become a bit of a tradition now, and everyone brings food, toward the end of the afternoon, when it's getting cooler and the beach is less crowded.

"Happy birthday, pet."

"Thanks Gran."

"Reg has got the cool boxes full of ice."

"Brilliant. There's more fizzy water in the car if we run out."

Having the beach hut has been such a boon. I'd forgotten the level of kit you need with a baby; we were just getting to the stage where I could leave the house with only my keys and my purse, and now we're back to bags of kits and buggies and spare hats. Not that Pearl will wear anything remotely resembling a sun hat unless she's in the mood, and a summer balaclava seems a bit drastic, so it's an ongoing battle. But having the beach hut means I can keep all sorts of spare kit ready, and the pink plastic paddling pool and a box of toys. She spends ages trotting backward and forward to the sea with her bucket, playing with the plastic cups and her collection of shells, which is exactly what she's doing now.

"Hi Jo. Happy birthday, love."

"Thanks Tina."

"Here, I've done you one of our vouchers, for a wash and blow-dry. It's from me and Linda."

"Thank you, so much, but you really shouldn't have. I thought we agreed no presents."

"I know, love, but it's not a proper present, not really, I haven't wrapped it up or anything. Where shall I put this? I've made a rice salad, like we said, and Linda's done a tomato one."

"Perfect, just put them inside on the table, where it's cool."

"Right you are."

"Christ alive, would you look at Cinzia."

"I know, Linda."

Cinzia's wearing her new red and white polka-dot bikini. She's wearing tiny denim shorts too, thank God, but she's still attracting a fair amount of attention.

"God, what I couldn't do, if I looked like that. Just for a day."

Tina smiles. "Like what, Lind?"

"Well, I would give my ex-husband a nasty moment, put it that way. Wipe the smile right off his face, that would."

Martin arrives with Elsie and Jeffrey, and with a large amount of Elsie's epic Tupperware collection. Rather brilliantly, the local council has ruled that dogs are not allowed on the beach until after 6:00 p.m. in July and August, so we are Trevor free. Hurrah. He's back at the barn, probably demolishing something.

"God, Martin, what have you done to your knee?"

He's got a huge bruise, and an impressive collection of cuts and scratches.

"I fell off the stepladder. I've sprained my shoulder too, I think. Just what I need when I was going to finish the roof of the porch while the weather holds."

Elsie sniffs. "You shouldn't be up ladders when you're on your own, Martin, I've told you. What if you'd knocked yourself out or something? You should wait until your father's around for jobs like that."

He ignores her and limps down the beach toward Graham and Mark, who've appointed themselves barbecue monitors, like they do every year.

Poor thing, what with the limp, and one shoulder higher than the other, all he needs is an eye patch and a parrot and he'd be a dead ringer for Long John Silver. I'll take him a beer, when Elsie's not looking. He looks like he could use one.

By five nearly everyone has arrived, and we're sitting in a collection of beach chairs, chatting and eating while the kids race around. Baby Maximo is being handed round in a newborn version of pass the parcel, and getting lots of cuddles while Connie's mum is proudly telling us how clever her newest grandson is. Mark has added his magic touch with herbs to the chicken and lamb, which I've marinated following his very detailed instructions, and Graham and Martin are busy cooking sausages and drinking beer. Reg is mixing up another jug of his killer Pimm's, and we're all starting to feel slightly soft around the edges.

"Mum."

"Yes, Archie."

"When we've finished our tea, shall I do my magic show?"

"I don't think so, love. You haven't got Peter here, have you?"

Please don't let him say he's smuggled him along in his rucksack.

"No, but I can do tricks with my cards."

He can do two tricks, neither of which is entirely convincing.

"Yes, but not on a beach, love, they'd get all sandy. I thought we could have a castle competition. I've got prizes, for the winners."

He races back down the beach to recruit sand castle builders for his team.

"Hello angel. This all looks very chilled out."

Christ, how does Daniel do that, keep appearing out of nowhere? Maybe he's going in for magic tricks too.

He kisses me on the cheek and hands me a large white shopping bag with black rope handles.

"Just a few things from the last job I did, nothing special, but I thought you could use them more than me."

"Thanks Daniel, you didn't have to. I've told everybody no presents."

"Yes, but I'm not everybody."

He kneels down to say hello to Pearl, who presents him with a pink plastic cup. "Dink?"

"I was hoping for something a bit stronger, my darling, but thank you. There's a couple of bottles of champagne in that cooler. Crack one open, would you Jo?"

Actually, there are six bottles. Crikey.

We drink a birthday toast, and then one to Maximo, and one to the chefs, and then the castle competition starts, which Graham and Travis are taking very seriously. They've brought special buckets, and sticks for decoration, while Mark helps Nelly and Archie, and Martin is on Jack and Marco's team.

"Do you want to make a castle, sweetheart?"

Pearl gives Daniel her hat.

He takes his battered old straw hat off and puts it on her head, and weirdly it seems to fit. It's too big, of course, but that doesn't seem to matter, it just shades her face more, and she trots about quite happily, in her flowery sundress, looking like she's off to a rodeo.

Daniel rootles through his satchel and retrieves a navy blue cotton baseball cap. "I came fully equipped. Hats to go, that's me. We love hats, don't we, Queenie?"

Cinzia smiles. "She is the Principessa."

"Is she, darling? Well both the principessas I know are total nightmares; one's as mad as a bucket of frogs, and the other one is busy drinking her way through the family cellar, so I think I'll stick with Queenie."

Cinzia adjusts her bikini top and gives him one of her best heart-stoppingly lovely smiles, but he's oblivious. I suppose spending so much time surrounded by supermodels has made him pretty calm in the face of such a small bikini.

"More."

"More what, angel?" He looks at me.

"She wants you to dig a castle."

"Right, well, I'll give it a go. It's all digging with you two, isn't it? How's the garden, still looking fabulous?"

"Yes, thanks, apart from the bits Peter's nibbled."

"Get a shotgun, that's my top tip."

"Thanks Daniel. The kids would so love that."

think I'll check on Martin, just to make sure he's okay with Daniel turning up. They've said hello, and it's all been fine, but still.

"Do you want another drink, Martin?"

"Yes please. My shoulder's really aching now. Have you got any aspirin?"

"In my bag, I think."

We both watch Daniel as he wanders off down the beach to select the perfect castle-building location, followed by Pearl, and Reg, who's decided he fancies a go too. Daniel looks tanned and relaxed, in old cutoff jeans and a white T-shirt. Martin looks, well, like Martin. And God knows where he got those enormous khaki shorts from, but wherever it was didn't have a mirror.

"That knee does look sore, Martin. Are you sure you shouldn't go to hospital?"

"It's fine, don't fuss. Is there any more of the rice salad?"

"Sure. Sit down, Long John Silver, and I'll get you a plate."

I kiss him on the cheek as I go to find the tablets.

The beach is getting quieter now as the day-trippers pack up and start leaving, and the light goes all soft. Maggie puts some music on, a medley of old classics, which is perfect. The kids are still beavering away on their castles as the tide starts to turn and their journeys down to the sea to fill their buckets get shorter and shorter. Daniel's taking photographs, wandering around and crouching down, taking pictures of the children with a battered old camera.

I'm sitting with Connie, enjoying a cuddle with Maximo, who's nearly asleep.

"It'll be Nelly's birthday next, Con."

"I know, and she wants a party, for her birthday, with all girls, and fairy costumes, and also Archie."

"Good luck with that one. I can't see Archie going for that, unless you tell him he can do a magic show."

"Can he do the tricks now?"

"No."

She laughs.

"I want to make it special for her, she has been so good, with the baby and everything, and I want it to be a special day. Mark is making her a fairy castle cake. Pink and pink."

"I'll help if you like; we can get loads of net at the market and turn your function room at the pub into a fairy palace. Tons of glitter, a few fake jewels, Pearl can wear her tiara. It'll be great."

"And Archie, he will come, yes?"

"Yes, if I stick him in the car and tell him we're just helping, and there'll be cake, I can probably get him in the door. Just don't mention the fairy thing, or he'll think we're trying to get him into tights."

Mark and Martin are making another round of burgers to keep the builders fed. Pearl's bored with castle building, but Daniel's still going strong and has been co-opted onto Nelly and Archie's team. He walks back up the beach, holding Pearl's hand.

"Jo, we need— How do you say it, Queenie?"

"Fezzers."

"Yes, feathers, for the castle. Don't you just love it? So, have you got any?"

"Not on me, no."

"Well, that's a poor show, angel. Can't expect us to create a masterpiece with no fezzers."

"There'll be a few lying on the beach, there always are."

"You mean I have to collect them?"

"Yes."

"I usually have Tony for stuff like that."

"I know."

He grins. "Come on, Queenie; let's go on a fezzer hunt."

onnie winks at me.

"What?"

"It is nice, seeing him with her."

"Yes."

"And Martin, he is okay with it, I think."

"Yes, he seems to be."

"Brava."

aura arrives, with Rosie, and Tom and Olivia. They've been working in the shop; we're opening on Sundays now, while the summer season is in full swing, and the café's doing really well, especially on cloudier days. Tom and Olivia are lugging one of Mark's big plastic boxes, full of ice cream in the little plastic tubs I bought at the market last week. Raspberry ripple, chocolate fudge, and honeycomb vanilla. And there's apricot sorbet too. Some of us, including me, have two tubs.

Cinzia's sitting with Tom, and puts her arm across his shoulder, which does not go unnoticed by Connie's mum. Damn: one step closer to a visit from irate Italians demanding to know what's going on with their daughter and my café staff. Connie and I exchange glances as Cinzia kisses him, a pretty chaste peck on the cheek, but still. She's smiling, and Tom looks very pleased. Bless.

Maximo starts to stir, and Connie takes him for a walk to settle him. Daniel is sitting on a blanket with Pearl, finishing his ice cream.

"This is great; I don't usually like it, but that apricot stuff was fabulous. Queenie's liking hers too, aren't you, sweetheart?"

She nods, still too busy with her little plastic spoon to bother speaking.

"I better make a move soon though; I'm working tomorrow, got to be at the airport early."

"Aren't you going to wait for the official judging of the castles? Gran and Elsie will be doing it pretty soon."

"No, I better head back. But if you get a chance, tell them we were going for Versace as our design motif. More is more, yes?"

"Sure. Like that will mean anything to either of them. Or me, come to that."

He grins. "Fezzers. And more fezzers."

Pearl claps her hands. "Fezzers."

"That's right, Queenie."

"Nutter."

"Out of the mouths of babes, Daniel."

He laughs.

"You've got quite a nice little collection of seventies cocktails going on here, haven't you, angel? Martini, Cinzano, very nice. Shame the Diva didn't turn up and we could have had a proper cocktail hour. She's a demon cocktail mixer."

"She's in Tuscany. So is Ellen. In different bits, at least I hope so, or Ellen will be trying to get an interview."

"I bet they haven't got ice cream as good as this though. I'll call you when I'm back, shall I?"

"Sure."

He kisses Pearl on her hand and stands up.

"Give her a proper kiss from me later, would you, only you might want to get some of that ice cream off her face first."

He says good-bye to Gran, and Reg, who rather sweetly shakes his hand, and waves good-bye to everyone who is busy putting the final touches to their castles.

"He's gone then, has he?"

"Yes Martin."

"Just a flying visit then, was it?"

"Yes, he's working tomorrow. Help me put these plates in the hut, would you? I'll come down and get the car tomorrow, I've had too much to drink tonight. Nice though, wasn't it?"

"Yes."

He kisses me. "Happy birthday, and I didn't know what to get you, so I thought a surprise?"

"If you've got me a dog, I'll kill you."

"No, I thought about it, but no, I thought I'd make you a new table, for the garden; the one you've got is in such a state."

"That's a lovely idea, Martin."

"It might take a while."

"That's fine, I'm sure it'll be lovely when it's finished. Come on; let's see who's won the competition."

I'm packing up the buggy for the walk home while Archie and Jack lobby Gran and Elsie to reconsider their verdict that the castle competition is a draw, so everyone gets a prize. They like a clear winner, do my boys, even though it's a draw every year. I wonder how long it will be before they realize everyone always gets a prize. Otherwise why would I bring so many little parcels of sweets already wrapped up? A few more years I hope.

I need to find Pearl's juice cup; she'll only drink out of the yellow one this week, and there'll be dramas if I haven't got it in the morning. Daniel's shopping bag is under my chair, so I have a quick look while I gather up all our other stuff; I didn't get a chance earlier, as I was trying to avoid unwrapping anything, but there's a huge bottle of Chanel No. 5, and a bottle of bath oil, some fabulous nail varnish in pink, and a lovely mint green, a tube of face cream, and one of hand cream. There are two scented candles, lemon and verbena, and lavender, and a tangle of beaded bracelets and necklaces, threaded onto ribbon. God, how fabulous. Pearl is going to love all the beads; I'll have to grab my favorite ones before she sees them or I won't get a look in.

"He's a nice man, that Daniel."

"Yes, Gran, he is."

"Will we be seeing more of him then?"

"I shouldn't think so, Gran, not much anyway, he's very busy."

"He's very taken with our Pearl. Which is as it should be."

"Yes."

"So have you had a lovely day then, pet?"

"Perfect."

"And did Martin tell you about the table? Won't that be lovely? He's been telling Reg all about it, and he's put a lot of thought into it you know."

"I know, Gran, and I'm sure it will be lovely."

She pats my arm. "He's a lovely man, your Martin. Come on then, let's start walking back. Reg is far too tiddly to drive, nice little walk will do us all good. Might have a cup of tea at your house to break the journey up the hill."

"Good idea."

"There might be a cake in your fridge if we look, with candles."

"Oh Gran."

"It's not a proper birthday without candles, pet. I've put her yellow cup in the bag, you'll need it in the morning."

"Thanks Gran."

And there's still cake to look forward to. How perfect.

··· 7 ···

Strangers in the Night

August and September

It's half past twelve on Monday morning and I'm at Ellen's house in Notting Hill, trying on frocks ready for the magazine piece on Ellen and her passion for knitting. In the end she decided to do one big interview and a photo shoot with *Good Housekeeping*, as it's the perfect hook into her target audience for the television series apparently, and they don't tend to run pieces where they completely stitch you up and make you look like a nutter. Which is reassuring. Despite having to catch the train at the crack of dawn, I'm still feeling the joy of being out for a grown-up day in London, with no small people needing anything. Ellen's child-free since Harry's taken Eddie out for an action-packed day of swimming and baby jungle gym, which I think is a more macho version of ordinary baby gym. Gran and Cinzia are with my three, having a morning at the beach before Gran goes off for her stint in the Lifeboats shop and Cinzia takes them home for an afternoon of films and pizza making. And even though I know the entire kitchen will be covered in a thin film of flour when I get home, I don't care. I'm finally getting a glimpse of what it must be like to be a mother seahorse. I'm child-free and not working, for what feels like the first time in years, and it's brilliant.

"That looks great on you, darling."

"Thanks Ellen."

I'm wearing a pretty smock dress, in dark navy blue silk with pink and orange splodges on it, which looks a lot nicer than it sounds, with one of my mohair shawls, in marmalade, draped artfully by the magazine stylist. I'm also wearing orange suede sandals with very thin straps. Not practical, impossible to walk in, and fabulous. I even managed to paint my toes yesterday, with some of the pink polish from Daniel's birthday bag. My legs are as tanned as they ever get, after all our school holiday trips to the beach, and my hair has been curled by a man called Fabrizio. So far, so good.

"Great colors."

"It feels lovely."

"Let's go with that then. Sophie, can you fix my hair, and then we can start."

The photographer is busy setting up his cameras. I think he's called Eden, or it might be Edam, which doesn't seem likely, but he's so laid-back he doesn't actually speak, so I can't work out how to ask him. I think I'll just try to avoid calling him the name of Dutch cheese and hope for the best. We're in Ellen's first-floor drawing room in her smart Georgian town house; in one of those posh squares which have a gated garden, just like in the film, although without Julia Roberts or Hugh Grant lolling about. It all looks very smart, with vases of beautiful flowers and the baskets of knitting and wool which I brought with me. The mantelpiece is crowded with pictures of Ellen and Harry with Eddie, and there's a huge arrangement of delphiniums and roses in the hearth.

I'm sitting next to Ellen on the gray velvet sofa.

"Why are you pulling that face, darling?"

"This is my being-photographed face. I told you this wasn't a good idea."

"Well pack it in; you look like you're sitting on something sharp. It'll be great. You look divine, I look divine, the knitting looks divine, relax."

In between having our hair tweaked and more face powder dabbed on, Eden/Edam takes what seems like hundreds of photographs, and then stands with the people from the magazine peering at a computer screen and agreeing that he's doing an amazing job.

Ellen seems oblivious to this, and we sit chatting. I'm telling her about how the school holidays have turned into one long endless blur.

"I'm so fed up with making picnic lunches, I'm half praying for rain."

"How much longer have you got before they go back?"

"Two more weeks, nearly. They go back on the Wednesday, and it can't come soon enough for me. I mean it's lovely, for the first week or so, and then they get bored, and I've still got the shop to sort, and Elsie had her week away, and well, basically, it's been a bit of a nightmare. I wish I could afford to take us all off somewhere, have a real break."

"Well do it then, darling."

"Maybe next year."

"Use up some of your rainy day money."

"Yes, but that's for rainy days, Ellen, not summer holidays. When the boiler blows up, or the car breaks down, that kind of thing. I'm not making enough money for holidays yet. Nearly, but not quite."

"Dear God, nearly but not quite? Give yourself a break. You're so boring, you know that, don't you? It's one of the things I love most about you. You'd be having a rainy day fund even if you won the lottery, wouldn't you?"

"You never know, Ellen. Life has a habit of smacking you into a tree when you least expect it, and someone has to be able to pay all the bills."

She leans forward and kisses me on the cheek, and Eden/ Edam shows a brief flicker of interest before he returns to the computer screen.

"That won't happen again, darling."

"I know. Because I've got my rainy day money stashed away. So it can't. If I disappeared tomorrow, Gran and Reg would have enough to bring the kids up. I've got my life assurance, and their savings accounts, and I've written a new will. It's all sorted, so I don't have to think about it."

"All right, little Miss Sunshine, you've got it sorted, I get it, and you're right, Harry made us do new wills too, but let's not think about it, it's far too upsetting. I can't imagine a world without marvelous me in it, and I don't want to try. I know, why don't we book a villa together next year? It really wasn't that expensive, not that I'm going back to Tuscany again, too many Brits wandering around with bright red faces wearing socks with their sandals banging on about bloody frescoes."

"Sounds just like Mum."

We both giggle.

"We could try Spain, that's bound to be cheaper. We could all go, and it would give Eddie someone to play with, so you'd be doing me a favor."

"Maybe."

"Don't sound so enthusiastic, darling."

"Sorry, no, it would be lovely, only I think my idea of a cheap holiday and yours might be a bit different. But let's see. It would be lovely if we could, really lovely, the kids would be thrilled."

"It's a definite then. We'll find something, and I won't tell you how much it costs, and then you can pay the same as a cheap package deal and we'll all be happy. And don't start saying 'yes but,' because that's what we're doing. I've decided. And I'm loving this cardigan, darling; I want to make another one."

Ellen's knitted a short pale pink cardigan in a silky cotton, which I sewed up for her because she tends to end up with bumpy seams and one arm shorter than the other.

"I've brought you the olive green you liked; it's in one of the bags."

"Thanks darling, and I want to make something for Eddie, do the full motherly thing. One of your blankets, if you'll do the sewing thing for me?"

"Of course."

"I'm really enjoying knitting again you know; it fills in time when I'm hanging about in the studio, and it means I've always got something pointy to hand if anyone annoys me. Christ, aren't we done yet?" She turns to Edam. "Five more minutes, okay, and then I'm throwing everyone out. We've got things to do this afternoon. Darling, hello, stop looking at that bloody screen, are we done? Because you've got about five minutes left before I turn back into a psycho pumpkin."

Ellen did the interview earlier on, and it all sounded great. The piece will be at least three pages, and there'll be an insert box with details of the shop and our website, and some pictures of knitting kits and our new range of tea cozies. Laura and I knitted a batch of pale blue and pebble white ones for Gus and Duggie at the Bay, with "The Bay" knitted in mint green, which inspired us to do a whole new range. So far we've done ones with "More Tea, Vicar?," "Keep Calm and Carry On," and "Time for Tea & Cake," with a small knitted fairy cake on the top instead of our usual pom-pom. We've lined them with cotton gingham, and they're selling really well, particularly at weekends, when the exodus from London brings all sorts of day-trippers into the shop. I've got Gran and Betty making more, and I'm doing a kit for the Tea & Cake ones, since they're the best sellers so far.

"I can't wait to see the magazine. It's for the November issue, so it'll be out in October, yes?"

Ellen checks with the magazine people, and a rather scary-looking woman who's wearing very bright red lipstick and various shades of black says yes, it will be November.

"But we won't actually still be sitting here then, will we, darling? Because a one-hour shoot does seem to be heading toward the third hour now, and I'm starting to get a bit pissed off."

"Sorry, we're nearly done, we'd just like one more set, maybe with you standing by the window, and Joanne sitting on the sofa; we think the contrast would work really well."

Ellen gives her a Look. Oh dear.

"It's Josephine, as in Napoleon and Josephine, and I'm Napoleon: small, but very determined. Happy to be violent when required. And no, I don't think standing by a window will work. Apart from anything else, I don't actually knit standing up. Authenticity is so important, isn't it, darling? Let me see what you've got so far. But I'm serious, ten more minutes and we're done."

—————

By the time we're finally done, it's half past two, but I'm the proud owner of the silk dress and the orange sandals, at a vastly reduced price, which Ellen has negotiated, which is a bloody good job because the dress alone costs nearly three hundred pounds in the shops.

"Right, let's go. Clothes shopping, then tea somewhere fabulous. Where does your train go from?"

"Charing Cross."

"I'll get my girl at the office to book the Savoy then."

"Can't we go straight to tea? I've already got a new frock, and shoes."

"No, we cannot. And don't forget, they pay expenses, so send me your train ticket and I'll get the office to sort it. There's a new wool shop I've spotted, which you'll love, all your sort of stuff, only three times the price, and then I want to go to Bond Street. There are some shoes I need to try on, and who knows, we might even find you some decent jeans."

"I've got jeans, Ellen."

"No, you haven't, not really, darling. Trust me."

She drags me round a series of shops, including the fabulous wool shop full of treasures at extortionate prices, where I surreptitiously take a few pictures with my phone, and then countless shoe shops and clothes shops, which all end up merging into one. But I do buy a new pair of jeans, which even I can see are somehow magically better fitting than my usual ones; and a new pair of green ballet flats; two new bras, after a rather unwarranted lecture from Ellen where I basically ended up buying them just to shut her up; and a floral A-line skirt, in blues and greens, which she insisted I buy practically on pain of death.

"I'm still not sure about that skirt you know, I don't really need it."

"If we only bought things we need, darling, we'd all look appalling. Clothes are meant to be beautiful, lift your spirits, that kind of thing, and that skirt is beautiful and it lifts my spirits, so shut up. The color works for you, the cut is great, and you can wear it with your boots in the autumn. It'll cheer us up in all that mist and rain you go in for down by the seaside. Let's find a taxi."

"Can we go to John Lewis? I want to look at new sheets for the boys, and maybe—"

"God, you're hopeless. Sheets are for online shopping, not wasting valuable drinking time. Let's do the Savoy tourist thing and have afternoon tea. At least they do a decent martini there. Or champagne? And if you say you want a nice cup of tea, I'm going to hit you with your new sandals."

The Savoy have stopped serving tea when we arrive, and a rather snooty waiter is about to glide away and leave us standing there until Ellen goes into full Britain's Favorite Broadcaster mode, and before we know it we're whisked off to the American Bar, and given a gorgeous array of dainty sandwiches and cakes, and a bottle of champagne.

"God, I love champagne, anytime, anywhere. It always hits the spot, doesn't it darling?"

"It certainly does."

"Have you had a lovely time today?"

"Perfect."

"Good, so have I. Just think, if you moved back to London, we could do this every day."

"Apart from the fact that I'd be working full-time to pay

for the nanny, and the massive mortgage, so we'd probably see less of each other than we do now. Talking of which, when's your new nanny starting?"

"Next month. We've settled on three days a week. She still does two days for her other family, and that's a good sign, that they want to keep her, yes?"

"Definitely. She sounds lovely. How long has she been with them?"

"Nearly ten years, so hopefully that will all work out. Harry's already happier now he can see the end is in sight; he hasn't completely loved the house-husband thing, not that I blame him. Total nightmare stuck at home every day trying to think of clever things to do with glove puppets. I hope she turns out be a total treasure, so he can get some freelance work. I'll be busy with the autumn series, and then we can decide about baby number two."

"I thought you had decided."

"I keep changing my mind. I'd definitely go for it if I knew I'd have a girl. Don't look at me like that, I'm just being honest; if I had another boy, I wouldn't put it up for adoption or anything, but I really want a girl. Why don't you have another one too? One of us is bound to get a girl, and if it's you we can do a swap. Actually, that's a brilliant plan. Otherwise all my expert shopping skills are going to go to waste. Eddie yells if I take him into any shop that doesn't sell food."

"I'm sure he doesn't, Ellen."

"He bloody does. He'll sit in the buggy quite happily at the farmers' market, or in the trolley at the supermarket, but anything remotely designer, he kicks off the minute I wheel him through the doors."

"He's a boy after my own heart."

"Yes, but my Pearly girl definitely has the makings of a fashionista, even if her mother doesn't."

"Not if it involves hats she doesn't. She buried another one on the beach last week. She digs a nice little hole and then pops her sun hat in when she thinks I'm not looking. She's as bad as bloody Trevor for digging bloody holes and burying things."

"At least she's stopped putting things in the washing machine."

"Not entirely. I washed two bits of Archie's train set on Sunday."

She laughs. "And how's Dovetail getting on? No more falling asleep?"

"No, thank you. He's fine; he's got a big job on at work, so he'll be away for three weeks, nearly four, all over the place, installing some new critical upgrade, something like that."

"So that'll be you stuck with that bloody dog? For three weeks? Jesus darling, that's a bit harsh."

"No, thank God, there's good news on that front. Jeffrey's setting up a workshop at the barn, in the old stables. He's got stacks of stuff in the garden shed which Elsie's been desperate to get rid of for years. So he's going to move it all, and that way he'll be there every day to look after Trevor. He's going to work on all the window frames, making new bits, and that'll take weeks."

"He's making his own window frames? Christ, they really go for it in the wonderful world of wooden things, don't they?"

"I know, but Martin's earning a fortune on this job, so he thinks he can take October off to finish the barn; well, perhaps not finish, but get the kitchen in, and the last bit of the roof done. So you never know, maybe there'll be less planks lying around next time you see it. He's looking after the kids tonight, when Cinzia goes out on her date. She and Tom are seeing each other properly now."

"Seeing each other, as in shagging? Christ, I'd never even thought about what my policy is on my domestic staff shagging. I suppose as long as it's not Harry, it's fine."

"She's not my domestic staff, not really, and anyway I'm trying not to think about it. I'm not sure her family back in Italy would approve."

She laughs. "Well, if you wake up with a horse's head in your bed, give me a call, darling."

"I woke up with a shoe on my pillow the other day; Pearl woke up early to rearrange the bottom of my wardrobe."

"See, that's why I need a girl, they get shoes in a way boys just don't."

She orders another bottle of champagne while I call home, but the line's engaged.

"Just one more glass, then I need to go or I'll miss my train."

"Cheers darling. Here's to us."

"Us what?"

"Us, being fabulous."

I raise my glass.

"Talking of fabulous, any news from Fitzcarraldo?"

"He's in Spain, in the mountains, doing some winter fashion thing, or he was the last time I heard from him. But he sent the photographs of us on the beach at my birthday, and they're lovely. There are some beautiful ones of Pearl, and the boys, and a really nice one of me holding Maximo, talking to

Connie. He's really good at taking pictures of kids; Maximo looks angelic."

"Quite good at grown-ups too, darling, from the number of awards he wins."

"Yes, but he doesn't make you pose, he just wanders around, and you forget he's there. Not like Edam."

"Who?"

"The photographer today."

She laughs.

"Erdenne. Though I'm calling him Edam from now on, it's much better. Yes, he was a bit full of himself, wasn't he? Come on, drink up darling. I've got to go to this stupid awards thing, and you've got a train to catch. Or we could stay here all night. Actually, let's do that. I'm sure we can find two busi-nessmen at a loose end who'd love to take us to dinner."

"No thank you. Loose businessmen aren't really my style. And we can take ourselves to dinner, can't we?"

"Yes, but it would be a laugh. A bit of off-the-record flirt-ing, just to keep your skills up."

She pours me another glass of champagne.

"What skills? No, it's tempting, but I really need to get home, Ellen, and you should go to the awards thing."

"Yes, but one more glass, to celebrate your new frock. And your proper girlie shandals."

"Shandals?"

"Yes."

"I'll drink to that."

Bugger. I've missed the 8:30 train, so I have to hang around at the station for nearly an hour, trying to make a cappuccino last and avoid sitting next to anyone who looks like they might be psychotic, which isn't easy. I have to move seats three times, and I try calling home again but the line's still engaged. I'm quite pleased with myself for not going into maternal meltdown and ringing every three minutes until I get through; I know Martin will call if there's anything up, and it's either Cinzia talking to her friends or Elsie calling Martin with one of her lectures. So I buy another cappuccino and pretend to read the paper, and then the bloody train stops at every single station and it's nearly midnight by the time I'm walking back up the hill from the station. Still, at least I've got new shandals.

Martin's half asleep on the sofa when I get in.

"God, I'm so sorry, Martin. I didn't mean to be so late."

"They're all asleep."

Poor thing, he's looking pretty irritated.

"Thanks so much, Martin. And I'm really sorry, it all took longer than I thought it would and then I missed the 8:30 by minutes. What time did Cinzia leave?"

"Around eight, after Pearl was asleep."

"Great, she said she'd wait until she'd put her down. Would you like a coffee, or tea? I think I'm going to have one."

"No thanks, I better be off. Nothing worse than when the paid help lingers, is there? Or the unpaid help in my case."

"Sorry?"

"I wish you'd called."

"I did, a few times, but the phone was engaged."

"That was Mum, and she was only on for five minutes."

I know Elsie has never made a phone call to Martin that only lasted five minutes in her life, but I don't think he's in the mood to be contradicted.

"Well I'm sorry, I did try, and you knew where I was, you could have called me if there was anything urgent."

"Yes, but that's me all over, isn't it? Nothing urgent."

"Shall we talk about this tomorrow? We could have a late breakfast, I'm in the shop for a while in the morning. How does that sound?"

"It sounds convenient. Like I'm being slotted into your busy day."

"Well I don't mean it like that, Martin, honestly."

"But I am, aren't I? Now Mr. Wonderful is back on the scene."

Oh, God. Now I get it.

"Nobody is back on the scene. He's Pearl's dad, so if he's around a bit more, that's got to be good, don't you think?"

"Oh yes, bloody brilliant, calling everyone angel and chucking money about like there's no tomorrow. While muggins here gets to stop in and babysit. I had hoped we'd be spending some proper time together now I'm less busy with the boat and everything. I thought that's what you wanted. Not to go jaunting off to London. Did you see him? Is that why you're so late back, loaded down with bags? Did he take you shopping? How kind of him."

"I'm too tired for all this right now, Martin."

"Well I hope you remember it was me that picked up the pieces last time. I was the one worrying myself sick in the kitchen that day, when you had Pearl. And where was he? Off shacked up with an actress living the high life."

"Martin, Daniel's in Spain, and I've been out with Ellen, just like I told you. And yes, I have been shopping, isn't that allowed? Let's talk about this tomorrow, when you're less grumpy."

"No, I want to talk about it now. I'm fed up of being good old Martin, who you can put to one side when anything better comes along."

God, he's starting to sound like Elsie now.

"Nobody is putting you to one side."

"Well it bloody feels like it."

"Maybe that's your problem, Martin, not mine. Look; I think you should go now."

Maybe he's been at the vodka or something, or he's extra tired. He has been working long hours on that bloody barn.

"You think you're so perfect, don't you? But you're not you know."

"I know I'm not perfect, Martin, but thanks for reminding me."

"It's high time someone told you a few home truths, coming home at this time, half cut and not a word, you could have been anywhere. No proper mother would carry on like you, do you know."

No proper mother? Bloody hell.

"Who's carrying on? The only person carrying on is you."

"It won't last you know, he'll soon get tired of you."

Oh sod this.

"I know but beggars can't be choosers, can they, Martin? Middle-aged women with three kids and one of them without a husband, well, they have to take what they can get, don't they?"

Trevor's looking at us rather anxiously now, and starting to whine. Just like bloody Martin.

"Shut up, Trevor. Just take him home will you, before he wakes someone up. You've made your point. No proper mother. How bloody dare you? Just piss off and take that bloody dog with you."

"I just meant—"

"No. I've had it with people just meaning. Everyone grabbing at me for what they need, their special project, their little problem, can I help, can I just fit in one more thing. It's my turn now. And if people don't like it—"

"Yes, but—"

"As long as the kids are happy, and they are, Martin, I always put them first, actually, first, second, and third. But in case it's escaped your notice, I do need to earn a living. Nick was off having affairs and taking out a second mortgage before he finally left us, pretty much up the creek without a fucking boat, let alone a paddle."

"I know, but—"

"And that's exactly what I've been doing. An interview with Ellen, to get more customers for the shop. And yes, losing Nick was a terrible tragedy, and of course I wish he was still around, for the boys, for all that, of course I do. But part of me thinks it was just bloody typical. When it really got tough, he drives into a bloody tree and leaves me to sort it all out. And that's exactly what I'm doing. So why don't you just go, and let me get on with it. It's been a long day, like most of my days actually, and I'm doing my best, although I know it's not perfect, thanks. But anyone who doesn't like it can just bugger off."

"I just think you need to—"

"No, I don't need to do anything, Martin. Good night. You can see yourself out can't you? Night Trevor."

Trevor wags his tail as I walk out of the kitchen toward the stairs.

Christ. I don't know why he's got himself into such a state, but he's got me into one now. And he did sound uncannily like his mother for a minute or two there. Bloody hell. If Ellen wasn't at her awards thing, I'd call her. So I go back and sit at the kitchen table instead, and write a list, eating half a packet of chocolate biscuits in the process. And Martin is definitely not on my list. Bloody cheek. No proper mother. Christ.

Elsie's standing with her arms folded when I get to the shop the next morning. Well, she can keep them bloody folded, because I'm not in the mood.

I don't think those aspirin I took earlier can have kicked in yet either. I still feel like I've got a very tight hat on.

"Morning dear, I told him you wouldn't like it."

"Sorry?"

"I told him to talk to you about it, not just go booking it, but he wouldn't listen. Mind you, it does look like a nice hotel, doesn't it dear? In the brochure, I mean. Four stars and your dinner for that price, and it'll do you good to get away for a weekend. And we can manage in the shop, it's just one day really and I know Saturdays get busy but I'm sure we'll be fine, and it's not until November, make a nice break just before Christmas."

"Elsie, sorry, I'm not—"

"I've always liked Brighton, and there's some tree he wants to see, on the way, did he say? In a village, hundreds of years old, a yew tree I think he said. So you can have a break and he can look at it on the way back. So that'll be nice, won't it dear? Only I did tell him he should have checked with you before he went ahead and booked it."

"Right."

"I mean, it's not that easy, is it, planning for a little holi- day, it takes thinking about."

"Yes."

"He was in right old temper this morning; I couldn't get a word out of him. I only got Jeffrey to drive me round with a bit of washing for him, a few shirts ready for this trip he's doing for work; he'll be in hotels all the time, and they charge a fortune, don't they? He still hasn't got that washing machine sorted out, you know. Stainless steel and flashing lights are all very well, but you need something to do the washing in. He says he's still deciding, but you want to tell him to get a move on. Can't cook a nice dinner without an oven, can you dear? Typical man he is; they never think of the practicalities, do they? His father's just the same."

"Right."

"I only said he should get the washer sorted because I won't always be around to do his laundry for him, and he nearly bit my head off. Not had a proper breakfast probably; he's always terrible when he hasn't had a breakfast. Shall I put that new silk mix out; it's just arrived, and that pale pink has sold out again."

"Yes please."

"We're a bit low on the mohair again, for the shawls. Shall I put it in the book?"

"Thanks Elsie."

Damn. He must have been waiting for me to get home so he could tell me about Brighton and his big surprise. Damn. I call Ellen.

"Silly sod, I hope you told him where to get off."

"Oh, I told him all right. But he had it all planned, Ellen. It's such a shame, I feel awful now."

"Why? If he thinks he can start giving you lectures, it's the beginning of the end. You don't need that, or deserve it, come to that. Still, he's gone up in my estimation if I'm honest. I didn't think he had it in him. I mean obviously he was talking complete bollocks, but you've got to give him credit for being a bit assertive."

"He can be assertive, Ellen. Just not aggressive and domineering, which is a good thing; it's one of the things I like most about him, well, usually. Actually, I think this might be more about Patsy than me, you know."

"Who?"

"His ex-wife, Patricia, the one who ran off with his sales manager, where he used to work, and now everyone has to call her Patsy, and she wears an ankle chain. I think he was so humiliated by it all, it's made him extrasensitive."

"Doesn't sound very sensitive to me. I mean you'd told him you were out with me and he still went into one, didn't he? And anyway, you can do what you like; you don't have to stay indoors with boring old Martin every night, darling."

"He's not boring, Ellen, he's just, well, he doesn't need to keep proving himself, he knows what he wants."

"Yes, and I bet it's made of wood. Maybe this is a sign you should be taking a step back, keep your options open. Tell Martin to sort himself out or ship out. On that stupid bloody boat of his."

"He probably wouldn't make it out of the harbor. Look what happened last time."

She laughs. "We can put the coast guard on alert, and find you someone new."

"No thanks, not unless they're a grown-up. I don't want anyone else with daft dogs and bits of wood everywhere."

"I think you're wrong on that one, darling. You don't need an older man moaning on about what time is his supper, and where have you been? You need a bright young thing, handy for Friday nights but not up for anything involving moving furniture, apart from in the bedroom."

"Ellen, please."

"No, seriously. A younger man would be perfect for you, and it would send out a very good signal to old Dovetail. Plenty more trees in the forest, that kind of thing."

"Where on earth do you think I'm going to find a younger man round here? I'd probably know his mother and she'd march into the shop and slap me silly. No thanks."

"I bet that Tom's got some fit young friends. But if you're sure, don't say I didn't offer. Look, I better go, darling. I've got a car waiting, but call me later, yes?"

"Sure, and thanks Ellen. I was worried I was being unfair, but you don't think I should ring him then?"

"No, I bloody don't. Definitely not. Leave him to calm down and apologize. Or bugger off. Yes?"

"Yes."

"Sure? If you get tempted to call, ring me first, promise?"

"Yes. I'm going to sort out the orders for knitting kits, and then take the kids to the beach."

"Good. Talk later, darling."

keep trying to decide whether to call him, or text, in between watching Pearl fill her paddling pool with sand while the boys build camps with their plastic soldiers. I don't want to leave it like this, whatever Ellen says, and I finally crack in the evening and send him a text:

HOPE YOU'RE OKAY. AM IN THE SHOP TOMORROW
MORNING IF YOU FANCY BREAKFAST BEFORE YOU LEAVE
FOR YOUR WORK TRIP.

But there's no reply.

Bloody cheek. Well, he's definitely off my list now.

It's Wednesday morning, and I'm in the shop upstairs in the office for a couple of hours before Cinzia brings the kids in and we go to the beach again. Martin's in Glasgow according to Elsie, and I'm not sure he actually got my text because apparently Trevor buried his phone again, so he had to get a new one. But I'm not playing that game; if he wants to call, he can. He'll have kept the same number, so he'll have got my text, eventually. He hasn't fallen down a crevasse; he can phone or text if he wants to. And he hasn't, so he's obviously still sulking, which is his problem, not mine. Ellen's been giving me pep talks, but actually I'm fine about it. Surprisingly fine, to be honest. I've got enough on my plate trying to get through the last bit of the school holidays, and keep the shop going, and the café stocked with ice cream. We had our highest sales ever last week, but Connie's mum has finally gone home, so Mark has been pretty full-on at the pub, and we're running low on the sorbet and the vanilla and fudge. I haven't got time to worry about stupid men who put two and two together and make fifteen. Either he gets over it or he doesn't. It's not something I can help him with.

The phone rings. If it's that rep who keeps trying to sell me horrible plastic needles I think he might be in for a surprise, because I'm really not in the mood.

"Morning angel."

Bloody hell, what is it with Daniel? Either he's turning up out of the blue or he's ringing when I least expect it.

"Hello Daniel."

"How do you fancy a few days in Devon?"

"Sorry?"

"I've got a job, some U.K. staycation thing, a magazine piece for next spring, how all the beautiful people are having holidays at home. You know the kind of thing, when you can't face being stuck at the airport for three days, getting one bottle of water from British Airways and then being told to sod off and wait in the tent outside for further information. Bastards."

"Well I hope they've got anoraks."

"British Airways?"

"No, the people staying at home for their holidays. I went to Devon once with Nick, and it rained the entire time."

"Christ, I hadn't factored in rain. Right, Tony, she says it'll be chucking it down, so let's make sure we've got all the gear for that too."

There's a pause and sounds of muttering. It doesn't sound like Tony's pleased.

"Tony says thanks a lot, that's just screwed up his whole budget."

"It might not rain."

"If we haven't got all the gear, it bloody will. Tony's always getting us stuck in the middle of bloody nowhere with half the kit we need and trying to blame it on the client. I don't know why I have him on the payroll really; cost of his food is enough to make you weep."

There's the sound of scuffling now.

"She says you're an idiot, Tony, and she doesn't know why I don't give you the old heave-ho, and neither do I frankly. Right, anyway, Devon. They want gorgeous people but in family groups, all bleached driftwood and trendy surfers. The campaign is for all-year-round holidays, so it won't be a total disaster if the weather isn't perfect. Tony's got all the details, but I thought since we'll be down there for a few days, you could join us and I could get to know my Pearly Queen a bit better."

"Not if you keep calling her your Pearly Queen you won't."

"I'd like to spend some proper time with her."

There's a pause. I know he knows that I'll find this hard to resist.

"We'll be staying in a five-star hotel, overlooking some pretty epic beach; well, I say five stars, but Tony's been wittering on about rosettes. What the fuck do rosettes stand for when they're at home?"

"It means they put parsley on your dinner."

"Christ, I haven't stayed anywhere like that for ages. You'll have to come, help us cope with the shock of partying with the parsley people."

"I'm sure you'll manage."

"Seriously, I think you all need a little holiday. I could come and spend some time down there, but we're so busy, and anyway that bloody Cinzano hates me."

"Cinzia does not hate you, she doesn't hate anyone, she's lovely."

"Not to me she's not, she likes Forrest Hump."

"Martin has not got a hump. I told you, he sprained his shoulder."

I don't think I'm going to mention that I'm not actually speaking to him right now, hump or no hump. It seems disloyal somehow.

"Whatever. So, yes or no? You and the boys and my beautiful girl, and that horrible Italian girl if you have to. Just get in the car, turn up, and we'll take care of everything else."

"Only a man who has no idea of how much kit three children need for a few days at the seaside could say that."

"All right, you, kids, horrible Italian, lorry following full of flip-flops and shorts. What do you say? We need to know now so we can sort out the suites."

"Suites? Daniel, I can't afford that."

"Don't worry about that, angel. The client won't care how many rooms we book as long as we don't go over budget, and thanks to Tony and his legendary scrooge act that won't be a problem. Seriously, it won't cost you a penny, or me either, before you start saying you don't want me shelling out, so the cost of the hotel's not a problem. You might need a few quid for ice creams, and that'll be it."

"Can I think about it?"

"Of course. Tony, give her all the details, she's coming, so sort it out, would you? And try to persuade her not to bring that bloody Cinzano."

Christ, Martin would go nuts if he knew. But actually it's got nothing to do with him, he's off in a sulk, and anyway, this is just a few days by the sea in a hotel, where someone else is in charge of all the cooking for a change. I'd be mad not to go. It'll be great for Pearl, and the boys, getting to know Daniel, even though he'll be working, and surrounded by models and magazine people. So there's no reason not to go. But still. Ellen's all for it, of course, but the real clincher is when Gran says she thinks we should go and a break will do us all good. I haven't told her that Martin and I have had what she'd call Words, but somehow she's sensed something is up. And then she said she thinks it's important for Pearl, and I can't argue with that.

The boys are so excited, partly about us having a proper holiday, but also at the prospect of finally going surfing. The beaches round here don't have the right kinds of waves for surfing, so they've been longing to go somewhere and have a go. They're practicing in the back garden on tea trays while Cinzia helps me pack; even Peter's having a go. Gran and Betty are going to cover for me in the shop, with Elsie and Laura, and nobody's asked me why we're suddenly off to Devon, although Laura seems to think I've just spotted a last-minute bargain break and was asking me where I found out about it. Elsie was listening, so I wasn't quite as forthcoming as I might have been and just said a friend had told me; so I wasn't technically telling a fib but at the same time there are no snippets for her to tell Martin, if she ever actually gets to speak to him; she's been moaning that he's working so hard he never calls. I know the feeling.

Cinzia staggers in with an enormous suitcase. She and Tom are back off again; she saw him having a coffee with that girl who follows his band around and threw a very Italian fit. Tom says it was only a coffee, but she says it doesn't matter, he was already being boring, so it is over. Again. They both seem fairly relaxed about it, Tom's doing a mild bit of moping but nothing serious, and Cinzia doesn't appear bothered at all. I think they quite like all the drama, so I'm keeping well out of it because I don't want to end up being the referee; I get enough of that with the boys.

"Here, is my clothes. Do you think too many?"

"We're only away for four days, Cinzia."

"Yes, but I have some things for the Principessa too."

"Oh, right, great. What have you got so far?"

It turns out she's packed one sundress, which Pearl usually refuses to wear but is one of Cinzia's favorites, and a couple of baby T-shirts. We unpack her case, repack it, and it seems fuller than before, and then we pack for the boys, and Pearl, and I end up with a small nylon bag for my stuff, as usual. Two pairs of jeans should do it, and maybe one dress, in case the hotel dining room is on the posh side, but apparently Cinzia thinks this is a joke, so we have to unpack her case all over again. By the time we're done I'm exhausted, and we still have to get the bloody things downstairs.

Cinzia grins. "I have a plan."

If it involves more repacking, she can count me out.

She returns with one of our largest tea trays, which the boys have been using for their surfing practice.

"Here, see."

She puts a case on the tray and slides it down the stairs.

She's thrilled, and so is Pearl.

"Brava. But let's carry the bag with all the toiletries in down, shall we? And let's make sure the boys never see, or they'll be shooting stuff down the stairs for weeks."

Crikey, what a difference a day makes. We're in Devon, after a nightmare journey, in heavy traffic including an epic queue at Stonehenge, which as Archie so rightly said is just old rocks, so why are all these stupid people here? At one point I thought we'd have to get out and walk to Devon the queues were so bad. But we finally arrived, late last night, and found ourselves ushered up to a suite of interconnecting rooms, with a beautiful, sparkling white bathroom that is bigger than my bedroom at home. A very late supper magically appeared on trays, which fortunately nobody tried to slide down the hotel staircase. The boys have got bunk beds, which they love, in their own little bedroom, with a separate room for Cinzia, which had a cot for Pearl in it until I moved it into my room. We've got all the doors open between the rooms, and

Pearl is wandering in and out, rearranging all our shoes. The view of the sea is beautiful; the hotel is perched on top of the cliffs, with a winding path down to the beach, and formal lawns, with loungers and umbrellas dotted about, and two swimming pools. Waiters are scurrying about serving coffee to people who are breakfasting outdoors. I think I may have died and gone to heaven.

"Shall we go down to breakfast, Cinzia?"
      She's wearing a miniature sundress; actually it may be one of Pearl's.
"Yes, I am having the full English I think."
I don't think she's going to have any trouble getting the waiter to take her order.
"That sounds nice."
"I want that too, Mum, only I don't want egg."
"Okay Jack. Put your shoes on, love."
After a search for shoes and a mini-strop from Pearl as we muck up her display, we finally make it to the dining room, attracting a fair amount of attention in the process, what with Cinzia and her dress and Pearl and her tiara. Daniel's already sitting at a huge round table by the window, chatting to Tony.
"Morning angel. Tiaras for breakfast I see, nice. Are you ready to go surfing, boys? Morning Cinzia, nice frock. Jesus, what's this music in aid of? It's enough to finish off the en-tente cordiale forever."
For some unknown reason the hotel has chosen to play accordion music in the background, which does give the break-fast buffet the flavor of French farce in among all the juice and cereals. Pearl is already waving a bread roll in time to the music.

Various versions of the ubiquitous full English breakfast arrive, along with assorted models, who are staying in other hotels apparently, because this one is full. We're only here at all because a big group canceled, although Tony does wink at me when he says this, so I'm thinking someone may have been downgraded at the last minute or offered a full refund, which makes me feel slightly guilty, but in a rather smug, aren't-we-lucky sort of way if I'm completely honest. I'm cutting up bacon for Pearl and trying to persuade Archie not to go back up to the buffet for a third croissant when an astonishing blond woman arrives, wearing a thin white muslin shirt, flip-flops, and a white bikini bottom. The man on the next table chokes, and is hit on the back by his wife, quite hard by the look of it. The vision in white leans forward and kisses Daniel.

"Where do you want me, darling?"

The man on the next table chokes all over again.

"In makeup. They're all down on the beach, and put a vest on next time you're floating around the hotel, darling. Bit too much information first thing in the morning, don't you think?"

She laughs. "You're the boss."

She kisses him again and turns to look at the small crowd of hovering waiters. "Would one of you be a complete star and show me the way down to the beach?"

They all step forward until the headwaiter barges through and says he will be more than happy to show her himself, if everyone else could just get on with the jobs they are actually meant to be doing.

"Doesn't she want any bacon?"

"No Archie, I think she probably had hers earlier on."

Daniel laughs. "I doubt it. She's not really a full English kind of girl, Archie."

Pearl starts throwing toast.

"Quite right, Queenie."

"Daniel, don't encourage her, and Pearl, stop that right now or you can't have bacon."

"Bit of bacon?"

"Yes, I'm cutting it up, see, nearly done, but no throwing things. Here, eat it nicely, love."

"More."

Daniel laughs. "She knows what she wants, doesn't she?"

"Oh yes."

"Good, I like that in a girl."

"Great, well you can be in charge of her breakfast then. She'll want some fruit any minute. So get peeling and cutting up, or she'll be throwing toast at you."

Tony laughs.

The beach is lovely, with literally miles of sand, and wonderful rock pools at the base of the cliffs. We don't really have any decent rock pools in Broadgate, so the boys spend a happy hour with buckets and nets, fishing for tiny crabs and little fish, while Pearl paddles in the shallows. She's loving the beach and her new pink bucket. She's also rather brilliantly decided that she's far too grown-up for nappies anymore. After a few attempts from me with trainer pants, which she point-blank refused to wear, she suddenly insisted on wearing a pair of Archie's underpants last week, and that was it. Done. Even at night. And so far not a single accident; Connie says Nelly did the same thing, but I'm still rather amazed, because it took ages with Jack and Archie. But she's very determined, my gorgeous girl, so part of me isn't surprised that she's done it her way. She's getting so tall now, maybe she'll be a model one day; they all seem to have legs like giraffes. She's also quite fond of wandering around naked given half a chance, which will come in handy if the antics on the beach during the photographs this morning have been anything to go by. They've put up a large white gazebo-size tent for outfit changes and hair and makeup, but it's so hot, one side of the tent is permanently open, and none of the models seem the slightest bit interested in shuffling about inside towels. They simply stand there, in full view of the beach, while clothes are taken off and new ones put on. It's all rather mesmerizing, and there's a growing collection of young surfing gods who always seem to be wandering past with their boards at crucial moments.

The male models are less convincing on the surfing front than the locals, but undeniably bronzed and gorgeous, so there's always something diverting to watch, and the children for the various family scenes arrive in a minibus along with their mothers, who all seem very determined to get their children into the shots. I'm trying to keep out of the way as much as possible, which isn't easy since Pearl's taken a bit of a shine to the silver umbrellas Tony and the other assistants keep putting into crucial places to reflect the light. Cinzia's busy flirting with the male models, but everyone's fairly relaxed, and there's a huge amount of hanging about with nothing much seeming to happen, so I can easily retrieve Pearl and take her for a paddle when she starts being a nuisance, leaving Cinzia to hone her flirting skills.

After lunch the boys have their first surfing lesson, and Cinzia takes Pearl for a swim in the baby pool. The surfing instructor, another bronzed Adonis called Ted, is incredibly patient with them, and seems to be able to leap through the waves and retrieve anyone who is the wrong way up in the surf in about five seconds, which is reassuring.

"Mum, did you see me? I nearly stood up."

"Yes, you did, love."

"And I did too."

"Yes Archie, I saw, you were both great."

"Tomorrow I definitely will."

"I'm sure you will."

We're renting wet suits, which are a bugger to get on, and off, but they're so thrilled with it all they don't go into the usual meltdown of wriggling and fussing, and the really fabulous thing is it exhausts them so much they can hardly speak by the time they get out. Archie's so tired we barely make it back up the hill to the hotel. I give them both a quick bath, and order pasta on trays since there's no way they're going to last until suppertime, and Archie actually falls asleep in the middle of eating. It's absolutely brilliant. They're both spark out, by seven. Tucked into their bunk beds like poster children for the Perfect Outdoor Life. Even Pearl's fast asleep by half past seven, after a rather mammoth tantrum when I try to wash the sand out of her hair and inadvertently remove her tiara without permission. I put the bloody thing on the top shelf of the wardrobe until people stop screaming, and then after a tearful sorry, and a reunion with the tiara and half a bedtime story, she conks out, clutching her squirrel.

I'm totally knackered, and it turns out the hotel's idea of a baby listening service is for you to leave the phone off hook in your room, and reception come and find you if they hear yelling. Which isn't my idea of a foolproof system, and anyway Archie would simply put the receiver back down and set about trying to get unsuitable channels on TV. So Cinzia and I are taking it in turns to go to dinner.

"You go tonight, I'm fine, Cinzia. I'm so tired I'll just have a sandwich. And maybe some hotel chips. I love those little baskets of chips you get in hotels. I'll see you later, but don't be out too late, all right?"

She grins.

Dear God. She's wearing a tiny white dress I haven't seen before. I hope the man that choked at breakfast isn't in the dining room, or his wife will be banging him on the back again for sure.

"Is that a new dress?"

"Yes, today, Emma, she said I can borrow."

Emma is the woman in charge of the wardrobe. Clever Cinzia has clearly made a useful friend.

"Well it's lovely."

"It is Armani."

That explains it; it's somehow classy while being teeny. Not an easy combination.

"Do you want a shawl, in case it gets cold later on?"

"Please."

"There's a blue one, in my wardrobe, or that pink one you like."

She kisses me, and goes down to dinner in a cloud of perfume. My Chanel No. 5 if I'm not mistaken.

But I've got room service, three sleeping children, a balcony with table and chairs, and a beautiful view of the sea. So I really don't care.

Bliss.

It's our last day today at the hotel, and I think they're going to have to remove me by force tomorrow morning. We've all had such a lovely time. Even the weather has been perfect, hot in the mornings but cooler in the afternoons; it was almost cloudy yesterday after lunch, which was perfect for the photographs apparently since they were doing a family picnic scene, with beach huts in the background, or rather the façades of the beach huts, since they had to bring in pretend ones. Lots of beautiful people with old-fashioned picnic hampers and children skipping happily about, with fake beach huts that weren't nearly as nice as ours back in Broadgate. These were too freshly painted, and too pastel; ours are much jollier—so that's one thing to look forward to when we get home. It feels like we've been away for weeks. And while I could definitely do with another week here, I'm also missing home, which is great; there's nothing worse than being on holiday and dreading going home.

I think I'll start saving up and try to bring us back here next year; the kids've had such a great time and they do family rooms, which while still being astronomically expensive, are just about affordable if I save something each month. There's a big barbecue on the beach tonight, for all the hotel guests, and the magazine people have invited all the models to join us, so Cinzia's in seventh heaven deciding what to wear.

The boys have had their last surfing lesson with Ted, and nobody has tried to winch me into a wet suit, thank God, so I've been able to stay on the shoreline making sure all my small people kept their chins above the waves, while Pearl and Cinzia have been having a marvelous time flirting, with pretty much everyone. They've taken to going swimming in the sea with the waiters on their morning breaks, with Pearl wearing her armbands and being surrounded by a gaggle of bronzed surfers who keep a close watch on her and boost her up onto their shoulders whenever the waves get a bit too big. She's adored every moment of it.

—————

We're walking back up the hill for an afternoon nap so everyone is awake for the barbecue later.

"Can we go for a swim later, Mum?"

"Yes Archie, once we've all had our sleeps, but in the pool, yes, not back down to the sea or we won't have time to get ready for the barbecue."

He doesn't even have the energy to tut.

Who knew surfing would be so brilliant?

Everyone is half asleep watching *Toy Story* after sandwiches and crisps in our room.

"I'm off to the spa, Cinzia, okay?"

Words I never thought I'd hear myself say.

"Yes, we will see you later, she is asleep. And Archie too, in a minute."

He mumbles something along the lines of "No I Am Not," but he's definitely dozy.

"See you in a bit."

I'm not sure the hotel's Driftwood Salon is what Ellen would call a spa; it's more like Tina's salon with a few side rooms for facials, but I'm loving it. The girls are all local, and lovely, and I get my hair washed and dried, which is a huge treat. All the salt and chlorine from the past few days have left it decidedly frizzy, but Denise puts some special conditioner on it, and spends ages drying it into soft curls, so it looks much better than it usually does. I have a mini-manicure and pedicure too; it's all very relaxing, and I'm feeling very pleased with

myself as I walk back through the hotel lobby, admiring my
new shiny nails.

"Hello angel. Nice hair. Do you fancy a coffee?"

"Lovely."

"Where are the kids?"

"Asleep, upstairs, with Cinzia. I'm really going to miss
those surfing lessons, you know. Archie is so much less trouble
when he's completely exhausted. They'll be down in a bit, for
a swim. Have you finished all the photographs?"

"Yes, thank God. Finally done, and everyone happy. The
light's great here, so when they're around later come and find
me and I'll take some more snaps."

"Shall I find Tony too?"

He grins; I've been teasing him about how he can't take a
single photograph without Tony on standby with a selection
of alternative lenses, and someone else hovering with a light
meter and adjusting various umbrellas.

"No thanks, I think I can cope. I quite like this family
holiday lark you know."

"That's good."

"It's pretty easy, isn't it?"

"Daniel, you've got Tony, and God knows how many other
assistants from the magazine, and a PA in your office, and I've
got Cinzia here too."

"I don't think Cinzano counts; she's still giving me filthy
looks."

"Only when you bring Pearl back covered in sand and
hand her over for someone else to de-sand."

"Yes, but I explained, that wasn't my fault, one minute she
was fine, playing with her bucket, and the next minute

she tipped it over herself and rolled around in the sand like a girl possessed. I don't know what came over her."

"That's what being a toddler is all about, doing daft things when people least expect it. Especially if they're annoying."

"Well apart from the sand thing, I'm enjoying it."

"Yes, so am I, and thank you, Daniel, it's been such a treat. But it's not always such fun, what with the washing and the cooking and the homework for school and finding all their kit."

"Okay, okay, don't go into one. Christ, no wonder all the men go bald."

"Is this another Daniel Fitzgerald Observation?"

"Yes, you only have to look at them, not the young just-got-married-and-sprogged ones, but the older ones, especially the ones with wife number two. They're all sucking in their stomachs, and going bald."

"Nice."

"There was a perfect example today on the beach. Never plays with his kids, you could tell, no idea how to chill out and spend time with them. He lasted about half an hour before he marched them back to the mum. Twat. Fancy missing out on something so precious."

"Yes, it's especially precious when they wake up at three a.m. and want a light snack. Preferably a bit of bacon."

"Yeah, sorry about that. Who knew her catchphrase from this holiday would be 'bit of bacon'?"

I smile. "It's better than *nutter*."

"True. She knows her own mind though, doesn't she? I like that in a girl. And she's going to be a stunner, you can tell. I can't wait."

"Wait for what?"

"For when she's a bit bigger and I can take her places,

without that bloody bag full of stuff I don't really know how to use. Wet wipers, special cups with tops that won't undo, all that baby kit that they design to make men look like prats."

"I'm not sure that's part of the design brief you know."

"No, but it's an added bonus that all you mummy mafia enjoy."

"True. There have to be some perks; it's a crap job otherwise: on call twenty-four/seven, no days off unless you spend hours arranging cover, and even then you spend most of the time worrying about them. And inbuilt redundancy."

"What's inbuilt redundancy when it's at home?"

"The whole point of being a mum is that you bring them up so they can bugger off. Unless you can pull off that extended family thing where you all live in one big house."

"Will you do that then?"

"Not unless I can afford a much bigger house, no I bloody won't. Jack will be fine, but Archie is going to go straight for the kinds of girls no mother would want him to bring home. And God knows what Pearl will be like, but I'm betting it won't be quiet and shy and making lovely pastry."

He laughs, and then suddenly stops. "Christ, I've just thought. Some little bastard is going to want to be her first boyfriend. Over my dead body. We want her having none of that until she's at least, I don't know, twenty-six? God in heaven, there's no way I'm going to be able to cope with that. You'll have to get a big dog; actually, get a couple. Any male over fifteen who comes round has to get past them. Rottweilers would be good. I'll get a couple, send them down, shall I?"

"No thanks, we've got enough trouble with Trevor, and he's basically just daft. The last thing I need is something designed to take chunks out of people's legs."

"God, I need a drink. The idea of some bastard like me trying to dazzle my lovely girl is really freaking me out."

"She'll be fine. Actually it's more likely to be the other way round; look what she's like with that waiter."

He smiles. Cinzia is particularly fond of one of the waiters, one of the surfing gods who works only part-time in the hotel and is nowhere to be found whenever the waves are good. Pearl's taken rather a shine to him as well and holds her hands up for him to lift her up and twirl her about whenever she sees him, which he does, whereupon she nuzzles into his shoulder, hugely envied by all the women under thirty. Actually, quite a few over thirty too.

"Well, I'm not having it. I'm going to research attack dogs, specially trained to repel teenage boys."

"Right you are."

"I am."

"You go for it. As long as they live at your house, not mine."

By the time we've had our swim, and a cream tea, and Daniel has taken hundreds more photographs, it's nearly eight. The hotel has hung fairy lights on the beach, which are twinkling across the sand, and there's a proper beach fire, and a huge gas-fired barbecue with two chefs with white hats, grilling fish and prawns and fabulous steaks while waiters scurry up and down to the hotel with bowls of salads and orders for drinks. It's like a Barbecue Plus, all the usual food, but better cooked, and ice in your gin and tonic. I'm definitely going to save up for next year, and maybe I can persuade Ellen to join us; Eddie will love it, and I can always warn her about the spa not really being up to her usual hot-stones-and-special-mud-wraps standards.

There's music playing softly, thankfully not the breakfast accordion medley, and people are starting to dance.

"It's like my poem, Mum."

"What is, Jack?"

"'Hand in hand, on the edge of the sand, they danced by the light of the moon.' Let's do dancing, by the light of the moon, can we, Mum?"

"Yes love."

Daniel looks at me and winks. He's been reading stories to Pearl, and the book of nonsense rhymes is one of her current favorites.

"We haven't had slices of quince yet though, have we Jack?"

"No, but eat a fair amount of mince though, don't we Jack?"

Jack giggles as Daniel stands up.

"Come on, let's dance. We've got the honey, and plenty of money, but God knows where I've put the runcible spoon, Queenie has probably buried it somewhere. Actually, what is a runcible spoon?"

"We did it at school, and people think it's like a fork and a spoon all in one, but I think it's a special golden spoon like Kings and Queens have."

Daniel lifts Jack up and twirls him round, and he laughs, and then he gives Archie a twirl too and they end up dizzy and delighted, and then one of the waiters turns the music up and the Beach Boys' "Surfing USA" booms across the beach and everyone starts dancing. The waiters form into a line, loosening their ties and taking off their rather shiny black jackets as "Help Me, Rhonda" starts playing, and they go into what seems like a well-practiced routine, which is brilliant and very funny, and also quite rude, but in a way that none of the kids will pick up on. Pearl is dancing, and is picked up by our breakfast waiter and twirled around for a quick jive, and Cinzia and Amber, one of the models from the photo shoot, are in the middle of the circle, dancing with all the waiters simultaneously. It's so perfect you almost want to clap. Actually, Pearl is clapping.

By eleven the kids are half asleep, despite pretending they're not, so we carry them up the hill, with Tony and Daniel carrying the boys and Cinzia carrying Pearl while I carry the bags.

"Are you coming back down, angel?"

"I don't know. Someone needs to stay with the kids, and I'm pretty tired."

Actually I'm still feeling a bit dizzy from all the dancing. I may have slightly overdone it on the gin and tonics, but I really don't care.

"Cinzia will stay with the kids. Come back down and have another drink."

Cinzia doesn't look that pleased. I think she's got plans with one of the waiters, which come to think of it is probably just the kind of thing her mother is hoping I'll be watching out for. Tom too, not that it's any of my business. But I have stayed in the room for the past two nights.

"Maybe, just for one more drink."

After a sleepy round of putting pajamas on, and tucking them into bed, we walk back down to the beach, and sit chatting and drinking and watching the fire, while people dance and melt away into the dunes.

"Fancy a dance, Jo?"

"Thanks Tony, but I'm fine."

"Have a dance with me, love, celebrate the holiday?"

"Okay."

He's so sweet, Tony. He puts his arms on my shoulders and we sway along to "No Woman No Cry." Which always makes me want to cry.

He kisses my hand as the music finishes.

"Thank you Tony, that was lovely."

"My pleasure, sweetheart. You've made this week a total treat. We should have you and the kids on all our jobs, makes him behave himself. No walking off in a huff if he doesn't get his own way."

"I heard that."

"You were meant to, guv."

"Charming. I bring you to all these nice places, and all you ever do is moan."

"Nice places? I was up at five yesterday sorting those fucking huts out."

"Yes, and they still looked like crap."

"Watch out, guv, she's coming over."

One of the models, Tanya, the one who wore the see-through muslin shirt to breakfast, comes and drapes herself across Daniel.

"I've been waiting for you to dance with me, darling."

"Have you?"

"Yes."

"That's a shame; I'm all danced out, but thanks."

Tony's staring at his feet and trying not to laugh.

We sit watching the fire, and I realize I'm nearly asleep.

"I think I'll go up."

"I'll walk up with you, angel, make sure you don't fall off that bloody cliff path."

We start up the hill, which seems much longer now.

"Bloody hell, angel, I'm way too tired for this. They should have a lift."

"Or one of those golf carts. I quite like the idea of whizzing up and down in one of those. The boys would love it too."

"I wanted to say thanks, angel."

"What for?"

"These past couple of days. Tony's right, bringing the kids and everything, it's made a real difference. I've loved it."

"Good, because we've had a brilliant time."

"You're a total sweetheart, you know that, don't you?"

And then he kisses me. A nice friendly kiss, which suddenly turns into something else.

"Sorry angel, I didn't mean to do that."

We're both smiling now as he moves a strand of my hair behind my ear and kisses me again. And I kiss him back.

Oh God.

"I think I should—"

"Yes."

"Cinzia will be waiting for me."

"Let her wait. Let's just stand here for a minute, look at the moon; it's so close you could almost touch it. Fancy a dance?"

He's smiling as I look up at the moon, and he kisses me again.

"Daniel."

"I know. But just for tonight, angel, just you and me?"

Oh God.

Bloody hell. It's half past two.

"Daniel, I've got to go."

"I know, just stay a bit longer. It's usually me who creeps out of hotel bedrooms in the middle of the night, and this is the second time you've done this to me, first Venice and now Devon. Takes a bit of getting used to. Stay a bit longer."

"But Cinzia will—"

"She'll be fast asleep, dreaming of waiters, and so will Queenie, and the boys will be dreaming of waves. Come here."

It's half past four by the time I get back to the room, with my hair in a total tangle and a strange mark on my neck.

Bloody hell.

Bloody bloody hell.

8

Diamonds and Pearls

September and October

It's ten o'clock on Tuesday morning and we're all still in our pajamas. The traffic on the journey home from Devon was so terrible we had to stop three times, and each motorway service station was worse than the last.

Archie's busy reuniting himself with Peter Rabbit, who seems have enjoyed his mini-break with Gran and Reg. I'm pretty sure Reg has cleaned out his hutch too, and put in fresh straw, so that's one thing off my list, which is a bloody good job because I've just finished writing it, and it was so long I needed a second sheet of paper. Jack and Pearl are watching telly, in between Pearl lining up all our shoes in the hall, so I put the second load of washing on and call Ellen.

"What time did you get back?"

"Really late. The journey was a nightmare; I got so desperate I almost let Cinzia drive, and she's only got a license for a scooter. I'm so knackered I feel like I need another holiday."

She laughs. "Well, if you will go having magic moments, darling. What did he say in the morning?"

"Nothing really. We were busy with the kids at breakfast, and then with all the packing we didn't really get a chance to talk. But it was okay; it didn't feel too shameful or anything."

"Of course not, darling, it's brilliant actually, but you do need to know what he's thinking."

"I don't even know what I'm thinking, Ellen, and anyway, he's off to New York. He said he'll call when he's back and fix a time to come down to see Pearl."

"Yes, but don't you want some time with him, just the two of you? Why don't you leave the kids with Cinzia and see him in town when he gets back? See how you go. Call him tonight and arrange it."

"Because I don't want to, not really. It felt right to be coming home. This isn't the start of anything, Ellen, I'm sure it isn't, and there'll be loads to do in the shop. I haven't even got their school uniforms sorted and they're back next week. And anyway, Cinzia's sulking."

"Why?"

"She had a hot date lined up."

"Not as hot as yours by all accounts. She'll get over it."

"I know, but I don't want to push it. She's got the day off today, so I'm hoping she'll be a bit happier tomorrow. Gran will be around, but I really need some proper time in the shop. God knows what they've got up to while I've been away, but I bet Elsie's ordered all sorts of tragic stuff."

"You're not feeling guilty about Martin, are you? Because you shouldn't, you know. All bets are off if he's too stupid to call you."

"It's weird, but I'm okay about that. I think because I know it's not real. If I thought it was the start of something, I'm sure

I'd feel really guilty. Look, I better go, we've got to get to the bloody supermarket if we want any lunch."

"Lucky you."

"I know. I'm so looking forward to it. I'll call you later."

"Well done darling, just what you needed, a nice little fling, and I still think it might be more than that."

"We'll see."

Actually, what I'd really like is not to think about Daniel or Martin or anyone over ten. I want a nice calm few days doing what Nick used to call my ostrich act. I can't cope with all this drama. I haven't got the time to go into a meltdown about me and my complicated life, not unless food is going to magically appear in the fridge and someone else is going to finish the unpacking and sort all the washing and work out where Pearl's hidden her sandals.

We finally get to the supermarket just before lunch, when everyone is hungry, so that's a great start. But Jack and Archie are luckily in helpful mode and find items on the list quite chirpily, which gains me a few admiring glances from other mothers busy wrestling unsolicited food off their kids. Pearl sits in the seat in the trolley, wearing her tiara and waving breadsticks in a rather regal fashion. It's all going quite well until we get to the dairy aisle. The boys are fed up and start bickering about whether we do or do not like chocolate milk, which we're not buying anyway, and then they both start lobbying me to buy cheese strings, which are so revolting I refuse to buy them on principle. And before I know it all three of them are yelling and Pearl throws down her tiara, as a prelude to a serious tantrum. It skitters across the floor and disappears under one of the freezer cabinets.

"Stop it, right now, all of you. Jack, get the bloody tiara, would you?"

Jack and Archie pause, midshove.

"Mum, you said bloody."

"I know I did. I'm very cross."

"Yes but—"

"No buts, Archie, just be quiet."

Jack's lying on his tummy, retrieving the tiara, and even Pearl has gone silent, although she's clearly considering whether to go into a Full Monty meltdown.

Jack hands me the tiara, and I put the sodding thing back on her head.

"Thank you, Jack. Pearl, no more shouting, we just need a few more things and we can go home. We can get chocolate mousse, for people who are not doing shouting, but there can't be any for people who are being silly."

Jack and Archie nod, recognizing the signs of a mother about to ban television for the rest of the day, but Pearl is oblivious and slowly removes her tiara and chucks it. Thankfully this time it lands in among the frozen peas.

"She's done it again, Mum."

"Thanks Archie, I did notice. Just ignore her."

I pick the tiara up and put it in my bag as she goes into a full screaming strop. She's kicking her legs and could probably propel the trolley round the shop all by herself. I move to the back of the trolley and push it from the side, a trick I learned with Archie, which attracts another admiring glance from a mum, but for a different reason obviously.

We move into the household supplies section, and the boys find washing-up liquid and fabric softener, and each time

I put anything in the trolley there's another round of shrieking and kicking. Jack and Archie, after initially quite enjoying the spectacle of their sister looping out, are now trudging along looking unhappy. I think they're genetically programmed to sympathize with whichever member of the family is having a strop with their mother. They quite enjoy someone getting a mini-telling-off, but anything more protracted than that and their allegiances definitely shift.

"I think you're being very cruel, Mum."

"Do you, Archie? Get a box of Shreddies please, love."

"I don't like—"

"I don't care, just get a box, and get Weetabix too please, and no, we're not having chocolate anything."

He tuts.

"Mum."

"Yes Jack?"

"Can I give her a breadstick, she's lost her others."

Pearl pauses, to listen to my response.

"She hasn't lost them, Jack; she's thrown them on the floor, which was silly. So no, I've got better things to spend my money on than food for people to throw on the floor. When she stops yelling, and says sorry, we can have a cuddle. But people who yell and kick and throw things can't have breadsticks. Or tiaras."

We get into another round of yelling and I'm starting to think I might have to cave and give her the bloody tiara when Annabel Morgan appears, pushing a trolley with Horrible Harry trotting along beside her. How absolutely bloody perfect. Harry and Archie glare at each other as Annabel scans the contents of my trolley and gives me one of her special condescending smiles. Thank God I didn't let them have the cheese strings.

"Supermarkets are so ghastly, aren't they? We usually shop at the farmers' markets, so super, aren't they? But we're just back from two weeks in France; Harry's French has improved so much. I suppose with your little shop it must be so difficult for you. Did you manage to get away at all?"

"We've just got back from Devon."

Archie nods and steps forward. Oh, God.

"Yes, and we stayed in a big hotel, with swimming pools and everything, it was brilliant, and we had fridges in our rooms, with chocolate in, and nuts. And Coke. And we did surfing, and Ted said I was very good, so I might be a surfer when I grow up, or a magician, I haven't decided yet."

He smiles, and gives Harry a rather menacing I-can-do-magic-so-you-better-watch-out kind of look.

Pearl has stopped yelling and is busy watching Archie, so I think this might be the perfect time for a quick exit before she starts up again. "Lovely to see you, Annabel, but we must get on."

I risk pulling the trolley from the front, while Pearl glares at me and then turns her head away, so she practically ends up facing backward, and we head into the biscuits and cakes aisle, which was very poor planning on my part because Jack and Archie start agitating for all sorts of packets of biscuits which we don't usually buy, and since I'm trying to be placatory, we end up with marshmallow teacakes and peanut cookies and a giant pack of Kit Kats, along with the digestives and custard creams for the shop, while I take the opportunity to solicit the magic word *sorry* from Pearl and reunite her with the bloody tiara, along with a large chunk of baguette. And then we're into the sweets and crisps aisle and things get even worse. Still, I'm sure they'll come in handy at some point, and I need all three of them out of full-strop mode so we can look at new school shirts and trousers in the clothing aisles at the back of the store.

After the usual scramble to find the right sizes, which are miraculously on the racks, we head for the till, and the end is in sight. Hurrah. Thirteen shopping bags later, I'm about to put my credit card into the machine when the till beeps and goes blank.

"The till's gone down. You'll have to go to another till and put it back through again."

The girl behind the till seems to find this amusing; she's about nineteen, and presumably child-free. Charm-free too.

"Sorry?"

"There's nothing I can do, you'll have to go through another till."

She's definitely smirking now. There are long queues at all the other tills, and Pearl's nearly finished eating her bread.

Actually, I don't bloody think so.

"Can you call the manager for me please?"

She presses a button, and a supervisor wanders over. Pearl is definitely moments away from another strop, and I'm about to join her.

"Sorry, there's nothing we can do, you'll need to go through another till."

"But we've got the total, it's still on the credit card machine, here's my card, just put it through and I can go."

"You need a till receipt."

"I really don't."

"We can't let you take things like that. How would we know what things you've bought? We need it for stock control. I'm sorry, but you'll just have to rescan everything."

"I think I need to speak to the manager."

"He's not here."

"The duty manager then. Now please."

She looks at me, and takes a mobile from her apron pocket as she walks away a few feet and turns her back.

"He says he's very busy, sorry."

"Well, could you ring him back and tell him I'm from Head Office and I'd like a word? Thanks."

I saw Ellen do this once, and it worked wonders.

She looks at me again and presses a button on her phone. "She says she's from Head Office."

She puts the phone back in her pocket, and we stand waiting, with Pearl glaring at all of us and dropping bits of bread on the floor, like we might need to retract our steps, while Jack and Archie lean against the checkout and sigh.

The manager appears, in a shiny suit, looking very pleased with himself. "Good afternoon, madam. Can I help?"

He's clearly waiting for my special Head Office credentials, but I've already worked out what I'm going to say. I'm channeling Ellen, which always works, well, nearly always.

"I'm a customer who spends a great deal of money here. I've got a trolley full of shopping, and your till has broken. So this is what we're going to do. I'm going to take my kids to the car, and you're going to sort it out. Here's my card, and my loyalty card. You can bring me my trolley and my receipt, with everything repacked, and if you're smart you'll bring me a bunch of flowers, to say sorry for the inconvenience and your staff appearing to think this is all highly amusing and somehow my problem. And then I'll tell you exactly who to call in Head Office so you can report in. But I do need you to do it, not one of your staff. It will give you some excellent practice in customer relations at the sharp end. Upskilling is so important. Thank you."

I hand him my card, pick up Pearl, who is now fortunately

silent. The supervisor winks at me, and the manager stands with his mouth slightly open.

"Come on, Jack, Archie, we're just going to wait in the car, I'm sure it won't be long. This nice man is going to sort it all out for us."

We walk to the car, and I'm half pleased that I've managed to be so assertive, and half terrified that security will appear and insist I leave the car park and we'll have to go somewhere else and get all the bloody shopping all over again. I've just sat down in the driving seat when my phone beeps.

Christ. Maybe they're texting me to tell me my loyalty card has been canceled and I've been banned for life.

"Jo?"

Bloody hell, it's Martin. What perfect timing.

"Hello Martin."

"How are you?"

"Fine thanks. Well, actually we're in the middle of a bit of a drama in the supermarket, but apart from that."

"Look, I just wanted to say I'm sorry, about the last time we spoke. I didn't mean half of it, not about you. I should have said it to Patsy, not you. But I think a break has probably been good, and I hope we can talk when I'm back? Can we?"

"Of course we can, Martin."

"Oh, thank God for that. Good, well, I should be home by the end of next week, so maybe we could meet up then?"

"Sure."

"This job has been mad. I'm sorry I haven't called before now, but Mum says you've been in Devon."

Here we go. Damn. I really don't want any more drama today.

"Yes. Daniel was working down there, so we had a few days in a hotel."

He hesitates, and then rallies. "That must have been nice."

"Yes, it was. The boys learnt to surf."

"Look, I better go, they're calling me into the next meeting, but I suddenly thought this is ridiculous and I should call you. I'll come round when I get back. And I'm really pleased, that you're still speaking to me. I'll call you soon."

The line goes dead.

Bloody hell. Part of me is really glad he called, and part of me thinks it's a bit of a cheek and I should have been cooler; he was totally out of order, and I'm not sure we can just go back to normal, whatever that is. But if I'm being strictly fair, I have managed to have another interlude with Daniel, which is exactly what he was accusing me of when I hadn't. Oh God, this is complicated. I think the ostrich thing is going to come in very handy if I can pull it off; otherwise I'm going to be a nervous wreck.

The manager from the supermarket taps on the window, which makes me jump. He's got the trolley full of bags of shopping, and a bunch of pink roses. Blimey; I didn't think I'd been that scary. How gratifying.

"Here we are, madam, and I do want to apologize once again."

"Thank you and I'll be writing to Head Office, to tell them how well you handled this. Let me just write down your name."

He hesitates, and then smiles.

"Thank you, madam. I thought you were one of our mystery shoppers for a minute there. Be just my luck for a till to go down for one of them."

Great, so that's something else to add to my list: write a letter to the bloody Head Office, wherever they are. Still, the roses are very pretty.

"I'll send you a copy of the letter, let me just write down your name."

He stands waving as we drive off.

I call Ellen, after bath time, which I'm celebrating with a small gin and tonic. I think I may need a little bit longer to get out of holiday mode.

"You didn't."

"I did. Thanks to your excellent example, I'm finally getting the hang of causing havoc in shops."

She laughs. "And how did Dovetail sound?"

"Fine."

"I still think you should have given him more of a hard time."

"I'm not into all that game playing, Ellen. I haven't got the energy."

"So what are you going to tell him, when you see him?"

"I've got no idea."

"That's my girl."

"No, I've literally got no idea. I'll see what he says, I suppose. If he's still being all pompous and sounding like his mother, he can bugger off. But if it was just a one-off, well, he's allowed to get grumpy once in a while, Ellen. We are quite a complicated package, one way or another."

"And Daniel?"

"There's no And Daniel. I never thought there was."

Actually I am slightly disappointed that he hasn't rung. Not surprised, but a tiny bit disappointed.

"See how it goes, darling; stranger things have happened at sea."

"True. Usually to Martin. Well I know one thing for sure."

"What?"

"Whatever happens I'm not getting a stupid orange anorak."

She laughs.

"Good decision, darling."

'm thinking about how mothers tend to get themselves into quite a few tricky situations on behalf of our children as I pour myself a tiny bit more gin. I'd never have gone to bloody Devon in the first place if it wasn't for Pearl. Still, tomorrow is another day as Gran says, and the boys are at school next week, so there are only a few more days of the school holidays before I can get back to normal. Hurrah. And as for anything else, I'm definitely not going to think about it.

t's Wednesday morning and the first week of the new school term, and just to add to the pressure of getting back into the swing of school mornings, I'm in my sodding tabard on the walking bus.

"Come on Archie, what are you doing, love?"

"Putting my bag in the hall for my sticker."

"Right, well that's good, but come and have some breakfast."

Bugger. We're running out of stickers. We've had a holiday amnesty over the past few weeks, so I better get some more or there'll be complaints to the management.

"I don't like my new school shirts, Mum, they're all scratchy."

"No they're not, Jack, they're just new."

And a size too big, since he's growing so fast. I even put all the new kit through the washing machine to get rid of that new-clothes chemical sheen that tends to bring on Jack's eczema on his elbows. Thank God they're only Aertex shirts and not proper ones or I'd have been ironing until midnight.

"Can I take Peter to school?"

"Don't be silly, Archie."

"I'm not. People walk to school with dogs, so we can walk with Peter."

"On the walking bus, are you joking?"

He grins. "Natasha's got a goat called Gladys."

"Yes, but she doesn't bring her on the walking bus. Now eat some cereal please."

Pearl has refused to eat cereal, so I've fobbed her off with a slice of toast.

"Bit of bacon?"

"Not today, sweetheart, but you've got lovely honey on your toast."

She throws her cup on the floor.

Great.

t's a perfect September morning as we make our way to the bottom of the High Street, sunny but not too hot, and Pearl's happily eating a second round of emergency toast after I diverted the beginnings of a second tantrum by silently cutting up apple and pear for people who weren't yelling. But I must add bacon to the shopping list, because there's only so many times she'll fall for a slice of apple, and I'd prefer a bit less tension on school mornings.

Connie's waiting with Maximo in his baby sling, fast asleep. She looks tired; she's definitely missing her mum and those enforced afternoon naps.

"Do you want me to have a go?"

"Yes please."

We carefully execute a sleeping baby plus sling transfer maneuver, and I keep moving, swaying from side to side like I might be about to start a slow waltz, which is pretty vital if we don't want him to wake up, which we seriously don't, and then we're off. Connie gives a modest baby-proof peep on her whistle, and Pearl starts singing her less baby-proof version of "If you're happy and you know it clap your hands," with accompanying clapping, as we walk up the High Street, collecting children as we go, like a maternal version of the Pied bloody Piper. Fortunately baby Max is oblivious, making an occasional sucking movement with his mouth, like he's feeding in his sleep. He looks adorable, and it's much easier walking with the baby in the sling when you're pushing a buggy, it gives you something to lean on, so I'm quite enjoying myself in the sunshine as Pearl moves on to singing "I'm a Little Teapot," despite the restrictions of the buggy interrupting her usual spout impressions.

The kids are excited about being back at school, however much they pretend they're not, and by the time we reach the school playground, they're all hopping and jumping and chattering away. Just one more reason to thank my lucky stars I'm not a primary school teacher.

"Mirabelle does not look happy."

I've shared Ellen's triumphant renaming of Annabel with Connie, and she's enjoying it almost as much as I am.

I'm still doing the maternal waltz and moving slowly backward and forward when Mr. O'Brien comes over.

"I wonder if we could have a quick word. Oh, is this the new baby, Mrs. Maxwell? Isn't he a little star being so quiet?"

He pauses and looks at the chaos in the playground. "Trent, please don't do that, it could be very dangerous. Could you hang on for a minute, Mrs. Mackenzie? Only Mrs. Berry and I would like a word."

"Of course."

Why does Archie's teacher want a word? Bloody hell, what now? It's only the start of term; even Archie can't have done anything yet.

"Here, give him to me. I will take the bambini to the café, yes?"

"Thanks Con, I'll be there as quick as I can."

We manage a reverse sling maneuver as Maximo starts to snuffle, so Connie sets off at quite a trot, with Pearl waving her tiara.

The kids are lining up now, sort of, after a great deal of bell ringing by Mrs. Tindall.

I wait by the main doors as they file in.

Mirabelle is giving me a very Hard look, clearly desperate to know why I'm lingering, no doubt hoping against hope that Mr. O'Brien has finally come to his senses and is about to expel at least one of my children, if not all three of them, if they can do advance expulsions for babies.

Mr. O'Brien is smiling. "That's better; I always forget how much noise they make. Let's sit in the staff room. Mrs. Berry will be along in a minute; she'll just get them settled with her new classroom assistant; nice woman, Mrs. Bentley, you'll like her. It was Mrs. Berry who thought of the idea, so I want to wait until she's here to tell you about it herself."

Bugger; I've got a horrible feeling this is going to be another in-school knitting project. Better than an issue with Archie of course, but I was half hoping it was a walking bus update or something boring like that. Even a quiet word

about how we can All Help Archie Be a Bit Less Lively would
be better than another bloody knitting project with mixed
infants. I'm trapped now, in a staff room that is looking very
first-day-of-term tidy. In a few weeks' time it'll be full of piles
of paper and half-drunk cups of coffee, and no doubt I'll be
knitting something annoying. Damn.

Mrs. Berry comes in, looking flustered. "Sorry about that,
they're all as high as kites. Your Archie's been telling me all
about his rabbit. Can he really do magic tricks with him?"

"Not so you'd notice, no."

She smiles and looks at Mr. O'Brien. "Yes, right, so the
thing is, we've been thinking about our Christmas play."

Double bugger; I knew it.

"Certain members of the PTA are very keen that we do a
proper Nativity play this year, as I think you know."

We all smile. Annabel has been lobbying for a proper Nativity for ages; I think she sees Harry in a starring role. Actually, he'd make a perfect Herod.

"So we've decided to do one, but not the usual, where only
a few children get the choice parts."

We all smile again. Bang goes her dream of Harry as Jo-
seph, or one of the Kings. I'm not really sure what other starring roles there are apart from the baby Jesus, and not even
Annabel could think Harry would pull that one off.

"We'll do it as a whole school project, where every class
makes something. We can use papier-mâché, and cardboard
for the stable walls and the crib, and we can make up bales of
straw, that kind of thing. But for the animals and the people
we thought some knitting might work, and then we can bring
everyone together to build a Nativity scene onstage, during
the concert."

"That sounds lovely but—"

"If you could help us, we'd be so grateful."

"I'm not sure I follow you. You want to knit a Nativity?"

Mr. O'Brien smiles, and Mrs. Berry nods. "Yes, there are so many lovely songs we can use as themes: 'We Three Kings,' 'While Shepherds Watched Their Flocks,' 'Little Donkey.'"

"So you want me to knit a donkey?"

She laughs. "Not life-size, of course."

"Thank God for that."

We're all laughing as Annabel opens the staff room door.

"So sorry, I didn't realize. I was just looking for the PTA folders. Good morning, Mrs. Mackenzie, is this a PTA matter? Because if so I'm more than happy to be consulted; as President I do try to keep up with any issues our parents might be worrying about. So often I can sort things out without taking up any of Mr. O'Brien's valuable time."

Mr. O'Brien stands up.

"No thank you, Mrs. Morgan, we've just finished a very useful curriculum planning session, and Mrs. Mackenzie is very kindly helping us again with her expert knowledge. We'll be starting a new project for our Nativity, none of that old-fashioned nonsense where a few children get the starring roles and everyone else is a sheep. Thank you again, Mrs. Mackenzie, for offering to help, and I'm sure the concert will be a triumph. I'll leave you and Mrs. Berry to start working on the planning." He ushers Mrs. Morgan out of the doorway. "Now then, Mrs. Morgan, I did want a word about the library. We'd like to order some more books with all the money we raised at the fayre, but the teachers do need to choose the titles, so they link into our literacy themes. Last time some of the books weren't quite what we were hoping for. I'm not sure who chose them, but there are some wonderful new books now, so I've drawn up a list." He closes the door as he goes out.

"Bloody hell he's good. Oh, sorry."

Mrs. Berry laughs. "No, you're right. Jim's great with her."

"He certainly is."

"Are you sure you can manage this knitting project? I didn't like to ask you because I know how busy you are, but what's that thing they say? If you want something done, ask a busy woman?"

"It'll be fine as long as we have enough volunteers, but I'm still a bit worried about the sizes. Are you sure I'm not going to have to work out how to knit a life-size sheep or anything?"

She laughs. "Perish the thought."

"Or cattle. Actually, I have no idea how you'd even start to knit a cow."

"As long as it's big enough to see onstage. But it needn't be huge. The children can hold things up before they put them into the display, and we'll get an army of helpers, I'm sure we will, like we did for our beautiful new banner. Each time I look at it, it makes me smile. Every single child in the school knitted something for it, that's the best thing of all. They're all so proud of it."

"So sort of normal toy size, that kind of thing?"

"Yes, and Mrs. Pickering will help, and Mrs. Johnson, and all the staff, well, most of them. We just need the ideas. Whenever I look in your shop windows, they're always so full of beautiful things, and so original. I loved the Teddy Bears' Picnic, and the beautiful seahorse."

"I'm not sure there was a seahorse at the Nativity, was there?"

She smiles. "Possibly not, but the one in your window is so beautiful, let's have one anyway. We can be as creative as we like, make whatever animals the children would like to make."

"I'm not knitting dinosaurs, thanks."

"Apart from anything Jurassic, or cartoon-based."

"That's clever. I'll knit you a seahorse of your own if you'd like one. It can be your Christmas present from Archie; it'll make a change from our usual bottle of bubble bath."

"I do wish parents wouldn't do that. I worry about the expense for some of my families, you know, and I get so much, it lasts me for months."

"Well, hopefully your new seahorse will last a bit longer. I'll put some lavender in, and then it'll be vaguely useful."

"Oh I'd love that. Did you know they're the only species where the males have the babies?"

"I did. And I'd like to know how they manage it, because if we can get men on the moon, surely we can give it a go! I can think of so many things that would change if they had to waddle about nine months pregnant."

"It would be terrific, wouldn't it? I'm sure they'd have special medals made, and maternity leave would suddenly be three years, at full pay. And I bet they'd all have epidurals, and six weeks in intensive care afterward."

Mrs. Berry has two teenage daughters and once told me, luckily after I'd had Pearl, that she spent twenty-nine hours in labor with the first one and bit her husband so hard he needed a stitch in his thumb.

I nod.

"Yes, or they'd go all competitive and be giving birth halfway up Everest, in a cagoule. Extreme birthing. They'd probably enter it into the Olympics; it would be a lot more useful than the hundred meters."

We're both giggling as we walk back down the corridor toward her classroom.

Bugger. So now I'm knitting an entire Nativity, possibly with
cattle, and a lavender seahorse. No pressure at all then.

I'll have to make a whole new list.

"A knitted Nativity?"

"Yes Gran."

"Well, isn't that lovely?"

Elsie's pleased too. Sometimes I think they both live on
an entirely different planet to me.

"We've got all those patterns for toy animals, that'll help.
I think there's a little donkey, and we've got the Nativity we
knitted for the window, to use as an example."

"Yes Elsie, but we won't be able to give them complicated
patterns. We'll have to do it like we did for the banner. They
can all knit squares, and then we can sew them together, something like that."

"I see what you mean, dear, yes, that might be best. Some of
the older ones might be able to manage a simple pattern though,
if we have a look. But who's going to pay for all the wool?"

"Last time we got the parents to donate stuff, and some of
the suppliers helped. I'll make some calls. They've still got all
the needles from last time, and I don't mind giving them some
stock, so we'll be fine on that front. It's how we get it all
done that's worrying me."

"I'll help, and I'm sure Mary and Betty will too?"

Betty's holding Maximo, having a quick cuddle while
Connie has a coffee and Gran pours more tea.

"Of course I will, pet, and Laura will have some ideas, it'll
look lovely in her folder for college, and we can ask that Mrs.
Peterson, do her good to get out more, and she'd like being in
the school, I'm sure she would. Take her out of herself."

"That's true, Gran. All right, well maybe it's not a total disaster."

Connie laughs. "No. But promise I am not knitting the donkey."

Cinzia arrives to take Pearl off for their morning wander, and Tom retreats upstairs to unload the dishwasher. They seem to be thawing slightly again; they went out for a drink at the weekend according to Connie, although Cinzia was home by ten. I'm not sure if all that flirting in Devon helped, not that Tom knows about that. But I'm definitely taking a what-happened-in-Devon-stays-in-Devon approach. Connie says something in Italian to Cinzia as she's leaving, with Pearl insisting on walking, which means it will take her hours to get home.

"What was that, Con?"

"I said she's like the weather, cold, then hot, then cold again. Poor Tom."

Betty giggles. "You've got to treat them keen to keep them mean, no, it's the other way round I think. Anyway, she might as well have a bit of fun while she's young, that's what I always say. We never got the chance."

"Oh I don't know, Betty; you seemed to have quite a nice time at all those dances at the Palace Ballroom from what I remember."

Betty smiles. "That's true enough, Mary, and I had some lovely frocks. I wish I'd kept them. I couldn't fit into them, of course, but I could look at them, couldn't I? But I wish I'd gone in for more dancing now. Anyway, we better be off if you want to get your shopping in and nip into the Lifeboats before we go to our first aid class at the church."

"Bother, I'd forgotten about that. I'm not sure I'm in the mood."

"Well, I'm not being bandaged again, that's all I'm saying. It took me ages to get the feeling back in my hand last time, and look what happened to poor Mrs. Winterton."

We all smile, and then feel guilty; Mrs. Winterton tripped over the demonstration dummy at their last class, and sprained her ankle, and somehow in among the rush of willing stretcher bearers, they managed to tip her off the church hall stretcher and fracture her elbow.

"They just got overexcited about having a real casualty to practice on. But it could be handy knowing how to jump-start someone."

Unless the Red Cross are going in for car maintenance now, I think Betty must mean resuscitate.

"Although you'd have to watch yourself round here; most of the time if they're on the floor down by the pier, it's because they've been at the drink. They sit there fishing looking like butter wouldn't melt and all the time they're swigging from their flasks and then they try to stand up and go down like skittles."

Gran smiles. "I've always got a clean hankie in my bag, so that'll be handy. You have to do that before you start the concussions."

Betty laughs. "You mean compressions, Mary. Chest compressions is what she said. You don't want to be giving them concussion on top of the heart attack, do you? Anyway, you'd need more than a hankie with some of them, unless you wanted it reeking of whiskey for days after. Ooh look, here comes Lady Denby."

Lady Denby comes in, in a state of high excitement, fortunately minus Algie and Clarkson.

"We've won, absolutely marvelous, had to come and tell you straightaway. Gold Medal, Best Seaside Town (Small). Knew we could do it if we all pulled together."

"That's wonderful, Lady Denby."

She's delighted, and before I know it we've got a little celebration going on in the café, with Lord Denby eating cake and making Betty giggle, and Gran and Elsie talking to Lady Denby about exactly when the medal will be presented and who will be invited and whether they need to wear hats.

By the time they've finished, it's nearly ten past twelve.

"Well done again, my dear, and good afternoon to you, Moira."

Elsie bobs a small curtsy at Lord Denby.

"Chap might get a bit of peace now; need to get back in the garden, instead of being dragged all round the town with frightful judges."

Lady Denby gives him a Look, and they wander off bickering; she's already told us how vital it is for us to retain our Gold Medal next year, so no doubt she'll be starting her new campaign as soon as the ceremony is over.

"I'll see you later then, pet."

"Yes Gran."

"It's lovely, isn't it, about the medal. It'll put a few noses out of joint, but I've always said you can't beat our pier."

"No Gran."

"Come on, Mary, or we'll be late for the class and we'll have to sit on those nasty metal chairs at the back."

Elsie's had such a lovely morning so far she even offers to tidy up.

"I'll just have a sort-out, shall I? Some of those shelves are in quite a muddle. I do wish people would put things back where they found them."

"Thanks, Elsie."

"We'll have to start thinking about our Christmas windows next, won't we? Be nice to have something new, for when we get our medal."

"Yes."

Damn. That's something else for the List. I thought we might make a kit for an Advent calendar, with a little knitted toy for each day, along with a gold chocolate coin, because I always think Advent calendars without chocolate are not really worth the bother: a bit like low-fat cake. And I want to knit more lavender bags, and Gus and Duggie want to sell tea cozies in their B and B; they've been so popular they want to start having a range to sell, with egg cozies too.

I'm in the stockroom checking the box of Christmas things from last year when Elsie comes up. "A courier just brought this for you."

It's a large package from New York.

"Thanks, Elsie, just leave it in the office. It'll be the brochures I ordered for Grace."

She looks briefly disappointed but goes back downstairs to share the glorious Gold Medal news with any passing customers, which is good because the last thing I need is her looking over my shoulder at whatever Daniel has sent. At least I hope it's from Daniel. I'm going to feel pretty stupid if it is brochures.

There's a large gray box inside the padded envelope, full of beautiful black-and-white prints of the children in Devon, along with some smaller color ones, which I'm sure Daniel would call snaps. They're still gorgeous. The black-and-white ones are the kind of thing you see in galleries. There's a lovely one of Pearl's hand, which I'd know anywhere even if she wasn't holding her tiara, and a beautiful one of all four of us sitting in the sand dunes, with Pearl on my lap and Jack and Archie either side of me, all of us looking intently into Archie's bucket of shells and rock pool treasures.

God, they're so beautiful I'm almost in tears. I'll get some of them framed; they're far too nice to keep hidden in albums.

I've got no idea if he's still in New York, or what time it is there, so I text him.

THE PHOTOGRAPHS ARE BEAUTIFUL. AMAZING. MAYBE YOU SHOULD TRY TO GET WORK AS A PROFESSIONAL PHOTOGRAPHER. THANK YOU, THANK YOU, THANK YOU JO X

I sit in the office and go through them again, and realize that there's a look on Jack's face in quite a few of the pictures, relaxed and happy and smiling, which I haven't seen enough of in the past couple of years. He looks younger somehow, and so does Archie. I'm trying to work out which photographs to frame when the phone rings.

"They arrived then?"

"Yes, and they're brilliant, Daniel, thanks so much. I'm going to get them framed. The only tricky bit will be choosing my favorite ones."

"Good. It's nice to hear someone's happy with my work. The tossers on that last job were total nightmares."

"Oh dear."

"It was worse than oh dear, angel. Even Tony lost his cool, and he never lets it get to him usually. He told the creative director to piss off."

"That doesn't sound great."

"It was actually. We won in the end; the client liked our choice not theirs. As bloody usual. When will they learn? Anyway, we're at the bloody airport again, off to Barbados, and it's hurricane season, so we'll probably get blown off the beach."

"Nice work if you can get it."

He laughs. "How are things in exotic Broadgate?"

"We've just won the Gold Medal in the Best Seaside competition, so I wouldn't mock if I were you. Everything's fine, apart from being recruited to knit a Nativity at school, which is going to be a nightmare of epic proportions. Knitting donkeys with a bunch of six-year-olds. I can't wait."

"Can you knit donkeys then?"

"I'm about to find out. The Gold Medal is good though, don't you think?"

"Brilliant. Maybe I should buy a house down there, before the prices shoot up. I've been thinking about it actually. The flat was only ever meant to be a short-term thing, I'd like a house. Maybe something fabulous by the sea?"

"Do you want to leave London then?"

"Not really, but it could be a weekend place. Actually, I've been thinking about that too, about Pearl and everything, and I want to tell people, I'm so proud of her, I haven't even told my mum."

Bloody hell, I'm not sure I really want another set of grandparents to deal with; Mum and Dad are more than enough. And Elizabeth and Gerald have hardly been a tower of strength in our hour of need. But I suppose if he's going to be part of Pearl's life, it makes sense that he'll want his mum to know. I just wish this wasn't so complicated.

"She'll think I'm a total trollop."

He laughs. "You're almost the exact opposite of that, angel."

"Oh, thanks. I quite like the idea of being a bit trollopy."

"Sorry, no can do. Not unless you change your entire wardrobe, and personality, and well, pretty much everything."

"I could be racy though, couldn't I?"

"Oh yes, definitely racy."

"Good."

He laughs again. "I've been having a think, angel."

"Oh yes?"

"This is something I really want to get right."

"I know."

"I want you and the kids to be part of my life, properly. Why don't you move up to town? We could get you a shop, and I could buy a decent-size house, and maybe a weekend place by the sea? What do you think? It's got to be worth a go."

Bloody hell. I'm not sure what he's trying to say.

"Give what a go?"

"I don't know, but I'm sure we could work something out. As long as I see my girl, that's a good start, isn't it?"

"Yes, but it doesn't work like that, Daniel, not with kids; you can't just give things a go and then move on to the next thing if it doesn't work out. The boys in particular have had enough changes to cope with."

"And you?"

"What about me?"

"That's precisely my point, angel. Just think about it. Look, I've got to go, they're calling our flight, but I wanted to tell you what I was thinking, hot off the press. We'll talk properly when I'm back, okay? I know I'm not making much sense, but I wanted you to know I'm ready."

"Ready?"

"To be a good dad."

"That's great."

"I'll see you soon."

"Okay."

Christ. I don't see how on earth I'm going to pull off my ostrich act now.

call Ellen, who inevitably is all for me racing up to London and waiting at whichever airport he's likely to land at when the Barbados job is finished.

"Don't be daft, Ellen. I don't even know when he's back, and anyway he's talking about Pearl, not me, even if he doesn't realize it. And even if he wasn't, who says it's what I want? There's this assumption that if he was really up for it I'd be mad not to up sticks and move in with him, but actually, I'm not sure that's true."

"Why not?"

"He's wonderful, in lots of ways, but he's not a grown-up. And that's what I want, a grown-up, someone who can fit in with our life, not dominate everything every bloody second. It would be just like Nick, only worse; he'd be popping in to pick up clean shirts and then he'd be off again."

"Worse?"

"He's a photographer, Ellen, surrounded by the world's most gorgeous women, day in, day out. Think about it. But actually it's not that, though that's enough to put any sane woman right off the idea. It was a fling, Ellen, a moment that reminded me that I wasn't just a mum, I mean not only a mum, I could have my own things too, a little secret interlude. I didn't fall in love with him or anything, and it's no use pretending I did. And he's definitely not in love with me, whatever that means."

"You know what it means, darling, and most of it is complete rubbish. He sets your pulse racing, he makes you laugh, he's solvent, and he loves the kids. And you'd live nearer to me so we could have jaunts. It's perfect. Look, don't make your mind up until you see him. You never know, he might surprise you."

"I'm sure he will, he's always surprising me. But there's no point pretending, Ellen. I love our life here, so do the kids, far too much to risk changing anything on a whim. And anyway, I already know."

"Know what?"

"Know who he loves; it's Pearl."

"Sweetheart—"

"No Ellen, it's true, and I'm fine with that, more than fine. She deserves that, of course she does."

"Still, nice to be asked, darling?"

"Yes, although I'm still not sure what he's asking, and neither is he. But nice, whatever it is."

Actually, it's not that nice; it's unsettling and complicated, and there's a tiny part of me that is half hoping it might be true, and we can all sail off into the sunset and play happy families while he flies round the world earning a fortune taking pictures before racing back home to us. But the trouble with being older and wiser: you know what makes you happy, and what makes your children happy.

It's a total bugger.

've just finished making supper and I'm having a quick cup of tea before I can face bath time, when Grace calls. She's nearly six months pregnant now, although she doesn't look it, and they've been busy filming in Northumberland, in a huge country house.

"How are you doing?"

"Rather brilliantly, darling, thank you. We've done most of the scenes where she's got to have a tiny waist, thank God, and now we're doing the newly married and up the duff bits."

"That's handy."

She laughs.

"Why do you think I chose the script, darling? It's looking very good, if I say so myself. There's something about acting being pregnant when you actually are which is rather mesmerizing, and the clothes are beautiful, all pin-tucked cotton and thin muslin shifts, and silks. Beautiful and floating, they fit my mood perfectly."

"And how's the gorgeous Colin?"

The newspapers have been full of the usual silly stories about her and her costar.

"Gorgeous. And not quite as devoted to the wife as he'd have us all believe, but I never mix business with pleasure, you know that, darling."

Actually, I know the exact opposite, but it's never a good idea to disagree with the Diva.

"Anyway, I've run out of wool again, so can you sort it please? Urgently."

Maxine has been texting me with snippets; and apparently in between flirting, Grace is knitting like a woman possessed.

"Max already put me on alert this morning, so there's a

courier delivering tomorrow. More of the baby cashmere and cotton, and some new patterns I thought you might like to see. But are you sure you're not overdoing, Grace? You are taking rests and everything, aren't you?"

"Yes, we've hired a nurse, who does my blood pressure, and everything is normal, so there's quite enough fussing going on with Max and her without you joining in, thank you. Tell me all the news. Max says the town won a medal?"

"Yes, for the Best Seaside, everyone's thrilled."

"And?"

"Not much else really. We survived the school holidays, we had a couple of days in Devon, with Daniel Fitzgerald actually, and now they're back at school and I've ended up with a knit-a-Nativity project, so that's a bit worrying."

She laughs. "So he's finally spent some proper time with Pearl. Good for him, not a total loser then after all. And?"

"Sorry?"

"How much time did you spend with the lovely Mr. Fitzgerald, one-on-one?"

"Grace, I don't."

"Don't try to kid me, darling. I know him. There's no way he'd be able to resist his very own Madonna and Child. You know he's not good enough for you, don't you? He might show some potential on the father front, I can see that, and he'd be mad not to, she's such a poppet. But he's nowhere near ready for anything else."

"You mean if I turned up on his doorstep, with the kids, and said, Right, here we are, he'd have the mother of all panic attacks and be on a flight before I'd even got the bags out of the car?"

"Exactly. Good for you, darling, I always forget how sensible you are."

"Can I ask you something? And be honest. If I was, well, more like you. Beautiful and—"

"Please don't, darling, or you'll have me in tears. I'm very tearful at the moment, the slightest thing can set me off, it must be all those fucking hormones. But if you were the most beautiful woman in the universe, it would still be the same. And by the way, nobody is ever as perfect as they want to be, ever. That way lies total madness."

"I sort of knew that, I just wanted to ask."

"You're way out of his league, darling."

"I know, I just—"

"No, you idiot, you're way above his league. You play for real; he's still stuck in the imaginary world of beautiful light and getting the perfect shot. Trust me, I know the type, I'm pretty similar myself, although I'd never admit to it. But you're more real than that. You just have to look at your kids to know that."

"What a lovely thing to say."

"My pleasure. It happens to be true. And anyway, I don't want to lose my knitting coach."

"Okay."

"I'll see you when we're back."

"Lovely."

"And darling?"

"Yes Grace."

"Tell him to watch his fucking step from me, okay?"

"Sure."

The boys come home from school on Thursday with some sort of mystery bug, so I have to race home early from my Stitch and Bitch group to rescue Gran from Archie, who always makes a huge fuss at the slightest sniffle. They spend the whole of Friday whining and moaning with slight temperatures and lots of coughing and sneezing, and then annoyingly perk up on Saturday, once they're sure it's not a school morning, whereas I feel like death warmed up. Archie brings me up a wet flannel, and a cup of tea made with cold water, which is obviously delicious, and then asks me if he and Jack can make pancakes. I can't actually think of anything better designed to get a sick mother belting downstairs than the prospect of two small boys flipping pancakes in a red-hot frying pan and filling the kitchen with smoke. I've been waiting for the cavalry to arrive in the form of Gran, with soup, for what seems like hours, but it's Martin who arrives, wearing his tragic anorak and looking completely filthy.

"I'm sorry to turn up like this, I've just been down to the boat to check everything was okay and Trevor got a bit excited."

He looks like he's been dragged through quite a lot of mud, which, knowing Trevor, he probably has.

"Where is he?"

"Dad took him home to wash him; he's in no state to go visiting."

He's grinning. "Mum will go nuts when she finds out. Anyway, can I come in?"

"Of course, sorry."

Bugger. I'm feeling worse and worse, but I can hardly let him in and then crawl upstairs and collapse, he'll think I'm making a point. So we sit in the kitchen, and he doesn't appear to notice that I'm still in my dressing gown and constantly sneezing while I make the tea.

"I am very sorry, you know, about the last time we spoke."

"It's fine, Martin."

"I just don't want to be dull old dependable Martin. I'm not a total pushover, you know."

I look at him, and he grins. "I might not be around forever, you know."

"Where are you going then?"

"I don't know, I might go somewhere on the boat."

We both smile.

"I realize I need to make more of an effort, with us I mean, our relationship."

"I don't think it should be an effort, Martin."

"No, sorry, I didn't mean it like that. I just think we should spend more time together; we could have a rota or something, make sure we go away for a weekend occasionally. Once I get the barn sorted, we can spend some of our time there too. We could write a list of things we want to do, places we'd like to visit, and then make sure we do them."

Great, another bloody list.

I pour the tea and hand him his cup.

"Thanks. I think we need to make more of an effort, that's all I'm trying to say."

Actually, the only effort I can make at the moment is to stay sitting upright, but he's oblivious.

"I do know what you mean, Martin."

"Do you? That's great; because I'm not sure I'm explaining it very well. Anyway, I should be able to get loads done on the barn when this job's finally finished. I've earned a fortune in overtime."

"That's good."

He starts telling me all about the plans for underfloor heating at the barn, and I can see he's so relieved we're back on what I'm sure he'd call an even keel given his newly found passion for nautical terminology that I haven't got the heart to stop him. Not that I want to. I just don't want to feel like we're back in a rut. But I'll have to talk to him about it an-other day, because I'm feeling on the point of hallucinating when Gran finally makes him leave and marches me back up to bed, with hot lemon and lots of lovely tablets. I catch sight of myself in the mirror on my chest of drawers and realize that I have a bright red nose, and my eyes are all puffy. So that's rather mortifying. But at least the upside of Martin being a tiny bit oblivious to normal social signals is that it doesn't matter if you happen to look like the dong with the luminous nose when he pops round for a chat. I'm still con-fused about Daniel, and whether I should be telling Martin about Devon, or if it doesn't count since we weren't techni-cally seeing each other then, what with him being off in a megastrop. Maybe when the room stops spinning and I've had a sleep, it will all become clear to me.

Or possibly not.

'm still feeling shaky on Sunday, but less feverish and tragic, not least because Gran has insisted on practically moving in with Reg and making me stop in bed all day. Just one more reason why I can't imagine how I'd ever cope without her. She's downstairs making egg and chips for supper; she sent Reg home for her chip pan earlier on. The boys are thrilled, and so am I. Egg and chips was our favorite supper when Vin and I used to come to stay with her for our summer holidays.

Jack comes up, holding the phone.

"It's Daniel, Mum."

"Oh, right. Thanks love."

He races back downstairs to keep an eye on the progress of the chips.

"Hello Daniel."

"I gather chips are on the menu."

"Yes, we're all thrilled."

"So I gathered. Well, save some for me. We might be down near you next week. I'll nip in and see Queenie if that's okay, for that job where we were looking at locations near you the last time I visited. The one that was on, then off, then back on again."

I know the feeling.

"How's it going, angel?"

"Crap, to be honest. I've had a horrible cold, I've still got it, actually. I look like the dong with the luminous nose, and I feel like it too."

"Had any thoughts about moving up to town?"

He's sounding nervous now. And I know, without him saying anything, that he's changing his mind, he's less keen on the idea now. And I don't even really mind.

"Yes. I've put the house on the market, but I've been thinking, and we should get married before we move in, don't you think?"

He's silent, but I'm sure I can hear him panicking.

"I'm joking, Daniel."

"Christ, you had me going there."

"So do I take it you've started to go off the idea? Be honest, Daniel."

"Maybe a little. Is that okay, angel?"

"Of course. You were never going to want to settle down, with a ready-made family and a middle-aged woman with creaking knees."

"I like your knees."

"Daniel."

"Well I might not have entirely got it out of my system,

this wandering-around-the-world thing. Not entirely. I might not be ready to totally embrace family life, in all its glory. But I want to be a proper dad."

"Yes, and I'm all for that, you know I am, as long as you don't keep appearing and disappearing, and making her feel insecure. Because if you muck her about, I'll have to kill you."

He laughs. "Yes, but are you sure?"

"We're not just talking about Pearl, it's me and the boys too, and that's quite a lot of pressure for one little girl. And anyway, I think we're worth more than that, Daniel."

"More than what?"

"More than living together. Because we like each other, and you love Pearl."

"I love you too, angel, I really do. I wouldn't have said anything if I didn't. You're so real."

"I know, and I love you too, but it's not real life. And when I'm even more real, in ten years' time? Can I ask you something Daniel?"

"Sure."

"How many women do you think you've had flings with, over the past ten years?"

"I don't know, angel, honestly. A few."

"And how many in the next ten years, if you were living with someone real and the kids were teenagers, and being, well, teenagers? How many models and bright young things would have moments in Venice, or Devon, or pretty much anywhere?"

"I don't know, angel. I'd try, I really would, but—"

"I'm not trying to catch you out. It's fine, but it's not the way I want to live. I've already done that with Nick. I don't want to feel second best, or feel that the thing you love most about me is my daughter."

He's silent again. "Good for you, angel."

"We can be friends, and Pearl's mum and dad. That's pretty good, isn't it?"

"Bloody amazing. You're the first woman I've ever really been able to say that about."

"I should bloody hope so."

"No, I mean the friends thing. I've never really seen the point before."

I laugh.

"Men don't, angel. They say they do, but they don't really. We don't want friends, not like women do. We can't sustain it. Too much talking, not enough, well, not enough not talking. But I don't want to miss being her dad, racketing around the world. I'll wake up and she'll be all grown up."

"Well don't then. We'll be friends and spends years and years watching her grow up, and being there for her, and each other, whatever happens, and I think that's brilliant, don't you? There's just one condition."

"Name it."

"Don't parade a series of gorgeous young things through my kitchen every time you come to see Pearl, okay?"

He laughs. "Deal. And you're still my jumbly girl, you know that, don't you? See, I read that bloody nursery rhyme book to Queenie so many times I know it off by heart now."

"Good, because for a minute there I thought you meant it looks like I get my clothes in jumble sales. But if you're quoting Edward Lear, that's okay."

He laughs.

"Jumble sales are Vintage, angel, very cool."

"Night Daniel."

"Night angel."

I have a quiet moment, feeling tearful, but I'm sure that's

just this bloody cold. There's a part of me that wishes things were different, that I was ten years younger and I didn't know what I know. But only a small part.

"Mum."

"Yes Jack."

"The chips are ready."

It just goes to show, to every cloud there's definitely a silver lining.

"Lovely darling, I'll be down in a minute."

t's half past seven in the morning, and I'm trying to finish the list for the birthday party tomorrow. I can't believe it's the middle of October already, and Pearl is nearly two and Jack is going to be ten. Ten; it's ridiculous, it seems like only five minutes ago when he was a baby. The past few weeks have passed in a blur of knitting and Nativity plans, but we've finally settled on Jack's favorite party theme, which is what he wants every year although he likes to take his time before he finally decides. A bonfire fancy-dress party with a Halloween theme, with Pearl being allowed to have her own cake and a share in the celebrations. I'm sure when she's bigger we'll be Princesses a-go-go, but this year she won't really care as long as I don't try to dress her up as a pumpkin.

call Ellen for a catch-up chat.

"I'm sorry we won't be there, darling."

"You'd be mad to miss the chance of a few days away, all expenses paid."

"I know, but the hotel is full of telly people, and Eddie didn't sleep that well in his travel cot last night. I'll have to book him and Harry their own room for tonight if he carries on; there's not much point spending all day in the spa if I'm awake half the bloody night. And I've got to give a speech later, Broadcasting Tomorrow Today, some bollocks like that."

"We'll see you next weekend, and we can have another birthday moment then."

"Okay, so you're sorted with the Village Hall and everything?"

"Yes, Gran fixed it. They get really booked up, but there was one Sunday afternoon slot pending for the Bowls Club, so she nabbed it. We can use the field at the back for the bonfire, Reg and Jeffrey are in charge of that, and the fireworks, and Elsie's volunteered herself for sparkler patrol."

"What's sparkler patrol?"

"Making sure nobody sets fire to their gloves."

"Good plan. Did you find the Halloween tablecloths?"

"Yup, and paper plates, paper everything, so in theory we can fill a couple of rubbish bags at the end and we'll be done. Mark's doing the cakes, and bringing some of his butternut squash soup for the grown-ups, and I'm doing loads of baked potatoes. Christ, I better add more baking potatoes to my list."

"Darling."

"Yes."

"Remember to breathe."

"That's easy for you to say, you haven't got nearly forty kids and God knows how many adults coming to a tea party. Just pray it doesn't rain, would you?"

"I'll do my best."

t's not raining. Hurrah. Martin's finally back from the last bit of his tour of the major cities in the U.K., so he's out in the field with Graham, rearranging the bonfire while Reg and Jeffrey set up the fireworks. They're enjoying themselves so much they were seriously discussing buying walkie-talkies for better coordination last week; I'm surprised they haven't bought special jackets.

The noise in the hall is indescribable. Gran and Betty are in charge of musical chairs, and then we'll move on to pin the tail on the Halloween donkey, and then musical statues to calm them down before we sit them at the trestle tables for tea. I've got three pass the parcels wrapped in my bag, just to keep everything going. If only the bloody cocktail sausages would cook in the antique oven, which seems to do stone cold or tepid as its two temperature options, we'd be fine. Pretty much everything else is ready.

"Do you need a hand?"

"No thanks, Tina. I'm just waiting for the sausages to cook and we're all done."

"You've put on quite a spread; it must have taken you ages."

"Gran and Betty love making party food, it's mostly down to them."

"Do you want a cup of tea?"

"Yes please, that would be great."

She puts the kettle on and rinses out the big catering teapot. "How many bags do I put in?"

"Six, and then everyone can have a cup, if they're not in the middle of musical chairs that is."

I give the sausages another anxious check, but the oven's finally warming up. "Ten more minutes, I think."

"Have a breather, love. Here, sit on that stool. I meant to tell you, have you heard the latest about Mrs. Bentley?"

The new classroom assistant for Archie's class has turned out to be a bit of a star. Mrs. Berry loves her; she's always been a great teacher and handles Archie brilliantly, but with Mrs. Bentley as backup, they've been doing all sorts of new projects. She's not only helping out with the knitting but she's also turned out to be Mrs. Bentley-Harrington, part of the local posh Harrington family, so Annabel has naturally assumed she'd become part of her coterie what with the snooty name and a rather good line in imperious glances. But the person she's been most imperious with is Annabel, which we've all been enjoying immensely.

"We were talking about it in the salon with Jane Johnson, and apparently Annabel invited Mrs. Bentley to one of her 'little kitchen suppers,' you know, those ones where she goes all posh and gets the silver out, like that one Cath went to by mistake when she first moved down here, only she turned her down flat, in front of Jane. She said it was brilliant, and Annabel was so furious she broke her pencil, snapped the end right off, Jane says."

"Archie likes her too. He says she smells of flowers, and when she reads stories she does lots of different voices."

Tina smiles. "Top marks all round then."

We're clearing the plates ready to bring the jelly and ice cream in when Daniel arrives.

"Hello angel, sorry we're so late. Tony got lost, again. Say sorry, Tony."

Tony steps forward, grinning, and hands me two birthday cards. "Sorry Tony."

"It's fine, Tony, and thank you, that's really sweet of you."

Daniel shakes his head. "It's not fine; I wanted to be here on time."

"You're in time for the cake, Daniel, and that's the big moment. Actually, you can carry Pearl's in if you like while I do Jack's."

"Really?"

He looks very pleased, and hands his camera to Tony.

"Much as it pains me, here, try and take some snaps with this, would you? Preferably where we all have heads, that kind of thing. The light's fine, so just don't touch anything."

Tony gives him a Look. "Who do you think fixes all your jobs when you're heading for disaster again?"

"Me."

He laughs. "I believe you, guv, thousands wouldn't."

The cakes are a triumph, Mark has really excelled himself. Jack has a giant J-shaped chocolate cake, with candles and indoor sparklers, and Pearl's is a pink extravaganza with edible glitter. She's completely thrilled. We sing "Happy Birthday" and then shepherd everyone outside to work off some of the sugar overload by racing round the bonfire before the fireworks kick off.

I'm making another round of cups of teas and coffee when Daniel comes in with two more cups. "Reg says he'd like one sugar this time."

"Okay."

"Great bonfire. Here, I got this for my girl, but I didn't want you opening it in front of everyone."

He reaches into his satchel and hands me a battered old leather box, in pale green leather.

It's a tiara, with a pearl in the middle, and what look like diamonds suspended in the middle of the flower shapes that surround the pearl.

"Oh, God, Daniel, it's gorgeous."

"It's a necklace too. That central bit unclips and there's a silver chain, in that little velvet pocket, see?"

"It's beautiful. She'll love it, but it's far too—"

"I know, but I couldn't resist it. It probably belonged to another Principessa. I found it in Venice. It just seemed so perfect, and I thought you could save it for her, for when she's bigger."

"Of course I will. Actually, she'd love it now, but I'd be worried she'd break it, it's so delicate."

"Good, I'm glad you like it. I told the guy in the shop it was for my two-year-old daughter. It felt great saying it, actually, and he went all soppy; you know what the Italians are like about kids. So I had to buy it after that. But we can't have our girl with better jewelry than her mum, can we? So here."

He hands me another battered box, this time in navy blue leather.

"Daniel, you shouldn't— Oh, my God."

It's the most beautiful necklace I've ever seen. A pearl necklace, with what I seriously hope aren't diamonds around the central pearl, which is huge, and beautiful pearl earrings to match. I should probably refuse it, but I can't. I love it too much already.

"Thank you, so much, it's absolutely beautiful."

"Great, so now you've both got diamonds. Girl's best friend, right?"

"Definitely."

Bloody hell, they really are diamonds.

"And you're still sure, angel? No second thoughts? There could be more diamonds, just say the word."

He's looking nervous.

"Don't worry. I'm not going to change my mind."

He grins. "But wherever you are, whoever you're with, I'm access all areas, yes? Well, not all areas but—"

"I know what you mean, Daniel, and yes. You're stuck with us now."

"Good. What did you get her by the way?"

"A plastic toddler-size kitchen, with plastic plates and saucepans and food. It's completely hideous. But at least it won't cause any damage if I put her saucepans on fast spin. Tragically stereotypical, I know, but she loves it."

"Whatever gets you through the night, right?"

"Yes."

He puts his arms round my waist and kisses me on the cheek, just as the kitchen door opens and Martin comes in.

Damn. They've been ignoring each other so far, not in any obvious way, but there's definitely been a tension. Which has just got a whole lot worse.

"Hello Martin. How are you?"

"I was fine, until you turned up. Can we have a word? Outside?"

Oh, God.

"Sure, what about? It's not about the wonderful world of wood, is it mate, because to be honest, it's not really my thing."

"I want to know what your intentions are. With Jo. I mean obviously Jo."

"Sorry?"

"Do you love her? Because if you do, well, that's fine. I

mean not fine, obviously, but I can accept that. But if you don't, then I think you should leave. It's the last thing she needs, the last thing the kids need, someone wasting their time. So, do you?"

"Sorry, you've lost me. Do I what?"

"Love her."

"I'm not sure I'm really comfortable discussing that with someone wearing such a ridiculous hat. Your mother made it, is that right?"

Martin goes red, and pulls his hat off.

"That's better. Now, where were we?"

Martin steps forward. "Will you just answer the question?"

"Or what? Christ, you're not going to challenge me to a duel are you? With special chisels or something?"

Crikey. So much testosterone, so little time. Actually, this is getting ridiculous.

"Daniel, stop it."

He smiles. "It's fine, angel. We're just having a chat. You need to channel it, mate, be a bit more assertive in your daily life, don't go round bottling it all up and then start venting at people."

"Daniel, I mean it. Stop it."

"It's all right. I'm just giving a few tips, man to man."

Martin looks furious.

Oh, God, they're glaring at each now.

Tony arrives, looking breathless. "What's going on here then? Come on, gents, let's break this up, shall we? I've always wanted to say that. Not much chance surrounded by models and bloody clients. Come on, guv, let's—"

"Fuck off, Tony. There's nothing to break up. He's come in, said his piece, and taken his woolly hat off. And now he's done. About time too, if you ask me."

And then Martin shoves him, and he lurches backward, and then he shoves him back.

It's so ridiculous I think we're all slightly stunned for a moment.

"Stop it, right now. Honestly, you're worse than the kids. Martin, go back outside, and Daniel, pull yourself together."

"Why do I have to be the one that goes outside?"

Daniel sniggers.

"Right, I'll go outside, and when you've both finished behaving like children, you can both bugger off home. I've had quite enough of this."

"No, it's fine Jo. I'll go out. I need to help Dad with the fireworks."

Martin glares at Daniel, picks up his hat, and slams the door behind him.

"What's his problem?"

"I quite liked him." Tony's grinning.

"Tony, you know that thing where I tell you to piss off, and you don't get it?"

"Yes."

"You're doing it right now."

"Oh. Right. I'm off for another little walk then. Only could you hurry up, guv? It's bloody freezing out there and we should be at the hotel for dinner with the client in about an hour. And it's at least a three-hour drive. See you later, Jo."

"Bye Tony."

"Well, that was a turn-up for the books."

"It's not a joke, Daniel."

"I know, angel. But wait for a bit, will you?"

"Wait for what?"

"Before you tell him that he's just made a total tit of himself and we're friends and nothing else. And don't tell him we were ever talking about, well, about anything else. I don't want him thinking he's seen me off."

"Daniel."

"Yes."

"You're ridiculous."

"I know that, angel. But I'm your kind of ridiculous, and anyway, we're going to be friends, and friends do favors for each other, don't they?"

"Yes."

"Well then, make him sweat for a bit, before you tell him he's won."

"He hasn't won. Christ I'm not a prize in a lucky dip."

He smiles.

"And if you ever behave like that again, I'm seriously going to lose my temper with you."

"Sorry. But he loves you, didn't you hear him? And that's a start, isn't it? And he's a decent enough bloke. Terrible temper, but you can't have everything."

"I've never seen him like that before."

"But girls like that sort of stuff, don't they?"

"Not really. Not if they've got any sense they don't."

"Oh, I get it. You don't know if you love him back?"

"I do, in lots of ways, but it's complicated."

"It always is."

"I know."

"All's fair in love and war, angel."

"Yes, and that's bollocks too. Fair is fair. It doesn't change just because love gets involved. And as for war, there'd be far less of that if men didn't think it was all right to go round shoving people. It's pathetic."

"True. And I promise I'll try harder to play nicely next time I see him, okay?"

"You bloody well better."

"I'll call you."

"Okay, and thank you, for the presents. They're, well, they're amazing."

"Nothing less than you deserve, angel."

He kisses me on the cheek and goes off back through the hall and out the main door.

I'm still trying to work out if I want to kick something or burst into tears when Gran comes in. "Was that Daniel leaving?"

"Yes, Gran."

"He's a lovely man, but that sort is always more trouble than they're worth, in the end. Like your Nick, too clever for his own good. He was bound to trip himself up in the end, too high an opinion of himself. The grass is always greener with men like him."

"Sometimes the grass *is* greener, Gran."

"Yes, and sometimes it's a collage."

"A collage? Do you mean mirage, Gran?"

"Yes pet, one of them too. But he does love our Pearl, anyone can see that."

"He's still going to be around, Gran. We're good friends, and he wants to be part of her life, properly."

"That's nice, but you want someone you can count on. Not someone who's always arriving and leaving."

"I know, Gran."

"Not that I mean you need to settle, if you're not ready." She looks at me and smiles. "Your Martin looked upset."

"Yes."

"He's a lovely man you know."

"I know, Gran."

"Well, good. But that doesn't mean you have to rush into

anything. There's plenty of time for that, you're still young. Look at me and Reg. You take your time, pet. You've got a whole lifetime ahead of you with the boys growing up and our Pearl giving you a few more sleepless nights."

We both smile.

"The thing is, does he take your breath away? Because I think you need that in a man, at your age. At any age, come to think of it. And Reg might not look like it, but he can still make me go all peculiar, and that's important."

"Yes Gran, but—"

"I don't mean in bed; I think there's far too much talked about that. No, I mean the things they say, the little things they do, things that make you realize you're important to them, that they'd turn the world upside down to find you. Anyway, that's what I think, pet."

"Nick took my breath away all the bloody time, and look how that turned out."

"Yes, but it was worth it though, wasn't it?"

She pats my hand.

"Yes Gran, it was."

"There you go then. I know people say you need someone as you grow older, but I don't know why. You don't want someone cluttering the place up and treading mud in from the garden and wanting his meals cooked unless you really love him, pet. Better to be on your own and have things the way you like them, far less bother in the end, unless you meet someone really special."

Gran's having a running battle with Reg over "mud" from the garden.

"Yes Gran."

"I just want you to be happy, pet. Don't listen to anybody

else. Just do whatever makes you happy, and then the children will be happy too, and so will I."

"Thanks Gran."

The fireworks are lovely, and Elsie makes sure nobody sets fire to their brother's hood, and then they're playing tag, while Pearl and Laura's Rosie play their own version, which involves running and then hurling yourself onto the grass giggling. Even Maximo is enjoying himself, transfixed by the bonfire and trying to get his gloves off.

Martin is standing by the fire.

"Have you calmed down yet?"

"Yes, I've had a walk round, and I'm really sorry about that, Jo, I really am. I'll ring him up and apologize."

"Good."

"Last time I was pacing up and down like that, I was in your garden and you were having Pearl."

"Yes."

"I was terrified."

"I wasn't feeling that calm myself."

"It was one of those moments, where you see everything clearly."

"Oh yes, and what did you see?"

"Well, you need your fence painted." He grins.

"I know I'm not very good at this. I tend to go off into my own little world."

"The wonderful world of wooden things."

He smiles. "Yes."

"That's okay, Martin. I'm getting quite fond of it now."

"Are you?"

"Yes, in short bursts."

"But you know I care about you, don't you? And the children? More than I can ever say."

"I know, Martin."

God, I'll be in tears in a minute. He looks so nervous.

"I know I'm not suave like him."

"Martin."

"No, I know I'm not. I'd ask you to marry me if I thought that was what you wanted. But it's not, is it?"

"No, I don't think so, not yet, maybe not ever, I don't know. I think I'd like to carry on just like we are and see what happens?"

"What do you mean like we are now? I haven't been speaking to you for the last five weeks."

"True. But that's because you're a twit."

He grins.

"So how do we carry on then? Sort of semidetached, muddling along, keeping the kids happy and trying to get some time to ourselves occasionally?"

"Yes."

"That sounds complicated."

"Sometimes complicated is good, Martin."

"So we just see what happens?"

"Yes."

"Okay, I think I can cope with that. I'll try as hard as I can."

I take hold of his hand.

"Do I really have to ring him up and apologize?"

"Yes, you do. He's going to be around a lot more, for Pearl."

He hesitates. "I suppose that's good, isn't it, for Pearl?"

"Yes, I think it is, Martin. But there's nothing going on, between him and me. There was a moment in Devon, I want to be honest with you, we—"

"Don't tell me about it. It's okay, but I don't want to know."

He's holding my hand quite tightly now.

"Okay. But whatever it was, it's all sorted now. We're friends, and Pearl's mum and dad, but nothing more."

"Good. And does he know that you and I are, whatever we are."

"Yes. He knows that you're the boy for me, Martin. Okay?"

He grins. "Am I?"

"We'll see."

He kisses me, and I kiss him back.

"Martin."

"Yes."

"That woolly hat is tragic."

He throws it on the bonfire.

Oh dear. I'm sure Elsie's seen him throwing his hat on the fire, so Monday morning in the shop might be a bit tricky.

But I really don't care.

"Mum?"

"Yes Jack."

"This was my best party ever."

"Was it, love? That's good."

"And Uncle Daniel gave me a whole twenty pounds."

"I know."

Actually it was fifty pounds, but he's never seen a fifty-pound note before, so he thinks it was a twenty. I could make a nifty profit there, if I was quick.

"And Mum."

"Yes."

"When we get home, I can open my presents from the party, can't I?"

"Yes love. But wait for me, so I can write down what everyone has got you for your thank-you letters."

"Yes, and then can we have toasted cheese, with no tomato?"

"I should think we probably can, love."

He gives me a hug and races off to tell Archie the good news.

Toasted cheese and birthday cake, and a birthday boy and girl to cuddle, along with my very own budding magician.

Perfect.

··· Reading Group Guide ···

Introduction

Knit One Pearl One, the follow-up novel to *The Beach Street Knitting Society and Yarn Club* and *Needles and Pearls*, continues the story of Jo Mackenzie's life in the scenic seaside village of Broadgate. Between her three adorable children, her ever-expanding knitting and café business, and her friends in high places, Jo can hardly find a moment of harmony in her crowded, hectic life. The arrival of Daniel, father to her young daughter, Pearl, throws a wrench into Jo's carefully planned day-to-day whirlwind. Should Jo take a leap of faith with the globe-trotting one-, well, two-night-stand Daniel, or should she settle for Martin, the hapless but earnest local carpenter? In *Knit One Pearl One*, one thing is certain: everyone in the close-knit Broadgate community is part of the family. And in the end, Jo realizes she doesn't need a man to make her happy—her busy life is already brimming over with love.

Discussion Questions

1. Have you read Gil McNeil's other *Beach Street* novels? If yes, which one did you like the best? If no, do you feel your reading experience would have been better with more backstory?

2. How did the author's British writing affect your comprehension or enjoyment of *Knit One Pearl One*? What words or phrases stuck out to you as particularly British?

3. Are you a knitter? If yes, did you feel particular kinship with Jo and the Stitch and Bitch ladies? If no, what drew you to this book?

4. A big part of the energy and heart of *Knit One Pearl One* comes from Jo's relationship with her three kids: Jack, Archie, and Pearl. If you've raised young children yourself, do you feel the author captured the experience properly? If you haven't raised children yourself, does this book change your opinion of raising kids?

5. When all three kids are playing harmoniously for a brief stretch, Jo thinks, "It's moments like this when it all makes sense" (p. 11). When you think back on hectic times in your life, what moments or experiences made you feel your sacrifices were all worth it?

6. Jo's family arrangement is an "untraditional" one, given that she's raising her kids without their father present. What are the benefits of raising her children without a father? Does Jo have more time for them? What are the challenges she faces?

7. Jo places a high value on being able to support herself and her kids, and she insists on being financially prepared to handle anything that life might throw her way. She says to Ellen, "I don't want to be beholden. Not to anyone. I never want to do that again. That way the world can't come crashing down again. See, I've got it all worked out" (p. 45). Do you

feel the same way as Jo? Have you taken any specific steps to create your own contingency plan? If yes, what steps; if not, do you hope to?

8. Knitting plays a large role in Jo's life—it connects her with other people, gives her financial security, and is a big stress reliever. Similarly, Jo observes that after Mrs. Peterson has been knitting, "Somehow she seems lighter, like it's not such a huge struggle to get through the day, which is great. I hope the knitting has helped, a bit" (p. 276). Do you have your own personal version of knitting—something you do in your day-to-day life that helps calm you down and bolster your spirits?

9. During one of her rare moments of quiet, Jo thinks to herself, "I've never liked the French; they're far too snooty about food, and they don't seem terribly good at laughing at themselves, which is a pretty vital life skill as far as I'm concerned" (p. 63). What do you consider your own vital life skills? Have you mastered them, or are you still working toward them?

10. When Pearl launches into one of her screaming tantrums, Jo is relieved to have fellow mom Connie around. As Jo explains, "Only another mum can really pull this off; with child-free people there's always that slight tension, where you know they think you should have some magic trick to stop the yelling, and if you don't you're clearly a crap mother" (pp. 64–65). If you've raised young kids yourself, do you empathize? If you haven't, do you ever feel frustrated around kids having loud tantrums in public?

11. Jo never told Elizabeth, her former mother-in-law, about the affairs and financial destruction that her late husband (and

Elizabeth's late son), Nick, had revealed to Jo right before he died. Do you agree with Jo's choice to withhold the upsetting information from Elizabeth? What do you think you would have done in Jo's situation?

12. During one of her many meandering conversations with Jo, Ellen starts talking about various "badges" that she feels she should earn throughout her life, ticking them off as she goes. Besides the motherhood badge, Ellen explains, "There's the Have a Proper Career badge, tick, Live Somewhere Smart, tick, Partner You Can Take to Dinner Parties, Not the Size of a House, Produce an Infant, tick, tick, tick" (p. 123). What badges are you hoping to earn throughout your life, in accordance with your own morals and values? Would you include any of Ellen's?

13. While reflecting on the nosiness she faced during her pregnancy with Pearl, Jo laments, "People seem to love dissecting other people's lives. Like most of us aren't just doing the best we can" (p. 167). Why do you think gossip is so compelling? When is it okay to gossip about someone?

14. When Helena tries to guilt-trip Jo about using disposable diapers, Jo replies, "To be honest, I think we should sort out the big oil companies, and air travel, things that make a huge difference, before we start guilt-tripping mothers about nappies" (p. 170). Do you agree with Jo? Do small actions add up to big impacts, or are they more of a gesture than anything else?

15. Are you happy with the way things worked out for Jo with Daniel and Martin? What did you hope would happen?

··· A Conversation with ···
Gil McNeil

Q: What parts of the book—settings, characters, plot points, relationships—are pulled from your own life?

A: None of them; they're inspired by my experiences, and those of my family and friends, but not based on them. I'm not interested in writing my autobiography, but I do have an annoying habit of scribbling down snatches of dialogue I overhear, which does make you look like an undercover agent and can attract the occasional worried glance.

Q: Which character did you have the most fun writing, whether because of their kindness or their delicious menace?

A: I love so many of them, but Elsie and Annabel Morgan were fun as mini-villains, and I did get a taste of what it might be like to be a superstar with Grace. Writing the children's voices was also always hugely entertaining.

Q: You describe the hectic-but-loving everyday existence of raising young children very convincingly. Are there any moments in the novel that are pulled from your own experience?

A: No, not least because my son would be deeply unimpressed by finding himself catapulted into one of my novels. But now I'm safely in the hinterland of parenting, with my son at university, I can remember the combination of exhaustion and constant negotiation with far more affection than I felt at the time. There are so many books out there telling us we're doing a bad job as mothers if we don't stay home and cook and clean until we've forgotten we ever had careers, and so many books that make you feel second rate if you're not out there wearing a tiny suit and very high heels, running a multinational while simultaneously mothering six-week-old triplets and making gourmet meals every night. I write for all those women who can't make their own mayonnaise, and don't care, and can't walk in high heels for more than ten minutes without falling over . . . in other words, women like me. One of the nicest things about being a writer is getting letters from readers saying you have made them laugh, and sometimes cry, too, which I always feel slightly guilty about, although I did once get a card from a reader saying I'd made her laugh so much on her journey to work she had to get off the bus because the other passengers were starting to give her odd looks.

Q: What parts of Jo Mackenzie do you see in yourself? Is she based on anyone in particular? If you could, would you trade lives with her for a year?

A: Jo is based on a mixture of friends and imagination, and I don't think I could live her life for a week, let alone a year—I'm far too selfish now, and need my time "off duty" in the garden, cooking, writing, and lolling about on the sofa, to be able to cope with three young kids. Looking after a friend's four-year-old for a couple of hours recently left me so exhausted I could barely speak by the time she came to collect him: I'd completely forgotten how traumatic arts and crafts with the under-fives can be . . .

Q: In a lovely change from many mainstream, female-oriented narratives, Jo finds happiness with her kids and her work, and doesn't feel that she needs a man to complete her. What led you to this choice?

A: I think, like millions of women around the world, Jo is happy if her kids are happy. It's as simple as that. Whether there's a man in her life or not, her children know they come first, second, and last. What happens in between doesn't really matter to them, or to Jo. She's not on a quest for Mr. Right, or Mr. Friday Night. She's just getting on with life, making the best of what opportunities come her way, and trying to remember where she's put the car keys . . .

Q: Your biography says you come from a long line of champion knitters. When did you learn to knit, and from whom? What are your favorite benefits of knitting?

A: My grandmother taught me how to knit; she knew a whole range of patterns off by heart, and could knit very quickly, which seemed like magic to me. She had a tough life, with six children and very little money, so she'd unpick a sweater belonging to one of her older kids, wash the wool, and re-knit it for one of the little ones. By the time she was knitting for her grandchildren, things were a little easier, and she'd spend ages knitting clothes for my dolls with me, using bright, sparkly yarns, which I thought were terribly smart. We'd be knitting by the fire, with my mum and my aunts all swapping patterns and working out complicated stitches, and me sitting cross-legged on the floor, concentrating hard, and they'd forget I was there, so I'd get to hear all sorts of family gossip usually reserved for child-free moments. It was fabulous.

Nowadays I love to knit presents for friends, and for new babies. I knit while watching TV, and whenever I feel particularly stressed—usually when a deadline is looming . . . I find the rhythm of knitting relaxes me and helps me rediscover that slower pace that comes when you feel calm. But it has to be the right kind of knitting; soft baby wool in soothing colors, with simple patterns that you get the hang of quickly—anything fiddly, or using different stitches and colors, or delicate yarn, is something I save for summer holidays and long weekends.

©Jerry Bauer

Gil McNeil is the author of *The Beach Street Knitting Society and Yarn Club* and *Needles and Pearls*. She lives in Kent, England, with her son, and comes from a long line of champion knitters.

ALSO BY GIL MCNEIL

"A warmly winning second-chance novel."
—Christian Science Monitor

the beach street
knitting society
and yarn club

A NOVEL

Gil McNeil

"Funny and sparkling
—a profoundly
moving study of
motherhood and true
love."
—Ruth Rendell

"A comfy, hopeful
yarn with believable
characters."
—*Publishers Weekly*

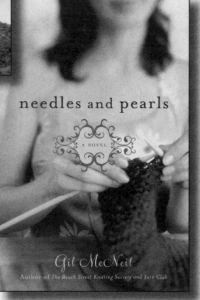

needles and pearls

A NOVEL

Gil McNeil
Author of *The Beach Street Knitting Society and Yarn Club*

voice